# A RUDE INTERRUPTION

Adrian wanted to take her. He saw no reason not to—they were alone on her bed, no one to answer to, nowhere to go. He would satisfy himself deep within her and bring her to climax again and again, letting his sorrow fade away in the sultry night.

She looked straight at him, and he knew she wanted it too. The tingling excitement of strangers choosing to have sex, except he felt somehow that he'd known her always.

On his arm, Ferrin suddenly morphed to his snake form and slithered across the bed. He touched Amber on the way, and she jerked, losing her hold on Adrian. "I *wish* he wouldn't do that."

Ferrin hissed, his body rigid. *Demon,* he announced, and then all hell broke loose.

# IMMORTALS: THE CALLING

## JENNIFER ASHLEY

LOVE SPELL  NEW YORK CITY

LOVE SPELL®

May 2007

Published by

Dorchester Publishing Co., Inc.
200 Madison Avenue
New York, NY 10016

ISBN-10: 0-505-52687-5
ISBN-13: 978-0-505-52687-8

Visit us on the web at www.dorchesterpub.com.

# ACKNOWLEDGMENTS

I would like to say a huge thank you to everyone who made this project possible. First to Robin Popp and Joy Nash for taking time out of their own busy writing schedules to write two wonderful books: *The Darkening* and *The Awakening*. Thanks to Leah Hultenschmidt, whose tireless editorial expertise brought the books together and made them a cohesive whole. Also to Brianna Yamashita for her promotions and ad design talents, and to the production department and the cover artist for the wonderful covers created for this series. Thanks in general to Dorchester for supporting the Immortals series and making it possible. And thanks, of course, goes to Forrest for his infinite patience, support, and love.

# IMMORTALS: The Calling

# PROLOGUE

Adrian's dream shifted from the fantasy of a naked woman on the other side of a soapy bath to a nightmare of haunting familiarity. The curvy young woman in his dream lost her smile, vacant eyes widening, and she vanished in a popping of soap bubbles.

The bathroom itself disappeared, and Adrian found himself on a wooded slope, naked and freezing in an arctic wind. He knew where he was—northern Scotland seven hundred years ago, after a battle to drive the monsters called Unseelies back into their own dimension. Adrian and his brothers could not keep them away forever and they knew it, but they could at least force them back through the gap they'd ripped between their world and the humans', and close it up behind them.

Adrian hated this dream, which could smite him unexpectedly and which always ended the same. *You'd think after seven hundred years I'd get over it.*

He heard sounds of the battle just out of sight where his brothers enjoyed themselves sealing up the Unseelies. Adrian's naked skin prickled as the wind cut him, his dreaming brain refusing to conjure clothes. His hand went to the silver snake-shaped band that clasped his upper arm in sinuous curves. At his touch Ferrin unwound himself, lengthening and straightening into a long silver sword.

His brother Hunter used to make jokes about Adrian's "extending weapon," and Tain had always leapt to Adrian's defense. *If not for Ferrin, you'd be dead ten times over,* he'd growl at Hunter. *Show some respect.*

Hunter would reply with the usual obscene gesture, and Adrian would say, *Lighten up, both of you. Go find a woman or something.*

Their bantering voices seemed to echo through the woods, fading before the knifelike wind. If the dream ran true to form, he wouldn't see any of them. He hadn't seen his brothers since the day Tain disappeared.

*Adrian!*

His youngest brother's voice ripped out of nowhere, screaming for help, the futility in his cry unbearable. In the real incident, Tain hadn't called for help. He'd simply disappeared. No body, no trace, no message, no hint, nothing. A witch had taken him away—that was the story the only witness had told him, and the witness had died moments later. Tain screamed for help only in the dreams.

*Isis, make it stop.*

Tain's face appeared out of the darkness, his once handsome visage twisted in agony. *Adrian, help me!*

Naked and alone on the Scottish hillside, sword heavy in his hand, Adrian shouted into the wind. "Where are you?"

The sounds of battle, of his brothers, of the dying, fleeing monsters faded, and all was silent but for the wind. "I'm trying to find you," Adrian called. "Help me find you."

*Adrian!*

Tain's scream was that of a being in horrible pain. Immortals could not be killed by normal human weapons, but they could be hurt and suffer as much as or more than the humans they resembled. Someone was torturing Tain. But as much as Adrian had searched the world for seven hundred years, he'd never found a trace of him. Adrian only had the dreams that reminded him, like a new wound on top of an old one, that he'd failed.

Adrenaline pumped through Adrian's body, raising his temperature beyond what a normal human would be able to tolerate. He wanted to fight, to kill—where was a good demon to slay when you wanted one? Creatures of death magic, those that fed on death, that were undead themselves—the vampires, demons, monsters of the dark imagination—all were fair game for Immortals.

Adrian braced himself for what would come next. Tain solidified in the air before him, still wearing the tattered remains of surcoat and mail from the battle long ago. Tain's body bled, his garments were soaked in blood, and blood leaked like tears from his eyes. "Why didn't you help me? Why didn't you come?"

"Tell me where you are. Damn it, I'll help you now."

"I trusted you," Tain spat at him. "I loved you. You're my *brother.*"

"Tain, I swear to Isis I'll find you. I swear this on my blood."

Tain grabbed the blade of Adrian's sword, crimson streaking his fingers as the blade cut him. "It is too late. You have killed me."

With amazing strength, Tain jerked the sword forward.

Adrian couldn't stop it, and with a hideous feeling of futility, he watched the point slide straight into Tain's heart.

Tain screamed with all the anguish of the worlds, and Adrian jerked awake.

Half awake. He was aware that he lay on his ultra-comfortable bed in his Los Angeles home, the cool sheets bunched around his bare thighs, the air conditioner blowing a stream of chill across his body.

But the dream was not over, or at least it had changed. He seemed to see an incredibly handsome man hovering over him, fists supporting his weight on each side of Adrian's head. The face was handsome enough to border on beautiful, and the man's long, silken hair spilled onto Adrian's chest.

The man's eyes were dark, almost black, his smile seductive. He had the hollow cheeks and sensual lips a male model would kill for, but his dark eyes held evil. He reached out a well-shaped finger and drew it down Adrian's face from forehead to lips, a seductive touch.

*Demon.* Adrian's skin crawled. The demon could be part of the dream, or he could be a true demon trying to manifest by coasting in on Adrian's dreams. Either way, Adrian felt his strength return, and along with it, glee.

*Something I can kill.*

As the thought formed, the demon morphed into a beautiful female, all lush black hair and warm nakedness, tight nipples grazing Adrian's chest. The eyes were the same, black pools of evil, and her lips curved into a smile. "You like this better?" she purred.

"Sorry, sweetheart, not interested." Adrian touched the cold armband that was Ferrin and started to pull it off.

The demon glanced behind her as though disturbed by some sound. An expression of vast annoyance crossed her face, and her fingernails tightened on Adrian's chest. Adrian peered into the darkness behind her and sensed a presence as well, but the dream was too foggy and he could see nothing. With a quiet sound, the demon vanished, and Adrian woke all the way.

The bedroom was silent. Curtains billowed at the open windows, the ocean below the house hissing as the tide rose. It had been a dream, another nightmare in a long line about Tain.

The demon, on the other hand, might have been real. It had turned its head as though hearing someone call its name, as though it had been summoned . . .

Adrian sat straight up, sheets sliding from his naked body. He reached out with his senses to the place the demon had fled and found a pinprick hole in reality. And on the other side of that hole, cold, rainy darkness—and a woman screaming in fear.

The pinprick shut, closing with a snap the portal to wherever the demon had gone. But at least Adrian had a direction to follow.

He sprang from his bed and began to dress.

# CHAPTER ONE

*Four weeks later*

Amber Silverthorne fell onto her back, stunned, as the man in the black leather coat crashed into the warehouse and started to beat off the demon.

The candles marking Amber's circle scattered, splattering wax across the dirty floor. The magic she'd invoked sputtered and died. Her terror at the demon's sudden appearance changed to amazement at the tall man facing her, a look of grim glee on his face, a huge silver sword in his grip.

He held the sword almost negligently, as though it weighed nothing, and as soon as the demon came at him, he swung it, slicing the blade across the demon's pristine suit. He laughed as the demon retreated, snarling.

The man's long black hair was bound in a tail at his nape and again halfway down his back, keeping it well out of the way of the fight. His face was nowhere near as handsome as that of the demon he fought, being more hard and square. A warrior's face matching a warrior's body.

The warrior and the demon were evenly matched in strength, speed, and agility. Each focused tightly on the other, the demon's black eyes sparkling with fury. The man's eyes were black too, like wells of darkness. The warrior chopped downward with the sword, and the demon spun away, black blood flying from a wound and splashing Amber's skin like acid.

Amber scrambled to sit up and gather her crystals to her, chanting furiously to re-form protective magic around her like a bubble. The man in black leather and the demon fought hand to hand, the man's sword swinging in wide, deadly arcs, the demon fighting back with the steel pole with which he'd tried to murder Amber.

"Immortal," he hissed.

The man gritted his teeth in a smile. "Good guess. What gave it away?"

"Who Called you?"

The silver sword went straight for the demon's throat. "No one. I happened to be passing."

Amber took her concentration from the crystals for a split second. *Happened to be passing?* A deserted warehouse between the tracks and the docks of Seattle? With a sword?

But good thing he was. There was nothing to distinguish this place from the other run-down buildings in the neighborhood, except that here, Amber's sister had died. Now, four weeks later, the police tape was long gone, the warehouse deserted, forensics and fingerprint takers finished. But no suspects had surfaced, and Amber refused to let Detective Jack Simon and the Seattle Police file away Susan's murder as an "unexplained paranormal death." So tonight she had gathered her supplies and come to conduct her own investigation.

The demon danced away from the warrior's sword, moving with the deadly speed of his kind. Undeterred, the warrior shifted his weight to one foot and kicked, catching the demon high on the shoulder.

Was the man here because of Susan? A boyfriend Amber didn't know about? Detective Simon had let her look at the notebook he'd found next to Susan. It had contained notes in a script Amber couldn't read, but she could feel how it tingled with evil. Susan had known damn well better than to mess with demons and death magic, but the evidence indicated she had done so anyway, and it had likely killed her.

Amber had cast a circle for her protection, calling on the element of Earth, to which her magic had the greatest affinity, to guard her. She'd used quartz crystals to enhance the vibrations left over from the murder so she might scry what had happened, plus salt to outline her circle and connect with the bones of the earth beneath the warehouse.

Not three minutes into the ritual, the demon had walked through the front door and tried to kill her.

She'd fought, futilely because demons were stronger than any mortal. This demon had seemed to radiate even more strength and evil than the demons who ran clubs in downtown Seattle, where foolish humans went to be seduced. He'd easily thrown down her protections and had been ready to bash out her brains when the warrior had come crashing in.

Amber focused her energy on the crystals, trying to find her center and shut out the death match happening five feet from her. Despite his wound, the demon easily whirled away and struck the warrior with his pole, landing a blow across the fine-fitting leather coat. The coat ripped, and the iron bar dug into the man's shoulders.

The warrior used the impact to bring his large fist around and catch the demon on the side of his head with a roundhouse punch. While the demon staggered, the warrior shrugged off his ripped coat and continued the fight in a T-shirt that molded to every muscle.

"Who are you?" he demanded of the demon.

To Amber's surprise, the demon chuckled. "That stays my secret."

"When I cut off your head, maybe I'll fish it out of your brain."

"I will not die this day, Immortal."

The man tossed his sword from hand to hand and gave the demon a contemptuous look. "You sound like a reject from a bad movie. How do you know about Immortals?"

"I know you seek one."

The declaration wiped the smile from the man's face. He snarled in fury and launched himself at the demon for an all-out attack. A dark cloud of death magic issued from the demon's hands, slick and foul like tar. It caught the man in the side and sent him shooting backward until he slammed high into a wall.

Amber winced, but the warrior sprang off the wall and easily landed on his feet. He lifted his sword straight out in front of him and bellowed, "Go!"

The sword shifted from a long blade into a five-foot snake, its mouth open, fangs gleaming. It flew through the air as though shot from a bow and sank its teeth into the demon's upflung arm.

The demon tried to shake it off, but the snake clung, biting deep. It must have been poisonous, but would its venom harm a demon? The demon flailed and cursed, his attempts to dislodge the snake sending him straight toward Amber and her circle. The demon slammed into the blue nimbus of magic, but Amber's protective bubble held, the shield glowing red where he struck it.

The demon's back and shoulders pressed the bubble as he looked up to find the warrior glaring down at him. The warrior's biceps were thick, a V of sweat plastering his T-shirt to well-honed muscles. He grabbed the snake by the tail, and it became a sword again, its tip slicing through the demon's silk shirt and into his chest.

The demon wrenched himself backward over the bubble, sliding down the other side. The man leapt after him, rolling across the shield an inch from Amber's head. The demon went down, and the warrior stood over him, sword point once more at the demon's chest. The man held the huge hilt in both hands, ready to shove the blade in.

"Tell me what you know," he commanded, voice hard.

The demon smirked. "About Tain?"

The warrior's eyes sent sparks into the dark. "What the hell do you know about Tain?"

"If you kill me, Immortal, you'll never know."

"Then I'll flay off every inch of your hide. Tell me what you know, and I'll be nice and kill you quick—er."

The demon laughed. He lolled his head back, his handsome mouth opening while his silky hair fanned across the warehouse floor. "Wouldn't you love to know what I mean?" He pointed at Amber. "Ask *her*."

The man glanced to where Amber sat under the faintly glowing shield, her mouth open. His face took on a look of absolute fury, and he spun back to the demon and rammed the sword through the demon's body.

Except the demon wasn't there. He dissolved into mist and vanished, his laughter ringing through the empty room, and then was gone.

The warrior stared in stunned silence at the space where the demon had lain. A few tendrils of mist lingered on the blank floor, dissipating in the cool breeze that blew through the warehouse.

Snarling in frustration, the warrior flung his sword across the floor, where it spun and rang and sparked into the darkness. Face drawn with fury, he balled his fist and punched a nearby steel girder. The metal groaned under the onslaught, but the man backed away, none the worse for wear.

Amber kept her protective bubble in place as the warrior stormed after his sword. He'd driven off the demon, but there was nothing to tell her he wasn't just as dangerous. The demon had called him an "immortal," and the only immortals she knew about were vampires. He didn't look like a vampire, but then again he might be some kind of super-vamp she'd never seen. When dealing with wielders of death magic, you couldn't be too careful.

He reached down and picked up his sword. His jeans fitted easily over his thighs, showing trim hips and one gorgeous ass. As soon as he touched the sword's hilt, it turned into a snake again and wrapped itself lovingly around his wrist. The snake lifted its head and looked at Amber, unblinking obsidian eyes fixing on her. It tested her scent with its tongue, then puffed its neck into a hood shape she recognized.

She choked out, "That—is a cobra."

"Yes." The man spoke a word to the snake, and it deflated and slithered up the man's arm. The cobra coiled around his bicep and morphed into a snake-shaped silver armlet that shone softly in the moonlight.

"Is it gone?"

"No." The man touched the armlet, and she heard a faint metallic ring. "He'll come when he's called."

"I'd appreciate it if you didn't call him, then."

He grinned tightly, then immediately lost the smile. In the split second before he closed his expression, she saw incredible weariness—grief and tiredness that went beyond anything she understood. He looked fairly young, about thirty, but his eyes held the strain of someone who had watched ages pass.

The heels of his square-toed black boots clicked on the floor as he walked to her. When he sank down to study her, she finally got a view of his whole physique. *Strong. Big.* The feeble adjectives welled up in her mind, but they kept her from blurting out, *Would you look at those thighs.* He was built like a wrestler, though not quite as bulked. His T-shirt stretched over tight, honed muscle, the neckline showing a dusting of black curls and an inviting sliver of chest. His hands were brown and sinewy, and a large silver ring she hadn't noticed before adorned the middle finger of his right hand.

His belt was of the finest alligator, and his jeans stretched enticingly over his groin. His face was hard and strong, cheekbones broad, his jaw square, nose broken more than once, black hair pulled back from a sharply defined brow.

His eyes arrested her. Cool darkness, a depth beyond anything she'd ever seen. Amber had some experience with otherworldly creatures—vampires with seductive eyes and werewolves with a golden gaze that trapped you before you could even think to run. But this man's eyes were different. She sensed something both ancient and as new as yesterday, a wisdom mixed with insatiable curiosity.

In spite of the spatter of black demon blood on his shirt and arms, he was utterly comfortable and unaware of his delectable looks.

"You like hiding behind that thing?" he asked, peering through the shield.

"Better safe than sorry, I always say."

He made a snatching motion at the bubble and it instantly dissolved, the light bleeding down into the salt outline before vanishing.

"Crap," she said softly. She wouldn't have time to charge the stones to raise another defensive barrier before he could strike. She was, as the phrase went, a sitting duck. No one should have been able to crack her shield like that.

"Your spells can't hurt me," he said, resting his hands on his knees. "And I won't hurt you, so don't strain yourself while I ask you questions."

She let her fear fan her anger. "Who the hell are you?"

"More important, who are you, and why are you brain-dead enough to summon a demon? Especially one of that caliber?"

"I didn't summon him."

He flicked his finger over her stones. "I see a circle. A chalice and knife, candles, salt, incense, stones. And when I came in, there was a demon. What, you wanted to cast his horoscope?"

"If you knew anything about witchcraft, you'd see this is a circle for protection only," Amber said.

"Which you just happened to cast in a warehouse in the middle of the night in a neighborhood of feral vampires. Not to mention rats, snakes, rabid dogs, and humans who'd roll you for a nickel." He leaned closer. "Why aren't you home tucked up in bed?"

"Why do you want to know?"

A corner of his mouth moved in impatience. "Just tell me."

"Tell me who you are, first."

He nodded once, as though her request was fair. "You can call me Adrian."

"Is that your name?"

"Close enough."

"Can you be more specific? Like what is an Immortal? Are you a vampire?"

He shook his head. "Sweetheart, I'm what vampires fear. When vampires tell each other scary stories, they're about me."

"I see. You're not full of yourself or anything."

To her surprise, he chuckled. The smile made his eyes crinkle, softening them into something almost human. "I'm not a being of death magic, if that's what you're worried about. I'm definitely about life magic, like you. Which is why I want to know why you're messing with death magic. This whole place reeks of it."

"You can sense it too?"

"Sense it? I can't breathe without inhaling a shitload of it. Do you have a car?"

The abruptness of the question made her jump. "Yes. Why?"

He rose to his feet with lithe grace. "I say we blow this joint and get some coffee and talk. That's what Seattle's known for, right? Coffee?"

"I hate coffee," Amber said automatically. A drawback living in twenty-first-century America, never mind Seattle. She was forever explaining she didn't like the taste and earning incredulous looks from her coffee-saturated friends.

"I'll buy you tea. Come on." He reached down a broad hand to help her to her feet.

"Aren't you afraid I'll turn you into a toad?"

"I'll risk it."

She studied him a while longer, wondering why she

even considered trusting him. He was a fine specimen of a man, yes, but she'd learned the hard way that looks could disguise any amount of badness. He should *not* have been able to break her circle without wielding powerful magic himself, but he did not feel like a demon, and she would have heard about any witch that strong.

His words about Seattle's coffee signaled that he was new in town, but why he should rush to this warehouse in the nick of time to save her was beyond her understanding. *"Happened to be passing,"* my ass.

While he waited, she felt a small push on her mind, a light fog that relaxed her the slightest bit. Was it from the backwash of magic? Or was he a telepath? Either way, she wanted to know more about him.

"All right," she answered. "I think we definitely need to talk."

Like a gentleman, he helped her gather her accoutrements into the carved sandalwood box she'd inherited from her mother; then he snatched up his torn leather coat, swirled it around his shoulders, and led her out into the night.

"Cobras eat toads, I bet," the young woman said. Her car, a Honda showing the wear and tear of living in a rainy climate, waited for them calmly in the warehouse's empty, gravel-strewn parking lot.

"Don't give him ideas." Adrian slung the box into the back seat and held open the driver's-side door to let her in.

She gave him a startled look with her incredible eyes but climbed in and started the car. Instead of speeding off and leaving him stranded, she waited for him to get himself into the passenger seat and strap on a seat belt.

He'd touched her mind a little, calming her and making her trust him—at least long enough for him to pry information out of her.

"Does your snake understand me?" she asked as she pulled away from the warehouse.

"Every word. At least that's what he tells me."

She gave him another startled look with eyes he wanted to get to know better. "He can talk?"

"Sometimes he never stops talking," Adrian said dryly. "You pick the place. Somewhere you like. You know the town better than I do, and I'll sit here and think about sampling Seattle's coffee."

Without answering, she pulled out onto a little-trafficked road, and he leaned against the window and contemplated her. Her long, slim fingers gripped the wheel as she sat upright and focused her gaze rigidly in front of her. He could feel the intensity of her, her fear, her anger—emotions she was not comfortable with. He sensed that these emotions hadn't plagued her much in her young life, and now she struggled to deal with them.

She had no taint of death magic on her. Some witches became seduced by it, the same way humans let demons or vampires seduce them in the back rooms of clubs in cities all across the world. It was a heady rush to command the sticky power of death magic, but it ultimately killed the witch who tried it. No witch was strong enough. But this woman seemed clean and free of it, a fact that had saved her life. Adrian would have killed her if he'd thought the death magic in the warehouse had come from her.

Short dark hair curled about her face and turned up naturally at the base of her neck. A face not beautiful but interesting, with high cheekbones, slim nose, wide mouth. Throat lightly tanned, long neck, strong shoulders under her light windbreaker. Her scoop-neck shirt showed a tiny tattoo on her collarbone, a butterfly in tasteful colors.

When she moved, he could glimpse firm breasts inside a lace bra. He'd appreciated the jeans hugging her curvy hips and long, long legs when he'd helped her gather up her things in the warehouse.

But her eyes most of all had made him stop. They were golden brown, almost the color of whiskey—a very good malt whiskey. But there was more to her eyes besides their pretty color. The slight tilt of them betrayed possible Asian ancestry, not unusual in the Pacific Northwest. She had something, some unwavering determination that had struck him hard when she'd first looked at him.

She didn't look particularly sexually adventurous. Except for her quick once-over when he'd crouched next to her protective circle, she wouldn't look at him. No sly glances, no assessing stares. She couldn't care less about him sexually, which was too bad. He would have to work on that. They had chemistry—he'd seen that when he'd knelt down and gazed at her through her magic shield. The light of the shield had shone around her, glowing out of her body with her clean, strong magic.

He was unable to shake the strange sensation that he'd seen her somewhere before. As she pulled onto a freeway, he opened the glove compartment and fished around until he withdrew her insurance card.

"Amber Silverthorne. That's you?"

"Yes," she said tightly. She didn't grow furious that he was digging through her glove compartment, but she wasn't happy about it either.

"A good witch name," he observed, shutting the ill-fitting door.

"It's my real name. My parents were witches."

"*Were?* Meaning they've passed?"

"My sister, too. She was murdered."

"In the warehouse?"

"Yes," she answered in a dull voice. "Four weeks ago."

"I'm sorry."

He truly was sorry. He remembered the sounds of what must have been her sister's screams in his waking dream and regretted he had been too late to save her. No one needed to lose everyone they loved, especially not to the darkness of violence. She acknowledged the deaths without breaking down in self-pity, but he felt the grief in her, the sorrow and the knowledge that she had to face the future alone.

He couldn't resist reaching out and rubbing her cheek with his fingers, trying to lend comfort. Her soft skin grew rosy under his touch.

"I lost my brother a long time ago," he said. "We never did find out what happened to him. I'm still looking."

She shot him a glance, surprise and sympathy in her eyes. "Goddess, I'm sorry. And his name was Tain?"

No reason to lie. He could make her forget all about him and what she knew later if he needed to. "Yes."

"And you thought the demon knew something about it?"

"Yes."

She returned her attention to the road in time to swerve around a truck. "So when you came to the warehouse, you were following him, not me." When he merely nodded, she asked. "How did you get here?"

"I flew."

She raised her brows and looked at his back as though checking for wings. He grinned. "In a 737. From Los Angeles. I've been tracking our demon friend since he showed up in one of my dreams a few weeks ago. I want to know everything you know about him."

"I don't know anything about him."

"You do. Maybe you don't know what yet, but you do."

She drove in silence, and he folded his arms and resumed his contemplation of her. She wore no rings but had three earrings in her right ear and two in her left, all silver. Wires and loops, as though she liked having things dangling and swishing around her ears. She wore a bracelet, again of fine silver, which softly clasped her wrist.

*Your eyes are going to bug out,* Ferrin's voice came in his head. The cobra spoke an ancient dialect of Egyptian, one that hadn't been heard in the world in several thousand years.

*She's worth looking at.*

Ferrin didn't answer. Maybe the snarky snake would go to sleep.

They moved through the city into quieter districts, where large houses with sloping lawns rested on dark wooded hills that wound above one another. In a neighborhood of flower-bordered walks and corner shops, Amber parked the car in front of a three-story Victorian Gothic structure with a tower and a wraparound porch.

"This is a coffeehouse?" Adrian asked dubiously.

"This is my house. Coffeehouses are closed at this hour. We'll have a cup in the kitchen, and we'll talk, and then you'll leave."

He touched her cheek again, letting a bit of magic ripple from him to her. "I won't hurt you."

She looked at him as though puzzled that he had to reassure her, but she was feeling his magic.

They left the car, and he carried her box of gear up to

the porch. She unlocked and opened the front door and started to step through, but he held her back with a hand on her shoulder. "Wait."

Her golden eyes widened as she stepped back and he handed her the box and went inside.

# CHAPTER TWO

Adrian found a foyer with a coatrack full of raincoats, an umbrella stand, and boots and a door on the other side with stained glass in its upper half. Beyond this lay a hall easily lit when he touched the switch behind the door. He went inside and began to explore the ground floor for anything that might be lying in wait.

The house was Victorian, but the inhabitants had updated it with the passing years. The walls were painted a cream color that complemented the hardwood floors and the green woven runner that lay the length of the hall. Open doors gave onto a huge, high-ceilinged living room on one side, an equally large dining room on the other. He found a kitchen behind the dining room, and an office tucked in the back of the house along with a glassed-in porch.

He felt the wards of protection that had been traced on every window and door and along the vents in the walls. Every crevice or crack that could lead to the outside was warded, and he sensed layers and layers of marks, new over old. They had been laid to keep out beings of death magic—vampires, demons, afreets, and other nasties—who would not be able to cross into the house unless they were very powerful.

He returned to the foyer and beckoned Amber in. "This house has been protected for generations."

She closed the door, shedding her windbreaker and hanging it on a hook. She kept the box of witch's tools under her arm. "Five generations. My grandfather's grandfather built it."

"All witches?"

"All."

"A hereditary witch. I'm impressed."

"You know a lot about witches."

"I know a lot about everything," he said. He slid off his leather coat, frowning a little over the rip the demon had made, then hung it on the hook next to her windbreaker and followed her to the kitchen.

Despite Amber's claim to loathe coffee, a coffeemaker rested on the counter, which she soon had perking away with gourmet coffee she pulled out of a cupboard. She filled a teakettle with water and put it on the stove for herself and filled a mesh ball with loose-leaf tea.

She moved with deft efficiency, her body lithe in jeans and short-sleeved shirt. In addition to the butterfly on her collarbone, she had a Celtic interlace tattoo around her upper arm.

He saw the tightness in her shoulders, tension from her sister's death. He suddenly wished he'd met her before the tragedy, when her mouth had turned up in ready smiles, when her laughter had echoed through this kitchen. He knew it had, because he felt it lingering. Adrian could also feel the remnants of shock and pain, and imagined her down here fixing herself a cup of tea after she'd learned of the murder, trying to calm herself.

The coffeemaker finished, and she poured him a cup of rich-smelling brew. At about the same time the old-fashioned teakettle whistled, and she poured the water into a teapot and brought it to the table with their cups.

"Sugar?" she asked belatedly. "I don't have cream, only milk."

He held his hand over the cup. "I like it plain."

"Good," she said, as if he'd passed some kind of test. She thumped down in a chair, positioned her tea mug on the table, and looked him full in the face, her dark hair in damp ringlets around her forehead. "Are you a witch? Maybe a long-lived one, which is why they call you Immortal?"

"No, not a witch."

"Then what?" Her tawny eyes flicked over his face. "Not a vampire, because I wouldn't be able to look at you without becoming your drooling lackey."

"Not a vampire," he agreed. "I am a creature of the night, though. And of the day too."

"Thank you, that's very clear," she said dryly.

He turned the coffee mug around on the straw place mat in front of him. "*Immortal* means I've been around a very long time. I was born on the Nile during what Egyptologists call the fourth dynasty, when Khufu made the great pyramid at Giza. I was brought up by Isis and Hathor, trained to fight the forces of death magic. I can sense death magic days after the creature has been there, and I can sense when a human or life-magic being has been dabbling in death magic. I can sense all magical creatures. For instance, I know there's a werewolf on your back porch." He lifted the coffee to his lips and took a sip.

Amber didn't show any surprise. "That's Sabina. She's a friend, and she likes to check up on me."

A young woman with a thick volume of blond hair was peering in through the glass half of the kitchen door, her hands cupped to see inside. She waved when Amber looked over, and Amber rose to let her in.

Sabina looked to be about Amber's age, but Adrian sensed an oldness about her that came with her wolf form. Werewolves were difficult to place age-wise because their human bodies were more resilient than normal human ones. She wore red sweats, probably easy to get in and out of when she shifted, and her wolf's eyes skewered Adrian, narrowing a little when she couldn't assess him.

"Hey, Amber," she said, her voice light but betraying caution. "Who's the hunk?"

"This is Adrian. Adrian—Sabina. My friend. He knew you were a werewolf."

"Yeah, well, lots of people do." Sabina fetched a cup, knowing where they were, helped herself to coffee, and sat down at the table with them. "Your date?" she said, running her shrewd golden gaze up and down Adrian. "He's good-looking at least."

"Not my date," Amber said with emphasis. "We were just talking."

"About what?"

"About the death of Amber's sister," Adrian said, setting down his cup. "Amber was just going to tell me everything."

Amber had no idea why she suddenly wanted to spill the whole story to Adrian. Sabina was giving her puzzled looks, clearly wondering, but to Amber it seemed the right thing to do. She'd kept what happened bottled up inside too long, where it pushed at her and hurt her.

She had grieved when her parents died, but with each

of them it had been a natural death, not sudden. No policeman had pounded on her door in the middle of the night to ask her to come identify a body.

She described how Detective Simon had taken her to the morgue and showed her Susan. Amber would never forget the smell of the place—heavy disinfectant that couldn't quite cover the odor of death. Susan had lain on the gurney with her eyes closed peacefully, but there were deep cuts all over her torso, and her face was bruised and battered, evidence of an ugly fight.

Detective Simon had shown Amber photos of the crime scene, mercifully without Susan's body in them, and asked Amber what she thought Susan had been doing in the warehouse. Susan had gone there to prepare a circle, complete with quarter candles and stones, herbs, salt, incense, and holy water, but what she'd meant the circle for and what magics she'd meant to do, Amber couldn't tell from the black-and-white photos.

Detective Simon had found a notebook next to Susan with sketches of the circle and notes for the ritual. He'd shown Amber the book a few days later, after the fingerprint takers and forensics had gone over it. Susan's notes looked like normal enough preparation for a circle of protection, but two pages had been covered with an evil-looking script Amber had never seen before.

"He let me copy some of it," she went on to Adrian. "But I haven't been able to figure out what kind of language it is. I haven't found anything like it on the Internet or in books, and no one I know has ever seen it."

"Show it to me," Adrian said. "I'm something of a linguist."

Without hesitation Amber rose, taking her box of accoutrements, and went upstairs to her bedroom to fetch the papers. The room next to hers, which she and Susan had used as a workroom, was cluttered with preparation for Beltane—ribbons and garlands and candles and robes that Susan would never wear waited. Amber wiped tears from her eyes as she thought of the celebration she and Susan were to have hosted together, as they did every year.

*Can't cry right now,* she told herself. *I want to find the bastard who killed her, and if this Adrian can help, let him. We'll make her killer pay, and at Beltane we'll dedicate the entire celebration to Susan.*

She carried the papers back to the kitchen. When she entered the room, Sabina was leaning over the table talking to Adrian in a fervent manner, her words too low for Amber to hear. Adrian lounged back in his chair, his long legs barely fitting under the table, fingers negligently encircling the coffee cup.

He looked utterly at home. He overwhelmed the kitchen like an ancient god—maybe Bacchus, patron of wine and revelry—who'd decided to relax and stay awhile.

Strange that she was thinking of Beltane rituals, which involved the coupling god and goddess, and now Bacchus. When Adrian looked up and caught her eye, heat burned swiftly through her. Why did his eyes have to be so sinful? They were deep and black, impenetrable as if they held ancient secrets, and he contemplated her as if he knew her every thought.

Sabina broke off when she noted Amber in the doorway. The werewolf folded her lips and sat back in her chair, taking an innocent sip of coffee. Amber plopped the pages in front of Adrian, with effort not looking into his eyes.

"The copies probably aren't that great," she said. "I was in a hurry and I didn't know what I was writing."

Adrian nodded absently. He perused the papers, his lashes flicking as he took in the words. "This script is very old."

"Like Old English, you mean?" Sabina leaned to him, her breasts pressing the table's edge. "Like *Beowulf*?"

"Far older than that."

"Egyptian?" Amber asked. "Not hieroglyphs, but the script—what's it called—hieratic?"

"Older even than that," Adrian answered. "This is a script from before the rise of human civilizations."

"How can that be?" Amber asked. "You have human civilization, then you have writing, not the other way around."

"I didn't say the writing was human."

Amber's gaze froze on him. "Demon, you mean?"

"Maybe. I can't decipher it, at least not here. I'll need resources. And possibly the rest of the pages."

Amber poured more tea into her cup. "I was lucky to get those, and only because I talked to Detective Simon fast and hard."

"I might convince him to give up more."

Sabina gave him a skeptical look. "Could you? Why is that?"

"Let's just say I have a way with people."

"Does it have anything to do with your snake?" Amber gestured to the silver cobra coiled around his upper arm. The sleeves of his T-shirt were cut short, baring the smooth bulge of his biceps, probably to accommodate the armlet. "What is your interest anyway? I'm grateful that you saved my life tonight, but I have to ask why you're so interested in what happened to Susan."

"Because this goes beyond your sister's death," he answered, regarding her gravely. "Something larger is happening, and I want to know why."

"Something larger?" Amber didn't like the sound of that. She had been noticing in the last months that the number of vampires in town had increased, that shadows seemed to lengthen, that dark alleys had become darker and people stayed indoors more at night, unusual because the weather was finally becoming warmer.

Adrian leaned forward a little, strong fingers cradling his coffee mug, his silver ring winking. "You feel it too."

She gave a reluctant nod. Sabina frowned as though she had no idea what they were talking about.

"Death magic is getting stronger," he said. "It should not be, the balance should be perfect. If it grows too strong, and the balance is tipped"—he held his hand palm up, then flipped it over, his eyes somber—"things could get bad. I mean very bad, like it hasn't been since this writing was created."

Amber touched the scrawled words, which seemed to twist into sinister lines before her eyes. She wondered again where the hell Susan had come across it, and why her sister, one of the most talented and careful witches Amber knew, had decided to copy a demon script into her working notebooks.

She also wondered how Adrian was so familiar with it, and what his connection was with the demon. She looked into his eyes as she sat back in her chair, but whatever he knew, he hid, and hid well.

Adrian watched Amber tense, her anger turning to worry. She puzzled him, because he should be able to make her relax and speak to him readily. No direct manipulation, just a gentle nudge to get her to talk to him and answer questions without terror. Amber kept rising out of his influence, and he wondered how that was possible.

He alone of his brothers had this power—they each had a talent the others lacked—and he used it either to calm people or to pry information out of them. It helped that he hadn't been created to live among humans—he came when Called, killed the threat, and departed without reward.

At least, he was supposed to. Adrian and his brothers had soon discovered they enjoyed remaining after the battle was over, dancing at the victory feast, answering the unspoken offers of young women with sly eyes. Adrian liked drinking wine and talking with grateful people, sharing their joy that death magic wouldn't carry off the children tonight or that the world wouldn't be destroyed for at least another day.

For the last seven hundred years, since he'd lost Tain and decided not to return to Ravenscroft where the Immortals had lived and trained, he'd dwelled in this world among humans, never settling in one place for long, leaving before people got too worried that he never aged. But even living among humans, he still hadn't been able to become like them, to enter into their world of families and close friendships. He was forever an outsider, unable to relate to anyone except his brothers, and even then he couldn't say he'd been close to any of them except Tain.

He glanced at the page of writing again, mundane notebook paper and ball-point ink, tracing shapes of letters so ancient and powerful they didn't have names. He couldn't read the words, but he had an idea what they were, and he didn't like it.

He looked up at Amber. Sweet chiseled face, tawny

eyes following his every move. Red, full lips touching her tea mug, her brow furrowing the slightest bit as she sipped the hot brew. Fingers long and strong, holding the mug with surety. He wondered how those fingers would feel moving down his torso, finding every hollow of him.

When Amber had been out of the room looking for the papers, the werewolf had told him in a vicious snarl that if Adrian had a one-night stand with Amber, taking advantage of her grief, Sabina would rip out his throat. She meant it, and as a werewolf, she could certainly do it—or try anyway.

Sabina didn't need to worry. A one-night stand with Amber wasn't what Adrian had in mind. Months, maybe, on a tropical island, watching her swim in the waves, laughing at night as they lounged by a fire. Waking up in the morning to see the sun on her face, moonlight licking her body at night.

Not a one-night stand. A very long association, and every hour worth it.

He reached with his thoughts toward Sabina and put forth the suggestion that she leave.

"I should go," Sabina said. Amber glanced at her in surprise, but Sabina shoved back her chair, clattered her coffee cup to the sink, and headed for the door. "I'll patrol the yard behind our houses and keep an eye on things. And if you need me, just holler. Or scream the house down. I'll be here." She shot Adrian a final dark look, then banged the back door closed behind her.

Adrian swallowed the last of his coffee and pushed the cup aside. "I need to shower. I have dried demon blood on me."

Amber's eye flickered at the abrupt change of subject.

"Are you staying at a hotel? Do you need me to drive you somewhere?"

He stood up. "No, I'm staying here."

"Oh, really?" Her gaze flattened him where he stood.

"I'm not leaving you alone. This house is well warded, but demons are tricky. Your sister likely died because of this." He touched the writing. "You don't need to die for it, too."

"Sabina will notice anyone trying to get in and come to help," she argued. "She noticed you."

"She's not strong enough to fight this demon, and she's mortal, which means she'll need to sleep sometime."

"Oh, and you don't?"

"I do." He enjoyed a moment visualizing Amber sleeping next to him, but her steely gaze told him she wanted him nowhere near her bed. He'd work on that. "But I can stay awake when it's necessary. For as long as it's necessary."

"Fine, then." She wasn't happy, but his subtle play with her mind made her agree. "The *guest* bedroom is at the top of the stairs, and it has an attached bathroom. Towels are in the linen closet at the end of the hall."

"Let me check the house again to make sure all is well, and then I'll take a shower."

"In that case, I'll get the towels."

Adrian got up. She tried to leave the kitchen at the same time he did, and they met at the door. He slid his arm around her waist. If he pulled her against him, they'd just fit, her head tucked under his chin. He felt her heartbeat beneath his arm, speeding like a rabbit's and not entirely in anger.

"After you," he said, changing his half embrace to a gentle push against the small of her back. Her cheeks stained red, and she ducked out the door and scuttled to the stairs. He watched her go, chuckling to himself.

Adrian walked the house, checking every door and window, while Amber rummaged in the linen cupboard upstairs. He saw her carry towels and pillows and bedding into the bedroom at the top of the stairs as he checked the windows in the hall. Farther down from the guest room, he found a bedroom filled with books and candles and framed art posters—controlled clutter. He caught a faint whiff of the perfume Amber wore and smiled.

Another bedroom displayed the same kind of organized chaos but held an air of sadness and disuse, tinged with the tiniest hint of death magic. Susan's room, he guessed.

He reinforced the wards on the window there, then went through the rest of the big house, including the staircase that wound to the top of the tower. He felt the history of the house as he wandered it, but none of that history had been tragic until Susan's death. The house held the usual succession of births, deaths, marriages, parties, happiness, sadness, everyday life.

Amber was still in the guest bathroom when he finished, running the water in the shower. She didn't hear him come into the bedroom, and he pretended he didn't see her.

Quietly setting Ferrin, who morphed into a snake, on a table near the bathroom door, Adrian shed his stained T-shirt, pulled his feet from his boots and socks, and peeled off his jeans before walking into the bathroom.

Amber jumped, pulse racing, when she turned around and found six and a half feet of golden muscle in the bathroom with her. He said, innocence in his voice, "I didn't know you were in here."

He looked down at her with eyes warm and enigmatic. His black hair flowed back from a strong face, caught in a sleek tail. The bare hollow of his throat enticed her, as did the black curls beneath it that spread across strong pectorals. She wanted to touch the planes of his body, explore his warm, male skin with her fingers.

She had no idea why she'd broken down and let him stay, but his arguments were so *convincing*. He exuded an aura of protection that she had the strangest impulse to cling to, much like her impulse to touch him.

When she did touch him, he closed his eyes, and she glanced around him at the mirror to view his strong, straight back.

She gasped. The mirror showed his back was covered with scars, wounds crisscrossed on top of wounds, some old, some new and raw. Some were shallow scratches on his skin and some were deep, where he'd been cut to the bone. There were so many, telling of countless fights.

Amber was no stranger to fighting. Being a witch, she'd had to learn to defend herself from beings of death magic who sometimes tried to attack her. She could fight if she had to with a short half-moon knife she fitted to her knuckles, and Sabina had taught Amber plenty of moves that might come in handy.

None of that preparation had readied Amber for the brutal attack of the demon tonight, a fight that Susan had lost and that Amber might have lost without Adrian. But her rare fights and even the struggle tonight were nothing compared to what must have caused the wreckage of this man's back.

She traced a triangular pucker of skin on his shoulder where someone had driven a sharp object. "Good Goddess, what happened to you?"

Adrian lost his half smile, his eyes filling with old pain. His eyes were black to begin with, and now they looked like a chasm into time itself. "A warrior has to expect to be cut now and again."

"Now and again?" she asked incredulously. "Some of this skin looks like it's been through a meat shredder."

He shrugged. "Swords, knives, arrows, bullets. No meat shredders."

Amber also noticed that an abrasion he'd sustained from the demon tonight was already closing, the wound a pink line. "What are you? And don't give me another lesson about ancient Egypt."

His gaze became more enigmatic still. "Something forgotten in this world."

"I could just ask your snake."

He started to laugh. "I thought you were afraid of him."

"I never said I'd stand close to him when I asked."

Adrian continued to laugh. He threaded his fingers through the short curls on the back of her neck and leaned down to kiss her. His lips slid across hers and his tongue swept briefly into her mouth. She tasted the sharp bite of him, and then he was gone.

He raised his head and rested his broad forearms on her shoulders, continuing to play with her hair. "I'm glad I found you tonight."

"I'm glad you found me, too. Or I'd be dead."

"You would be," he said without boasting. "I'm happy I reached you in time."

She touched his jaw. His whiskers were sandpaper rough, like a human's would be, but then, vampires shaved and could behave like normal humans, as she'd discovered the hard way when she was younger. A vampire could glamour a person's mind to accept them as a human. She'd been in love with Julio for six months before Susan had removed the glamour and she'd learned the awful and humiliating truth.

Susan wasn't here anymore to get rid of glamour spells and protect her little sister. Amber lightly stroked Adrian's jaw, feeling the strength of the muscles beneath his skin.

The pulse beating hard at his throat told her he was very much alive and no vampire. But neither was he a werewolf. She had known Sabina since childhood, and Sabina had always exuded a wolflike air. Her wolf's eyes would narrow in thought, as if she'd caught sight of a rabbit she particularly wanted.

Adrian had nothing of the wolf about him. He had a predatory air, but one that said he fought alone. Amber sensed that his aloneness was not his choice but something he had learned to live with. The sheer loneliness she felt from him was overpowering.

His hand grew firm on the nape of her neck as though he would stop her from falling. "I'm sorry," he said. "You aren't ready for what I am."

She wasn't quite sure why he was apologizing. She continued to look into his eyes, but the feeling of vast emptiness gradually lessened, and she simply looked at a strong man's strong, dark eyes.

"I need to shower." He slowly withdrew his fingers from her neck. Then, before she could stop him, he slipped his briefs to his ankles, stepped out of them, and walked casually to the shower stall.

No way could she not look. The scars couldn't lessen the beauty of the muscular triangle of back from shoulders to hips, strong legs, firm mounds of backside. His black tail of hair hung to the base of his spine, the end curling now in the damp air of the shower. On his left buttock was a tattoo of a pentacle, an upright five-pointed star surrounded by a circle.

He glanced at her, mouth quirked, knowing she couldn't stop staring, and entered the steam-filled stall. Smiling another smile that crinkled the corners of his eyes, he shut the opaque door, steam swirling around his pale body.

She remained staring. What she'd seen stirring between his legs as he stepped into the shower had been firm, well shaped, and incredibly erotic. She couldn't stop imagining him standing in front of her, his staff rising to her hand while he touched her with languid fingers, those dark eyes promising sin.

In the shower, Adrian started to whistle. Amber swallowed hard and made herself turn around and walk deliberately from the room.

By the time Adrian finished his shower, Amber had disappeared. He dried himself off and pulled on his jeans, softly walking through the guest room to the hall.

The door to the bedroom he'd identified as Amber's was tightly closed. He sensed her behind it, in bed perhaps, her breathing too rapid for sleep. He grinned and retreated to his own bedroom.

He sprawled across the double bed, hands locked behind his head. The taste of her kiss had been delectable. The feel of her gaze on him as he'd entered the shower was even more delectable. She'd wanted to see him, she'd wanted to touch, which gratified something deep inside him. He didn't frighten or unnerve her—she wanted him in the raw, basic way a woman wanted a man.

He wanted her with the same intensity, and he was

certain she felt it. Witches carried nature and a part of the mother Goddess in them, and he could feel Amber's solid connection with the earth. Even her name, *Amber,* grounded her, the stone used in magic rituals for healing, protection, and strength. Her magic would complement his when they coupled, and it would be rough and pleasurable and hard to forget. He looked forward to the moment they could shed their clothes together and enjoy a little carnality.

As soon as he judged Amber to be asleep, Adrian rose, and in only his jeans and bare feet, went softly down the hall to Susan's bedroom. As he'd sensed when he'd first explored, this room felt different from the others in the house. Susan had obviously begun to explore negative energies, drawing them to her like a porch light attracts moths.

Dabbling in death magic drew death magic, a fact she'd obviously known, because she'd put a stand of black candles across her windowsill in an effort to keep negativity from crossing. It hadn't worked. Adrian could smell a taint in the air, which was absent in the rest of the house. There had been no tendrils of death magic in Amber's room, and he was willing to believe she was innocent of whatever Susan had been doing.

No, he wanted to believe it. He wanted to find someone who was exactly as she seemed with no duplicity to her. Most witches he met were eager to tap into his power, and often suggested complex sex rituals through which they could. Sometimes he let them, holding his magic back so he wouldn't hurt them, but the aftermath always left him unsatisfied.

Of course, if Amber wanted to practice sex magic with him, he'd throw himself down and invite her to come on in.

He paused in the center of the bedroom and stretched his senses to feel all of it. Susan had been dabbling in many things—from hieroglyphs of a cult of Apep, dark serpent god of Egypt, to the demon language. Why the demon script? She would not have been strong enough to withstand such death magic if she invoked it, and she must have known it.

He wondered where Susan had come across the script at all. Was it an ancient text hidden before Adrian and Isis had destroyed their writings? The script had been used by demons to write rituals to their own gods, invocations that contained strong death magic and unbelievable evil. Only a very powerful demon, or one very old, would know or understand the language. The knowledge that the demon he'd faced tonight was an Old One chilled him to the bone.

One of Adrian's tasks was to keep demons from overrunning the world. He could not kill them all, much as he wanted to, because life and death magic had to stay in balance. Too much of one or the other could unmake the world.

In ancient times, death magic had been very strong, nearly wiping out living magic and the world time and again. Isis had contrived with a priest of Amun to bear a child—Adrian—a demigod who would take on immortality and help humans fight death magic that became too strong. She'd wanted him half-human so that he'd have compassion for humans, and half god to have the magic and life of a god.

A hell of a life. His other brothers had come along one at a time, sired by priests and a different aspect of the mother Goddess. A family of warriors, Immortals, living out of time until summoned by a Calling. At first they'd done nothing but answer the Calls, unaware that they had a choice.

So much had happened since that time, so many world changes, populations rising and falling, then rising again. So much had happened to Adrian, from unbelievable loneliness to unbelievable joy. Now here he stood in a Victorian house in the Pacific Northwest, thinking of the kiss of a woman in a way he'd not in a long time.

He shook his head as he began opening drawers and going through them. He found what he'd expected to find in a witch's room—boxes of candles sorted by color, herbs tied up into bags or loose in jars. Ready-made sticks and cones of incense, plus jars of incense she'd mixed herself. A mortar and pestle and common plastic spoons to measure out various herbs when she needed them. A broom stood in one corner, its handle decorated with streamers.

And books. Shelves upon shelves and piles of books from the latest popular press on Wicca to old texts on herb lore, folklore, folk magic. Susan had marked up her books, highlighting lines or circling rhymes, folding down pages or marking them with scraps of bright paper. None of them bore the demon script, or any reference to it.

In a drawer he found Susan's notes in three-ring binders, one notebook per year. Each notebook was neatly organized into seasons, rituals, notes of tarot readings and scryings, spells, and esbat workings.

"I've already been through all those," Amber said from the doorway.

# CHAPTER THREE

Adrian didn't start at Amber's voice. He'd heard her footsteps in the hall, caught her scent on the air, and felt the unmistakable touch of her aura. He would always be able to sense her coming.

He flicked slowly through the notebook from the previous year without looking up. "I know you have. But I might see something you missed or didn't understand."

She came to him, feet whispering on the carpeted floor. She wore a long nightshirt loose at the neck, which gave him a glimpse of the soft woman inside.

"How could I not understand?" Amber asked. "She and I were trained together."

"I meant you might miss the significance of something, or she might have hidden it from your eyes."

"With a glamour, you mean?" Amber moved uneasily as she peered at the page he read. "I would detect any glamour Susan cast."

"Not if she really wanted to hide something from you."

"And have you found anything?"

"Not here." He closed the notebook. "If she wanted to

hide something that much, she'd put it someplace more secret, especially if she didn't want *you* to find it. Hiding in plain sight sometimes works, but probably not with you, not from her."

Amber's brown-gold eyes held caution. "You know so little about her. And I know nothing about you. You say you want to help, but why should you? Susan's murder has nothing to do with you—you aren't even from around here."

"Because as I told you, this goes beyond Susan's death," he explained patiently. "It's about death magic and its wielders, not the murder of one insignificant witch."

Tears softened Amber's eyes. "She wasn't insignificant to me."

"I know."

Adrian set aside the notebook. He turned Amber to face him and peered down into the depths of her eyes to a place most people kept closed off from the world. He easily opened her doors, reaching into the essence of her. Her brow furrowed; she knew he was doing something but was not quite able to understand what. Her response made her different from most people, who never felt a thing when he probed them.

"You have such innocence." He brushed her cheek-bone with his thumb.

She made an effort to blink back her tears. "I did some pretty wild stuff in college."

He didn't laugh. "Trust me, you are innocent. It's like a shining light in a world of darkness."

"That sounds poetic."

"I'm a bad poet. I'm a fighter. I don't have a way with words."

"Seems to me you're doing fine," she said.

He leaned down and kissed her, taking his time this time. A taste of lips, smooth and warm with sleep, then the spicier bite of her tongue.

She made a faint noise of acceptance and her hand came up to rest on the back of his neck. She pulled him closer to deepen the kiss, and wanting thrummed through him. Adrian knew how to keep sex casual. He fulfilled his needs, and his partners fulfilled theirs. Mutual pleasuring, nothing beyond.

He already knew that one short burst with this woman would never be enough. He'd want her again and again and again, and that would be foolish for both of them.

She wormed her fingers beneath his hair. "So, do you have a girlfriend?"

He drew back a little, surprised. "No."

"Wife, fiancée, significant other?"

"No."

"Just checking. I don't either, by the way. Have a significant other, I mean."

"I know."

She frowned, her lovely eyes so close. "How could you know? I might have a boyfriend."

He flicked his tongue across her lower lip. "If you had someone, his pictures would be in your room. His clothes would be lying around, and you'd have beer in your refrigerator. There's nothing masculine in this house, and the only pictures of a man are ones of your father in the living room."

She shot him a look of grudging respect. "Are you a detective or something?"

"Let's just say I like to solve problems."

"And you want to solve mine?"

He smoothed her hair from her forehead. "I find that I do."

"You seem like you want to solve *one* of my problems." She leaned a little into him, where his obvious arousal pressed his jeans. Good thing he'd left Ferrin behind in the bedroom. The snarky snake would laugh himself sick.

Adrian wanted more than anything to pick her up and carry her back to her bedroom and lay with her across her bed. He would run his fingers through her short hair, smiling to see it curl around his fingertips. He would kiss her brows, her nose and mouth, her chin and throat, and nuzzle the opening of her nightshirt. He would strip the nightshirt away altogether and let his hands drift over her body, learning its curves.

He could go farther, ease his fingers inside her, gently stroking her to arousal, and then enter her. He'd be surrounded by the scent, taste, and feel of her, and he'd not let go until they climaxed together.

A nice dream. Her kiss told him she wouldn't mind it, but then, he hadn't really let her have her own thoughts since he'd broken through her circle in the warehouse. He could make her do this for him, and he could even make her forget afterward.

*But I'll remember.*

Her fingertips grazed his biceps while she circled her tongue in his mouth. His bare skin was damp with sweat, her touch raising goosebumps. His sex was plenty hard, and the tip would poke above his waistband if he didn't stop this. What if she slid her hand down his torso and found it there? Would she flinch and back off? Or would she run her fingers around the shaft, flicking her thumb back and forth over the top, rubbing the excitement already there?

"No," he said under his breath.

He broke the kiss and tried to make himself hold her

at arm's length. It didn't work; he only got a hand's-length away from her warmth. "Like I said before, you're not ready for what I am. Not yet."

Hurt flashed in her eyes, quickly masked by an indifferent look. She was trying to signal to him, *No great loss.*

He held her with his hands at the small of her back. "Not because I don't want you. Believe me, I want you. I want you right now, and to hell with discovering what's going on with death magic. But I can't always have what I want. Never, in fact."

Her brows shot up. "Never? What does that mean?"

"It means that as much as I tried to break away, I never can. I can be bad-ass and refuse to come running when the goddesses call, but I'm as defeated as if I'd gone back to Ravenscroft like a good boy and pretended my brother was dead."

"Ravenscroft?" She jumped, her eyes widening, as though she'd only heard the one word in his entire speech.

"You know that name?" Most mortals had never heard of it, the Valhalla where he and his brothers had grown up and trained, where they'd waited to be Called. Those were the old days, when everything was as neat and organized as Susan's notebooks, when Adrian had thought his life had a purpose.

"I found mention of it in Susan's notes when I searched her room the day after she died. What is Ravenscroft, and what does it have to do with you?"

Under her touch, Adrian went very still. The enigmatic darkness of his eyes showed nothing, but the fierceness of his expression gave her pause.

"What is it?" she asked.

"Show me what you found," he said.

His teasing, provocative tone had vanished, and in place of the man who'd just kissed her thoroughly stood a hard warrior who'd faced down enemies she couldn't imagine. She'd only half believed him when he said he'd been alive since before the great pyramids of Giza, but now she realized she was in the room with an ancient being, one powerful enough to erase her with a thought.

He wasn't a vampire or a werewolf or even a demon. He was something stronger, and she should be terrified of him. She dimly realized that her mind was half in fog and had been since she'd met him. She knew deep inside that she should have run screaming from him and his cobra a long time ago.

She had the sudden knowledge that helping him further would be a great mistake. She should let Susan go, continue the preparations for Beltane, and forget she'd ever met Adrian.

"Show me," he repeated in a hard voice.

She found herself obeying. As she padded back to her own room, where she'd taken a few of Susan's notebooks, part of her wanted to run down the stairs and out of the house, to find Sabina, to stay with her tonight for protection. Instead she led Adrian to her bedroom, opened the door, and let him inside.

Amber laid the notebooks out on her rumpled bed, and Adrian sat down next to them. She noted that no underwear showed above the waistband of his low-slung jeans. As he lifted the first notebook and started flipping through it, the glare of her bedside lamp highlighted the mass of scars on his back and across his shoulders. He'd fought plenty of demons, likely werewolves and vampires too, that had scored his skin and never killed him. What the hell was he?

She sat beside him, the mattress dipping under their

combined weight. He skimmed pages quickly, flipping them in rapid succession before she could focus on more than two words on each.

He stopped so suddenly it startled her. Over his shoulder, she read: *Ravenscroft. Is it real? Not enough data. Waterhouse mentions it as a mythical place of the Immortals, but no further reference. Waterhouse deceased now, so can't ask him.*

When he turned the page, Adrian went rigid beside her, his eyes focused with dead stillness on the next sheet. It was covered with sketches of a man, with a note: *Images from riding between, February 28.* Susan had drawn sketches of a man with an incredibly handsome face and long hair, who looked so much like Adrian that Amber gasped.

The next page had a note only: *Nearly caught while riding between last night by a demon stronger than I've ever known. But learned a name. Tain. If I am right, he was an Immortal, and if I am right, they must be stopped. If his intent is what I think it is.*

On the next page, Susan had drawn a circle with a line through it, with a caption: *The end of the world as we know it.*

Adrian looked up, his eyes throwing sparks into the dim room like they'd done in the warehouse. "Show me the rest. Show me every single thing she ever wrote down, no matter how unimportant you think it is. Don't hide anything from me."

Amber jumped at the ferocity in his tone but held on to her courage. "You saw everything. I left all her journals in her room except these two."

He leapt up. "We need to search the house." He kept his thumb on the page with the drawings, and he held the book so tightly his fingers were bloodless white. He was huge and strong, a half-naked warrior in her bedroom, body firm under skin that had been ravaged by the same battles that honed his muscles. He could do anything, but he held back, even in his anger.

"Wait," Amber said as he left the room. She slid off the bed and caught up to him in the hall. His eyes still sparked, white-hot specks swimming in the darkness. "Is this why Susan died? Because she knew about Tain, your brother?"

"Yes," he said, his voice cold. Amber almost expected the air to freeze as he spoke. "This is exactly why she died." He turned on his heel and headed for Susan's bedroom.

Adrian wasn't kidding when he'd said "search the house." He started in Susan's room, peeling up floorboards, peering into every crevice before demanding a hammer and chisel so he could pry off the baseboards too.

Amber tried to weave a spell around him to at least make him slow down and explain why Susan knowing about Tain and Ravenscroft was important, but when the spell touched him he only looked over his shoulder in irritation and kept on wrenching up boards.

At one point, he held out his arm and snapped his fingers impatiently. Amber wondered what he wanted; then she heard a slithering sound on the hallway runner and looked down to see Ferrin bending himself around the door frame. She jumped backward, knocking her elbow painfully against the doorknob. The snake looked at her with its glittering black eyes, and if snakes could smirk, this one was smirking.

Lowering his head, Ferrin slid along to Adrian, who grabbed him and fed him into the hole he'd created, telling the snake to report back what he found.

Amber decided to make Adrian coffee rather than watch him tear her family's house apart one piece at a time.

When she came back upstairs with a cup for him, Ferrin was coiled around Adrian's biceps again as the silver armlet. Adrian sat on his heels in the middle of the floor, his fingers tracing the sketches in Susan's book. His huge body shook all over, his naked back heaving as if he were having a seizure.

Amber plunked down the cup and hurried to him in alarm. Not until she knelt next to him, touching his shoulder, did she see that he was crying. Not just crying, weeping, his eyes screwed shut, his mouth drawn in grief, his cheeks wet with silent tears. Sorrow poured from him in waves, a grief that threatened to knock her over and maybe pull down the house with it.

"Adrian?" she whispered. When he didn't respond, she lifted a lock of hair from his wet cheek. "You all right?"

He didn't acknowledge her. He was lost in some world of his own, his fingers blindly tracing the drawings as if he could feel every stroke of the lines.

*Riding between,* Susan had written. Riding between was dangerous, and only very strong witches attempted it. It meant riding dreams in the world between the conscious and unconscious mind, the astral plane, but the witch had to be firmly anchored to her body or she'd be lost forever to the ether. The witch could travel along ley lines, using the tendrils of power that snaked around the earth to keep them tied to their bodies.

The fact that Susan had been doing it and not telling Amber chilled her. A witch often asked another witch to sit with her while she rode, so that if her mortal body showed any sign of distress, the other witch could wake her and pull her back home before it was too late.

Susan had seen this man while riding between, and something about him and Immortals had worried her very much. Very likely she had gone to the warehouse to understand what she'd found in the dream, maybe even to learn how to stop it. Susan had been a very strong witch, often attempting dangerous magic that Amber begged her not to.

Susan usually won through on strength of will, which only bolstered her confidence to try things even more dangerous. Amber was a more practical witch, learning how to earn their bread and butter from reading rune stones or performing cleansing spells, using magic to make their lives roll along. A "domestic witch," Susan always called her. Susan had the talent and creativity, and she and Amber had shouted through many arguments about what the Craft was truly for.

"Adrian." Amber gently stroked his shoulder. Whatever he'd suffered had been terrible, and he'd suffered it alone.

He opened eyes that were wet and shining like dark jewels. He traced the drawing of the man again, his mouth pulled in sorrow.

"That's your brother?" she asked.

He nodded slowly, finally acknowledging her. "In seven hundred years, this is the first trace I've ever found of him."

Amber made him drink the coffee. She convinced him to stop tearing up the room and return to her bedroom, where she sat cross-legged on the bed with him and watched him sip the steaming liquid. Adrian drank thoughtfully, stopping to wipe away fresh tears when they leaked from his eyes. Unlike most males she knew, he seemed in no way ashamed of crying. Amber understood. Some grief was too important to keep bottled up.

"Are you going to tell me about it?" she asked.

"This is dangerous knowledge, Amber."

"I figured that. I also figure I know too much already, so you might as well tell me the rest."

He reached out and grasped her hand, his fingers warm from the coffee mug. She felt his pulse beating through his hand, his heartbeat quick and hard, his skin warmer than a normal human's. "I'll do better than that. I'll show you."

"How do you plan to do that?" she asked nervously. "Psychic projection?"

"No." He cupped her cheek and tilted her head so she looked straight into his eyes. "Stronger magic than a parlor trick."

She couldn't have looked away even if she'd wanted to. He held her with his black gaze, which promised her the secrets of the universe if only she learned how to read them. She sensed the room whirling away from her, but it was all right, because she was with him. His strong hand warmed her face, and she found comfort in falling into the darkness of his eyes.

The first thing she felt was cold. Bone-chilling, icy cold from wind that had swept across an Arctic sea. She stood on a wooded slope that tumbled to a clear blue lake at the bottom, a vast sheet of water that curved out of sight around a jagged mountain. She glimpsed a castle in the distance, something square and squat. It was a fortress, not a fairy-tale castle, grim and faceless, meant for fighting. Adrian was nowhere in sight.

"Adrian?" Her voice rang in the sudden emptiness.

Her breath didn't mist, though it should have in that climate, telling her she was only magically there. In truth she must still be in her bedroom with Adrian, his hands cupping her face, his dark eyes making her see what he wanted her to see.

She started down the slope, noting that she still had to step over brambles and fallen branches, though they didn't cut her feet.

"Adrian, where are you?" she called.

No answer. She gritted her teeth and kept hurrying down the hill, for some reason believing that she'd find Adrian, or at least an answer to where he'd gone, at the bottom. She never got out of breath or hurt, and she thought it unfair that she had to search for him at all.

Unless something had gone wrong. This was somewhat like riding between—Amber had attempted it twice in her life. Even with Susan supervising, it had scared her senseless both times. But this was different. She could not feel any ley lines tethering her to her own body, didn't feel weightless and able to flit from place to place with a thought. Riding between had always left her slightly motion sick.

"You might have warned me I'd have to hike," she muttered. "Whoever you are, Adrian, you're driving me insane. Which only proves you're *male*."

She heard shouting, deep hoarse shouts, and the clash of metal on metal. Skidding to a halt, she peered into a clearing that led to the shores of the lake.

A dozen creatures with bent backs and leathery wings circled above a lone warrior. The warrior stood six foot six and wore mail covered by a surcoat stained with blood. He had a chain-mail hood and greaves on his arms and legs. He hefted a huge sword Amber had seen earlier that night at the warehouse.

Adrian turned in a wary circle, watching the demons, his sword held ready. A word swam in Amber's brain: Unseelie. Large, strong, bad-smelling Celtic nasties that killed cattle and stole children and did other traditional evil things. Right now they were ganging up to kill Adrian.

Amber had no way to tell whether this Adrian was from the past, which meant she already knew he'd live through the fight, or if he was the Adrian she'd met tonight, pulled into some kind of bizarre game their demon had started. The Adrian in blue jeans slung low across his hips was nowhere in sight.

The Unseelies all charged him at the same time from different directions. Amber shoved her hand in her mouth to stifle her scream as they lunged at him. She started to conjure magics in her mind, but they petered out, reminding her this place wasn't real, it was Adrian's memory. Her magical body and mind remained on the bed in her house.

A warrior's cry rose from Adrian's throat and echoed from the clearing to ring across the lake and surrounding mountains. Adrian swung his sword in a furious arc, slamming into first one monster, then another. The Unseelies struck back without remorse, using their advantage of aerial height. This was no choreographed Hollywood fight, where the crowd of villains politely waited for the hero to take them one at a time. The monsters swarmed him, determined to kill.

Adrian methodically beat them back. Amber saw talons rake his shoulders, some foiled by the chain mail while others sliced through it to find blood. She understood his scars now, from battles like this and many others. He didn't stumble or go down, he fought relentlessly, shoving the sword through bodies, a ferocious smile on his face.

The creatures dropped dead at his feet as they were stabbed, the odor making Amber gag. The remaining Unseelies, instead of running away, kept at him, as though they couldn't leave until either he or they were dead. Adrian shouted again, his strong voice rolling off the mountainside, and then Amber realized he was laughing. He thought this was *fun*.

When all the monsters had been slain in a circle around him, Adrian stood still a moment, chest heaving; then he whooped in victory and tossed his sword in the air, end over end. He caught the sword by the hilt, its blade black with blood.

"Tain!" he shouted. "I'm done. 'Twas easy, as you said." The words were not English, but she understood them inside his memories.

Adrian's laughter rolled across the lake. "Tain!" he called again. He waited, listening, but everything was silent except the faint roar of the trees. "I thirst. Let us hie to the village and drown ourselves in a barrel of ale."

He waited another moment, then began making his way toward the lake, pulling off his chain-mail hood and letting the wind stream through his long hair as he went. "Tain?"

Amber listened too. At first she heard nothing but the trees; not even a bird call split the silence. She thought a whisper floated on the wind, a faint sound that could have been words, but then it was gone.

Adrian had heard it too. He halted, staring out over the lake to the castle at the far end. Resting the sword over his shoulder, he started to walk, then to stride, and finally to run.

Amber made a noise of frustration and scrambled after him, but suddenly the woods whipped away from her, and she landed on her feet inside a dark stone room. The walls were made of huge blocks of stone, not well finished, and she guessed that she was now inside the castle.

Adrian was there too. So were about ten people who lay on the floor, their bodies still with death. Some were bloody, others looked as though they'd just dropped in place. Adrian said a foul word and strode across the room, sorrow creasing his face as he stepped over the bodies.

One young woman was still alive. Her gown had been made of a fine material, thick against the weather, and she wore the tattered remains of a fur cloak. Adrian knelt over her, raising her head to his lap as Amber moved closer to hear.

"Where is Tain?" Adrian asked urgently.

"Gone."

Again, they didn't speak English, probably a dialect of old Gaelic, but Amber understood.

"Gone where? He abandoned you?"

"No." The girl tried to grip Adrian's arm, but her hand fell back, weak. "She took him. She took him, and her demons killed us."

"Who did?"

The girl's voice was a faint whisper. "Nimue."

Adrian showed no surprise at the name of the sorceress who had seduced Merlin of legend and sealed him in a cave. Only the tightening of his muscles betrayed his anger. "Tell me what happened." His voice was both gentle and urgent.

"He protected us until the end. But there were too

many. He couldn't fight them off and protect us too. Then *she* came." The girl swallowed, her eyes moving back and forth as though she could no longer see Adrian. "She took him away. He went with her, he didn't fight . . . She must have enchanted . . ."

Her voice trailed off. Adrian stroked her hair comfortingly. "Stay still. Help will come."

The girl opened her eyes again. "No, I cannot . . ." Her voice broke, and this time she went still with death.

Adrian's expression changed from one of gentle comfort to rage so pure it radiated from him like magic. White sparks danced in his eyes, the incredible power Amber had sensed in him earlier coming to the surface. He closed the girl's eyes with his gloved fingers, then bowed his head, his hand splaying across his face as though he prayed for her.

Amber let out a sigh of sympathy. The poor young woman had believed that Tain and Adrian would defend her, but her words had not blamed either of them in the end.

Adrian looked up suddenly, his white-hot gaze focusing on Amber. He *saw* her, even though he shouldn't be able to—this was a vision, a memory, and he was from the past.

"Leave them be," he snarled and flung his hand out, fingers open.

Power streamed from him like waves on a pond and sent Amber flying backward. She screamed and flailed, and then instantly was on her feet on the wooded slope, gasping for breath. Silence flooded the valley, and Adrian was still nowhere in sight.

Another blast of freezing wind poured down from the mountains, making her teeth chatter, even though she knew that her between state kept her protected from the real cold. With the wind came a cry, a haunting scream of anguish and pain she couldn't begin to fathom.

*Adrian! Help me!*

The cry was so full of torment that Amber wanted to rush to his side, wherever he was.

*Adrian!*

"You can hear him?" Adrian asked beside her.

Amber jumped, heart in throat. He stood next to her as though he'd always been there, dressed in the mail and tattered surcoat, his sword held point downward between his huge hands.

"He didn't cry out the day he was taken." Adrian scanned the valley, his dark eyes flickering. "Only in my dreams. It's haunted me for centuries."

Amber rubbed her hands over her arms, trying to scrub warmth into them. "Let me get this straight. Tain was lured away by Nimue the sorceress?"

Adrian shook his head. "The girl could have seen anyone—a goddess, a demon in woman's form, a witch. The girl knew the stories and decided she'd seen Nimue. I saw no reason to argue with her."

"She said Tain went willingly, without fighting."

"I know." His deep blue surcoat stirred in the wind, his face incredibly sad. "Though I've started to wonder whether he did go willingly. He'd fallen in love with a woman, wanted to stay with her. I was annoyed, lectured him on his duty, and he defied me. It's obvious that the Unseelies attacking the valley were a diversion to get me out of the way while he went off with her—leaving those people to die. She'd never have taken him if I had been there. That's what I've had to live with all these years."

"You don't know that," Amber pointed out. "You don't know you would have been able to stop it."

His eyes were somber. "I do know." His clothes changed to the blue jeans, his torso naked to the wind. "From that day to this I've never found a scrap of evidence of him. Me, the great Immortal warrior," he finished bitterly.

"How did Susan find out?" Amber wondered.

"That is what I need to know. And more to the point, *what* she found out."

Amber reached out and slid her fingers through his. "I'm sorry, Adrian. I wish I knew more. I wish Susan would have told me what she was up to. She was probably trying to protect me from dangerous knowledge. I wish I could help you better."

Adrian gave her a puzzled look. "You care about this."

"Of course I care. I just lost my sister—I know what you went through. The shock, the hope that it's all a mistake, that she'll come walking through the door, laughing that she played a joke. The question of whether I could have done something to prevent it. Was it my fault? The constant *why?* and *what did I do wrong?* Am I close?"

"Yes." He stroked her fingers with his thumb. "The only difference is, I know that somewhere Tain is still alive, trapped, and in pain. I have to find him."

The wooded hills spun away along with the cold, and the two of them were sitting on her bed again in her warm house in Seattle. Adrian ran his hand through his hair that was tangled by the wind. His eyes still held tears as though their journey had lasted but a second—and maybe it had.

"Now I remember," he said, voice soft. "Where I'd seen you before."

Amber knew she should stop herself, but she decided not to. She closed the space between them, moved onto his lap, and wrapped her arms around him. He stiffened in surprise. Then his arms came around her, and he held her close.

# CHAPTER FOUR

Adrian buried his face in Amber's neck, taking comfort in her sweet scent. He'd become so used to being alone in his grief that her burst of compassion startled him.

Showing her what happened on the day Tain disappeared had been harder than he'd expected. A brief flash, then it was gone, though to her it had happened in real time. But even the short moment reliving the shock of Tain's disappearance cut at him.

She was right; when people lost someone to violence they blamed themselves for not preventing it. *I should have known, I should have seen, I should have been there.*

He still wasn't certain why he'd confided in her, but finding sketches of Tain in her sister's notebooks had pushed him over the edge. How had Susan seen him, and what did the demon writing have to do with it?

Amber raised her head and looked at him. He knew that she was offering comfort and compassion, but her tawny eyes held depths of promise—a sensual woman who didn't realize how sensual she was. When he kissed her, she didn't resist, and she didn't resist when he pushed her down onto the bed and stretched out on top of her.

She tasted as sweet as she smelled. He nuzzled her throat, and she slid her fingers to the back of his jeans and dipped her hand under the waistband.

"I knew it," she whispered. "I knew you weren't wearing underwear."

Her smile did things to him, from warming his icy, lonely heart to warming other parts of his anatomy. His erection rose as her fingers explored the bare skin of his backside and the hollow between his buttocks. He'd only met her a short while ago, but he wanted her in the worst way, and he hoped to Isis that finding her wasn't a trick of the demon.

But she felt real, not like a demon manifestation. There was nothing in her eyes and in her mind but herself, and nothing evil in this house but what her sister had been dabbling in. Amber's room felt only of her own clean magic, of the devotions she said every morning to the Goddess and the God, of layers of magic that had overlapped each other as she grew.

Her fingers worked magic of their own. His skin heated and his cock rose. He needed her. "If you don't stop that . . ."

She looked up at him, eyes bright. "What? I'll regret it?"

"I hope so," he growled.

She removed her hand from inside his pants and teased fingers over his back, tracing the scars. She was the only woman who understood what his scars meant. Most women closed their eyes tight after they saw his back, or were so busy squealing under him that they never noticed. Amber noticed, knew his scars were part of him, and wasn't afraid of them.

He nipped her neck, breathing her spice. The sensation caused her to wriggle, her body moving in a good way under the loose nightshirt, soft curve of breasts rubbing his chest.

"You told me you weren't a vampire," she admonished teasingly.

"That doesn't mean I don't want to taste you."

To his surprise, she licked his neck from collarbone to jaw. "You taste good too."

He parted the placket of her nightshirt, feathering small kisses over the hollow of her throat. Her scent and warmth enticed him to slide a hand inside the nightshirt and cup her breast. The nipple rose, warm and taut, to meet his palm.

She moved her hand around to the front of his waistband, popping the button. He shifted so she could explore, and stifled a groan when her cool hand found his hot, hard shaft pressing against the zipper.

Her eyes widened behind thick lashes. "Goddess. What are you, size twenty?"

He gave her a puzzled look. "There are sizes?"

"I've heard it corresponds to shoe size."

He wanted to laugh. He still had tears in his eyes, still felt the anguish of Tain begging for help, and she made him want to laugh.

She slid awkward fingers into the tight place between his stem and his abdomen. She found niches and stroked them, wicked sensations tingling from her fingers to heat his blood. When he took her it would be satisfying, deeply satisfying, and he wouldn't stop after just once.

He unbuttoned and unzipped his jeans, widening his legs so she could reach more of him. Her breasts lay open to the light, lovely and firm and beckoning his mouth.

As much as he wanted her to play with him, he wanted to explore her too. He propped himself on his elbow, and while she continued to stroke him, he brushed his tongue around her aureole, suckling it to make it dark and tight.

His temperature rose as her fingers continued dancing on his shaft. He balled his hand in the bedcovers as she found a bead of moisture in his slit and smoothed it across his tip. He was going to climax just from her touching him. Ferrin would laugh. *Adrian, the mighty warrior. Always in perfect control.*

Amber smiled up at him, eyes languid. "Thank you for rescuing me."

He clenched his teeth against the climax rising to take him and answered thickly. "I always enjoy sticking a sword through a demon."

"I'm sorry he got away."

"I'll find him," he promised. "And make him answer questions." He groaned, fighting off his climax as Amber's hand tightened on his shaft.

"I'd like him to answer one question," she said in a hard voice.

Adrian eased her fingers open a little. "Remind me not to piss you off. You have a dangerous grip."

"Sorry." She gentled her touch, and her gaze turned thoughtful. "If you were born in the time of the first Egyptian dynasties, how is it you speak modern English slang?"

"Because you wouldn't understand me if I spoke ancient Egyptian," he said. "Phrases haven't changed much in six thousand years. We fall back on the very basics when it's most important."

"Are things important now?"

"Meeting you is one of the most important things

that's happened in a long, long time. I don't know exactly why it will be important, but it is."

Her brown-gold gaze studied him as though she wanted to penetrate his defenses and see all the way inside him. He couldn't let her, not yet. What he was could hurt her, and the last thing he wanted to do to this innocence was hurt it.

He gently nudged her mind to not want to wonder about him, and she let her eyes drift closed. She continued to skim her fingers over his cock, and Adrian lay back and let himself enjoy the feel of what she did to him.

The urge to climax eased, but the excitement didn't cease. He moved his hips, letting his shaft slide through her grip. She made a little noise of satisfaction, as if what they were doing made her feel good too.

He wanted to take her. He saw no reason not to—they were alone on her bed, no one to answer to, nowhere to go. He could satisfy himself deep within her and bring her to climax again and again, letting his sorrow fade away in the sultry night.

She looked straight at him, and he knew she wanted it too. The tingling excitement of strangers choosing to have sex, except he felt somehow that he'd known her always.

On his arm, Ferrin suddenly morphed to his snake form and slithered across the bed. He touched Amber on the way, and she jerked, losing her hold on Adrian. "I *wish* he wouldn't do that."

Ferrin faced the window and reared up, his hood flaring.

"What is it, my friend?" Adrian asked, coming alert.

Ferrin swayed, his black eyes fixed on the window. *By the pricking of my thumbs, something wicked this way comes.*

"You don't have thumbs," Adrian quipped, but he rolled away from Amber and zipped up his jeans. Amber pulled her nightshirt closed, as watchful as Adrian.

"It might just be Sabina," she suggested. "She said she'd be prowling."

"No." Adrian felt the surge of death magic, the sudden draining of light and hope and anything worth living for. "It's not a werewolf."

Ferrin hissed again, his body rigid. *Demon,* he announced, and then all hell broke loose.

Wind exploded through the bedroom, strong as a tornado, picking up books, trinkets, papers, candles, and ornaments and hurling them through the air. The bed shook and started to rise, the furniture coming off the floor. A blackness rose with the wind, twining through the debris like it wove a net to strangle them.

Adrian grabbed Amber and rolled with her to the floor behind the bed, protecting her with his body and hoping the bed didn't leap up and land on top of them. Ferrin slithered past him, the snake's body cool and rigid.

A chair smashed into the wall, raining splinters onto Adrian's bare back, stinging his flesh. Amber huddled under him, but she wasn't crying or fearful—her golden-brown eyes snapped in rage. "This house is warded. How can death magic get in?"

"He rode the vision back with us. I brought him in." Adrian ducked suddenly to shield her as a shelfload of books sailed over and fell on top of him.

"But even going between, the wards should hold against death magic," Amber shouted over the noise.

"Not after your sister let some in."

The whirlwind picked up crystals and smashed them against the mirror above her dresser. Shards of glass slashed around the room, as deadly as bullets, cutting Adrian's skin. One splinter got past him, and blood blossomed on Amber's cheek.

Adrian's rage flared. He flung himself to his feet, dodging the lamp that came flying at him at a hundred miles an hour. Ferrin slithered under the bed. *Coward.*

Adrian spread his arms and bellowed an ancient word of command, his voice ringing over the commotion and the howling of the unnatural wind. The sound roared out of his mouth, filled with his rage. It was a word of power he rarely used, one from the dawn of time that hadn't been heard in the world in thousands of years. It was dangerous, telling the unseen things of the world exactly what he was and where he was.

The wind abruptly ceased. Amber's books and papers and crystals hung in midair for a moment, then dashed to the floor. Glass shattered, paper fluttered, and suddenly everything went silent.

Amber put white hands on the side of the bed and pulled herself up to look over the mattress. "Is it over?"

"For now. You can come out, Ferrin."

The snake poked his head out from under the bed. His tongue flicked as he tested the air. Then he slid quickly up the bedpost and hid under a pillow.

"Pack up some clothes," Adrian said. "And as much of Susan's research as you can."

Amber looked dismayed as she surveyed the complete mess of her bedroom. "What for?"

"We can't stay here. The demon coasted in on our vision, and he'll find a way to coast in again. We need to get whatever Susan found away from here."

"But you stopped the attack."

"I slowed him down a little." He took Amber's hands and pulled her up. "This is no ordinary demon. He's something ancient, an Old One, a demon from before my time. My brothers and I were created to stand against such demons, and we did, but it took our combined power to do so. I hadn't thought demons of that caliber still existed."

"A demon worse than your garden-variety demon?" Amber asked, eyes widening. "Terrific."

"He killed your sister and he's after something—her knowledge of Tain, maybe. So we need to find Tain before the demon does."

Her dark brows furrowed. "Why would an ancient demon be interested in your brother?"

"I have no idea. If I can decipher the writing, maybe I can find out."

Amber took his hand. Her fingers were warm against his—she was always warm. "What I mean is, why is he looking for your brother when *you* are right here in front of him? If he wants an Immortal, why not take you?"

Adrian shook his head. "I don't know. I'm pretty powerful, and not easy to take. Tain has been missing for seven hundred years. If a demon is suddenly interested in him, I want to know why."

"I can't just leave, Adrian. I have clients. And I have students to teach how not to blow themselves up doing candle spells."

"They'll be safer without you near them."

His warrior's body hummed with the need to act, not argue. He'd been pent up, ready to climax under her erotic touch, then had to force a huge amount of magic through himself to close the gap against the demon. He wanted to rush Amber to safety, then turn and fight. It was what he was made to do. Well-reasoned debates weren't his style.

"Where can we possible stay?" she went on. "This

house has been warded for a century and a half. And if the demon can get in here, where are we safe?"

"My house."

Her eyes widened. "Don't you live in Los Angeles?"

"Yes. You don't need to pack many clothes. We can buy what you need when you get there."

Amber looked at the mess again, pulse beating in her throat. It reminded Adrian just how delectable her skin tasted. His adrenaline and his need for her crashed in a maelstrom inside him.

"What about my house?" Amber asked, oblivious of his desire to throw her down to the mess and take her, never mind they didn't have time. "What will keep the demon from totally trashing the place?"

"He'll be following us, so he'll leave it alone."

"That's supposed to make me feel better?" she asked.

"The safest place you can be is with me." Adrian restlessly crossed the room and pulled a suitcase out of the closet. He tossed it onto the bed. "Start packing, or I'll do it, and you know I'll pick the wrong things. Forty-five hundred years observing humans and I still don't know what clothes females consider important."

Amber looked like she wanted to argue some more, but she finally turned to the dresser, which the wind had shoved sideways, and opened a drawer. "Last-minute plane tickets will cost a fortune. Unless you have a private jet standing by?"

"We won't fly." He pushed aside the enticing thought of snuggling with her in the back seat of a plane, kissing her as he pressed her against a bulkhead. "I'd rather not be trapped on a plane with a powerful demon chasing me. Plus, we'd bring danger to the other passengers and the pilots. He could use their lives as blackmail."

"I notice you feel free to put *me* in danger," Amber said as she stuffed handfuls of lingerie into her bag.

"You are already in danger, and I'm not letting you out of my protection. We'll take your car."

She blinked. "That will be safe?"

"As safe as anything. You ward your car, don't you?"

"Of course, but it's, what, a sixteen-hour drive to Los Angeles?"

He lifted the notebooks he'd dragged to the floor with them and tossed them into her suitcase on top of her underwear—her lacy bikini underwear. "I think so. But that's all right, I can drive and you can sleep. Bring some CDs if you want. I like Stevie Ray Vaughan."

Half an hour later, they were speeding south through Seattle toward Oregon and California beyond. Amber glanced at Adrian, who sat calmly behind the wheel, dark eyes flickering as he watched passing traffic, strong fingers steering with a light touch.

Sixteen hours, give or take, to his house with a demon chasing them all the way, and he was worried about CDs. She felt herself inexorably pulled into something bigger than she was, bigger even than Susan's murder, and Adrian, the being who dragged her firmly into the mire, was now the only one who could protect her.

City lights glared on the windshield as they rolled through town, barely any traffic to slow them down. This early it was cool, and Amber was glad of the windbreaker she'd snatched up. Fog floated in patches from Puget Sound, wisping across the headlights like ghosts.

Adrian leaned back in the seat, one arm resting on the wheel as if he enjoyed driving. He'd brushed his black hair and rebound it, letting the tail hang loose down his back. His square face and sinful eyes made him look like a hero out of a romance novel, but experience had imprinted him, sharpening his edges. He'd seen much, he'd fought much, and he was no pretty-boy.

He wore his black coat over his still-stained T-shirt, and the leather gaped where the demon had pummeled him with the steel pole. She traced the gash across his shoulders as he steered the car around a curve.

"Sorry about your coat," she ventured. They'd said nothing to each other since pulling onto the freeway that led through the city.

His body rippled with a shrug. "I have another one."

He fell silent again, eyes moving as he assessed the few cars around them. They hadn't heard from the demon since Adrian had tossed Amber's suitcase into her car and told her to get in.

"How did you get rid of the demon?" she asked. "I've never felt power like that before. You stopped the storm cold."

"An ancient spell," he said offhandedly, as though he tossed around such magic all the time. "The magical equivalent of tear gas." He rubbed the sinewy hand that rested on the steering wheel. "Hard to call up, though."

"It seemed easy for you."

"Not really. My brother Hunter is better at words of power than I am. Probably because they allow him more time to sit on his ass."

"He's an Immortal too?" When Adrian nodded, she asked. "So why haven't I ever heard of Immortals if you've been around so long?"

He gave another shrug, leather creaking. "Much knowledge about Immortals has been lost."

"Enlighten me," she said impatiently. "It's a long trip."

Adrian gave her a sideways look. For a few moments,

she thought he wouldn't answer her. Then he settled back and let out his breath.

"There are five of us. Kalen, Darius, Hunter, Tain, and me. Created millennia ago to keep death-magic creatures from overrunning frail human civilization, which was just getting started. You're a witch—you know that life magic and death magic have to remain in balance or the universe whirls into chaos. Call us the balancing act. In the beginning, demons were incredibly powerful and always ready to pull the rug out from under the world. They love chaos. And death. Vampires came along about that time. No friends of demons, but they also feed on death. You should have seen the vampires' faces when they encountered their first Immortal. I enjoyed myself."

"Like you did by the lake when you killed all those Unseelies?"

"More. The vampires and demons I faced in the beginning thought they were invulnerable. I taught them otherwise."

He wasn't boasting, just stating a fact.

"Vampires and demons are still with us," Amber pointed out. "By the score. But I've never heard of an Immortal."

Adrian took a turnoff to another freeway, and the city began to recede. "The vampires and demons we have now are pale shadows of what they were. We killed the worst of them thousands of years ago. The ones who exist now are strong enough to keep life and death magic in balance, but not strong enough to tip the balance to their side. We haven't been needed in a long time."

"Where are the rest of them? Hunter and Darius and . . . ?"

Adrian shook his head. "I don't know. Kalen has always done his own thing; he had his special people to protect. Hunter walked out about the same Tain disappeared. Darius went back to Ravenscroft, but if he could have returned to the world, I don't know. He hasn't bothered to look me up. None of them have."

His expression was bland, but she sensed tension behind his *whatever* attitude.

"I'm sorry they haven't." She couldn't imagine not being close to her family.

"I've never bothered to look them up either," he said, still sounding offhand. "There's nothing for us to say. Kalen never had much use for the rest of us anyway. The Etruscans made him a god." He snorted in derision.

"I never understood why he always thought building aqueducts was more important than battling evil. Goddess, we used to fight . . ." He went silent a moment, as though sifting through memories. "Darius is a well-oiled fighting machine—he has tattoos all over his body that can change to weapons at his touch. He's a stickler for duty—doesn't trust anyone but himself to do the job right, and that includes me.

"And Hunter . . ." He broke off and shook his head. "Hunter is just crazy. Kali is Hunter's mother. She gave him some of her force of whirlwind destruction. We're brothers—half-brothers really, born of a human male and a manifestation of the mother Goddess. Darius is from Sekhmet, Kalen from Uni, Hunter from Kali. So we're brothers, but at the same time loners. Hard to explain."

"So you haven't seen each other since about 1300?"

"About then, yes."

"What were you doing before?" she asked, growing interested. "I mean from 2500 or so BC to AD 1300? Fighting evil?"

"Fighting evil, training, playing cards, drinking the fermented beverage of the day, living at Ravenscroft. Waiting to be Called. It used to be that witches or beings of life magic could form a circle and say a chant and *poof,* Immortal warriors were at their beck and call to fight the bad guys."

Amber gave him a look of alarm. "So if someone does a Calling spell right now, you vaporize and go? Leaving me in a driverless car speeding down the road?"

He gave a short laugh. "The Calling hasn't happened in centuries, and the secret of the spell has been lost. Not that I care. Once the goddesses let on that they didn't give a damn if we ever found Tain, I left. Even Cerridwen, who created Tain, shrugged her Celtic shoulders and let him go. So I basically said, 'up yours.' The goddesses can do their own work."

"What if someone is truly in need of help?"

"I still fight evil," he rumbled. "I can sense truly ferocious evil when it manifests. Like the demon when he killed your sister." He paused, the lights of an oncoming car shining briefly in his eyes. "I was dreaming of Tain that night. And the demon, except the demon part of the dream was real. He was going to try to kill me from inside my mind. He got distracted by something and fled.

"I think Susan had started her ritual, and he zipped through a portal before I could grab him and killed her. I don't have the magic to move through portals unless someone drags me. We can all go back and forth to Ravenscroft, but only Kalen can travel by portal unaided. So I had to get on a plane and track the demon to where I sensed him in the warehouse. When I got there, I realized the dream had been time-distorted. You were there, but he'd gone to kill your sister almost a month before."

Amber hugged her arms over her chest. She still couldn't fathom why Susan would summon a demon—and of all demons, *that* one. She didn't like the picture Adrian painted, of the demon turning aside from trying to kill Adrian to swat Susan like she was an annoying mosquito.

Tears filled her eyes, blurring the oncoming headlights.

Adrian pried one of her hands loose and closed his around it, his warmth comforting. "I'm sorry I couldn't stop him. I tried, but he was gone. He is incredibly powerful."

Amber gripped his callused fingers, drawing strength from them. "Do you know which demon he is? If he's that old and powerful, he probably has a name and a legend attached to the name."

"Most likely many names. A name would help in tracking and binding him. We'll find it."

He spoke with confidence, but Amber felt none. She supposed that if Adrian had lived as an invulnerable warrior for forty-five hundred years, he'd seen pretty much everything and thought he could do almost anything, even find and kill a demon with more strength than anything Amber had ever seen.

"You're trusting me with a lot of knowledge about you," she said.

He glanced at her in surprise, his tail of black hair sliding across his jacket. "Nothing you couldn't find out with research. The Immortals used to be common knowledge—still are, among the undead. Humans and life-magic creatures like werewolves have forgotten, though."

He pressed a heat-tingling kiss to her hand, then released her. "What I don't know about is you," he said, his eyes darkening. "Tell me all about Amber Silverthorne. And don't leave anything out, it could be important."

Amber again felt the strange compelling touch on her mind, and she started to talk.

# CHAPTER FIVE

"Not much to tell," she began, self-conscious.

"Not true," he answered in a quiet voice. "I think there is a lot you can tell me."

The push on her mind strengthened, relaxing her limbs and her tongue. He wanted something from her, but he wouldn't reach into her head and drag it out. He wanted her to tell him, to offer it, like a gift, just as she'd lain beneath him on the bed and let him touch her body with his strong, battle-scarred hands.

"I've always been a witch," she started, not sure what he wanted to hear. "I learned the Craft at the same time I learned to read. I knew I'd never be as skilled a witch as Susan, but I didn't resent her. I always wanted to be like her, and Susan taught me much more than I'd learn studying with a coven. After I graduated from college, Susan and I started doing magical services for others to make a living. My parents died about ten years ago, and since then it's just been Susan and me."

Adrian glanced at her, his faint smile as seductive as it had been when he'd slid his hands inside her nightshirt on the bed. "That isn't about *you*. Tell me about your first time. How did you feel?"

Amber stared in surprise, but again she felt the subtle encouragement to bare her soul. *It will be all right,* the unspoken urge said. *It's only Adrian.*

She let out a breath. "All right, then. Technically my first time was with Stephan Cade on the football field behind the bleachers at two in the morning. The grass was wet, and I don't think we did it right. The real first time was with a vampire. Except I didn't know he was a vampire until it was too late."

Adrian's amusement died, his eyes narrowing as he focused on that piece of information. "You couldn't sense the death magic of a vampire?"

"Not at first." That had been almost ten years ago, when she'd been eighteen, first year away from home living in the dorm downtown at the University of Washington, with the freedom to be herself. "He was very, very subtle. I was flattered that an older guy was interested in me—I didn't realize how *much* older he was."

She remembered Julio, dark eyes and blond hair, good-looking but not in a showy way. He'd been a sweetheart, bringing her flowers and taking her to nice dinners, but not so overly attentive as to arouse suspicion—what man was really that romantic without an ulterior motive?

"Imagine my surprise when he bit me," she finished. They'd been making love. The best time she'd ever had, no exceptions, until Julio had bared his fangs and sunk them into her neck. She'd fought him off, angry and humiliated.

Susan had been suspicious of him. Before Amber had left on her last date with him, Susan had slipped a charm into Amber's pocket, a length of knotted string over which Susan had chanted while tying the knots. When the glamour dropped from Julio, Amber had seen what he really was, a soulless dark creature with evil eyes.

"He tried to make you a blood slave?" Adrian asked, voice holding an angry note.

"*Tried* is the operative word. Didn't succeed."

Some people went out of their way to beg a vampire to make them a blood slave, and vampires took care of their every need, including financial. Sex between a vampire and a blood slave was supposed to be mind-blowing. Plus, things could get creative. Ménages were common, she'd heard. But she shuddered at the thought of existing solely to provide sex and blood to a vampire until she was used up.

"Interesting," Adrian commented.

"Not the word I used at the time."

"Did you kill him?" He sounded matter-of-fact.

"I set his hair on fire. *All* his hair, if you know what I mean. He survived. But while he was running up and down the hall screaming, I threw on my clothes and got out of there."

Adrian gave a short laugh. "I wish I could have seen his face. He must have been a strong vampire, to glamour a hereditary witch and not expect her to retaliate. Why a fire spell?"

"First thing that came to me." She had to admit she'd furiously enjoyed the sight of Julio dashing naked from the room with flames dancing around his head and his balls. He'd scared her, but more than that, he'd enraged her. It had been a long time before the humiliation of falling for a vampire's charm had faded.

"I always wondered why he chose me," she said.

"I wonder too." Adrian's voice was quiet, thoughtful. "You are damn sexy, so I'm surprised every creature of the night isn't out to seduce you, but he must have known what a powerful witch you were. So why did he want you?"

Amber blinked at him, surprised by two phrases—*damn sexy* and *powerful witch.*

"He glammed me easily enough."

Adrian shrugged again, the power of his moving muscles distracting her. "You were young, and vampires are skilled seducers. But he must have known that if you decided to fight him, he'd be toast." He grinned. "Literally. I still wonder why he wanted to make you a blood slave. Why did he need such a strong witch under his thrall?"

"I don't know." Amber leaned against the corner of the seat. "I never saw him again. No, wait." She paused, remembering. "I thought I saw him again when I went to a movie once with Susan. There was a huge crowd, and I can't be sure it was him. I didn't fancy an encounter, so I left."

"Better safe than sorry?" he asked.

"What?"

"It's what you said to me when you hid behind your protective shield in the warehouse. Which was pretty powerful, by the way."

"You broke it like it was an eggshell. A *thin* eggshell."

"Yes, but I'm an Immortal," he said, his dark gaze moving to her. "Until I made it go away, the shield held very well." He paused as he drove around another knot of traffic. "You brought stones with you, didn't you? I want you to be able to make a protective shield any time you need one. If this demon is an Old One, I want you to stay as safe as you possibly can."

Amber reached into the back seat and dragged out her overnight bag. Rummaging in it, she took out a small plastic box. "I haven't had time to charge them. A quickie charge will work, but not as good as if I had time to consecrate them and leave them in moonlight awhile."

Adrian reached out his large hand. "Give them to me."

Amber upended the contents of the box, about eight stones in all, quartz and amber and amethyst, into his large palm. He closed his fingers around them without slowing or taking his other hand from the wheel.

For a moment, nothing happened. Then a humming noise began, swelling to fill the car. White light spilled between his fingers, falling to the floorboards like it had weight. Bright balls of it danced at Amber's feet; then there was a sudden flash followed by dense darkness.

Adrian held his hand out to Amber again. She gulped and thrust her cupped hands out to catch the crystals. They fell into her palms, one after another, the center of each holding a glowing ember of light. Adrian returned his hand to the wheel and kept driving as if nothing had happened.

The crystals vibrated with sheer power. She'd never felt such magic inside them, impatient magic that wanted to get out. "What on earth did you do to them?"

"Charged them. That's what you need, isn't it?"

"Yes, but Good Goddess." She placed each crystal back into the box—carefully. "How did you do that?"

"I did the same thing you do, just faster. Witch magic can be slow."

"Slow like a mountain," she said automatically, used to having to explain her affinity with magic of the earth. She could work some other magics, like the fire spell and spells of air and water, but she was best with stones and the bones of the earth. "Or tree roots."

"You don't always have time to wait for tree roots to

strangle an enemy," he said, an amused smile pulling at his mouth.

"Well, I wasn't gifted with a fancy sword that turns into a snake." Amber closed the box and slid it back into her bag. "I have to use what I've got. Tree roots might be slow, but they never stop. Neither do mountains."

He nodded once. "Good point. Cars stop, though, when they're out of gas."

He flicked his finger at the gas indicator, and Amber saw the needle resting on the E. Adrian slid the car onto the next off-ramp. Dawn was still an hour or so away, and the entire intersection was brightly lit with a truck stop, gas station, motel, and a sign flashing *Food. 24 Hrs.*

Adrian got out of the car and pumped gas. He did it like any normal man would—a man with jeans stretching tight over his groin and firm ass, which were at Amber's eye level while he filled the tank. He did it as though he'd not just expended more power than she'd ever hope to achieve in her life. And never broke a sweat, as if he did it all the time.

Adrian finished with the gas, then pulled the car into the empty diner parking lot. Amber scanned the few tired-looking truckers under the glare of lights and the passing cars on the highway. "Shouldn't we press on?"

"I'm hungry." Adrian unbuckled his seat belt and hauled himself out of the car again. "I can't drive all the way to L.A. on an empty stomach and no coffee. You raise a protective shield around the car, and we'll go inside and have pancakes."

"You're immortal," she said, even as she reached for the vibrating crystals. "I take it that means you won't starve to death."

"But you will." He gave her a smile through her open window, eyes dark and hot. "Besides, do you really want a hungry, under-caffeinated Immortal warrior in the car with you all day?" He straightened up and sauntered away, as though never doubting she'd follow.

His torn leather coat and rugged jeans outlined a body of masculine beauty, but she couldn't forget the mass of scars that marked his back and shoulders. He was a fighting man, a true warrior, as she'd seen in the battle in Scotland, and he wanted something from her—what, she had no idea.

He wasn't staying just to protect her in case of a demon attack. He'd sounded almost offhand when he asked about her personal life, but he probed for something, and she had the feeling he wouldn't stop until he got it. An Immortal warrior had plenty of time to make her do as he liked.

He'd already manipulated her mind a little, not to mention the heat of his kisses and his touch burning her all over. She had the feeling he'd try everything, from magic to seduction, to pry what he wanted from her. Not that she'd fought off the seduction—the memory of his body hard over hers, his lips hot and bruising, made her shiver.

On the other side of the parking lot, Adrian casually opened the door of the diner, the glass flashing under the yellow lights of the truck stop. Amber's stomach stirred with pangs of hunger, and she couldn't deny that a short stack sounded great about now.

She put one of the pulsating clear quartz crystals on the dashboard and concentrated on it to raise a protective shield around the car.

Power shot up and around the car so fast the backlash threw her against the seat, electricity jolting through her. She gasped, feeling the hair on her arms stand up and her skin crawl with power. *Holy Mother Goddess.*

It was the most powerful shield she'd ever raised.

When she sliced through the air with her finger, giving herself a slit through which to exit the car, the magic crackled and sparked.

She slipped shakily out and to her feet, hoping she'd not screwed up anything when creating the shield, or she'd have to take it down and do it again. She wasn't sure her body could take two of these power raisings so close together.

She moved her finger across the bubble again to zip it up behind her. A faint glimmer surrounded the car that would be invisible to all but another witch and maybe Adrian. A normal protective bubble would deter would-be car thieves and vandals, but this bubble could probably keep out a charging elephant. Amber had never touched such raw power in her life.

Adrian waited for her just inside the door, dark eyes calm, as though he had no doubt she could handle raising the shield. He didn't even ask if she was all right, as though he knew he didn't need to.

A waitress holding coffeepots in both hands told him to take any seat while she bustled behind the counter to serve the truckers there. Adrian led Amber to a booth well away from the truckers, and when the cherry-cheeked waitress approached, he requested four orders of pancakes—one for Amber and three for himself. When the food arrived, he poured half a pot of maple syrup over the first stack and began to eat steadily as if this were a normal meal for him.

"When I asked you about your first time," he said when he started stack number two—with blueberry syrup, "I wasn't talking about sex. I was talking about your initiation into the Craft."

"Oh." She stopped chewing, cheeks scalding. "Then

why did you let me go on about who I went to bed with? You could have stopped me."

Adrian poured more blue-black syrup over the half-eaten helping, carefully not looking at her. "I didn't want to interrupt you. Besides, you told me that intriguing tale about your vampire."

Her cheeks burned redder. "Thanks a lot, Adrian."

"Never be afraid to talk to me about sex." He raised his gaze at last, his dark eyes burning her. "Or anything else, for that matter. I do want to know all about you."

"Goddess, I swear if we weren't in public I'd throw something at you."

"I'd probably catch it. My reflexes are well honed. But you were going to tell me about your initiation."

"I didn't do it naked, if that's what you want to know," she growled.

"Do not be angry." He made a small gesture, and suddenly she wasn't angry. Silly to be—she'd misunderstood him and started blathering to him, which wasn't his fault. "Tell me."

She chewed a mouthful of her own pancakes. "My dedication I did alone in the woods north of town near a cabin my parents owned. My initiation was a year and a day later, at Samhain in the same place. My parents and my sister were with me, as well as a few other solitary witch friends."

"Which aspect of the Goddess did you dedicate to?"

"Hathor," Amber said. "I always liked her."

"Good choice. I'm sure she was flattered."

"I hope so." Amber had taken a long time to decide to dedicate her studies and devotion to Hathor, a goddess who was not only wise and powerful but had a good sense of humor.

"I will ask her when I see her," Adrian remarked, starting on his third stack of pancakes.

Amber coughed. "When you see her? You *know* Hathor?"

Adrian nodded, firm jaw moving as he chewed and swallowed. "She helped train me, she and her priestesses. When I was small, Hathor let me ride on her back when she was a cow."

Amber hastily gulped her orange juice. "I never know whether to believe all this stuff you tell me or not."

"You are a witch, and undead and other magical creatures walk the earth. Why should I not know gods and goddesses?"

"It's different . . ." She trailed off.

Vampires and werewolves and Sidhe and witches were part of everyday existence. Gods and goddesses watched from afar, even though she'd sensed the presence of the Goddess and Hathor in her rituals and in the magic workings she'd done with Susan. But she'd never seen Her or imagined Her training Immortal warriors to fight battles.

"True, the goddesses have removed themselves more in modern times," Adrian went on. "They are pleased with the resurgence of Goddess cults in the world. They were so long forgotten."

"I suppose you are on speaking terms with the God, too."

"Oh, yes." Adrian nodded and attacked his last stack of pancakes. "We hunt together sometimes."

"You are the strangest man I have ever met."

"Probably," he conceded. He ate steadily, not looking stuffed or uncomfortable with all the food he'd consumed. "I've met beings far stranger than you, and not nearly as pretty."

The look he gave her was full of sin. Her thoughts flashed back to how he'd suckled her on the bed, at the same time spreading his legs to give her full access to himself. His cock had been huge and hot, and her hands had wanted to go on and on stroking it. She'd felt the pulsing behind his balls. He'd been ready to come, right before the demon had interrupted. Damn demon.

Adrian's eyes darkened. He licked a drop of syrup from his fork, tongue curving to flick the sweet substance into his mouth.

"I'm sorry we're in a hurry," he said, voice low with seduction.

Warmth pooled in her belly, and she shoved her plate away with more force than necessary. "We'd better go."

He took a last sip of coffee, eyes closing as he enjoyed it, throat moving in a slow swallow. He set down the cup and licked a drop from his lips.

"I'm ready."

Amber resisted saying, *I'm ready too,* and made herself stand up and walk steadily to the counter.

Adrian paid at the cash register, dipping into a full wallet. He slid his hand to the small of her back, warm against the early morning chill, and guided her out the door. When they got to the car, she could possibly cast a slight glamour so no one would look their way, and she could get her sudden need to kiss him out of her system. She imagined his tongue, sweet with syrup, sliding into her mouth, moving in slow seduction.

The scenario was spoiled when a half dozen young men, some with women clinging to their arms, came out of the shadows to surround the car.

The men wore low-slung jeans and T-shirts and jeans jackets. The young women had more variety of dress, either short shorts and cropped tops or black leather skin-hugging pants and Lycra shirts that pushed their cleavage toward their chins. All wore dead white makeup, black eyeliner, and black lipstick.

*Gang kids,* she thought at first, but then she felt the taint of death magic. Not just gang kids—vampires.

"It's all right," Adrian said. "The car is protected."

"But we're not *in* the car," she pointed out.

"So many together," Adrian said softly, almost to himself. "They are gathering in strength and numbers, and not just here. Why?"

Adrian suddenly moved ahead of her, lengthening his stride, and Amber, with a sigh of exasperation, half jogged to keep up with him. The vampires lounged around the car, smiling. It was nearly dawn, but they smirked with confidence, convinced they'd make an easy meal of Amber and Adrian and get underground before the sun rose.

The waiting group was not all vampire, she saw as they drew nearer. The four girls and two of the young men were human, likely blood slaves, but that didn't make them less dangerous. Blood slaves would fight to the death for their vampire masters, and they'd fight dirty. They did whatever it took to keep their masters alive.

"Can we at least come up with a plan?" Amber panted.

"Are you afraid?" Adrian stopped and looked down at her in surprise, as though she'd confessed fear of the geckos that hung out on her back porch. "They're only vampires."

"There are ten of them, including the blood slaves, and only two of us."

He nodded. "Not very good odds for them, I agree. They should have brought more."

She looked for a flicker of humor in his eyes and found none. He was perfectly serious. "You truly think the vampires are the ones in trouble?"

"They are."

She stared back at him for a long moment. "Must be nice to be an Immortal."

"Not really."

Without explaining the cryptic statement, he started again toward the car and the vampires waiting around it.

A power began building inside him in a magnitude of which she'd never sensed before. The magic was a little like the light that had flowed from him into the crystals, but much, much stronger. A man who grew up riding on the back of Hathor and being trained by Isis probably had no need to fear something as paltry as modern-day vampires. One blow from the immense power she felt radiating from him, and the vampires and blood slaves would be dust.

"Do you plan to kill them?" she asked conversationally. "Or just blow them across the parking lot?"

She was close enough for the vampires and blood slaves around the car to hear her. Their grins began to fade. The vamps should be getting a tingle of the magic inside Adrian now—bright life magic, stronger and more concentrated than anything Amber had ever encountered.

"I haven't decided," Adrian answered. "They're not very strong, but I don't want them lingering to retaliate on the innocent because they're pissed at me." He studied the sky. "I can always hold them in place until the sun comes up. Letting them melt away won't be pretty, but it will be effective."

The vampires heard them. Two of them began to back off.

Amber's confidence started to rise, a giddiness tingling in her fingertips. She'd never had to face a gang of vampires before, but Adrian's calm assurance that they were easily dealt with made her heart speed in anticipation of the fight.

"Vampires flying all over the place will attract a lot of attention," she pointed out.

Adrian looked at her. If she hadn't grown used to the fathomless darkness of his eyes, she'd have stepped back—no, sprinted away from him. Incredible magic filled every space in him—even what she glimpsed in his eyes was terrible. He held more magic than any witch she'd ever known, any werewolf, any vampire, even any demon.

She asked the question she still hadn't gotten a satisfactory answer to. "What *are* you?"

"A son of Isis. And you are right, using my power in this way will attract too much attention. The demon will focus on us when he feels it, like he did before. I wouldn't be surprised if he encouraged the undead to look for us so he could pinpoint us when I fought them."

His immense power began to dampen, the pulsating magic receding. Fear left the vampires' faces, their grins returning.

"All right, so what do we do?" Amber asked. "Politely tell them to move so we can get in the car?"

"That might work," Adrian said. "But I believe we'll have to do this the old-fashioned way."

He held out his arm. Ferrin slithered to his hand and solidified into a sword, the blade catching the yellow lights lining the truck stop's parking lot. The vampires stopped smiling and formed into ranks, the blood slaves behind them.

Adrian lifted the sword over his head. Giving the fierce

and gleeful shout she'd heard rolling through the mountains on the wooded slope of Scotland, he attacked.

Vampires understood this kind of fighting. They met Adrian's attack, swarming upon him despite the silver sword that cut straight for them. The blood slaves, four women with madness in their eyes, turned to Amber. All had knives in their hands and the determined look of women ready to defend their men to their last breath.

"Adrian!" Amber shouted, backing away. "We're still outnumbered."

Adrian slammed his sword across one vampire's neck, neatly severing his head from his body. The torso fell to the ground, where it began to decompose. Not rapidly—the stench was horrible.

"You are right," Adrian said as he swung to slice at the other vampires. "You'll have to do a spell."

"Spell? What spell?"

One of the women began to keen, her edge of sanity snapping. The dead vampire must have been her master. Wailing, she tore at her own eyes, and the woman behind her screamed and charged at Amber, flailing madly with her knife.

Amber jerked her half-moon knife from her jacket pocket and deflected the blow. *Do a spell? Oh, sure.* Spells required accoutrements, tools to hone the concentration, and they also needed focus and quiet, plus time to slide into the fabric of the universe. All three were in short supply here.

"Use the spell you told me about in the car," Adrian shot at her before turning and ferociously slicing another vampire in half.

He meant her story about Julio. She remembered lying in bed with candles flickering eerie light through the room. Julio had pinned her with strong hands, while his mouth came down on her. She remembered her terror and shock when Susan's anti-glamour spell had kicked in and she'd finally seen Julio's lips peeling back from glistening fangs. She remembered her fear, then rage, and then—fire.

Two of the vampires burst into flames. They ran, shrieking, desperately clawing at their hair, and their blood slaves abandoned the fight and dashed after them. Amber slashed her knife at the remaining blood slave. The girl danced out of the way, leaving open the way to the car.

Amber brought her finger down sharply, slicing an opening in her protective sphere, then dove through it and yanked the car door open. The last blood slave followed her, viciously flailing with her knife. She stabbed Amber's shoulder to the bone just as Amber dove into the car.

She yelled in pain and kicked the girl's leather-clad legs out from under her. The blood slave's eyes were wide with grief and rage, bloodshot and terrible. She raised her knife again.

Amber clenched her shoulder, pain weakening her, and pointed at the bubble to seal it again. The magic closed with a snick just before the young woman could strike. The blood slave screamed in rage and threw herself against the bubble, but she was mortal and not a witch, and couldn't breach it. The girl pounded insanely at the sphere, but the magic held.

Amber rummaged in the glove compartment for her first-aid kit, happy she always made sure it was well stocked with antibacterial wipes and adhesive bandages. The cut she'd taken was deep, she saw when she eased off her windbreaker and cranked her head around to look, although the bleeding had already stopped. She'd need stitches—and some painkillers, she thought, wincing—but she could hold it together now with a big square bandage.

Adrian faced the last vampire. He held his sword loosely, moving on the balls of his feet, his face set in the ferocious grin he'd worn when he'd slaughtered the Unseelies on the mountainside. Amber wiped off the cut and slapped a gauze bandage over it, clenching her teeth against the pain. Outside, the vampire snarled at Adrian and launched himself at him, extending his fingers like claws.

If the vampire thought he'd dive under Adrian's reach, he was wrong. Amber watched as Adrian easily dispatched the vampire with one wide sweep of his sword, leaving it to decompose on the asphalt. Then he turned to face the last blood slave, his blade stained black with vampire blood.

The blood slave's eyes widened. Howling, she turned and sprinted into the woods after the others, and Adrian lowered his sword, looking satisfied.

Amber closed her hand over the crystal on the dashboard and opened the protective circle so he could slide into the car. Ferrin changed back into the snake as Adrian closed the door behind him. The snake studied Amber with his black lidless eyes, then wrapped himself around Adrian's bicep and became metal again.

Adrian started the car. "Are you all right?"

"I will be." Amber tossed the first-aid kit back into the glove compartment.

"Let me see." Adrian started to lean toward her, but Amber caught movement out the front window and froze.

"Adrian . . ."

From the woods poured a horde of vampires,

dressed like the others. They converged through the silent parking lot toward the car, their intentions clear.

Adrian started the car. "I'll take care of it later. Will you be all right until we get farther down the road?" He waited for her answer, making no move to put the car in gear and get the hell away.

"Fine, I'll be fine," Amber said hastily. "We should go now."

Adrian turned from the wheel again, sliding his arm across the seat like they had all day. "I don't want you to be hurt, especially not because of me."

"That's nice. Can we talk about this later?"

He remained studying her, his dark eyes glittering with the fierce joy of the fight and the magic inside him. "There's syrup on your lip," he said.

Amber put up her hand to wipe it away. Adrian leaned down and gently moved her fingers aside, then brushed his tongue softly over her lips.

In spite of danger running toward them at vampire speed, Amber sank back into the seat, her feminine places warm and hungry. Adrian parted her lips so his tongue could slide in and explore her, and she welcomed him. She made a noise of satisfaction, the pain in her shoulder forgotten.

Adrian finished the kiss and eased back, his eyes softening. "You taste sweet, with or without the syrup. But syrup would be pretty on you."

Amber's heart sped, and the warmth between her legs became out-and-out fire. "You're flattering, but shouldn't we be going?"

Adrian brushed his thumb over her cheek. "Yes. Regretfully. When we reach my house we'll—discuss things."

He was perfectly confident they'd reach L.A. with no

problems, despite the fifty vampires who flung themselves against the car just then.

Adrian flashed her another warrior's grin and gunned the engine. "Hold on," he said.

Amber grabbed the seat, thankful she'd already buckled herself in. Adrian slammed his foot on the gas, released the brake, and tore into the vampires, ramming the ones foolish enough to be in front of him. The car fishtailed around the parking lot, then sped back toward the highway, the speedometer needle rapidly reaching sixty, then eighty, then a hundred.

Adrian threw his head back and laughed with the confidence of one who knew he couldn't die. The car flung off the last of the vampires and hurtled up the on-ramp of the happily empty freeway.

Heart in her throat, Amber clutched the seat and looked through the back windshield to the swiftly receding truck stop. But the parking lot was deserted, and all the vampires had vanished. The sun was just streaming over the horizon, its first rays flushing the empty lot with healing light.

# CHAPTER SIX

Amber's car died fifty miles down the road. Adrian felt Amber's accusing stare as he pulled the car to a stop in a patch of weeds studded with dew from the morning. Trucks rumbled past on a highway now bathed in sunshine of full daylight. At least they wouldn't have to worry about vampire attacks.

Amber hopped out and glared at the car, hands on hips. She was furious, her brown-gold eyes flashing. What a beautiful woman she was, Adrian thought, and he hadn't been wrong about her tasting damn good with syrup. He imagined her lying under him, her body firm and deliciously curved, while he dripped syrup between her breasts, drop by drop.

He hated the sight of the bandage on her shoulder, stark white against her skin. At least it hadn't been a vampire blade, which would have stabbed death magic into her. Blood-slave weapons had no magic.

"This car wasn't meant to take that kind of speed," she spluttered as he pulled himself out of the driver's seat.

"It's just something to get me from place to place in the city."

"I'll buy you a new one," Adrian promised, slamming the door. "What kind would you like?"

She stopped in mid-rant, mouth open. "Are you kidding?"

"Tell me what make and what color, and I'll buy you a car when we reach Los Angeles."

She stared at him a moment longer, then nervously turned her back on him, folding her arms and studying the tall trees beyond the road, thumbs rubbing her elbows. "Nice of you to promise, but how are we supposed to get to L.A. now?"

Adrian pulled a cell phone out of his leather coat. "Easy. I call a friend to pick us up."

Amber looked suspiciously up and down the road and along the empty greenery to either side of the highway. "He lives nearby?"

"No, but he'll get here quickly." Adrian hit his speed dial and listened to a long series of electronic ringing on the other end while Amber watched, unconvinced.

The phone finally clicked. "Hello?" came a deep and wary voice that sounded as if its owner had just climbed out of sleep.

"Valerian!"

There was a pause, then, "Oh, Goddess." His words were melodious and hollow and dismayed. "It's Adrian."

"It is. My old friend, I need a favor . . ."

Half an hour later a black Mustang slid to a halt in front of Adrian and Amber, its motor thumping. The black-tinted passenger window slid silently down to reveal a hulk of a man with blond hair and brilliant blue eyes. "Hey. Need a lift?"

Amber looked from Valerian to Adrian doubtfully, not softened by Adrian's reassuring nod. Amber, her face white with exhaustion, said she'd crawl into the back and sleep. Adrian wanted to have a better look at her wound, so he got in back with her after tossing the bags in the trunk, cramming his long legs into the small space with difficulty.

"Nice car," Amber observed as Valerian swung the door shut.

"It's a rental." Valerian's rumbling voice filled the car with a bass timbre. He swiveled around and looked at them, his blue eyes alert as he gave Amber a once-over. "I always like to rent something flashy. I would've got a Ferrari, but we wouldn't all fit. Where to, pilgrims?"

"My house," Adrian answered. "Quick as you can."

Valerian settled his muscular body into his seat and launched the car onto the highway with a spin of gravel.

"There are faster ways to travel," Valerian remarked as he sped along the lightly trafficked road.

"None that avoid attention."

Valerian's azure eyes met Adrian's in the rearview mirror. "What? Adrian the Unstoppable wants to avoid attention?"

"I have precious cargo."

Valerian's gaze moved to Amber again, lingering so long he nearly ran up the back of a slow-moving RV. "Cute cargo," he said, swinging out to pass.

"She is."

Valerian waggled his brows. "Are you two—you know?"

"Not yet," Adrian answered seriously.

"Good. Still a chance for me, then."

"I said *not yet.*"

Amber opened her eyes, tawny and sleepy in the

morning light. "I can hear you, you know. I'm still awake."

Adrian drew her closer. "Good. Let me look at your shoulder." Without waiting for permission, he began easing the white bandage from her flesh.

"What happened?" Valerian asked him.

"Vampire attack," Adrian answered.

The blue eyes widened. "She got bit?"

"Stabbed. By a blood slave."

"Whew. That's bad, but could have been worse."

Adrian agreed. He briefly explained about the vampire attack as he peeled back the bandage to reveal the gash. Amber's head lay on his shoulder, her soft hair tickling his nose as he leaned over her. Even running away from home and fighting vampires hadn't erased her sweet scent.

The shoulder wound wasn't too bad, but Amber was human and mortal and such a thing could fester. He opened Amber's box of crystals and picked out a few amethysts, their centers glowing with dark purple light. Enclosing them in his left hand, he let their healing vibrations build before he transferred them to his right hand and put his closed fist over the cut.

Amber was watching Valerian. "What is he?" she whispered.

"A friend. A shape-shifter."

"Not a werewolf," she said with conviction.

Adrian agreed that Valerian's scent and vibrations were absolutely nothing like a werewolf's. "No."

Amber waited for him to explain, but Adrian closed his eyes and concentrated on the crystals, and Valerian drove in silence. She'd find out what Valerian was sooner or later—no sense scaring her now.

Under Adrian's hand, the wound began to close.

Cleansed by the healing magic of the crystals, her skin knitted together from the depth of the wound outward until only a red line indicated where the cut had been. Amber opened sleepy eyes, then suddenly rubbed her shoulder like it itched.

Adrian moved her hand and soothed his own over it. He kissed her cheek. "Go to sleep. All is well now."

She stared at him a little longer, not instantly obeying, no matter how much he brushed her mind. She could resist his compelling mind-touch like no mortal he had ever known. She probably didn't even realize she did it. At last she settled her head on his shoulder and closed her eyes, but because *she* chose.

He looked up at the sunlit morning rushing past the heavily tinted windows. He could understand Amber's wonder at Valerian. The man was built like a wrestler with thick blond hair he kept tamed into a braid, and eyes so blue they were like pieces of the noonday sky. His eyes were a little larger than most humans' and the irises wider, so when you looked into them you saw nothing but color.

Adrian had been sired by a rather jovial young priest, who'd had no problem with Isis taking him as a lover, but Valerian had nothing human in his makeup. He could assume human shape, but that was as far as his humanity went. Even werewolves and vampires were more human than Valerian.

Valerian glanced into the rearview again. "Septimus was looking for you last night," he said, naming a vampire who owned several very upscale, exclusive clubs in Los Angeles. "He didn't say why."

"I wouldn't expect him to."

"He asked me to call him if I got in touch with you, but I figured you'd talk to him in your own time."

"Thank you."

Valerian, though he had his own agendas, would never betray Adrian to a vampire. If Adrian wanted to trust Septimus, kingpin of his part of town, that was Adrian's business, Valerian thought.

"There's some weird shit going down," Valerian continued. "Can't point to anything specific, but I'm right."

Adrian stroked his fingers over Amber's curly hair. "I know. Weird shit has been happening all night."

"I'll get you home," Valerian promised, speeding the car around a slow-moving semi. "And we'll figure out what to do."

After the events in Seattle, Adrian had the feeling that the home they were heading toward would only be a temporary refuge.

Amber opened her eyes to a sea of white. As the blur of sleep cleared, she saw that she lay in the middle of a bed which stretched a long distance on each side of her. Piles of pillows in soft white and a cool down coverlet, also white, completed it. The walls of the room and the vaulted ceiling were painted a soft yellow, capturing the sunshine that glinted off the sea and poured in through the open windows.

When Adrian had mentioned his home in Los Angeles, she'd pictured a boxy residence in the suburbs. This, she realized as she climbed out of the vast bed, was a huge house perched on the side of a bluff not twenty feet from the sea.

As she stepped to the windows that opened out onto a deck, she saw the bedroom occupied the entire end of the house. The rest of the house bent in a U shape away from her, the wooden veranda curving from the bedroom to floor-to-ceiling windows of a living room and to equally tall French doors of a bedroom opposite her. To her left, a wooden stairway went down to an empty stretch of beach.

The sea slid up to the golden sands, the rushing sound of the waves under the half-gray sky soothing. Amber now understood Adrian's offhand comment that he'd buy her another car. *What kind would you like?* He must have Money with a capital M.

The breeze from the window felt cool against her bare arms and legs. She realized she was in her underwear, a white lace bikini panty and matching bra that she'd thrown on before Adrian had dragged her out of her house in Seattle. The last thing she remembered was falling asleep in the Mustang driven by the huge man with large blue eyes. She recalled Adrian's comforting shoulder cradling her head, his lips in her hair.

He'd healed her. Amber turned to a mirror mounted on one wall and peered at her shoulder. The wound had closed completely, leaving only a pink-tinted streak. Her arm felt whole and strong, no infection from the blood slave's blade. She didn't know any witch who could heal another that completely and quickly, not even among those who specialized in healing.

She remembered the incredible power she'd sensed building within Adrian as they'd walked toward the vampires at the truck stop. If he'd unleashed that power, the vampires would have died instantly, along with the vamps who lingered in the woods waiting to see if they were needed. She had the feeling he'd have been able to channel the power to kill only the undead and leave the humans alone if he wanted.

An Immortal. A son of Isis. A demigod. A being with

more power inside him than she'd ever seen in her life. More dangerous than anything she'd ever faced.

Yet he'd been protective of her from the moment she met him. This house felt protected, far more than her own home had been. Her witch's sight could discern no wards over windows and doors, but it was as though he'd encased the house with a veneer of power to keep bad things out.

The mirror told her another thing, that her hair was matted to her skull, that her face and arms were dirty. Great. Who had undressed her? Adrian? Her body grew warm with the thought. She remembered his mouth on her breasts, the firm suckling that made her arch to him and want him inside her. The thought of him gently stripping her, his strong hands on her body, made her glow with excitement.

She wanted him, this erotic stranger with incredible powers. Ever since she'd met him, she'd been half consumed with lust for him. She hoped that the dirt and grime from the fight hadn't turned him off.

The bathroom off the bedroom contained a huge shower stall with a shower head on each end, a deep whirlpool bathtub, acres of cool marble tile, a pile of fluffy towels, and an equally fluffy bathrobe resting on the counter.

Amber showered, scrubbing with the loofah she found hanging from a hook, enjoying the fresh-scented soaps and shampoos waiting for her, unused, on the shelf. She emerged and dried herself with the huge towels, then bundled into the bathrobe. It too was large, made for a man. Why did it relieve her that he didn't have a woman's bathrobe handy?

Of course, none of her clothes were handy either. The

bag she'd hastily packed wasn't visible in the room, nor in any closets she opened. She wandered out to the main area of the house, noting that it was very quiet but for the rushing of the ocean in the background.

The living room ran the length of one side of the U, large and airy and open to the veranda and the sea. Beautiful. Amber stepped outside, breathing the fresh salt air, and enjoying the sounds of the morning, before she heard quick footsteps and turned to see who had entered the room behind her.

A Barbie doll. A perfectly shaped, tall young woman had come traipsing in, dressed in a white linen sleeveless dress that set off a perfect tan, and high-heeled sandals. Her blond hair was loose and short, but the windblown look was as perfect as the rest of her. If she wore makeup, it was artful enough not to draw attention to itself while highlighting her eyes and high cheekbones.

She had a model's angular face and sensual lips, and eyes that had intelligent thought behind them.

"Hello," she said in a beautiful contralto voice. "I'm Kelly O'Byrne, Adrian's next-door neighbor. Adrian asked me to come over and keep you company."

"Ah," was all that came out of Amber's mouth. She now recognized Kelly from a movie she'd seen a few months ago with Susan, a romantic comedy with the usual big stars. Kelly hadn't been the lead, she'd been a secondary character, but had played the wise best friend of the heroine with clarity. The next Meg Ryan, people were calling her.

Amber suddenly felt awkward in the oversized robe with her hair wet and no makeup next to this poised beauty. When she'd asked Adrian whether he had a wife or significant other, she'd neglected to ask, "How about a to-die-for beautiful next-door neighbor?" Well, this was

Los Angeles. Maybe Kelly was gay. Was is polite to ask, even in L.A.?

Kelly gestured to the bright kitchen behind her. "Would you like something to eat? I brought Manny, my cook, with me. Adrian never has anything to eat."

She said it like she waltzed over here and checked out Adrian's refrigerator all the time. Like a woman who had a key to his house.

Amber tried to shrug. "Sure, why not?"

Kelly smiled with a confident air and led the way through the living room and down a short hall to a broad, sunny kitchen in the front of the house.

Manny was a black-haired Italian, and he threw pots and spoons around Adrian's kitchen with professional ease. "I cook you the best frittata you ever eat," he assured Amber without looking up.

Kelly sat down at the breakfast bar and poured sparkling mineral water into a glass. Manny, without being asked, poured another and slid it in front of Amber. A paper-thin slice of lemon floated on top.

"Adrian said you liked tea," Kelly said. "Manny is brewing a pot." She took a delicate sip of mineral water, barely wetting her perfect lips.

"Where is Adrian?" Amber craned her neck to look around the enormous kitchen. She couldn't sense his presence in the quiet house.

"He went out somewhere," Kelly answered. "He didn't tell me where, just asked me to come over. He didn't want you waking up and finding yourself alone."

Amber took a drink of the water. Not her morning beverage choice, but she had to admit it wasn't bad. "Gallant of him."

"Adrian is gallant. I worked at a vampire club a few years ago, as a dancer," she added.

Amber tried not to blink at the non sequitur. She had the feeling Kelly said anything she wanted about anything at any time.

A "dancer" at a vampire club could mean a stripper or it might not, depending on what kind of club it was. Kelly didn't have any scars on her neck from bites, so she likely hadn't been a blood slave, although plastic surgery could have repaired her skin.

Kelly went on with her story. "After I started getting good acting jobs I quit dancing and moved up here. But the vampire who ran the club considered me his property, and he sent his boys to drag me back. Adrian came over and told them to get lost. I was scared for Adrian—I had barely met him, and I thought they'd kill him. But you know what?" She smiled, showing perfect white teeth. "Those vampires took one look at Adrian and hightailed it out of there. I couldn't believe it. Not an hour later, the vamp who owned the club pulled up in his limo. Adrian met him at my front door, and the two of them had a long, long talk. The vampire never even tried to see me. He got back in his limo and drove away fast and never bothered me again."

She watched Amber with her almond-shaped eyes, waiting to see what Amber made of that. Amber imagined Adrian stoking up the incredible power inside him, just enough so the vampire could feel it, and explaining carefully that he'd better not find vampires anywhere near Kelly again. The head vampire had probably tried not to wet himself.

"You're right," Amber said, taking another sip of water. "He is gallant."

"I wanted you to know that. Also that we aren't lovers and never have been."

"Um, that's all right. I mean, it's none of my business—I just met him."

Manny kept on cooking like he was used to Kelly talking about her lovers. The eggs were starting to set up, so he threw on a handful of sliced red peppers, some mushrooms, and an assortment of cheeses and shoved the pan in the oven.

Kelly tapped her glass with tapered fingernails and gave Amber a sharp, assessing look. "I'm telling you because you look like you might be good for him."

"I see." Amber toyed with her water glass, not trusting herself to drink. "Why do you think I'll be good for him?"

Kelly laughed. "Simple. He's never asked me to come over and look after someone before."

Amber realized that behind the Hollywood body and perfect face, Kelly still had a woman's matchmaking instincts. She softened to Kelly a little.

"Adrian and I are—just friends," she ventured.

Kelly's smile wrinkled her nose. "Whatever you say. If you want to do some shopping, my chauffeur will drive you wherever you want to go. Adrian said he dragged you down here without much and that you'd need clothes."

Manny grabbed the frittata from the oven, slid it expertly onto a plate, and placed the porcelain in front of Amber on the breakfast bar. "Adrian said she stays here," he said, flashing Kelly a dark look.

"Yes, but men don't understand about clothes."

Amber thought about the protection she'd sensed in this house as soon as she woke up. Vampires couldn't get at her in broad daylight—as long as they weren't outside, she corrected herself. Demons didn't have the daylight restriction, and neither did blood slaves, who would kill if their vampires ordered them to. Unless Kelly's chauffeur had superpowers, maybe she should stay put.

She was hungry anyway. She attacked the frittata and smiled at Manny, who hovered, waiting for her opinion. It really was the best she'd ever had and she told him so. Manny nodded modestly, as though he hadn't been worried, and went back to banging pans.

"I don't mind staying here," Amber said, looking around the beautiful, airy house.

"Suit yourself," Kelly said. "I can call a boutique and have them bring the clothes here if you want."

*Must be nice,* Amber thought. "I'll let you know. How long have you known Adrian?"

"About five years now, I guess." She grinned knowingly. "What do you want to know about him?"

Amber decided to stop being coy. "Everything. Absolutely everything."

Kelly laughed. "I thought you might." She crossed her legs and held her water glass daintily. "Well, it's funny. He lives pretty high on the hog, hosts fabulous parties with the top echelons of Hollywood and the wealthiest men in town, even vampires, but he still keeps himself to himself. He disappears for weeks at a time, never saying where he's going, and when he comes back he's depressed. He never says that, but you can tell. He hires staff to look after the house, but they're a service that comes in, does their job, and leaves. This place is almost like an office, not his home."

"I noticed that."

Adrian had decorated the house to be light and bring in the sea air, but there weren't many personal objects in sight. No photographs or mementoes, no scattered books or magazines, nothing about *him*. Amber sensed his protective aura around the house like a cocoon, but other than that, anyone could have lived here. You'd think a man who'd been alive as long as he had would have collected a few trinkets.

But Adrian was a warrior. He'd come up to Seattle with nothing but his sword—maybe he traveled light, used what he needed, and discarded it. An efficient way to live, but lonely, she would have thought. No ties to the past.

"So how did *you* meet him?" Kelly asked, wanting to know.

Amber found herself telling Kelly about Susan's death and Adrian finding her while she investigated at the warehouse. She omitted the part about the demon and Adrian's being an Immortal, not knowing how far Adrian wanted Kelly in his confidence. Kelly seemed genuinely sorry for Amber over Susan's passing, and confessed that she'd lost a brother when she was ten. Amber was sorry Kelly had had to experience that, but the story did make her seem more human and less doll-like.

After Amber finished breakfast, she decided to discover how far Adrian's protection extended. She walked out on the back deck barefoot in her robe, breathing in the cool air and listening to the rush of the waves. Kelly remained inside, saying that the salt air was bad for her skin, but possibly she sensed that Amber wanted a few minutes alone.

The aura of protection extended all the way to the beach, Amber found to her delight as she walked down the stairs to the sands. She could walk a little way to either side of the house, around the curve of trees to Kelly's house on one side, and on the other to a brick wall that enclosed another house.

The ocean rippled dark blue to the sky, the ball of sun

behind her to the east. It had been early morning when Valerian picked them up in southern Washington, and the drive should have taken another fourteen hours or more after that, depending on whether Adrian had Valerian stick to the back roads or take the freeways.

It was mid-morning now, which meant she'd slept the whole day's drive and the entire night after that. She didn't feel as if she'd been out of it that long; she felt refreshed. But then, she'd been attacked by a demon, astral-traveled with Adrian, been in a vampire brawl, and stabbed through the shoulder. All that could make a person need a good, long sleep. She remembered Adrian whispering the suggestion in the car, and her overwhelming urge to obey.

Her senses began to tingle with his magic; then a pair of strong arms came around her from behind, and Adrian's warmth.

"Hello," he rumbled. She felt his lips in her hair, and his long, strong body against her back.

# CHAPTER SEVEN

She knew she'd never get enough of him. His body was hard behind her, his arms corded with muscle as he gathered her against him.

"Hello," she responded in a slight daze. "What have you been up to?"

"Buying you a car."

She turned in his embrace, looking up into his fathomless black eyes. "I didn't think you were serious."

His smile made all kinds of promises. "You said you liked the car Valerian rented, so I got you one just like it."

"But you can't just give me a *car*. I can get my old one fixed."

"It would have given up the ghost soon anyway," he said quietly. "If you don't like black, I can have it painted. It looks good black."

"Holy Mother Goddess, Adrian."

He took a set of keys from his pocket and pressed them into her hand at the same time as he leaned down and kissed her. It was the kiss of a man not yet ready to push her out and say, *It's been fun*. It was the kiss of a man thinking, *Time for bed*.

His hair was warm, the back of his neck damp with sweat. He'd dressed in another T-shirt that stretched tight over his shoulders and chest, outlining the hollows and planes of his body. Her fingers found the ridges of old scars, the body of a fighting man who'd healed but would never be completely whole again.

A demigod, kissing her and touching her as much as she touched him. He licked the corner of her mouth, tongue hot, his hands sliding to cradle her breasts, thumbs stirring the tips to life.

She curled her toes in the warm sand, her female places heating as he continued to caress her. She adored the thought of lying on the beach with him, maybe on top of the loose bathrobe, him making love to her. The thought of all his power, the imagined delight of when he moved his hips against hers made her shiver.

"Your protection doesn't keep the neighbors from seeing your stretch of beach, does it?" she whispered.

He smiled, his mouth touching hers. "Afraid not."

"Damn."

"I'm happy you want it." He slid one hand around to cradle her backside. "If I had the power to slow time, I would, to be with you longer."

"That's a good line," she said, kissing his lower lip.

"That doesn't stop it from being true."

"Mmm, you really are a sweet-talker, you know that?"

He nuzzled her cheek. "Is it working?"

*Yes.* She turned to look out to sea again, liking him holding her from behind. The sea in front of her was tranquil and beautiful, peaceful, and behind her stood the rock-solid strength of Adrian. So easy here to let her mind move away from demons and vampires, violence and fear, death magic and sorrow.

Adrian's strong hands moved to her abdomen, right over the tie that held the robe together. It was the perfect romantic moment, the sun bright on the sea, the cool breeze ruffling her hair, his strong arms around her, his lips on her neck.

He was a powerful being, holding more magic than she understood and motives beyond her comprehension. He bought her cars and nibbled her skin like a lover. He'd fought battles since the dawn of civilization, crumpling vampires and demons like paper dolls.

The fact that he was a demigod didn't make him good. She was simply lucky he chose to be kind to her. The power inside him was terrifying, and if she were his enemy, he would have no compunction about turning that power against her.

The sensible part of her said, *Slow down, find a way to get out of this.*

The wild part of her that had almost died with Susan's murder said, *Enjoy the danger. A chance like this will never come again.*

She lay her head against his chest as his fingers slid inside the robe. His warm hand moved down her abdomen, tracing the indentation of her navel, fingers feathering down to the curls at the joining of her thighs.

The touch made her feel wild and wanton. This was a public beach, even if it was a secluded part, shielded by Kelly's house and that of his walled-in neighbor. But they were outdoors, and he was touching her bare skin beneath the robe with no hesitation or shame.

"You smell good, sweet witch," he said in her ear.

Her hips moved as his fingers found her rising nub, already slick with what he did. "I used your shampoo."

"It's yours now. I will give it all to you, this house and everything in it, if you want it."

She tried to shake her head. "You're crazy, you know that?"

"I will have to move on soon—I've stayed here too long already. I'd like to think someone lived in this house who would like it and remember me a little." He kissed her neck again.

"Remember you a *little*?" she asked in amazement. "How could I forget you?"

His voice was somber. "I can make you forget if you want. I can make you forget your sorrow and your fear—and me."

She looked up at him. She could never read what went on behind his eyes. Black and enigmatic, the windows to his soul were shut and closely guarded. "I don't want to forget you."

"You might later, when you no longer like what you see. When you want to forget, you tell me."

She started to protest, but he leaned down and teased her earlobe with his tongue. "Hush now. Enjoy my gifts."

Did he mean the car, the house, or his fingers on the sensitive places of her body? *And does it matter?*

His skilled touch moved on her, his fingertip rocking back and forth on her button until her body tingled with fire. She leaned back into him, finding the obvious erection rising beneath his jeans. She liked that what he did aroused him as much as it aroused her, and she rubbed her backside playfully against him.

He growled low in his throat and punished her by redoubling his efforts. His fingers splayed on her thighs, palms spreading her legs so he could dip his forefinger into her cleft. She moved her hips against him as she curled her toes into the sun-toasted sand.

The breeze made a nice a contrast to the heat burning her from the inside out. His sharp teeth fastened on her neck, sexier than any vampire bite because he gentled himself for her. He wanted her pleasure, not her life. Vampires took; Adrian gave.

Some of the magic she'd performed in her life had been heady, but Adrian's skilled touch wound her higher faster than any magic, and certainly no sex she ever had could compare. She'd once thought Julio the ultimate in sexual partners, but his memory faded fast as Adrian swirled his fingers and spiraled her toward climax.

He pressed his hand against her, two fingers now dipping inside her, the breadth of them pressing her open. He stroked her hard, harder, his fingers working magic.

She rose on her tiptoes, the wind skimming the curls on her head. Dark fire rocked through her, and she moved back and forth on his callused hand.

"Goddess, Adrian," she breathed.

"Feel it," he whispered. "Feel it for me."

She let out a scream that the wind dragged away. She rocked her hips faster and faster, wanting the sensation to go on and on. "I love it," she crooned.

"Good."

She cried out again, her head thrown back on his shoulder, his hand clamped hard between her legs. It felt wonderful, as if she could fly and at the same time stand still on the hot sand with the sun beating down on her.

She held on to her climax as long as she could, liking the intense sensation she'd never quite achieved before. Memories of Julio splintered and disappeared. The vampire couldn't compare, and Adrian had only touched her.

"That's it," Adrian murmured into her ear, his teeth sharp on her lobe. "That's what I want."

She sighed and stretched against his body, her climax winding down. His erection rested firmly between her buttocks, pressing through the robe and his jeans.

She tried to reach for it, to begin to pleasure him back, but he turned her around and kissed her instead. She felt his heart pounding beneath his hard chest, his skin warmer than a normal human's.

His breath warm on her lips, he began to peel the robe from her shoulders. She gasped, "Adrian."

"None will see," he whispered.

A tingling filled the air, a transparent wave that glittered as the wind touched it. A magical canopy, she sensed, somewhat like a well-cast witch's circle that obscured those within it.

The thought that no one could see them out here, that his magic kept them out, made her feel wicked and daring. She untied her robe and let him push it all the way off her.

The sun touched bare skin with fingers of warmth, wind tickling her all over. He didn't touch her, but looked at her from head to toe, his eyes warming. He was barefoot himself, his feet sinking into smooth sand.

"You are beautiful, my witch."

Amber's heartbeat quickened with the naughtiness of what she was doing—standing under the sun, naked, letting him look his fill. She stepped closer and touched his face, feeling the roughness of his jaw, the smoothness of his lips.

He put his hand on her waist and pulled her close, her bare body against his clothed one. The denim of his jeans and his cotton T-shirt rubbed erotically across her sun-drenched skin. He slid his hand down to cup her buttocks, pulling her up to kiss her.

The kiss went on and on, he tasting her mouth with slow thoroughness. She couldn't help but press her body against his, the hardness in his jeans a pleasing ridge. He made a sound low in his throat, his large, warm hands splaying over the small of her back.

She wormed her hand between them and rubbed his erection, smiling when his eyes went darker than ever. Swirling lights appeared in the very depths of them.

"You said you want me to forget you," she said as his lips brushed her mouth. "Do you want to forget me?"

"Never." The word ground out of him. "I never will."

"That's pleasing to know."

"It is the truth."

He leaned to her, his thigh sliding between her legs, and opened her mouth with hungry, practiced kisses.

She popped the button of his jeans and dipped her fingers inside. His cock was wide and hard and hotter than the sunshine on her back. He made a sound of pleasure as she traced her fingertips around his shaft, and his kiss turned fierce.

He dragged her against him, his strength barely contained. Making love to him would be the ultimate sensual experience, his large body covering hers, his hardness thick inside her.

He moved his hips against her, seeming to like the way she played with his shaft. He caressed her backside, fingers playing in the crease until dark shivers blanketed her.

"Adrian," she murmured. "I never want to forget *this*."

In silence he kissed her, rubbing her as she rubbed him, a man and a woman pleasuring each other on an empty beach.

He groaned suddenly and jerked down the zipper of his jeans, seizing himself in his fist. Amber eased his fingers away and took up the task herself, stroking his cock between her two hands as his head rocked back and his hips moved.

She felt his seed building at the base of him, shuddering pulses beginning.

"Amber, Goddess help me."

"You made *me* come," she answered softly. "Payback."

"Witch."

"Always."

He groaned. He suddenly pushed her away from him, sending her stumbling back in the sand. Her surprise turned to a grin as he kicked his jeans all the way off and ran toward the waves. His body was beautiful to look at, the white T-shirt covering his back until just above his ass, his tight-muscled legs working as he dashed across the sand.

He splashed into the water, and she distinctly heard another heavy groan as he dove into the waves. She ran after him, cold water striking her and making her shriek. Adrian surfaced, water slicking his hair back and plastering his T-shirt to his body.

She caught up to him, and he crushed her against him and kissed her hard, the salt water letting them float without much effort.

When they drew apart, she laughed at him. His brows drew together as he brushed her hair from her face, his fingers points of warmth in the cold water.

Amber threw her arms around his neck and floated with him. "Don't make me forget this," she said breathlessly. "I'd rather keep memories and learn how to live with them than let you wipe my brain."

He kissed her forehead, but didn't answer. Whether he'd do as she wanted or not, she couldn't tell.

She rested her head on his chest and watched the sea, sunlight on the water lighting a sparkling path to the cloud-lined edge of the world. It felt so good to be here with him like this, alone amid serenity.

She knew it couldn't last. They could stay in this bubble of protection for now, but the demon was still out there and dangerous.

"How is it you want me to help you?" she murmured, relaxed against him. "You hint that I'm a powerful witch, but Susan had all the power. She belonged to an order called the Coven of Light, a couple dozen damn strong witches from all over the world, who do spells together by connecting with stones or mirrors or water scrying. They held a memorial with me for Susan."

Adrian put his fingertips to her forehead, and she felt a flicker of magic move across her skin. "You're wrong. You have great power, untapped maybe, but you have it. You stayed in the shadows, didn't you, while Susan shone?"

"A little bit." She flushed. "Not because I felt inadequate, but because she was so compelling. If you'd known her, you'd understand."

"If you want to avenge her, to not make her death a waste, it's time to come into the light." He brushed a lock of her hair back, and again she felt the flicker of magic.

They stayed there for a while, floating with each other, trading kisses and learning each other's bodies. Then, as though by mutual agreement, they moved back to shore, Adrian leading her by the hand up onto the beach.

She tried not to stare too hard at his strong legs and thighs, the tattoo moving on his buttocks as he leaned over to pull on his jeans. He slowly zipped up and buttoned his pants and watched with obvious interest as Amber slipped back into the robe.

"By the way," he said, resting casually, hands on hips. "I have to meet with a vampire lord tonight at his club. I want you to come with me."

Her eyes widened, her fingertips growing cold. "To a vampire club?" She thought about the clubs in Seattle where humans went to get high on being suckled by vampires. A dangerous addiction, like the similar demon clubs, except demons fed on life essences, often while having sex with their victims. Making love with a demon was supposed to be the ultimate in sexual experiences. Vampires and demons had no need to rape, because their partners came to them eager and willing. "With vampires eyeing me like fresh meat?"

"You'll not be touched. I want Septimus to meet you, to understand that you're mine. His vampires will obey him to the point of fighting other vamps to keep them away from you."

She raised her brows. "That I'm *yours*?"

He nodded, hair glistening from his swim, a bronzed and beautiful god under the sun. "You have my protection."

His dark eyes gave nothing away, as though he saw nothing wrong with the statement he'd made. She belonged to him. He'd decided, and it was so.

"And you're friends with this vampire?" she asked as she moved across the sand to him. Crumbles of sand stuck to her bare feet.

"Not friends. Allies, maybe. I've told him that as long

as he keeps his vampires in line and intimidates the others in town, I won't wipe him out."

"How nice of you." She stuck her hands in the pockets of her robe, the breeze suddenly cool. Adrian stood straight and tall against it, despite the T-shirt plastered to every contour of his body, his nipples tight and brown against the fabric. She could look at him forever.

"Another reason I want to talk to Septimus is that he might know what the writing says," he said. "He's an Old One himself."

"Making me want to meet him more and more."

"He'll be fine as long as I am with you." He leaned down and kissed the corner of her lips, his eyes sparkling. "Besides, I want a kick-ass witch beside me if I'm going into a vampire's lair."

The kiss turned deep, his mouth slanting across hers, showing her just how sweet he tasted. Making love to him would be wild excitement and deep fulfillment. She determined then and there to make sure he understood just how ready for him she could be.

At nine that night, Amber rode with Adrian, who drove the Mustang into the heart of downtown Los Angeles and the upscale vampire nightclubs that had blossomed there. Valerian had stuffed himself in the back to accompany them.

Amber still didn't know quite what to make of Valerian. He exuded life magic—a shape-shifter, Adrian had said—but he wasn't like any shape-shifter she'd ever encountered.

Valerian was a big man, attractive in a brutal sort of way. Like Adrian, he was a fighter, but again, the similarities ended there. Adrian had enormous power within him, and Valerian had raw physical strength. Valerian's magic, she sensed, only let him shape-shift, while Adrian's could blast everyone out of his path if he wanted it to.

She'd brought some of her charged crystals and a few amulets and herbs with her, kept in a drawstring bag on her belt. Adrian seemed amused that she wanted her accoutrements, but no way was she walking into a vampire club without having magic backup. The fire spell she could throw was minute—*potentially* deadly to a vampire who could die by fire, but usually easily doused. She wanted far stronger magics than that on her side.

Adrian had not brought the demon writing with him, saying he wouldn't take something that reeked that much of death magic into a vampire club, where its power could be enhanced. He'd ask Septimus to come to the house to look at it, which in Amber's opinion wasn't a much better idea. The thought of a vampire invading Adrian's protected nest didn't leave a good taste in her mouth.

Amber was dressed in new clothes—a blouse over a tight, cropped tank top, jeans, and high-heeled sandals. Adrian still hadn't wanted Amber to leave the house even to go shopping in a public place, so Kelly had called her couturiers and asked them to come to Adrian's. The clothiers knew Kelly for a rising star and happily came running.

Adrian had bought Amber a slew of clothes from casual to dressy, all chic, all form-hugging, all sexy. She'd tried to stop him, but he'd ignored her and handed plenty of money to the clothier, who was more apt to listen to Adrian than Amber.

"Gee, I always wanted a sugar daddy," she'd said, mimicking a little-girl voice.

Kelly had laughed and said, "Honey, take what you can get. Men always treated me like shit." She'd laughed again. "Now I buy *them* presents."

Adrian parked the car and came around to open the door for Amber before the vampires in suits at the door could. Valerian piled out behind them, smiling dangerously. The vampire doormen pretended to ignore him as they opened the dark stained-glass doors and ushered the three inside.

In the black-painted vestibule, a pair of vampires demanded they hand over all weapons. That included not only knives and guns, but swords, stakes, crosses, and holy water, they were told. Valerian just smiled and spread his arms, declaring he was clean, daring them to frisk him. The vampire doormen gave him baleful stares but didn't touch him.

They demanded Amber's bag of magical equipment.

"It's not a weapon," she said hotly.

"Could be." One weapons taker peered into the bag, very carefully touching nothing. "Witches can stir magic against vampires. No magical implements allowed."

"In other words, if things get ugly, I can't defend myself."

The vampire gave her a deadpan stare. She carefully looked at his left cheek, not about to be sucked in by vampire eyes. "Rules of the club protect you," he said. "No human to be killed on the premises."

"Septimus likes to avoid problems," Adrian told her. He pulled off his armlet, which changed into Ferrin the snake the moment Adrian dropped him to the counter. "He likes wine, but be careful. Too much makes him cranky."

Ferrin wound into a coil and raised his head, flattening his neck into a hood. Both vampires stepped back uneasily.

"The poison won't kill them," Amber whispered as they walked toward the club doors in the rear of the vestibule. "What are they afraid of?"

"It can make them sick for a long time," Adrian answered, holding open the door. "And if they're too sick to feed, they'll starve to death. A human bitten by a cobra has a cleaner and quicker end."

Valerian rumbled behind her, "That's why I love you, Adrian. You're so *evil.*"

"Years of experience," Adrian answered, and Valerian laughed. The laugh was swallowed by a roar of music as they entered the club.

Whatever harsh, staccato, beat-into-your-brain music was popular that month blasted from hidden speakers in the middle of a black-dark room pierced here and there with spots and strobes. The lyrics, sung by a low-voiced female, moved from suggestive to blatant and back again. Tables lined the dance floor, and a bar, lit from below with red lights, glowed along an entire wall. Amber smelled the tang of alcohol—for the humans, although vampires liked it too.

She didn't actually see any biting going on between the couples huddled at tables in the shadows, though some came damn close. Doors opened off the other side of the dance floor, probably to private rooms, from what she'd heard about these types of clubs. Biting definitely went on back there, and likely sex, not always between only two people.

Vampires loved sex and didn't like the idea of limiting themselves to one partner at a time. Blood slaves had to get used to that, but from all accounts, by the time a person was addicted enough to a vampire to become a blood slave, they didn't care.

Adrian reached behind her and grasped her hand, his muscled arm like a lifeline as he led her through the crowd and the dance floor to the doors beyond. Looking around, Amber saw that she was underdressed—or overdressed, however she wanted to view it. Some women wore tiny black leather dresses, showing off generous bosoms and long legs in impossibly high heels. Others wore still scantier clothing, halter tops or cropped shirts and miniskirts, or jeans riding so low that string bikinis showed over their waistbands—on those who'd bothered with underwear. Amber's blouse over cropped tank that showed her tiny butterfly tattoo seemed almost matronly.

Valerian's presence faded behind her, and Amber looked back to see the big man stop to talk with a woman in a black leather dress and a collar. He put his hand on her hip, and moments later they were dancing together, so close that molecules of air couldn't have slid between them.

Adrian didn't notice, but pulled Amber after him through the dark and the dense music to a door flanked by a pair of vampire thugs. They straightened up and gave Adrian a respectful look, but blocked the way to the door. "Mr. Septimus wants to see you alone." They glanced meaningfully at Amber.

Adrian returned their look, staring down at them, and the vampires shifted nervously.

"It's all right," Adrian said, half to Amber. "I know you'll be perfectly safe out here." He trained his gaze straight on the vampires, not worried about their powers of the mind. He could look a vampire in the eye, and it was the vampire who cringed and backed down.

"Yes, sir," one of the vamps said, and he moved aside to open the door.

Adrian leaned to Amber. "No one will touch you, and Valerian's here. Enjoy yourself." He gave her a smile as though they were at a harmless picnic in the park, then turned and slipped through the door, leaving her alone with the vamps and their sexy music.

# CHAPTER EIGHT

"Hey, you're new here, aren't you?" came a cheerful, almost perky woman's voice.

Amber gave the vampire guards a last look, careful not to meet their eyes, and turned to see who'd spoken to her. A young woman wearing shorts cut halfway up her backside and a white tank top so tight her nipples pressed dark circles against it smiled at Amber. She had short red hair, freckles, and green eyes made luminous with colored contact lenses. A tattoo of some winged creature spread itself across her upper chest, and she wore black lipstick.

Under the makeup and the "have sex with me now" clothes, she looked clean-cut and almost cute. Her neck did sport scars from past vampire bites and two bright red spots from a more recent feeding. She didn't have the half-crazed look of a blood slave, but sometimes they hid it well.

"Yes," Amber responded neutrally. "My first time here."

The girl examined Amber's neck, brightening when she saw no teeth marks. "A vamp virgin? Girl, you're going to have some fun tonight. I'm LaChey. Want to dance?"

She started wiggling and bumping to the music, lifting her hands in the air. Amber glanced at the closed door with the two vampire guards, and at Valerian, still leg-locked with the black-leather-dress woman. LaChey looked harmless—a girl out on the town, enjoying her favorite addiction. No drug tracks scarred her arms, her eyes were clear, and she didn't reek of smoke or alcohol. A good-girl Goth?

"What the hell," Amber said.

LaChey laughed and wriggled her way out to the floor. The music was catchy, the lights beating almost in time with it. Amber followed her until they were dancing in the middle of the floor. The vampires seemed to ignore them, focusing on women or men who were lifting necks to them, almost begging to be bitten.

Amber tried to ignore them and dance, enjoying herself for the first time since Susan's death. No, not really *enjoying,* she thought. Letting loose. Dancing in a pool of danger, shaking her booty while sharks circled. They must know that she'd never been fed on—a vamp virgin, as LaChey had called her—and they must know she'd come with Adrian.

Someone danced up behind her. She felt a body brush her back, legs in black leather curving inside hers, mimicking her movements. She looked over her shoulder to find a bare-chested vampire in very low-slung black-leather pants dancing tightly against her, his long black hair flowing over muscular shoulders. He moved his hips so his groin brushed her, dirty dancing with her.

LaChey laughed. "That's Bryan. With a Y. Hi, Bryan." She waved.

Bryan flashed liquid dark eyes at her before going back to being too sexy for his fangs. His sharp white teeth showed against his sensual mouth, and he slowly licked his lips.

"I didn't come in here to get bit," Amber told him.

"You wanted vampires," he disagreed, his voice low and sultry. "Or else you'd have waited in the car for your man."

He had a point. Adrian could have left her in the protection of the car with Valerian if she'd asked, but she had been curious about the club. She spent her time avoiding or fighting off death-magic creatures, never seeing them behind the scenes. As much as she didn't understand people wanting to be blood slaves, she could see the attraction. Bryan was certainly beautiful, and he probably made the feeding a sensual, magnetic experience.

"Really, I don't want to be a blood donor tonight," Amber yelled over the music.

"You're mean to tease." Bryan sidled closer, his hips and thighs brushing hers. "Let me give you a little nip. I'll erase the marks so your boyfriend will never know."

She felt his breath on her neck, his cool lips, the tiny scrape of his teeth as he scratched them across her skin.

Valerian's voice suddenly rumbled from on high. "Oh, goody. An excuse to kick some vampire ass." His big hand closed on Bryan's shoulder, prying him away from Amber.

Bryan hissed, his sensuous face clouding. "Lick me, lizard man." He turned on his booted heel and swayed away, the pants so tight that every curve and crevice showed.

Valerian scowled after him. "Bloodsucker. Amber, Adrian needs you. Septimus sent me a message to bring you in."

"Sent you a message? Why couldn't he ask me himself?"

Valerian laughed. "Vampires are the ultimate chauvinists. They can only think in terms of vampire and blood slave. Dom and submissive. If you're not one, you're the other."

"How flattering."

Valerian lifted his hands in a gesture of surrender. "Hey, I didn't make vampires complete assholes. But whatever you think of him, it's a bad idea to keep Septimus waiting. Adrian too, for that matter."

"Fine," Amber said. "Let's rush to see the big, bad vampire."

LaChey waved from where she danced with another leather-clad vamp, this one blond. "'Bye. Come back and dance later."

Amber returned the wave and walked away with Valerian. "Lizard man?" she asked as they neared the door through which Adrian had disappeared. "You're not a were-iguana, are you?"

Valerian gave her a deprecating look. "I love a witch with a sense of humor."

He hadn't answered the question, but they'd arrived at the door and Amber didn't have a chance to ask again.

The vampire guards let them into a short hallway with plush carpeting and expensive-looking artwork, then to a door at the far end of the hall that led into a lavish office. The office had black marble walls and no windows, all the better for a vampire to keep working during daylight without the inconvenience of sunlight.

The office was ultra-chic—clean lines, black and white with splashes of red to relieve the monochrome. Adrian lounged in a black armchair, his long legs stretched out in front of him, but he got languorously to his feet when she entered.

Another man rose from behind the polished granite-topped desk, as tall as Adrian and what she expected from a vampire: powerful build, sensual face, dark hair, dressed in a black silk suit.

She felt from him a wave of death magic so strong she thought she'd be sick. He didn't deliberately throw it at her; it surrounded him and pulsated through the air. She wondered how Adrian, as full of life magic as he was, could stand to remain in the room with him. She noticed Valerian's tension. Maybe he wasn't as disgusted as she was, but certainly wary.

As though Adrian read Amber's distress, he came to her and put a comforting arm around her waist. "Amber, meet Septimus. He's evil but helpful."

"You're too kind," Septimus said. He held out his hand to Amber. "Ms. Silverthorne, I've made a promise never to hurt you, though I assure you, your neck is quite bitable." He said it the way a human might compliment her eyes or face.

Amber barely touched his palm with hers. Her first quick glance told her his eyes were blue as a deep lake and promised all the delights of fragrant grass crushed under bodies as they twined together, mouths seeking each other's. Her gaze began to travel upward against her will; the need to look into his blue eyes was compelling, though she knew she'd be lost if she did.

Adrian's hand on her waist burned through her thin shirt, and the vision snapped away. She dragged in a breath and dropped her gaze.

"She is strong," Septimus said to Adrian in admiration. "I congratulate you."

"She is very strong." Adrian guided Amber to a chair and eased her into it. He perched on its arm, putting his backside near her line of vision, a preferable sight to

Septimus's dangerous eyes. "I noticed that the moment I met her."

"When the demon attacked her." Septimus rested one hip on his desk, dangling his long, well-tailored leg. "You say he was an Old One?"

"I haven't felt anything like it in centuries. He ran away instead of trying to incapacitate me, but I think that was because he simply didn't want an out-and-out fight, not then. As though he didn't have time for it."

"An Old One?" Valerian demanded. "What is an Old One?"

"Shit you don't want to mess with," Septimus responded.

Amber remembered Adrian explaining that Old Ones had come from ancient times, even before Adrian had been conceived.

"He's something even the gods were worried about," she put in. "Am I right?"

"Well, that sucks," Valerian growled.

"It explains much," Septimus said thoughtfully. He reached across the desk and swung his flat-screen computer monitor around so they could all see it. "I've felt the balance of magic tipping, death magic creeping in more than it should. Too many human deaths, too many vampires made."

"That should suit you," Valerian said. "You feed on death."

"I don't like chaos," Septimus responded. "I like death to be orderly and useful. Random, out-of-control dark magic is as annoying to me as a huge influx of living magic. And I hate living magic. It's all I can do not to lose my dinner with the three of you in the room."

*Interesting,* Amber made a mental note. The information that she made him as nauseous as he made her might come in handy some day.

Septimus almost delicately clicked the mouse next to the computer and brought up a multicolored chart, red and yellow waves running evenly on top of one another. "This is a record of vampires Turned versus human deaths in Los Angeles County a year ago. As you can see, it's fairly balanced. There were no more human deaths than usual, no upsurge of the vampire population. Now this . . ."

He clicked to pop up another chart. In this one both lines were higher, and the red-shaded area was much larger than the yellow.

"This is vampires made versus human deaths in the last eight months. As you can see, the death rate for humans has risen sharply. But the rate for vampires appearing has risen even more sharply. Many of those vampires likely came from the surplus of dying humans, but vampires are multiplying at an unprecedented rate. Most of these I knew nothing about. They were certainly not authorized."

"You have to authorize vampires to Turn someone?" Amber asked.

"In my jurisdiction, yes," Septimus answered. "A vampire is allowed two Turnings a year in my area, and only under certain circumstances. Violation means death, for both the vampire and the Turned."

His handsome face remained neutral, a corporate CEO explaining why employees got fired. They break the rules, they're out.

"Are all vampire neighborhoods run this efficiently?" Amber asked.

Septimus quirked a smile. "No. Or rather, I don't know.

I concern myself with my territory, and that's it. How others choose to run things is their business. I like rules, and rules keep Adrian off my back."

He shot Adrian a glance that held a measure of respect, but Amber sensed simmering tension behind the calm eyes. Adrian had him tamed for now, Septimus was thinking, but if Adrian's power ever slipped . . .

The vampire calmly turned away and clicked up another chart, this one black and white with solid and broken lines rising on a graph. "And this is the recorded demon activity in the last eight months. Demons enslaving humans permanently, deaths in demon clubs." He added in disgust, "The vermin can't regulate anything."

"I've been noticing the same thing," Adrian put in. "Too many instances of the undead where they shouldn't be, too many deaths by violence of living magic creatures. An entire werewolf pack was slaughtered near San Luis Obispo. They'd lived there for generations."

"Oh," Amber said in sympathy. She thought of her friend Sabina's family—their close ties even when they fought among themselves, the honor they'd extended to Amber in accepting her as one of the pack. "How awful."

Septimus looked as if he had no kind thoughts to spare for werewolves, but Valerian glowered. "Shapeshifters are being picked on, like someone knows they're the strongest of living magic creatures."

"The Sidhe are pretty strong," Adrian said. He really did have a very nice backside, molded by denim jeans that left little to the imagination, Amber observed afresh. "They don't leave their territory much, but they rival the shape-shifters in power."

"But you never know what some of the half-blood Sidhe will get up to," Valerian pointed out. "If they think it would be fun to watch a death-magic creature take down a living-magic one, they'll make bets and sell tickets."

Septimus's expression didn't change. "There are no Sidhe, half-blood or otherwise, in Los Angeles, so I do not know if they've been affected. But death magic is growing, Adrian. You should be pleased; I've heard you complain that fighting ordinary demons is boring."

"It is. No challenge to it."

"Immortals." Septimus shook his head.

"Have you known more than one?" Amber asked him.

Septimus put his fingers to the bridge of his nose and gave a little shudder. "I met Hunter once. We battled for three days and nights, and would he stop to negotiate a truce like a civilized being? No. Your brother is crazy, Adrian."

"I know that. He's a warrior through and through. Why talk when he'd have more fun killing you?"

"When I finally got away, he didn't bother chasing me. He was bored by that time, I suppose. A failing among Immortals. You like stimuli all the time."

"My brothers might disagree with you." Adrian slid his enticing backside from the arm of the chair and got to his feet. "Are we done here?"

Septimus looked briefly from Amber to Adrian and nodded. "I think so. Thank you for your courtesy in stopping by."

"If you want to think it courtesy, go right ahead," Adrian said. He helped Amber to her feet, then guided her to the door with his hand on the small of her back. Valerian came behind them.

"She'll be protected," Septimus said. "I gave you my word."

Adrian only nodded, and they said good-bye. Once again, Amber fought the compulsion to look into Septimus's very blue eyes. *Peace,* she seemed to hear. *You'll like it here.*

"Amber?" Adrian stepped in front of her, blocking her view. He was smiling, but his eyes held understanding.

*Thank you,* she mouthed.

"Don't be afraid of Septimus," he said in a soft voice, and then suddenly, she wasn't. Septimus now had no control over her, and she could look at him or turn her back on him, just as she liked.

She chose to turn her back and walk out of the room with Adrian, Valerian hulking close behind.

Once the vampire guards had guided them back to the main part of the club, Amber turned to Adrian. "What were you and Septimus talking about before you let me in? No, wait, before you *sent* for me."

"An agreement to make you untouchable to any vampire, in his jurisdiction and beyond. He'll put out the word that you belong to me."

She eyed him coolly, still unsettled by the heavy pall of death magic in Septimus's office. "I'm not a blood slave. And I don't belong to anyone."

Adrian gave her a look of surprise, and Valerian guffawed. "You really know the way to a woman's heart, Adrian. Real smooth."

"I told you, I need to protect you," Adrian said to Amber, brows lowering.

She liked that she didn't have to avoid looking into his eyes like she did the vampire's. She could meet his gaze all she wanted, drown in the black depths and enjoy every minute. "Protection is fine. I don't really want to end up as a vampire snack. But *belong* to you? Why do you keep saying that?"

"It is what a vampire would understand," Adrian explained.

He met her gaze, a challenge in his eyes, which she met with one of her own. "You're not a vampire," she reminded him. "And if you offered me the car and the house so I'd be your adoring slave, take them back. I wouldn't do that for a vampire, and I'm not doing it for you."

His brow furrowed, sparks floating in his eyes. "I offered them as gifts. They mean nothing to me."

"Oh, gee, thanks." She swung around and marched away.

Behind her, Valerian bellowed with laughter. "Good, Adrian. Five thousand years old, and you still don't know anything about women."

Adrian's answer was a grunt drowned by the rapid thump of music. The music nearly drowned another cry Amber heard, this one from a woman, a scream of pain and fear coming from behind one of the closed doors. "No, please! I don't want to. Let me go!"

Amber's fury built to a breaking point. This club was all about coercing people into being food for vampires, no matter how civilized Septimus pretended to be, no matter how businesslike he was with his charts and his concern about rising chaos. All she knew was that a woman was screaming for mercy that no vampire or blood slave was going to give her—and it sounded like the freckle-faced LaChey.

Amber grabbed the doorknob, feeling faint surprise that the door was neither locked nor guarded, and burst inside. She heard Adrian and Valerian coming behind her, trying to stop her.

"Get away from her!" Amber shouted to the black-haired, naked vampire firmly pinning a woman beneath his large body.

Bryan looked up and snarled, his pointed canines, upper and lower, gleaming red with blood. He was definitely en flagrante delicto, both in sex and feeding. His open mouth and the hiss that came out of it, and the fury in his eyes, made him look like what he was, a beast pretending to be human.

The woman under him cried out in relief. It wasn't LaChey, but a woman with long black hair. A red dress lay in a heap at the end of the bed on top of Bryan's sexy leather pants.

Adrian looked over Amber's shoulder, swore, and dodged in front of her.

"What's wrong?" Valerian asked. "He's only a vampire. Just break the creep's neck."

Adrian remained standing rock solid in front of Amber. "Not him. *Her.*"

The woman looked up and laughed. A laugh that Amber had heard before, even though then it had belonged to a man. The demon, now in female form, sat up and looked at them with black eyes containing unimaginable evil.

# CHAPTER NINE

"Bryan, get away from her!" Amber cried, this time in alarm. Bryan, not comprehending, hissed again, and the demon woman sprang at him.

She threw Bryan across the small room and into the wall with such force that he crashed through plaster and brick and out into the alley beyond. The demon rose, her body lush, breasts full, hair gleaming black. She slammed a fist into the wall, and the rest of it broke away, leaving a gaping ten-foot hole into the night. Bryan remained facedown in the alley beyond, but the demon woman faced Adrian and Amber with a gleaming smile.

Adrian held out his arm and shouted for Ferrin, his eyes flashing sparks that glittered in the darkness. Amber felt the intense alien magic building inside him with the ferocity of a volcano preparing to erupt.

"Holy crap," Valerian muttered. Life magic was building up in him as well, the tension of it cutting into the room.

Septimus came running in and stopped in dismay, though Amber wasn't sure whether it was because of the demon or the hole in his wall. He took on the pained look of a man calculating the cost to repair it.

"Adrian," the demon female purred. "I have a message from your brother Tain. He says that he loves you very much."

Adrian's voice went flat, anger radiating from him like a solar flare. "Where is he?"

His tone should have struck terror into any creature, but the demon laughed a sultry laugh. She sauntered to Adrian, her perfect breasts swaying with her hips. She radiated death magic far stronger than what Amber had felt from Septimus, a sticky, sickening power that was as compelling as it was nauseating.

"Adrian, don't let her touch you," Amber said, her heart pounding with fear. Even Septimus, as filled with death magic as he was, backed away.

The demon turned to Amber and smiled a wide smile. "You care for him. How delicious." She raised her hands like claws, and dark magic shot out of them, snaking straight for Amber.

Adrian's magic burst toward the demon with a sound like a sonic boom. White-hot energy blasted the demon backward through the hole, bringing more of the wall down. The backlash sent Amber staggering into Valerian and Septimus.

The demon landed on her feet in the alley, morphing into a beautiful naked man, taller than Adrian and glowing like a god. His penis was erect, as though facing them excited him. "Tain also wants you to die," he said.

"Stay here," Adrian said over his shoulder to his companions as he strode into the alley. "Remember, he's an Old One."

Valerian's sigh sounded as if it came from the depths

of his boots. "Hell, I'm pretty old myself." He stepped out into the alley to flank Adrian on the right.

"I too am an Old One," Septimus said quietly and stepped out to stand near the broken wall with the other two.

Amber chewed her lip, wondering what she could do to help. She could fight a little, but she was not a warrior woman. Her weapon was magic, and she couldn't fathom what she could do against the demon that Adrian couldn't. But she also couldn't just wring her hands on the sidelines. She had to do *something*.

Ferrin slithered past her on his way to answer Adrian's summons, Amber's bag of accoutrements clenched between his teeth. He dropped the bag at her feet, and she could swear he smiled.

"Thank you," she said awkwardly.

"A snake who fetches," Valerian said, looking back. "How cute."

Ferrin slithered into the alley and Amber followed, clutching her bag of stones. The snake leapt onto Adrian's outstretched hand and became three feet of gleaming, deadly sword.

"Go back inside, Amber," Adrian said, not looking at her.

"No, wait, I have an idea." Amber rummaged in the bag for crystals, an amulet, and a little bag of salt. The crystals still glowed with the magic Adrian had infused in them. "Keep the demon busy for a few minutes."

Valerian barked a laugh. "Sure thing, sweetheart." He swung a bola around his head, the two flaming balls at the end of the rope burning with the bright blue purity of life magic.

Trying to ignore them, Amber hastily drew a circle

around herself on the ground, outlining it with salt. A blue nimbus rose around the circle, protecting her from the death magic outside it—barely. She dumped crystals on the ground, picking out the ones she wanted— onyx and clear quartz. To these she added more salt crystals, laid an amulet on top of them, and began to chant.

Beyond the magic barrier, Amber saw Septimus crouch down, daggers in hand. The three men advanced on the demon, Valerian laughing as he swung his fiery weapon. Adrian let loose another *boom* of built-up magic, a white energy field that raced away from him like ripples of water and struck the demon hard.

The demon flew backward but landed upright, balancing on leathery wings that shot out from his back.

"Oh, great," Valerian muttered. "Now the roach flies."

Death magic flowed from the demon like black mist, engulfing the alley and the fighters in it. Fingers of darkness pushed at the blue of Amber's magic shield, and she had to divert her energy from the spell to keep the circle whole.

Adrian sliced through the demon's dark magic, his sword a white band of light. With a roar, Valerian let his bola fly. Fiery bands wrapped around the demon's throat, briefly dimming the blackness of his magic. Valerian held up his hand and the bola flew back to it, blue fire still burning.

While the demon recovered, Septimus darted in, daggers in hand, and stabbed the demon full in the stomach. Black blood poured out of a huge wound, and Septimus danced away from the flow, more to protect his suit than his life.

The demon laughed as his wounds began to close. "You'll have to do better than that, vampire."

Tendrils of inky mist wound around Septimus's throat and chest and closed tight. The vampire wouldn't choke, but the demon could easily slice Septimus in half, which would kill him.

Adrian came in with his sword, hacking at the ropes of magic, freeing Septimus, the severed strands of death magic dissipating. Blue-white light glowed out of Adrian's sword, and the same white light shot from his eyes. Power built inside him that could destroy city blocks when he unleashed it.

Amber felt the power of Goddess nudge her, bringing her attention back to the amulet she was preparing. Then something happened that had never before happened in Amber's circles.

An unseen hand traced a pattern in a blotch of spilled salt—a pair of horns, the sign of Isis. She stared at the symbol, remembering that Adrian had told her he was born of the Goddess in the form of Isis. She had come to help her son.

Amber broke off her ritual chanting to babble, "Make it work. Please make it work."

Something warm and quiet touched her, a serenity and a surety, and then it was gone.

"Adrian, wait," she called.

Adrian paid no attention. He released his power, which knocked the demon across the alley and into a brick and steel wall that bent under the onslaught. Adrian followed up by sailing after the demon on a wave of magic.

"Where is Tain?" Adrian demanded as he sliced down with his sword, his words ringing through the alley. Sanity had left his voice. "Where is he?"

The demon, despite Adrian's attack, laughed, death magic dancing in his hands. "He sends his love. And says he'll never forgive you. Not even if you give him your body to flay alive."

"No!" Adrian roared, and plunged his sword into the demon. The demon dissolved into black mist, only to re-form a few feet away and swat Adrian aside. Adrian landed heavily, Ferrin flying wide to clatter across the alley floor.

Amber's spell was ready. "Ferrin, help me!" she cried.

As Valerian and Septimus assisted Adrian to his feet, the sword on the ground—now bent into the sinuous waves of the snake—slithered to her, sliding through the gap she created for him in the circle. Gingerly Amber looped the amulet's small chain around one of Ferrin's fangs.

"Get it on the demon somehow," she whispered.

The snake regarded her with intelligent eyes, then slipped noiselessly through the trash in the alley, unheeded by the demon, who curled death magic in his hands to throw at the three men grouped before him.

With the mindless bravery of cobras, Ferrin sailed straight at the demon and buried the amulet in the wound Adrian had opened in him. The demon grabbed the snake in a strangling hold, but Ferrin turned into a sword again and cut into the demon's hands. The demon's hands began to smoke, and he snarled and let the sword clank to the ground.

Amber watched her spell take hold. The demon's eyes glittered black fire, and his focus moved past the three men now on their feet and landed with acid sharpness on Amber standing alone.

"Ah," the demon said. "*Interesting* choice."

Valerian said to Amber, "Please say you're corroding him from the inside out."

Adrian said nothing at all. Silently he retrieved Ferrin

and moved to block Amber from the demon's deadly stare. Adrian's face was beaded with sweat, his shirt soaked with it. His black eyes still swam with sparks, his anger focused and lethal.

"What is your name?" Amber called out to the demon. She prayed that the truth spell she'd infused into the amulet was strong enough to get some answers out of him, ones they could use against him.

The demon laughed. "I go by many names. I am a son of Apep."

"Who's Apep?" Valerian hissed to Adrian.

"A snake god of ancient Egypt," he answered, his gaze pinned on the demon. "Always trying to swallow the sun."

"Nice to know," Valerian murmured back.

Amber called to the demon again, "Why did you kill Susan?"

The demon answered as if he didn't mind the question. "She knew too much. Like you do. I don't like people who get too close." He made a crushing movement between thumb and forefinger.

Swallowing her anger, Amber went on bravely. "Where is Tain?"

He laughed, the sound echoing along the buildings. "You think your spell can make me tell you? To reach inside me and bring forth the truth? But there are many truths, earth witch. Which one do you want to know?"

"I want to know where Tain is. Where are you keeping him?"

"No one likes a clever witch."

"You must answer," Amber said, putting a stern note in her voice. She didn't feel at all stern—she was terrified—but spells worked better when you were firm. "I command you to give me the truth."

The demon laughed again, rising on his wings. He

seemed to grow larger, a being of shadow and smoke that filled the alley.

"I'll do better than tell you. I'll show you." He pointed a long finger at her, and death magic poured out of him. *"Ice,"* he hissed, and shot up into the sky.

"Oh, shit," Valerian said. "You had to ask."

A huge sphere of ice closed over the alley, advancing and thickening so rapidly that it crackled and groaned. The wall of the club was coated over in seconds, the ice ceiling bearing down on the four in the alley at hideous speed.

Septimus struck at the wall, which only chipped despite his vampire strength. Adrian swung his sword, but Ferrin only carved a few grooves without doing much damage. The blue fire of Valerian's bola did about the same, and Amber's desperate attempt to throw her fire spell did still less.

"Valerian," Adrian said, his voice commanding.

"Yes, all right, give me a second."

He threw down the bola and started taking off his clothes. Septimus saw nothing strange in this but stopped trying to punch his way out. Ice shifted and began to enclose the vampire, but he stood and waited. He couldn't be smothered with it, but the ice would trap him, and he'd be there when the sun rose if no one hacked him free.

"What is he doing?" Amber asked; then her voice died as Valerian kicked off his jeans and stood up to full height, stark naked, his blond hair falling loose.

"Look out," Adrian warned, and then Valerian changed.

*Lizard man,* Bryan the vampire had sneered at him. As Valerian's body exploded into ten tons of scales, haunches, claws, and above all, dozens of huge pointed teeth, Amber understood.

Not lizard. *Dragon.*

She had time to gasp before Adrian threw her to the ground and landed on top of her. A second later, Valerian blasted incandescent fire straight into the ice canopy above them.

The ice groaned, then shattered. Several tons of water cascaded down to the alley below, Adrian grunting as his body took the brunt of it. Amber groped for breath and got a mouthful of water instead.

Adrian was soaked to the skin with freezing water, his hair plastered to his scalp. He eased off Amber, and she hunched into a ball to shiver in the breeze that swept down the alley. Septimus wiped off his ruined suit with his hands, looking disgusted.

Valerian settled onto his haunches, lowering his great dragon head to stare at Adrian with enormous blue eyes. "Happy now?" he rumbled.

Adrian paid no attention. He was looking upward, water beading on his lashes, scanning the sky above them. "He's gone."

"A circumstance devoutly to be wished," Septimus said. He tried wringing out his cuffs, then gave up. "I don't mind playing your games, Adrian, but letting an ancient demon wreak havoc in my club is a bit much."

Adrian got to his feet, still looking up. "I'll pay the damages."

Septimus opened his mouth, as though he'd say, *That's not the point,* but shut it again. He trudged back to the club and the fearful spectators who had peered outside to watch the fight and its aftermath. "Start getting this wall sealed up," Amber heard him say.

A creak of scales filled the alley as the dragon morphed back into Valerian, arms folding over his nude body. "What now?"

Adrian finally looked at him. His eyes were opaque black again, the sparks gone, the thoughts behind them obscured. "Valerian, get Amber home safely," he commanded.

Without another word, he strode off down the alley, heels grinding on the dirt and gravel and water on its floor. Amber started to call out, but Valerian stopped her with a heavy hand.

"Best to leave him alone when he's like that."

Amber watched Adrian disappear into the darkness at the mouth of the alley. She still wanted to rush after him, but she was able to sense when someone truly wanted to be alone.

"I want to help him," she said. "He saved my life."

"I don't know if you can help him." Valerian sighed. "He's the ultimate loner—there's no one in the world exactly like him except the other Immortals, and you don't see them around anywhere, do you? Not rushing in to hold big brother's hand. Now, me, I like people. When you need someone to talk to, you can always talk to me."

Amber dragged her gaze from the darkness and choked back a shaky laugh. "You're not exactly the boy next door. And could you put your clothes back on?"

"What?" He looked down at himself, all six foot and change of solid muscle. "Oh. I forget sometimes when I first shift back. Clothes seem unnatural."

Amber averted her eyes while Valerian walked away to find his wet jeans and shirt.

"My shape-shifter friend Sabina is like that, too," she said, averting her eyes while he pulled them on. "She grumbles when she has to re-dress herself."

"Mmm." She heard a soft zzz sound as Valerian zipped up his jeans. "I wouldn't mind meeting her."

"She's a werewolf. She's picky about who she takes up with."

"Don't think she'd like lizards?"

"I have no idea. It's never come up in conversation." As she talked, Amber gathered her stones and rubbed out the now-sodden salt on the alley surface, resolutely trying not to think about Adrian and what he might be encountering out there in the city.

As she turned to go back into the club, her gaze fell on Bryan, who still lay unconscious on a pile of bricks.

"We should take him inside," she said.

Valerian gave her an incredulous look. "What for?"

"If they forget him, and he's still here when the sun comes up . . ."

"He'll decompose. Oh, well."

"It's not a fair way to die."

Valerian scowled again, but moved to Bryan's inert form and heaved him over his shoulder. "You're a soft touch, witch."

He carried Bryan back into the ruined room, and Amber followed. In the club proper, the vampire staff was trying to come up with ways to wedge the door to the ruined room closed and seal it before the sun came up. LaChey pushed through the guards holding the crowd back and ran for Valerian, calling Bryan's name.

Valerian dumped Bryan in another room just as the vampire was coming around. LaChey held Bryan's hand and began crooning to him. Amber left them quickly. When Bryan woke up, hurt and groggy, he'd likely want to feed right away and not care much who he sank his teeth into or how hard. LaChey seemed to have enough experience with vampires to keep him under control— at least, Amber hoped she did.

They left the club and Valerian took Amber back to Adrian's house. He offered to stay, but Amber felt protected enough with Adrian's magic, and the dragon-man looked tired from shifting and fighting.

After he departed, Amber went to the white guest room and lay awake on the bed waiting for Adrian to come back, but by sunrise, he hadn't returned.

Manny, Kelly's chef, came over the next morning to cook breakfast. Kelly didn't because she wasn't an early riser, Manny said, and she had to rest up for an upcoming movie that would start shooting soon.

Amber ate the fantastic breakfast without tasting it, then wandered the beach hoping to feel Adrian's arms come around her as they had the afternoon before, but he didn't appear. She refused to be worried. Adrian could take care of himself—right? He had more power than anything she'd ever encountered. Nothing much could stop him.

Except for one bad-ass demon who had already murdered her sister. Maybe Adrian's demigod status made him unkillable, but he could always be hurt or ensorcelled or trapped somewhere.

Now she was worrying.

She hoped Valerian would meet up with him, but that hope was dashed about noon when Valerian called to see if Adrian had come home. When Amber answered that she hadn't seen him, Valerian treated her to a thoughtful silence. Then he said gruffly that he'd keep an eye out for him and hung up.

*Crap.* Valerian was worried too.

Restless, Amber explored the house. The place was huge but didn't have very many rooms. The living room took up the whole middle of the house, and the kitchen opened into its own wing in the front of the house. Two oceanic bedrooms lay one on each side of the living room, the two bathrooms both twice as large as the dorm room she'd shared with a friend in college.

That was all except for the locked door.

She found the door in Adrian's room, nestled behind the bedroom door. Adrian's bedroom looked much like the guest room—white, airy, large bed with white sheets and plump pillows. His bathroom contained nothing more personal than a razor left haphazardly on a shelf in the shower and a toothbrush on the vanity. Nothing of *him*.

Which made her very curious about the locked door. It wasn't a closet. Adrian had a walk-in closet off the bathroom without many clothes in it—a few well-made suits, jeans, shirts both casual and dressy, motorcycle boots, dressy shoes that looked as if they didn't get much wear. She assumed the cleaning service must extend to his closet, because the shoes were lined up neatly on shoe racks, and no man she'd ever known would bother to do that.

The door might lead to nothing more exciting than a water heater or a space under the house, but she had to know. It was Adrian's own fault for leaving her here alone and worried and edgy.

She was a good enough witch to spell a lock, drawing a simple circle around the doorknob and speaking a word into the keyhole. The door opened, revealing a wooden staircase leading down. Cautiously she made her way down; then her heart began to thump excitedly when she stepped off the last stair. She'd found something of Adrian's at last.

# CHAPTER TEN

The room stretched the length of the house, enclosed and paneled, the ceiling supported with dark beams. It was as though she'd stepped into an Old English hall, except instead of a long table and warriors feasting, glassed-in cabinets ran along the walls, holding bits and pieces of the past.

A thick woven carpet covered the floor; it was a tapestry, she realized, used as an area rug. Part of the tapestry depicted a medieval-looking Adrian hefting a silver sword.

In the glass cabinets she found a tattered surcoat, a pair of gauntlets, a topper from the Victorian era, calling cards with names she didn't know, a lady's fan, a pocket watch, a faded map of eastern America about the time of Elizabeth I, letters in Greek and Russian, an Egyptian scarab, and what looked like a Fabergé egg.

Things he'd collected and kept, things that must mean something to him. She wondered who the lady was, what the letters said, where he'd come by the map.

The souvenirs were scattered haphazardly in the

cases without a discernible organization, no sorting of trinkets by era or place. Just things he liked locked behind glass where he could look at them when he wanted.

She caught a flicker of movement in the corner of her eye and swung around. He was sitting in the shadows, reclining in a chair, his long legs stretched in front of him, his hands resting limply on the arms. He didn't move when she looked at him.

"Goddess, Adrian." Amber pressed her hand to her chest, her heart beating swiftly beneath her fingers. "How long have you been down here?"

"I don't know." The answer rasped from him, and when she approached him she saw that he was bruised and battered, his face lined and white, his shirt bloody from hundreds of cuts. "I don't remember."

While Amber's golden eyes widened in horror, Adrian reflected how glad he was to see her. He'd returned here after he'd found the demon and fought him, fought him and lost. He'd followed the demon's magic trail to the desert outside the city, using a Harley borrowed from one of Septimus's patrons.

Without having to worry about hurting Valerian or Amber or even Septimus, Adrian had let loose, fighting with every ounce of his strength and energy. He'd fought Old Ones before and knew how cunning and strong and twisted they were, and he knew what he had to do to best them.

But this one he couldn't beat. Not alone. They'd battled hard, neither he nor the demon holding back, washes of magic flaring into the sky like the aurora borealis. No human had come to investigate—they either thought they saw heat lightning in the desert or realized it was something supernatural and shied away. Sensible humans had learned not to mess too much with the paranormal.

Adrian had fought until he couldn't feel his arms, grown numb from swinging his sword; until Ferrin's blade was nicked and warped; until his magic weakened and he fell to his knees. Even then he'd grabbed the demon before he could flee and rained blows into his face, demanding that the demon take him to Tain.

He'd done plenty of damage to the demon, but the Old One proved to be stronger than Adrian ever could be. With a last blow that sent Adrian tumbling across the desert floor, he'd skimmed into the air, expanding his wings, and disappeared through a mist. Adrian couldn't sense where he'd flown to or follow his trail; he was simply gone.

Adrian had gotten himself back to the city on the Harley, left the bike at the club, and walked home. He could make people avoid him if he wanted them to, and he wanted them to. He wanted to be alone to think and decide what to do. This was the closest he'd come to finding Tain in seven hundred years, and he didn't want to throw away his chance. But for the first time, he wasn't certain how to proceed.

He'd wanted to be alone until he'd seen Amber step tentatively into his collection room and look with wondering eyes at the mementos of his life. She'd gazed in fascination and delight at the treasures he'd never shown anyone else.

"What happened?" she asked in a near whisper. She knelt next to him, resting gentle hands on his thigh, all sweet-smelling from a shower, her hair scented with honey and aloe.

"What did he mean?" Adrian asked, half to himself.

"When he showed us the ice, what did that mean? I've been across the globe a hundred times since Tain was gone, and never found a sign of him. I don't know what it means."

She looked up into his face, her eyes trusting. "Don't worry. We'll work it out. We'll figure out what he meant."

Adrian wanted to laugh, and in fact a fierce chuckle escaped him. Her tawny eyes warmed him, her voice so sincere, so matter-of-fact. *Don't worry, we'll find Tain.*

Such a contrast to her fury when she'd turned on him in the club, demanding to know what he meant when he said she belonged to him. So ardently independent, knowing she was a weak human and defying anyone to take issue with that. She didn't understand the joy it gave him to explain to Septimus that she was his, because no one had ever belonged to him before.

He slid his hand to her shoulder. Her skin was smooth, her arms warm, while he felt cold and spent. She touched his face, her palm comforting. "You're hurt. You need help."

"I heal quickly." Already his metabolism had closed most of the wounds except for the angry stripes from the demon's talons as he'd knocked Adrian flat the last time.

She wasn't convinced. She snatched the hem of his ruined shirt and started pushing it up his body. He assisted, lifting the tattered T-shirt over his head and dropping it to the floor. Her breath slid over his skin as she looked over his torn and bloody torso. "The demon did this to you?"

"The wounds will be healed in a few hours." Already the horrible sting of them had started to fade.

"But he might have poisoned you. At least let me get my crystals."

She started up, and he seized her wrists in a bruising grip. "Not yet. I need you to stay."

"You need healing."

"I need you."

Amber stared at him. She wouldn't understand, and he couldn't explain his overwhelming urge to protect her, his intense craving for her presence. He'd felt it coming on ever since he'd seen her crouched inside her circle in the warehouse. A wanting that grew stronger every minute he was with her, even when he knew he'd never be able to fulfill it.

"I need you," he repeated.

"Come upstairs with me." She whispered it against the side of his mouth, giving him a brief kiss on an un-bruised part of his cheek.

He shook his head. He transferred his grip to her hips and pulled her onto the chair with him, shifting her to straddle his legs. He kissed her slowly, opening her mouth and fastening his lips around her tongue. She made a noise in her throat and rocked against his hard-ening groin.

Then she took his tongue and did back what he'd done to her. "Good," he murmured.

"Good what?" she asked breathlessly.

"Good that you like to suck."

Interest and desire flared in her eyes. He tugged her shirt from the waistband of her jeans and skimmed it off. Beneath she wore a small bra of white lace that barely cupped her breasts. "Take this off."

She gave him a faint smile, and for a moment he hoped she'd ask him to do it for her. Not that he could with his clumsy, battered fingers, but he wouldn't mind fumbling with it for a while with her resting against him.

Before he could suggest it, she reached around her back and unhooked the bra with a soft *click*. He pushed the slim straps down her arms and tossed the lace thing away.

Her breasts were firm and round as he remembered from the night on her bed, nicely fitting his hands. He lowered his head and traced the colorful outline of the butterfly on her collarbone with his tongue, then gently nipped it. The smell of honey and the taste of her were delectable.

This was different from when he'd kissed her in the bathroom of her Seattle home, when he'd teased her by undressing while pretending he didn't know she was there. Those kisses had been playful, testing the waters. Even the exploring they'd shared on her bed had been tinged with a sense of wonder and newness, two people getting to know each other.

Now he wanted her with a mindless urgency, as though the only way he'd ever heal was with her touch.

Amber moved her hands across his shoulders, careful of his bruises. She stroked his hair, fingers twisting it free of its bindings.

He lifted her with hands on her waist to take the hard point of her nipple in his mouth, showing her it wasn't only her tongue he liked to suckle. The aroused bead pressed his tongue, and he wanted to lick and suck until he was completely satisfied. Just rubbing her aureole could make him climax, but he wanted to do so much more before that happened.

*Savor her.*

She arched to him as if she wanted to bury herself in his mouth. Her fingers played in his hair, smoothing its tangles, brushing it from his cheek. She felt like soft velvet and tasted like warm chocolate, and the only reason he wanted to stop licking her breast was to taste other parts of her, too.

He slid open the button of her jeans, his fingers clumsy on the zipper. When they'd kissed on her bed in Seattle, she'd worn a nightshirt with nothing underneath, and he remembered how silky her bare skin had been under his hands. This time, in his house protected by his own magic, they'd have no demon interruption. Even Ferrin lay sleeping across the room in a lined box, recovering from his injuries.

"Do you want these off too?" Amber asked, fingers on her waistband, her eyes heavy with languor.

He could only nod. She slid from his lap, her breasts moving softly, and finished unzipping her pants. Then she hesitated, holding on to the loosened jeans.

"Don't be afraid," he said. "I would never hurt you."

"I'm not afraid. I'm shy."

The incongruity made him laugh. Grinning hurt, but he couldn't stop. "You stripped for me on the beach. I've seen you." Taut, strong body, long, luscious, firm legs. He wanted to lick them from thigh to ankle.

"I know, but . . ."

*That was playing,* he thought. *This is real. No stopping, no holding back.*

"How about if I strip for you at the same time?" He leveraged himself to his feet, his back protesting painfully.

He unbuttoned, unzipped, and opened his jeans before she had time to object. Her eyes riveted on his groin and his briefs that left nothing to the imagination. He'd been rock hard since he'd seen her come off the stairs into his secret room, and the small piece of fabric wasn't anywhere near large enough to contain him.

He pried her fingers from her waistband. "How about if I strip you too?" he asked.

Not waiting for her answer, he peeled the jeans from her legs, going down on one knee so she could step out of them. Instead of getting to his feet, he remained kneeling and grasped the lace panties that matched her bra. "These too."

"Take them off me," she whispered, voice strained.

"Happy to." He slid them down, skimming the backs of her knees, flattening his palms against her calves, enjoying every inch of her legs. Still on his knees, he lay his hand against her abdomen and dipped his head to lick the twist of curls between her legs.

Honey, nectar, food of the gods. Nothing came close to what she tasted like. She was already wet with excitement—he had known that when he first touched her. Need vibrated through her body, and he was grateful for it. She wasn't coming to him out of pity or a misguided need to help, but because she wanted him as much as he wanted her.

Plenty of women in the past had been fascinated by him, and Amber was fascinated as well, but she looked beyond the demigod who thoughtlessly bestowed gifts on her. She saw Adrian the man.

When he'd told her about the car and his wish that she take his house when he moved on, she'd only stared at him as if he were crazy. No groveling, no gasps of delight—she only gave him that puzzled frown and shook her head as if she couldn't believe his naiveté.

He wanted to give her everything. She should have everything. She was beautiful, and she tasted so damn good, and she'd touched his face and told him not to worry. They'd find Tain and everything would be all right.

She believed it. For that alone he could fall in love with her.

She moaned as he swirled his tongue across her clit, pleasuring her at the same time as he took pleasure in tasting her. She was wet and needy, her feet sliding apart so he could reach her better.

He could drink her forever. His thumbs found the sensitive flesh of her inner thighs, stroking softly to arouse her even further. She rocked into his mouth, repeating his name as if she couldn't stop herself.

He wanted to be in her, to feel her legs rising to pull him inside, to lose himself in her. He wanted it—no, he needed it. Soon.

The warmth of her filled places that had been empty too long. He moved his tongue faster, both wanting her to feel the excitement of it and to ready her to take him. He wanted this to be pure pleasure for her, no pain, and he knew he was big enough to hurt her.

She still wore her sandals, and looking at her while he drew back to take a breath was nearly enough to trigger his climax. Naked from head to ankles, she was tall and lovely. Her waist curved under his hand, and her breasts were plump, her hips delicious.

She looked down at him with half-closed eyes, the gold-brown of them gleaming from behind long lashes. "Take them off," she said. "I want to see you too."

He gave her a feral smile. He rocked to his feet and slid out of his briefs. He was already barefoot, and now he was completely nude, tense and hard.

Her gaze did not drop instantly to his groin, and for some reason that pleased him. She took her time examining his shoulders and chest, his abdomen and arms, his fingers as they flexed and curled. Then she looked all the way down at his feet, skimming her gaze slowly up his legs and thighs. Finally she finished at his cock, erect and large and dark. His balls were tight, pushing forward between his legs, more than ready for him to get on with it.

Not yet. He wanted her to come first, for her body to be open and eager for him. He sank to his knees again, bracing his hands on the backs of her thighs and coaxing her legs to part. Then he got down to business.

He licked and nipped her, dipping his tongue inside her tight opening and flicking it fast over her button, varying the techniques so she wouldn't know which one was coming when. He spread her wider and suckled her, first her clit, then her opening, licking and tasting and gently using his teeth.

She abandoned herself to it, no longer trying to stifle her cries. He felt her body tighten as she wound toward climax. Then she nearly sobbed, "Goddess, help me," and came.

Her honey flowed into his mouth, sweet and hot, and he couldn't get enough of it. He felt gooseflesh rise on her hips and back, her entire body tingling with what she was feeling.

Before she could recover, Adrian scooped his arm behind her and gently lowered her to the tapestry on the floor. She went willingly, her body fluid and warm, supple with climax.

He positioned himself over her, hands on each side of her head, smiling when she wrapped her legs around him and pulled him down. They lay hips across hips, his rock-hard staff resting between them, outside of her.

"Amber, do you want me to give you a child?" he asked in a low voice.

Her eyes widened, golden specks swimming in the

brown of her irises. "What?" Her voice was broken, still hoarse from her release.

He spoke quickly. "I can give you a child, or not, as you please. I give you the choice. Do you want a child to come from this coupling?"

She responded with her characteristic astonishment. "Good Goddess, Adrian. Do you always start making love with that question?"

He was already shaking his head. "I can choose whether or not to create a child. I always thought it best not to."

"Then why are you asking me?"

"You are the first I've thought I'd want one with."

Her mouth remained open, but the glitter in her eyes softened. "The first you thought . . ." She blew out her breath. "Great Mother, I never know what you're going to say next."

"What is your decision?"

His heart beat hard while he waited. He'd never thought it wise to leave a child behind that he couldn't take care of, as much as he was tempted to create something of his own—a *family*. But he had no way of knowing whether the child would be immortal or human, or would even survive. He'd seen what had happened to his brother Hunter, who had sired two children long ago, and who'd been killed before they could grow up. Hunter had been out of his mind with grief, and Adrian didn't think he'd ever truly recovered.

And never had Adrian been with a woman he would want to raise his child. He'd learned to confine his sexual needs to women who viewed intercourse as physical only, women who wanted pleasure without emotion. Amber was the only human woman he could think of who he'd want to hold his child in her arms.

Amber drew her tongue across lips that shook a little. "I think—not this time. But maybe later. I mean, if I were going to have a child, I'd want it to be yours."

That stunned him almost as much as his question had her. "Would you?"

"Well, yes. Why not?"

He could think of a hundred reasons, but decided not to pursue it. Not now. Later when they were calmer and could examine the question, he might casually ask her what she meant.

He spread her wider with his hand and slipped his tip inside her. Her warm walls cradled him, begging him to thrust all the way in.

"Are you ready?"

"Yes." She drew a sharp breath. "Please."

"Be certain."

She gripped his shoulders. "Don't tease me, Adrian."

He touched her face, wanting to watch every nuance of it as he slid himself straight inside her.

Amber drew a sharp breath as he penetrated her, thick and heavy and spreading her wider than she'd ever been spread. She clutched his shoulders and felt again a mist in her mind intended to soothe and relax her.

"No," she said, voice low. "Let me feel it."

His expression turned startled. His mind's touch slowly drifted away, like a drug wearing off, and she then felt every inch of him pressing her open.

He moaned low in his throat, a small sound as if he were trying to hold his pleasure tight inside. Amber rubbed her palms over his shoulders, willing him to let it out. He moved his hips slowly, drawing the length of his cock back before sliding it firmly inside again. She gasped in pleasure, raising her hips to meet his.

His long hair fell to pool on her bare chest. She loved the feel of it, raw silk on her fingers. The dark of his eyes were impenetrable, his irises ringed with a rich chocolate brown.

He kissed her with possession, recalling his words to her in the club: *You belong to me.* He hadn't asked her politely, he'd simply declared it, darkness dancing in his eyes.

She drew him closer as he began a rhythm of hips that sent their thighs together and him penetrating high into her. He braced himself on brown arms lashed with thin white scars. He'd faced so much hurt, and yet he could make love with tenderness. She appreciated that he gentled his strength for her, but her body shuddered as she wondered what it would be like if he truly let go.

He bent his head, eyes closed as he rocked himself into her, arms and shoulders taut. His mouth twisted as he felt it, a low sound coming from his throat. Amber arched to him, wanting to drag him deep inside, deeper than ever.

She wanted to be part of this man who was so strong and so powerfully magical, and yet so vulnerable. With his power he might have broken himself free of the ice tonight and gone after the demon right away, but he'd turned away to save her and his friends. His obsession to find his brother ate him up, but even so, he'd first made sure that Amber was safe.

No man—no person—had ever done that for her.

He raised her leg to hook over his arm, opening her wider. Her eyes half closed as the position made him penetrate her farther, making her realize just how big he really was.

She started to say his name, again and again, the syllables faster and faster. He was sweating now, his face damp, his eyes still shut.

She pressed her hand to his cheek, gasping. "Look at me, please."

His jaw clenched harder. "You don't—need—that . . ."

"I do. Please. I want to see your eyes when I come."

He looked at her as though he couldn't stop himself, and one glance into the black depths showed her why he hadn't wanted to. She found herself suddenly swept away under swirling stars, floating with nothing beneath her, a void dropping away beneath her back. She screamed until she realized he held her, strong arms keeping her from falling.

He was the only thing between her and the darkness. He pumped into her and took what he pleased, as though he couldn't hold himself back anymore. He didn't look away, those deep black eyes holding her in place, sparks of his incredible power dancing on their surface.

"Come for me," he said. "I want you to come before I do. I want all thoughts of that asshole vampire Julio out of your head."

"They have been," she said in surprise. "There's only you."

"Then come for me, sweetheart."

He wanted mastery. He wanted to control everything, even this.

Amber gave him a sly smile, then reached between his buttocks and found the hard tightness of his balls. She gently squeezed and was rewarded with him swelling inside her, his eyes growing even more intense.

"*Witch*," he hissed, and then he groaned. "No."

His seed shot into her, hard, harder, and Amber climaxed under him. They met each other thrust for thrust, bodies locked around each other. Incredibly, she felt his climax in her mind as well as her own, dark, maddening swirls wrapping her brain and plunging her into the wildest love she'd ever experienced.

And then suddenly they were back on the prickly tapestry carpet, she gasping for breath, and he smoothing the hair from her face with shaking, sweating hands.

A little later, Amber felt herself being lifted and carried, up and up and up, and then settled on a vast expanse of sheets. She gripped Adrian's arm, afraid he'd lay her down and leave her, but he got into bed beside her.

He touched and kissed her some more, hands strong and firm. She slid her fingers over his back and found his wounds closed, faded to ridged scars.

"I guess you do heal quickly," she murmured.

"You healed me."

He slid his thigh across her and made love to her again, a slow, sensuous lovemaking that left her breathless, but this time they remained firmly on the bed, no floating in black space.

She didn't think she would come so hard so soon again, but before long she was screaming with wanting, dragging him against her as she thrust her hips to meet his. After that, they both wound down from breathless climax and lay in the bed, she drowsing, he watching her with eyes black as sin.

The plain white sheets looked much better tangled around his limbs, the mounds of his backside rising above a fold, the pentacle tattoo on his left buttock stark against his skin. He watched her like a man would watch his lover, a small smile on his lips as he contemplated her nude body stretched out and tired from what they'd done.

"You look pleased with yourself," she said.

"Why not? A beautiful witch in my house, in my bed."

She ran her hand up the tightness of his smooth bicep. "I've wanted you since you were sitting in my kitchen drinking coffee at the table. Did Sabina warn you off that night?"

"She threatened to rip out my throat if I touched you."

"I notice you didn't listen." She thought of how not fifteen minutes later, he'd stripped himself bare in the guest bathroom and kissed her while steam roiled from the shower.

"I decided to risk it." When he got that teasing light in his eye, he looked like any normal male patting himself on the back for seducing a female he wanted

"You told me then I wasn't ready for you," she said. "Because of the . . . floating in the middle of the sky or whatever that was."

He shook his head, his cheek pressing his forearm. "That never happened before."

"Oh." She thought about how he'd kept his eyes firmly closed at first. "Because it never happened, or because you didn't want it to happen?"

"I don't know." His smile faded. "Amber, come with me. . . . No." He turned his head. "No, never mind."

"Come with you where? To find your brother?"

Silence stretched so long she thought he would refuse to answer. "I started to ask you to come with me when I move on. When I take another house in another place and keep pretending to be mortal."

She laughed lightly. "I don't think anyone believes you're a normal human being, Adrian. You radiate supernatural power—they're just not sure what kind." She playfully tapped the tip of his nose. "You're not fooling anyone."

He didn't smile. "A millennium means nothing to me. But it's different for you. I don't go after what I want, because I know I can't have it."

"Meaning if I go with you, I'll age and die and you won't."

"Meaning if I keep you with me, I'll have to leave you. The longer I stay, the harder it will be for me to go."

Amber sat up, crossing her legs and drawing a piece of sheet over them. "Tell me something in truth. Do you make this speech to every woman you go to bed with?"

He looked puzzled. "No, I've never asked a woman to stay with me."

"You haven't actually asked me. You stopped yourself."

"I know."

Amber rested her cheek on her palm, studying him. He was a beautiful man, brown limbs lying against sheets like a perfect sculpture, or an art photo that could hang on a gallery wall. Even the scars on his back didn't mar him. The Goddess had done a damn good job on him.

"After we find your brother, come with me to Seattle," she said. "You could help me do psychic readings or something, or help teach my students how to deal with death-magic creatures. Then you can decide whether you want to stay."

*"After we find my brother,"* he repeated her words, his eyes becoming opaque again. "You speak as if it's a certainty."

"Well, we're close. The demon resisted my truth spell by being cryptic, but he couldn't resist altogether. So the ice he conjured must mean something. And we have Susan's notes. She definitely saw Tain while she was traveling between. The demon wanted Tain to stay hidden, and so he followed Susan and killed her." Amber's throat went tight. "That means she got too close, which means it's possible for us to get closer. I'm a decent witch, I know how my sister thought, and you have incredible power. I don't see how we can fail."

"Amber." His deep voice cut through her words. "This isn't your fight, or your quest."

"My sister died for it. I think that makes it mine."

"Finding Tain, which I've come to realize is an impossible task, won't bring Susan back to you. It won't solve anything for you."

She huffed in exasperation. "I know that. But it will help you. If I can help you not lose a brother, then she wouldn't have died for nothing."

"It's a different thing," he said sternly. The muscles tightened all over his body, under smooth skin. "Tain walked away seven hundred years ago. If he'd wanted to be found, I would have found him by now. My dreams are just that—dreams; me driving myself crazy. He doesn't want me to find him. That's what I've realized in the past few days."

"Meaning he asked the demon to keep you away? Oh, come on, Adrian."

"I'm right."

She bounced onto her knees and faced him, clenching her fists. "No, you *want* to be right. You're trying to make it easy for you to walk away from the nightmare. Well, I'm not walking. I'm going to find him for you. Then if he doesn't want you, that's his business."

His voice went cold. "It's something to be solved between me and my brother. I'll keep you safe from that demon, but you're staying out of it. It has nothing to do with you."

"So what? Am I supposed to hide because it's not my fight? Am I not allowed to help someone because I care about him?"

He went still, his eyes dark and enigmatic, no longer letting her in. She thought with a little regret that she'd never again see the starry night she'd seen when they made love. He was shutting her out.

"If you mean you care for me, it's a mistake," he said, voice quiet.

"Don't flatter yourself." She made her words hard. "Don't suppose that I'm madly in love with you, or that I'll die without you. I can help a friend because I care, or even a fellow human—I mean, a fellow being."

She grew nervous as he continued to study her, his brown arms folded across the pillow. She started to babble. "I mean, you're a great lover, but hey, I'll get over you in no time. I've got men lined up waiting to eat out of my hand."

His brows pinched. "They'd better not be."

"I thrive on going out with the supernatural, Mr. Immortal One. I even dated a vampire, buster."

"By accident," he said in mock outrage. "I'm going to find this Julio and turn him into dust. Septimus probably has connections in Seattle."

Amber stopped her joking. "So it's all right for you to be protective of me, but I'm not allowed to be of you?"

"It's dangerous, Amber." His voice took on the flat note again. "This is far more dangerous than anything you've ever been involved in, and don't tell me about being friends with werewolves and sleeping with vampires. This demon is an Old One who can squash you

between his fingers. He is dangerous, and I am dangerous. And if anything happened to you, I'd . . ." He broke
off, going silent.

"You'd what?" She leaned closer, her heart beating
hard. "You've only just met me. Why should you care if
something happens to me?"

"Because I'd care."

"And I'd care if something happened to you." She
raked the short ends of her hair from her face. "What are
we going to do?"

He touched her thigh, sliding his finger along the fold
of her knee. "I didn't want this to happen."

"I didn't want it to happen either. But it did."

The fierceness in Adrian's face softened a little, and
he slid his hand to her waist. "Come here."

She pushed aside crumpled sheets and lay next to
him. The kiss he gave her was deep, his palm cradling
her head. She could fall in love with the taste of him, a
bite of spice like young wine.

When he eased away, his eyes were lighting, power
growing with his arousal. "I want to make love to you
again."

"I won't say no," she said.

"You should say no."

She nibbled on his lower lip. "But I won't."

He rolled over on top of her and slid his hand between them, giving her a look of satisfaction when he
found her wet and open. "You give in to me too easily."

"You're a powerful Immortal being, as you keep point-
ing out. What chance do I have?"

"None at all," he said, and then they both murmured
in satisfaction as he entered her. "You're always so tight.
Damn, you feel so good."

Amber's thoughts were too scattered for answer. He

began to love her, driving deeper and harder with every thrust until Amber came apart again.

Just when things were at their most interesting, the bed moving in earnest and the night table in danger of toppling over, someone rang the front doorbell.

# CHAPTER ELEVEN

Adrian pulled on his jeans, secured Ferrin on his arm, and padded to the living room to open the front door.

On the doorstep stood Amber's werewolf neighbor from Seattle and a fortyish man with short black hair wearing pressed slacks, a dark shirt, and a tie. The man's light blue eyes held wry intelligence as he took in Adrian, noting the lack of shirt, jeans riding low over underwearless hips, and mussed hair. No doubt the man could smell lovemaking on him. Sabina obviously could, because her wolf's eyes narrowed.

Before Adrian could speak, he heard Amber come out of the bedroom, her footsteps quick, breathing agitated. She stopped short a few feet behind him.

"Detective Simon," she said in surprise. "What are you doing here?"

"I could ask you the same question, Ms. Silverthorne." Detective Simon's gaze focused on her, his blue eyes going hard. "I'm still looking into the circumstances surrounding your sister's death, and I really didn't want you to leave town."

"I'm not a suspect, am I?" Amber came forward, her frame lost in Adrian's bathrobe.

Adrian saw the man's nostrils flare and realized in a heartbeat that he was angry about more than Amber leaving town. Simon's eyes held the uncomfortable rage of a man who had hoped a woman would become his, and was now confronted with evidence that she preferred another. He tried to hold it in, to tell himself that what Amber did was her business, but he couldn't quite tamp down his reaction.

Simon cleared his throat. "No, but—I wanted to question you further."

"How on earth did you find me?" Amber asked. She switched her glare to Sabina. "And what are you doing here?"

"I came to see what this guy was up to." Sabina pointed a long finger at Adrian. "He comes over one night, and the next morning, you've disappeared into thin air. Then someone reports finding your car abandoned on the side of the highway. What was I supposed to think?" She walked into the house, past Adrian, who returned her scrutinizing look. "What is he, Amber? I don't like him."

"So you called Detective Simon?" Amber asked, sounding annoyed. "And came down here looking for me? How *did* you find me, by the way?"

Adrian motioned Simon to come in. Simon did so, not looking happy about it, and Adrian closed the door. "I called the detective. Did you bring them?" he asked Simon.

The man nodded. He reached into his coat and pulled out two battered spiral notebooks, and Amber's eyes widened. "Those are Susan's." She looked at Adrian in confusion. "What did you do?"

"I needed to see the actual writing Susan copied or used," Adrian said, taking the books. He ran his hand over them, feeling the taint of death magic on them. "You told me the police kept the notebooks, and we couldn't find any more of the writing in the house. So the answer has to be here."

He walked to the table in the big kitchen and slapped the notebooks down. He opened one and flinched when he saw the demon script, the sharp points and downward dips of the letters unnerving. He could read only a word here and there, but the script held death magic that turned Adrian's insides. He knew the magic was dampened—this was something copied by Susan from something else—but even so, death magic permeated it. On his arm, Ferrin morphed into a snake and let out a warning hiss.

"I know, my friend," Adrian murmured. "But it must be done."

"What the hell is that?" Simon demanded. His hand was under his coat, the leather of his shoulder holster showing against his shirt.

"This is Ferrin," Adrian said. "He's fine once you get to know him."

Sabina moved her gaze to Amber. "Are you all right? Did he kidnap you? If he did, say so and I'll take him out." She turned a glare to Adrian, her scent changing as her magic built with her intention to shift into wolf form.

Adrian pressed her mind, less gently than he did with Amber, but he needed Sabina to understand. He saw her eyes flicker as he showed her very clearly where she stood in his world. Her throat moved, her hackles lowering, but she still gave him a warning look, which amused him. She was certainly Amber's friend.

"You should return to Seattle," he told her and Simon.

"This evidence is dangerous to possess, and you will be safer once you leave it with me. Amber is more protected in this house than anywhere else in the world, so here she stays."

Detective Simon bristled. "I'm investigating a murder."

"And I am trying to keep Amber from being slaughtered by the ancient demon who killed her sister. These books will help me do it. There's plenty of food and drink in the kitchen, so you can fill up before you go. Help yourself."

He turned back to the notebooks, ignoring the startled looks of the others.

The visitors didn't leave. Sabina decided to take him at his word and rummaged in the kitchen for coffee and tea. Detective Simon sat down with coffee to watch Adrian, his aggression palpable, but professional curiosity was mixed with it.

Amber shut herself in the guest room for a while and emerged dressed in the sexy clothes Adrian had purchased for her, though she tried to play down the sexiness by wearing a crocheted poncho over the cropped tank and low-riding jeans. Detective Simon glanced at her once, then away, but Adrian didn't miss the hunger in the man's eyes. It wasn't feral hunger, but the simple desire of a man for a woman, tinged with sadness because Simon now knew the lay of the land.

Adrian could explain that he was the one who should feel sad. Amber was a beautiful and compelling woman, but Adrian could only have her for a little while. He would go on being an Immortal warrior, chasing demons and vampires, and Detective Simon would remain behind with his normal life and no tendency toward centuries-long quests.

Watching the no-nonsense way Amber dragged out

Adrian's laptop and fired it up, he sensed she'd be the perfect wife for a hardworking cop—using her skills to help her detective husband solve a crime, the two of them celebrating a victory. *Hell.*

Adrian didn't bother getting dressed beyond the jeans he wore. He sat next to Amber where he could watch her skilled fingers skim the keyboard and her eyes flick over the information on the screen. He turned the pages of Susan's notebook, which was blotched and grimy from the warehouse floor.

Deciphering the writing proved nearly impossible. Adrian knew some of the demon words, but in context they made no sense. Either it was a language their ancient demon knew that no one else did, or else it was encrypted. Amber searched the Net for different texts, not finding much, but what little they did find didn't compare to what Susan had written.

Adrian tried not to let his frustration boil over. He liked Amber's warmth next to him, liked whenever their thighs touched when they studied the computer screen, her breath on his cheek when she turned to say something to him. Once when she did that, he kissed her, not minding Sabina's glare.

Amber seemed to sense when his frustration and anger built too high for them to continue. Sweet woman, she got up, stretching, saying she needed a break, and suggested a walk along the beach. Sabina abandoned her coffee and went with her, but Detective Simon stayed behind.

The two young women left through the back doors in the living room, Amber leading the way down the staircase off the deck. After a while, Simon rose and helped himself to more coffee, glancing at the notebooks on the way.

"This writing—you think it is the key?" he asked.

Adrian nodded, leaning back in his chair, his bare feet curling on the cool tile floor. "It will tell me what the demon is looking for, which I suspect has something to do with where my brother is. The demon killed Susan to keep her from finding out."

Simon stopped, the coffee cup halfway to his mouth. "Which means he could kill Amber for the same reason."

"He has already tried to kill Amber. Which is why I brought her here, to a place where he cannot get at her."

Simon nodded. "Well, I'm grateful you helped her, but what is to stop *you* from getting at her?"

The man was angry, but his anger came from concern for Amber, which mitigated Adrian's own anger. When Adrian gently touched Simon's mind, he discovered a man tangled in emotion—a strong compulsion to bring in the demon who'd committed murder, coupled with anguish on meeting Amber and wanting her. All that combined with the need to help Amber and knowing he couldn't.

"I'd never hurt her," Adrian said.

Simon answered stiffly, "I think you already have."

Adrian closed his notebook, hiding the demon words. "She already knows the lay of the land. I've tried to convince her to stay out of it, but she won't."

"You haven't tried very hard," Simon observed.

Adrian thought of their last lovemaking, how he hadn't been able to hold himself back. He shouldn't have touched her at all, but he'd *needed* her. He was unfamiliar with need like that. "You're probably right." He met the detective's eyes.

"So what do you want me to do? Drag her back to Seattle?"

"No, she's safer here. But if I can't make sure she's not

hurt, maybe you can. You can take care of her when I'm gone."

"Or you could let me make my own decisions," Amber said as she stepped alone through the open door. "And not pass me off like a used library book."

Simon turned hastily, embarrassed and red. "That's not what I—"

"It's not you I'm mad at, Detective." Her golden-brown glare burned through Adrian. "It's the annoying alpha male next to you."

Adrian was faintly aware of Ferrin sniggering, switching to snake state on his arm to watch. "I'm new at this, Amber," Adrian said.

"New at what?" she demanded.

"Caring about someone."

She remained standing silently in the doorway, her expression a mystery, and Sabina, unaware of the conversation, had to push her way around her. "Now, what's going on?" she demanded.

"Nothing." Amber shook herself and strode to the kitchen. "I'm making more coffee. And tea."

"I'm coffeed out." Sabina combed fingers through her wind-mussed mane and looked curiously at the closed notebooks. "You figure it out yet?"

Adrian shook his head. "Septimus will arrive after dark. He knows the old languages better than I do."

"Being one of the evil undead himself," Amber said as she filled a pot with water. Her back was ramrod straight, her hair also mussed from the wind, the dark curls sticking every which way. Adrian longed to cross the room to her and smooth each lock, kissing it as he went.

"This Septimus is a demon?" Sabina asked, wrinkling her nose.

"Vampire," Amber answered.

"Even worse."

Sabina in innocence began to talk about vampires, she with the natural prejudice of werewolves against the death-magic vampires. Amber answered her, voice bright, her laughter too brittle. Detective Simon had gone back to studying the notebooks, a stain of red clinging to his cheeks.

Falling in love was alien to Adrian, even though he could love. He loved Isis and the happy-go-lucky Hathor. He'd loved the priest his father, and he loved his brothers—more or less, some of whom were harder to love than others. But he'd never let himself fully experience sexual and emotional desire for a woman, because he knew he could never have it. Why tear himself apart to have a few hours, a few years maybe, of love?

Sabina made a vampire joke, and Amber lost her anger long enough to laugh. Her laughter filled the kitchen like silver chimes, which wrapped around Adrian. Too late. Much, much too late to run.

He went into his bedroom to dress and then to take a long, long walk.

The vampire arrived at the same time Kelly did, just after dark. Septimus cruised up in a limo with all the windows dark and emerged flanked by two vampire bodyguards. The guards walked a discreet distance behind him to the door, standing just out of the circle of the porch light.

Kelly walked over across the beach and in the back door just as Adrian opened the front door for Septimus.

"I can't come in," Septimus said, sounding annoyed. "Far too much life magic in there, plus your house is warded against beings like me."

Amber idly watched Adrian, fully dressed now, his

hair combed and bound. He cocked his head at Septimus, enjoying his discomfort. "You're always welcome here, Septimus, but just you."

Septimus glanced at the door as though waiting for a green light, then nodded once and crossed the threshold. "I'm trusting you completely, Adrian. If you wanted me dead, you'd have already killed me."

"You're learning wisdom." Adrian closed the door and beckoned him into the house. "I need you to help me, so I won't stake you right now."

"Thank you," Septimus said dryly, then stopped, his lips pulling back from gleaming fangs. "Who let the dog in?"

"Soul-sucker," Sabina growled. The hint of wolf rolled strongly from her, and Amber expected her to grow fur, claws, and teeth at any moment.

"You mean bloodsucker," Septimus answered smoothly. "Soul-suckers are demons."

"I thought those were lawyers," Kelly said, her screen-perfect voice blending into the room. "I know you, don't I?" she asked Septimus.

He inclined his head politely. "You danced at the club of a colleague. He was sorry to lose you."

Kelly gave a dainty shrug. "Time to move on."

"He was quite angry when Adrian told him to leave you alone. I killed him, by the way. He had stepped out of line, coming after you, and Adrian had to have a phone conversation with me. I didn't like that."

Kelly's eyes widened. "Oh."

"I was glad of the excuse—he was a fool." Septimus rubbed his well-formed hands together. "Now, Adrian, where is this writing you want me to look at?"

Hours passed. Septimus and Adrian pored over the texts, using the computer to aid them as necessary, Septimus's fingers moving elegantly on the keyboard. Detective Simon seemed interested in deciphering the words as well, coupled with embarrassment over the end of the conversation Amber had overheard between him and Adrian, so he pretended to ignore her. Kelly sat apart from the others, her gaze glued on Septimus.

After a while, Amber and Sabina wandered down to the beach again, staying within the bubble of Adrian's protection.

Amber had previously told Sabina about the demon and why they'd fled Seattle. Sabina could feel the protective magic of Adrian's home as well, so she didn't argue about the wisdom of staying there. *Use an ancient being to stop an ancient being,* was her philosophy.

"So, you and Adrian," Sabina said, and sighed. "I really hoped you'd make Detective Simon happy. I mean, he has those blue eyes and that sad smile."

Amber kicked off her sandals and dipped her toes in the white-foamed waves. "If you like him so much, why don't you go for it?"

Sabina shook her head. "I've dated normal humans before, and it was always a disaster. Do you know how hard it is to explain to a man why you're compelled to have sex every full moon—a lot of it? Oh, and I might morph into a wolf at any second, too?"

"Most men wouldn't mind the sex part."

"They say they don't, but then they find out what you really mean." Sabina, wrinkled her nose. "And they run. Fast. Far. Nope, no more relationships with non-shape-shifters. I don't care how blue his eyes are."

"I don't have much luck with non-magical people either," Amber said glumly. "Men think me being a witch is *cool* until they get a taste of real magic. I dated a witch once, but all he could do was talk about the sex magic techniques he'd perfected, but they needed three or more participants to be effective. Then when it came time for real sex, he always had a headache."

"I remember him. What a jerk."

Amber sighed. "The best relationships I've had were with a vampire who tried to trick me into being his blood slave, and an Immortal warrior with other things on his mind. My luck is terrible."

"Mine isn't much better. Adrian's neighbor, now—she seems a little taken with the vampires. She doesn't seem the type."

"I don't really know her well enough to tell," Amber answered. The ocean water was soothing, the waves tickling her feet. The moon was nearly full, a sphere of silver, shining with the light of the Goddess.

Amber thought of how Adrian had tried to pass his protection of her to Detective Simon, then the warmth in his eyes when he'd told her he was new at caring. She'd been torn between anger and lust and wanting and caring ever since she'd met him only two days ago. *Men.*

"Hey, who's that?" Sabina pointed toward the house.

In alarm, Amber swung around, but she saw that Sabina pointed at Valerian hulking in the lighted windows of the living room. He threw back his head and laughed at something, the sound reaching them on the beach.

"Come on." Amber snatched up her sandals and led Sabina back up the stairs and across the deck into the house.

The atmosphere had changed. Adrian's eyes were sparking, not in anger, but excitement. Septimus had his head down over a page, and so did Detective Simon, the natural antipathy between human and vampire gone as they jabbered about what a phrase really meant.

"Did you figure it out?" Amber asked.

"Almost," Adrian said, his voice warm. "I'll need you for the last part."

As she raised her brows in a question, Valerian noticed Sabina behind her. "Hey, a werewolf. A cute one, too. I bet you're the one Amber told me didn't like to put her clothes back on after she shifted."

Sabina looked him up and down, and Amber saw a gleam of interest behind her pretended scorn. "What are you supposed to be?"

"Transportation," Adrian said.

Valerian lost his grin. "Oh, no. Don't tell me you need me to fly you somewhere." He pointed to his backside. "Do you see an airline logo on my tail?"

"I'll *maybe* need you to fly me somewhere. Amber." Adrian beckoned to her. "I need you to do a spell. We can almost make out the words, but they're magically encrypted. We need a spell that lifts obscurity. Can you do that?"

"I can," Amber answered dubiously. "It's not that difficult. But are you certain we should try magic with it?"

"Yes. Do you understand now?" His eyes gleamed, and Ferrin on his arm sat up to listen. "*This* is what Susan was doing in the warehouse, not summoning a demon or trying to find Tain. She wanted to clear up the encryption in the text, and feared that she'd bring too much death magic into your house if she tried it at home. She found the text after she'd seen my brother while riding between and wanted to figure out who and where he was. The demon heard her begin the spell to unravel his secrets, so he went to stop her." He broke off. "What I don't understand is why she didn't tell anyone.

She could have raised formidable protection against the demon if she'd worked with other witches."

"Like the Coven of Light," Amber agreed. "But I know why she didn't." She sighed. "It would be just like Susan. She liked to challenge herself, to go beyond her powers, and then to boast afterward about what she'd accomplished. She'd never been wrong about her capacity before."

"This time, she was dealing with a demon who knows how to control an Immortal," Adrian said. "He knows where Tain is, and he's hiding him from me."

His eyes flashed fire, the light of it tearing briefly through the room and causing the others to shield their eyes. Septimus ducked the dose of life magic, swearing.

Detective Simon was the first to point out the problems. "So if the demon heard Susan using the decryption spell, he'd know Amber was doing it too. And he'd attack, just like he did Susan in the warehouse."

Valerian blanched. "Oh, that wouldn't be good. He was pretty nasty in the alley even with all three of us ganging up on him."

"This house is protected," Adrian said. "The magic of Isis is stronger than that of a demon. He can't enter here."

"But he can sneak into my club and tear out a wall," Septimus said dryly.

"I said I was paying for that. Amber?" Adrian threaded his fingers through hers. "I won't ask you to do this if you really don't want to."

He wasn't speaking about fear. He knew how she'd grieved at losing Susan, and now he was asking her to do the very thing that had gotten her sister killed.

Amber also knew that Adrian could simply make her do the spell. He could cloud her mind as he had before and coerce her to perform the magic. His words promised he wouldn't do that, as much as he needed her help.

Amber kissed his cheek. "See, when you're not being an overbearing Neanderthal, you're not so bad. I'll do it, Adrian. I told you I'd help you find your brother, and I will. I need you to clear off the table and find me a lot of salt."

# CHAPTER TWELVE

Adrian had built his house right over a ley line. Amber had realized it only abstractly because Adrian's power was so great it overlaid all vibrations of it. But when she drew her circle and tapped into the natural magic of the earth below the house, she felt the line, shining and thick, like a vein of gold.

She set out her stones and the salt Adrian had brought her—crystallized salt in a fancy container. The stones Adrian had charged during their journey from Seattle still glowed in the center.

She drew the circle around the table with herself and all she needed inside. She asked Valerian and Sabina to sit in the circle with her, because their strong life magic would help give power to the spell. She did not ask Adrian because she knew she'd never control any power she tapped into from him. The whole circle could explode, maybe taking part of the house with it.

Septimus had retreated to the other side of the room so his death magic wouldn't interfere with the spell. He looked pleased to stand as far away from what he termed "goody two-shoes magic" as he could. He wouldn't leave altogether, because he was too interested to see what happened. Kelly stood with him, talking to him quietly, but Amber noticed the woman was practiced at not looking directly into his eyes.

Sabina had helped Amber in rituals before and knew when to light the candle and say her lines to call her quarter. Valerian obviously had never participated in witch magic, because he kept asking questions and moving the candle and stones after Amber had carefully placed them. Sabina slapped his hand, and he glared in mock pain.

Amber piled quartz crystals around the base of a yellow candle, which would aid in bringing clarity and understanding to her spell. She began to chant under her breath, words to summon the elements, earth, air, fire, and water, signaling Valerian to light the candle for fire, Sabina to light the one for water. Earth and air she lit herself.

She asked the Goddess and the God to attend, to send their aid as well as their protection. She felt an answering tingle inside her, which she recognized as the two deities touching her and telling her all would be well.

She studied the depths of the stones, letting the glow inside them mesmerize her. She built magic energy inside herself, then reached out to tap the latent power of Sabina, then Valerian.

Sabina's power, as always, felt sharp and strong, but was tinged faintly with light blue, as though Sabina's essence hovered in a constant state of amusement. It went with Sabina's sarcastic sense of humor, which sometimes hid her good heart.

Valerian had a different kind of energy altogether. His aura was bright yellow with brilliant flickers of blue and red streaking through it. She'd never felt anything like it. The energy that rolled off him was strong, with the raw brute strength of a predatory animal. No matter how much he looked human, he wasn't. His essence was dragon through and through—powerful, hungry, primal. Valerian was happiest fighting an enemy and feasting on its carcass afterward.

The energies of the two were amazingly similar, and Sabina and Valerian kept shooting covert glances at each other as they felt their auras touch.

Amber drew their energies into herself to add to her own and called upon the energy of the crystals and the candle flame. She chanted her spell, then picked up the charged crystals and scattered them, releasing the energy of the spell.

Instantly she felt different. Images became sharper in her head, Valerian's dragon form and Sabina's wolf form clear, with their human shells insubstantial. The pretty green light in the corner was Kelly, the black smoky thing next to her, Septimus. Detective Simon was blues and purples, a kind man at heart frustrated by the evils of life.

And Adrian . . . She couldn't even look at his aura. It blazed white and so bright she couldn't believe the house didn't explode with it. Adrian had learned to contain his power, but looking at him was like looking at an angel—or in this case, a demigod. She was wise not to have tried to tap into him to do the spell; she might have blown them all into the middle of the Pacific.

She pulled the notebook to her and focused her new clarity of vision on it. At first the lines of demon script only swam before Amber's eyes; then the squiggles suddenly smoothed out and she *understood* them. She snatched up the pen and paper she'd set out next to her and began to translate.

This was easy. How could they have not known what the script said? The words were so obvious. Her pen scratched quickly, her hand barely able to keep up with the words pouring through her head.

But what she wrote troubled her. Verses about sex and erotic satisfaction, some implying that death was the ultimate in eroticism. She wrote of insatiable need mixed with pain and confusion, the need being for both pain and sexual fulfillment.

A lament ran: *I sit in my prison of ice which has become not a prison but sanctuary. Here I do not hurt, here I am at peace until he comes. But she helps me when he is finished, and I love her, or maybe I love him, I do not know.*

"Prison of ice," Detective Simon murmured, having moved closer to watch her. "What does that mean?"

"Ice?" Valerian repeated. "Interesting, eh?"

Amber kept writing, her hand moving faster and faster, sweat beading her brow. Adrian stood behind her, his white-hot aura touching her, watching the words form as she wrote them.

*North, north, and north, where nothing lives, where the world is death, where I belong, under ice and water and ice again. No one will find me, they will never find me. I am death.*

The words came out at lightning speed, Amber's fingers cramping. The paper ripped as her pen underlined the last words, though she never told herself to underline it.

The pen flew out of her hand like a bullet, breaking the nimbus of the circle. Detective Simon ducked as the pen rocketed past him and struck the wall with a splinter of plastic.

Valerian stared at the ink splotch on Adrian's pristine wall. "What the hell was that?"

"What does it mean?" Sabina asked, leaning forward. "Under ice and water and ice again?"

Amber sat back, breathing heavily, and massaged her hand. "I don't know. Polar ice, maybe? An iceberg? Something under water?"

Adrian stepped over the broken circle and sat down next to her. He took her shaking hands in his, warm fingers moving over her skin. Her forehead was still wet with sweat, her stomach fluttering.

Now that the spell was broken, she saw everyone's human form, but Adrian still seemed to contain white light, the same that sparked from his eyes when he was enraged or excited. She doubted she'd ever look the same way at him again.

She glanced back at the writing, which was quickly blurring into indecipherable squiggles. But it had tapped something in her, the words holding more magic than just the thoughts of the person who'd written it. She felt a tug of her body in a certain direction. *North, north, and north, where nothing lives, where the world is death.*

She knew who had written those words. Susan had copied them, possibly from something she'd seen while riding between. Then she'd tried to decipher what she'd copied, hoping to find the elusive man who haunted her dreams.

Adrian was staring at the paper in slight disappointment. "That's it?"

Amber shook her head and pulled the notes toward her, her handwriting wild and unlike her usual neat style.

"I didn't just copy out the words mindlessly," she said. "When I was writing I *saw* everything. It was as if magic had let me envision exactly what the words meant—I wasn't so much translating as writing down what they showed me." She crumpled the papers in her sweaty palms, unable to keep excitement at bay. "I saw your brother, Adrian—what Susan must have seen. I think I can take you to him."

"Are you up to it?" Adrian asked Valerian as they stood with Amber and the others later on the beach.

The night air was cool next to the ocean, and Amber shivered even in the parka and heavy clothing she'd donned for their trek northward. Amber and Adrian would follow the trail Amber had sensed while Detective Simon and Sabina stayed in Adrian's house to wait for their return or to render assistance, whatever was needed. Detective Simon hadn't looked as though he liked staying put, but he didn't argue. He seemed to know that Adrian was right: They were safest in the well-warded house.

Both Adrian and Amber had hoped the writing would reveal the demon's name—something they could bind him with—but there had been nothing. Adrian studied Amber's crumpled notes by the glow of a flashlight while he waited for Valerian's answer. Adrian wore a leather coat—not the one ruined by the demon—thick jeans, and motorcycle boots.

"I don't know," the dragon said. "If I fly too far north, my blood starts to freeze. I'm a tropical dragon. You know, you could get a flight to Alaska and—I don't know—do sled dogs from there."

"I wouldn't ask if there was another way," Adrian said. "You can help fight off a demon. An airplane full of innocents can't. Even a private plane contains a pilot who can be killed."

Valerian sighed, then studied the sky with a resigned look, no longer arguing.

"So why didn't the demon attack?" Sabina asked. "When Amber did the decrypting spell, why didn't he attack us? Adrian's power notwithstanding, he could have just waited for us to come out of the house."

"I don't know," Adrian answered absently.

"Terrific," Valerian growled.

"Maybe he no longer cares whether you find your brother's whereabouts," Septimus suggested.

Adrian folded the papers and put them in his pocket. "I think he has his own reasons. Are you ready to go?"

He directed his question at Valerian, who stood with hands on hips, his blond hair bound in its usual braid. Valerian heaved another aggrieved sigh and walked a little away from them down the beach.

"Don't stare, I'm bashful," he called over his shoulder before he started stripping off his clothes. Amber averted her eyes, but she noticed Sabina watching him blatantly.

Valerian didn't morph into a dragon like shape-shifters did in movies, body elongating and changing from human skin to scales. One moment he was a man, the next simply *dragon*, his huge body crouched on the beach, long neck curved to an enormous head with razor-sharp teeth. Pointed leatherlike wings sprouted from his back, which he spread wide to float back toward them.

"Ready," he said. "If I freeze like an iceberg and fall out of the sky, it's your own fault."

Adrian didn't bother to answer. He brought out rock-climbing harnesses he'd pulled from a back closet and now contrived a way to secure himself and Amber and a duffle bag with provisions and Valerian's clothes on Valerian's back. The dragon muttered and rumbled as they climbed up on him and latched themselves on to his body.

"Strangle me, why don't you?" he said. He turned his brilliant blue eyes to Sabina. "Don't wait up for me, darling. I might be a while."

Sabina wrinkled her nose, but her eyes had widened, her amazement at him apparent.

Adrian tapped on Valerian's neck to indicate they were ready, and the dragon, without preliminary, launched himself into the air. Amber bit back a scream as the ground dropped away, the world falling as Valerian angled out over the dark ocean.

Adrian lay half over her, gloved hands holding hard to the nylon straps that kept them from falling to their deaths. Valerian heaved his wings upward until they almost touched at the top, then brought them down with a huge flap that propelled them at incredible speed. Each time he pumped, they accelerated a little faster and a little farther until they were speeding along like a small jet.

Amber clung to the straps, glad of Adrian's warmth and bulk holding her in place. Swirls of white dove by her, clouds that froze her breath. She hunkered into Valerian's neck, finding his scales surprisingly soft and warm, almost silken as they moved with his body.

Adrian seemed unaffected by the cold, his large body sheltering her from the worst of the wind.

They flew on and on, the pale line of the coast quickly falling behind, the ocean below dark and cold. Amber was exhausted by her spell-casting, coupled with lack of sleep. The only sleep she'd had in the last twenty-four hours was when she'd drowsed on Adrian's bed after lovemaking.

The remembrance of lassitude warmed her limbs and threatened to loosen her hold on the straps. She clutched at them, and Adrian's hard body shifted to cover hers completely.

"It's all right," he said into her ear. "I've got you."

She really had to stop obeying him. At least, her body had to stop obeying him. She felt the faint fog in her mind, and her eyes drifted closed. Rocked by the sway of Valerian's body under her, and protected by Adrian, she slid into sleep.

She jerked awake to find Valerian rapidly descending. Adrian still held her tightly, his body keeping hers in place. She tried to ask what was happening, but the wind stole her words as fast as they formed.

Valerian folded his wings tight as he plummeted straight down into a thick-canopied forest. At the last minute, he shoved his body upright and landed with a thump on his haunches.

They'd come down in deep pine woods, and Amber's exhausted mind guessed they might be in northern Washington or maybe somewhere in British Columbia or perhaps a national forest in southern Alaska. In any case, it was a place that hadn't been developed by city people wanting to escape the rat race, or by huge companies looking for lumber, minerals, and oil.

Adrian unhooked her straps and helped her climb to the ground. Amber expected Valerian to morph back into human form, but he simply curled into a big ball of dragon, nose pressed to tail, and closed his giant blue eyes.

Amber's legs shook as she tried to stand, and she gave up and plopped on the ground. The earth was relatively dry under the thick stand of trees, a faint breeze stirring the boughs high above them, the smell of resin thick.

"What's he doing?" she asked, voice unsteady.

"Recouping his energy." Adrian put his hands on his hips and studied the woods around them. Amber sensed him sending out tendrils of magic, searching for danger. "We still have a long way to go."

"Maybe we should have reconsidered the private jet thing," she said once she'd caught her breath. Adrian started to shake his head, and she held up her hand. "I know, too dangerous. But if I fall off Valerian's back, it will be dangerous to *me*."

"I'll never let you fall," Adrian said.

She believed him. His power was like a safety net, though she knew she should feel anything but safe. Here she was, out in deep woods, far from civilization, her only way out on the back of a dragon who'd decided to settle in for a nap. They had no food and no shelter. And yet her foolish mind bleated, *It's all right, Adrian will take care of me.*

"I don't like being taken care of," she said out loud.

Adrian turned from his examination of the woods. "Why not?"

"I don't know. Putting your fate in the hands of someone who might abuse your trust and hurt you is a bad idea. Better to learn to take care of yourself. Fall in love for love, not security."

His fathomless gaze pinned her. She wanted to squirm under it, knowing she babbled things that had nothing to do with him and herself. She was talking mostly to keep her teeth from chattering, saying whatever came into her head.

After a time, Adrian asked, "You think I will hurt you?"

She shook her head. "No, but I don't know whether that's because I believe in you or you're still messing with my mind."

One dark brow twitched. "You can feel that?"

"Yes, but maybe that's because I'm a hot-ass witch. Do vampires eat meals?"

He blinked, dark eyes curious. "Old Ones do. The lesser vampires don't bother."

"So my vampire Julio was an Old One."

He nodded slowly. "I suspected so, if he was able to glamour a powerful earth witch like you."

"You're saying that to make me feel better. I *should* feel like an idiot, because I didn't know he was a vampire. I probably saw all the signs, but chose to ignore them."

He shook his head. "You were young and he was strong. I know why he tried it. Having a witch as a blood slave would have made him powerful indeed."

"What do I make you?"

He stopped, studying her for a long time with his unreadable eyes. Then he swiftly cupped his hand under her chin and gave her a long, searing kiss. "Alive," he said.

She gave him a stunned look as her mouth and the rest of her body savored the kiss. He turned away, staring off into the woods again. Keeping watch? Thinking deep thoughts? She glanced at the sleeping dragon, whose breathing was surprisingly quiet.

"How long is he likely to sleep?"

"Not long," Adrian answered. He looked at her again, folding his arms over his chest. "While we're waiting, perhaps you will tell me precisely where we are going." His eyes were sharp.

She raked her hand through her hair, condensation dripping through her fingers. "The problem is, I don't know. I can't draw you a map. I only have a sense of direction, as if a compass had been magicked into me when I translated the writing. I point to Tain. Perhaps Tain wanted that and was reaching out the only way he could."

Adrian said nothing, but his grim look heightened. Amber guessed what he must be thinking: *Why didn't he reach out to me?*

"Maybe he couldn't," she said to his unasked question. "If he was spirited away by whoever it was, if this demon is trying to keep his whereabouts secret, then Tain couldn't call to you. When he wrote those words, they were for Susan to find when she was riding between."

Adrian's words were low and grating. "So if the demon kept Tain hidden away, why was Susan able to see him? Why could she suddenly see him and copy this writing, when I found nothing of him for centuries? And Sabina's question was a good one: Why didn't the demon attempt to attack us when you did the spell, or when we decided to follow it?"

Amber considered this, or pretended to, because the sour taste in her mouth indicated the answer. "Because it's a trap. The demon wants to trap us."

"Not *us*," he corrected her. "*Me.*"

"Yes, but . . ." Panic welled up inside her along with ideas she didn't want. "I was the one who could do the translation spell. I'm the only one who can follow the trail."

"I know. That's why he led me to you in the first place."

Amber swallowed the burning in her throat. "Wait a minute. You're implying that the demon killed my sister, that he let her find out about Tain and then murdered her for the sole purpose of getting you into his trap?" Tears she hadn't let herself shed began to leak from her eyes. "You are saying Susan died because she was *bait*?"

Adrian said nothing, because there was nothing to say. If he was right, then the demon had used Susan to entice him out of Los Angeles to come rushing to Seattle to find out what Susan knew. The demon had crushed

Susan's life out to make Adrian investigate what she'd been doing. Susan had meant nothing to the demon—she'd simply been the means to an end.

Silent tears wet Amber's face. "He could have used anyone. He could have left her alone and chosen someone else. Why did he have to pick her?"

"No, not anyone," Adrian answered, his deep voice gentle. "He wanted Susan in particular, and you. He needed both of you."

Amber got to her feet. "What are you talking about? We weren't leaders of powerful covens, we were young women with some competence in magic—but others have more. Some of the witches in the Coven of Light are ten times more powerful than I am. That's crazy—you can't be right."

He held her gaze as though willing her to understand. "You told me that Susan was creative, that she liked to reach beyond her ability, to dare. And you were able to take anything Susan discovered and turn it into powerful practical magic. You would do anything, including help an Immortal who should terrify you, to avenge your sister."

"I don't believe it. How could the demon know that? Why would he want us—there are plenty of witches out there who care about each other, sisters, friends, lovers—"

"I believe he hired a vampire, an Old One, ten years ago, to seduce you and discover what you were made of."

The air left her lungs. "Julio."

"Julio must have been desperate, if he deigned to help a demon. Old vampires don't have to feed as often, but when they do, their need is nearly insatiable. The demon might have promised Julio unlimited victims if he'd do him the favor of finding out what made you tick."

Tears slid over her lips, the salt taste thick on her tongue. "That was ten years ago. You think he planned that far in advance?"

"What is ten years to an Old One? They live millennia like you live weeks. I'd bet he investigated quite a few witches in the Coven of Light before he hit the right combination. He found Susan, then saw you and knew I'd want to protect you and keep you with me. A match-maker, is our demon. I well believe he took that long and was that thorough to set up a trap."

Amber wiped her eyes with the heel of her hand. "Then why are we walking into it?"

Again Adrian looked off between the trees, and she sensed him closing to her as he sometimes did. "I want to see what the son of a bitch has in mind. If he knows where Tain is, I'll make him take me there."

"And if he succeeds in trapping you, he'll have two Immortals in his power."

"Tain is not as strong as I am. He never was. I'll turn this trap around and release my brother."

Amber clenched her fists, anger and fear twisting into a hard ball in her gut. "But the demon is damn strong. You've fought him several times—the last time, I found you with your body slashed to ribbons."

"I wasn't trying to kill him then," he said absently. "I was trying to get information out of him. If he's waiting for us, with or without Tain, I will kill him."

His eyes sparked with grim determination, but he wouldn't look at her. He wanted this battle, she saw that in the hard line of his mouth. He'd fight until he could fight no more, and it chilled Amber to think what the de-mon might do to him if Adrian fell under his power.

She was tired of losing people she cared about to this damn demon. There had to be a better way than simply springing the trap on the demon, though Amber had to admit she had no idea what.

Adrian would try to protect Amber from the demon, probably recruiting Valerian to help him, but she had a few ideas about that. She'd taken the measure of the dragon's aura when he assisted her in the spell, and now thought she could gain Valerian's loyalty. Or at least coerce him into being on her side. Blackmail if she had to.

At that moment, Valerian came out of his sleep, scales sliding as he uncoiled himself. The animal sounds of the forest immediately ceased, small creatures aware of the huge predator in their midst. "Ready to go?" he rumbled.

Adrian and Amber shared a look. Adrian turned away and said nothing as he helped Amber strap herself to Valerian before they took off again into the freezing atmosphere.

Valerian could only fly as far as a small fishing town in northern Alaska. After that his dragon blood would freeze, he said, but Amber still had not pinpointed Tain's location.

"Farther north, that's all I know," Amber said.

They found a small motel on the main road near the town's one stop sign. The woman at the front desk with two squalling children in the room behind her eyed them with suspicion. They were obviously not locals or the usual sport fishermen who ventured this far north.

Adrian paid for the one room the motel had available, the rest of the rooms being occupied or in need of remodeling. A petite maid came around later with a pile of towels and tried to peer past Amber when she answered the door, clearly curious as to what the three of them were up to in there. The maid seemed disappointed to see Adrian only using the phone and Valerian sprawled in a chair idly flicking through television channels.

"They really need to upgrade their cable," Valerian said.

His human face was drawn and haggard, the toll of the thousands of miles he'd flown wearing on him. Amber had placed a big order of Chinese food from the restaurant that seemed to be the mainstay of the town. Now Adrian was on the phone trying to rent or buy cold weather equipment.

Valerian yawned, stretching his beefy legs. "I could sleep for a week."

"You might have the chance." Adrian hung up the phone. "Amber and I will have a long way to go, depending on where she leads us. I just set us up with some motorbikes for land and skis to get us across ice."

"Sorry," Valerian mumbled.

"You've done enough," Amber said reassuringly. "Eat and rest and catch up on your soaps."

Valerian grinned. "Hey, maybe that maid will want to keep me company." He laughed, sounding a little hollow but stronger. "Better idea would have been to bring the werewolf along." He waggled his brows, giving them little doubt what he would have brought Sabina along for.

"She bites," Amber warned.

"That's what I'm hoping." Valerian's grin was infectious. He yawned again, oblivious to the tension between Adrian and Amber. "Where's the food?"

Not long after that, the delivery arrived. Even though it was late April, a light snow fell. The sky was still light, the northern clime anticipating the coming midnight sun.

Valerian consumed most of the meal. Amber found herself not very hungry despite their long journey, and Adrian didn't eat at all. She picked through her beef and broccoli while Valerian inhaled at least four orders of kung pao chicken and ate what was to have been Adrian's mu shu shrimp. After that, the dragon-man stretched himself out on the bed, flung one arm over his eyes, and went to sleep.

Adrian studied a map sent over from the place that had rented him the bikes. The roadmap showed lots of white space with tiny, mostly unimproved roads. Adrian unfolded a contour map, which Amber couldn't read well, though she could make out their town at the edge of a lot of nothing.

"Does the rental place have a GPS positioner?" Amber asked over his shoulder. "I'd hate to get lost out in all that ice."

"We will not get lost." Adrian kept his black gaze on the map.

"I wish I could point to a specific place, but all I can say is, that way." She made a vague gesture against the blankness of the map.

"Then we'll go that way," Adrian said. He turned to her, taking her in with his eyes. She felt his brush on her mind, his attempt to make her do what he wanted.

She leaned down and kissed his lips, feeling heat stir between her legs and wishing there'd been two rooms. Adrian returned the kiss, his tongue sweeping into her mouth like a bite of spice.

"Sleep now," he commanded, and instantly her limbs grew heavy. "I'll wake you when we need to go."

Amber tried to fight his suggestion, but her eyes were sandy and she yawned. In her clothes, she crawled under the rough sheets and thin blanket of the second bed, watching Adrian's broad back as he leaned over the map. As she drifted to sleep, she saw him raise his head and speak to the air. She thought a thin mist formed in front of him, but the more she strained to see, the more tired she became.

He turned and put his hand palm out toward her. "Go to sleep, Amber."

This time, the compulsion was too hard to resist, and Amber tumbled into sleep. When she woke, both men were gone.

# CHAPTER THIRTEEN

Adrian watched Amber emerge from the seedy hotel, her black hair tossed by the strong, straight wind. The parka and boots did little to hide her long-legged beauty, and her measured stride showed her determination to see this through.

He hoped to Isis she hadn't been lying when she'd said she couldn't point out precisely where Tain was and so had had to come with him. The demon was doing what demons did—hurting the innocent to get what he wanted. The demon had planned well to use Amber, a witch who had a good chance of snaring an Immortal's heart.

First Adrian wanted to discover *why* the demon wanted him and Tain both. Was he starting a collection of Immortals? For what purpose? Adrian mused on his brothers Darius, Kalen, and Hunter, and wondered whether the demon was busily trapping them as well.

Tain was not as strong as Adrian, but the two of them together could easily best a demon, even an Old One.

All five Immortals working together could turn an ancient demon into dust just by sneering at him.

But the demon had survived this long, meaning he had been strong enough to resist the Immortals and the goddesses all those years ago, or at the very least, had successfully hidden from them. In ancient times, demons had trembled before the might of the Immortals. Adrian had been cocky and enjoyed slaughtering them in various ways, liking that they begged for mercy. *Like your own victims begged you?* he'd asked them. *I'll give you the same mercy you gave them.*

It had felt good to be a demon slayer, felt good to let Ferrin the sword taste demon blood. His brother Hunter had shared Adrian's fanatical need to slow the number of demons and vampires on earth, never letting a demon get away even if he had to follow it to the ends of the earth.

Hunter was a stalker and a killer who took no prisoners and gave no mercy. He had an affinity with animals, able to read their thoughts and send his to them. In many ways, he got along with wild animals better than he did with humans, or even his brothers. Predators had a kill-or-be-killed instinct, and Hunter shared it.

Valerian glanced at Amber as she leaned into the wind to walk to them. "She's one stubborn lady, Adrian. And cute. How'd you get so lucky?"

"If I needed you to knock her out and take her back home, would you do it?" Adrian asked him.

Valerian rubbed his upper lip. "I don't know. I have the feeling she'd be pissed when she woke up."

"Are you afraid of a human witch?"

"Not afraid exactly. But what if she put a curse on me to always wear my underwear on the outside or something? That would play hell with my reputation."

Adrian didn't smile. "I might need you to take her anyway. If she were killed because of me, I'd have eternity to regret it."

Valerian lost his grin. "That hard?"

Adrian said nothing, because Amber was within earshot, but he gave Valerian a pleading look, and the shifter nodded.

Adrian had purchased and rented cold-weather gear for their trek north. He'd obtained goggles, lined parkas, pants and boots, a compass and GPS device, an Arctic tent they could anchor to ice, a saw-edged shovel that folded, Arctic-rated sleeping bags, walkie-talkies, MRE rations, thermal bottles of water, lighters, fuel bottles, batteries, lanterns, cross-country skis, and a few other things to make life out on the ice floes a little easier. He'd also added flares.

He'd rented motorbikes, which they could ride through packed snow until they came to the ice floes, but also through mud if they had to cross melted areas. Spring came late this far north, but thaws happened.

Even a motorbike helmet and goggles couldn't make Amber look any less delicious. Her fingers shook a little as she fastened the chin strap and mounted the bike, her long legs straddling the saddle.

They said good-bye to Valerian and rode out of the motel parking lot. The maid and the desk clerk came out to watch them go, as they turned onto the road. Valerian raised a big hand in farewell, then ducked inside out of the cold.

Amber wished she had a better direction than "that way," but it was all the spell had given her. Adrian made her ride behind him, far enough back so that he wouldn't throw snow and exhaust in her face, and she gave him changes of direction through a walkie-talkie.

The road ended after about ninety miles, and from there on it was cross-country driving, but the motorbikes had been made for offroading, with thick, deep-tread tires and motors made to resist freezing when temperatures dropped. Fortunately, the sun stayed out longer these days, so darkness would only last a few hours.

They rode for miles, Amber hunched over her handlebars in an attempt to keep the wind from slowing her. She and Susan had dirt-biked all over the Northwest during college summers, days of freedom. They'd camped at night and talked magic, trying out new spells they'd written.

Amber had learned how to be a biker, resting her body in different positions so her shoulders and back and legs would be less stiff. In a way, a bike gave her much more freedom than a car, and there was nothing like speeding down the road like a biker chick while the world rushed by.

This trip was a little different because she was bundled tight against the cold and she strained to keep Adrian in sight. His bike kicked up snow and mud, obscuring his taillight. If she dropped too far behind, she might lose him in the glare of all the white. Also, the direction she needed to follow changed from due north to east. She radioed the information to him and went on, paralleling the Beaufort Sea and heading into Canada.

They rode all day, and when Amber began to droop with exhaustion, Adrian broke the ride and they made camp. Adrian erected the tent, and they ate and drank before he built a shelter for the bikes and their supplies.

Amber had a sleeping bag to herself in the tiny tent, but Adrian snuggled up behind her and draped his sleeping-bagged form over her for extra warmth. She tucked her head under his chin and slid her backside against his thighs, wishing they had more room. When she felt his lips in her hair, she turned sleepily and gave him a full kiss.

She hadn't thought they'd be able to do anything sexual in the confined space, but Adrian got them out of their bags and undressed quickly. He made love to her on the nest of sleeping bags, their combined warmth filling the tent and making her sweat.

Out here in the middle of nowhere they had no need to be quiet, and he quickly had her screaming louder than she'd let herself before. Adrian for the most part was silent, using his mouth to lick and suck her flesh, his hands molding to her body. She gazed into his eyes and experienced the floating sensation again, the two of them suspended in blackness as stars whirled by.

When he came, he groaned hard, setting his teeth in her neck as he liked to do.

They spiraled down from climax together, but before she could drift into sleep, he made love to her again. This time he pinned her hands above her head and rode her with quick, rough thrusts. She lifted her body, wanting as much contact with his as possible.

When they relaxed again, she drew languid fingers across his cheek. "The polar bears must be laughing at the bouncing tent."

He kissed her throat. "I am keeping all the wild creatures away. You'll be safe here."

"Maybe, but they'll still laugh."

He raised his head, his eyes quiet. "You like to laugh, even though you hold so much sorrow. It's one of the lovable things about you."

In the happiness of afterglow, she let the word *lovable*

flow over her. She couldn't believe she'd just had wild sex in an Arctic-rated tent in the middle of nowhere on the Alaska-Canada border.

A twinge of uneasiness cut through her comfort.

"If the demon used me and Susan to bring you to him, is what I'm feeling for you part of his power?" she asked. "Making sure I stick with you?"

He traced the bow of her lips, his dark eyes unreadable. "What are you feeling for me?"

"I think you know."

His gaze took on the deep sadness she'd sensed in him when she'd first met him. "Amber, you can't fall in love with an Immortal."

"Can if I want to."

"When we are finished, I will make you forget me, as I've promised. You will go back to your life, and I will cease to exist for you."

She glared at him, the cozy afterglow dissolving. "Why do you get to make all the decisions?"

He gave her a puzzled look. "Decisions?"

"First you decide I belong to you, and then, *snap*, you're finished? You must be king of the one-night stands if you can make your lovers forget about you in the morning."

His brows lowered. "That is not what I mean."

She knew it wasn't, and she knew this was his way of keeping her from hurt, but it angered her all the same. "First the demon manipulates me, now you want to keep me from remembering I was manipulated in the first place. I'm tired of being screwed around by ancient beings."

She half pushed him away, stuffed herself into her sleeping bag, and zipped it up. He remained on his side, facing her, looking like the gorgeous demigod he was, black hair flowing over tightly muscled shoulders, his eyes gleaming in the light of the battery-powered lantern.

She could gaze at him forever, taking in the perfection of his body, marred only by the scars of battles long past, his tight abdomen leading her eyes to the brush of hair below his pelvis and his thick erection still hard for her.

What woman would not want him, even if her price was forgetting him in the morning?

Annoyed at her own inconsistency, Amber rolled over so she wouldn't have to look at him. "We have a long day tomorrow, and this mortal woman needs her sleep. Good *night.*"

He said nothing. For the longest time, she felt his gaze on her, his big body still, his breathing quiet. A half hour passed as she lay rigidly, expecting him to snarl at her, or laugh at her, or even throw her down and make love to her again.

At last, a little disappointingly, he clicked the light off, zipped himself into his own sleeping bag, and quietly dropped off to sleep.

Morning came excruciatingly early, and the sun was full and bright by the time she and Adrian moved on. Adrian was grateful for the goggles because even with his powers, he would have been snow-blind in ten seconds without them. This far up, where perpetual glaciers and sea ice were the norm, spring was nowhere near.

They went east and then north again until they reached packed ice. At the end of the day, Adrian knew they'd have to leave the bikes behind. Ice alone lay beyond this, and they'd proceed via cross-country skis.

Toward the end of their second day on skis, Adrian turned his head just in time to see Amber silently begin skiing perpendicular to their path, even though it led to thinner, greener ice. A spike of adrenaline raced through his body, and he swung around to follow her, hoping to Isis she didn't charge out to a freak thaw and fall through. She'd be dead within seconds of hitting water that cold.

Amber halted so suddenly her skis moved a bit forward before she dug the poles in and pulled herself upright. Adrian stopped himself before he ran into her.

"Is this it?" His voice was muffled behind his goggles and ski mask.

Amber nodded. She wore the same kind of goggles and ski mask, which completely hid her face, and her parka hood covered her head. A mute stuffed into layers of nylon and padding.

She pointed with a mitten to what looked like snow-brushed ice-floe, not much different from the rest of the ice around them. She looked up at him, and he could just make out her wide eyes behind the tinted goggles. "What do we do now?"

Adrian threw down the pack he'd been carrying, unfolded the saw-edged shovel and the small pickaxe he'd brought with him. "We dig."

He saw her mouth form a grimace behind the ski mask. She took up the pickaxe and made a few strikes at the ice. She made a small dent or two, then threw down the axe in disgust and pulled off her insulated mitten before Adrian could stop her.

He understood what she was doing when she shot a burst of fire at the ice's surface, then quickly popped her mitten back on and tucked her hand under her arm. Adrian took advantage of the melt she'd started and banged the shovel through the ice a few inches before it began to harden again.

As soon as her hand warmed, Amber threw the spell again; this time Adrian was ready with the pickaxe. They worked this way for a while, exposing Amber's fingers to the harsh cold only long enough for her to pop her small fireball over the ice.

When Adrian had made a hole large enough to satisfy him, he dug out two stones from Amber's hoard, a topaz and tiger's eye, both of which would carry warm, radiating magic. Though they still held the charge he'd infused on them in her car, he wanted her magic in them too, so he asked her to infuse them.

Amber cupped the stones in her mittened hands and faced the sun, her head thrown back to catch its rays, and closed her eyes. The sun shone brilliant and strong here, despite the bitter, powerful cold. The sun God in all his glory still ruled, even where the earth was dormant.

Amber handed him back the stones, which vibrated strongly with the combination of her earth power, the power of the sun, and the fire element of the stones themselves. Excellent.

Adrian dropped the stones into the hole he made, then pulled Amber out of the way. He built up power deep inside him, as Isis had taught him long ago on the banks of the Nile, and spoke one word.

Power flowed out of him in a concentrated arrow, seeking the stones in the ice. The two stones absorbed, magnified, and gave back the power in one mighty burst.

The ice moved and groaned, and Amber fell, catching herself on hands and knees. Adrian flung himself over her just as a sudden explosion of ice and freezing water burst from the hole and fell in thick shards all around them. The razor-sharp ice rained down on them, deflecting off Adrian's padded clothing, hissing and splintering when it hit the ground.

After about five minutes, the ice shower lessened, and finally everything grew quiet. Adrian raised his head, and Amber crawled out from under him, both of them staring in wonder.

In place of the flat ice and the small area they'd dug out was a hole about three feet in diameter. Below it was a tunnel, its walls made of smooth, thick green ice that curved downward and away from them at a slight angle.

Adrian made a *down there?* motion with his thick glove, and Amber nodded. He placed his hands on her shoulders and looked down into her eyes.

"Stay here. If I don't come back in half an hour, radio Valerian for help. He'll send someone if he can't come himself. He can't fly, but helicopters can."

"In this wind?" The stubborn set of her shoulders only got more stubborn. "You need me with you."

"I need you safe."

"You want me to abandon you to the demon? To go back to a motel and be warm and dry while he skins you alive and leaves you in a bank of ice?"

She worried for him. No woman had ever worried for him before. Not that it mattered; she could do nothing from this point on but keep herself out of it.

He didn't bother with an answering argument but simply turned, lay down on the ice, and dove arms-first into the hole. At the last moment, he felt Amber's grip on his ankles, and then they were both sliding down, down, down through a tube that snaked for several thousand feet before dropping them into a wide cavern carved deep into the ice.

Amber peeled her fingers from Adrian's ankles and sat back in awe. The cavern was enormous, like a stone cave with stalagmites and stalactites, except that everything was made entirely of ice. It was a magical place. She could feel magic permeating every crevice and frozen droplet of water. Instead of the darkness she would expect, the entire cave glowed with a crystalline light that was glass green, its beauty intense.

The cave was also relatively warm. Sheltered from the howling wind, situated beneath a ton of thick ice, the cave let Amber peel off her goggles and face mask in comfort. She pushed back her hood and gazed around her.

Adrian also removed goggles, mask, hood, and gloves, absently stuffing them into his parka. Amber expected him to glower at her for following him, and maybe toss her back to the surface on a wave of his power. She imagined herself popping high out of the hole like a cartoon character and landing hard on her behind on the ice.

Adrian seemed to forget all about Amber as he turned in a circle, his dark eyes roving the place. He scanned every facet of it, every icicle hanging from the roof, every nook and cranny in walls and ceiling and floor.

But other than Adrian and Amber, the cave was uninhabited. No Immortal, no demon, nothing.

Adrian continued to study the cave, head tilted back as he gazed up at the droplets of ice that hung like diamonds. Amber felt that he looked not so much with his eyes as with all his senses, testing the air with his magic.

"He was here," he whispered.

Amber scanned where Adrian had looked, but was unable to see anything beyond the green glowing ice. The magic from the decryption spell had shut off, leaving her blind.

"He isn't here now," she said, her voice echoing hollowly. "We should go."

Adrian pressed his palms directly to the ice, closed his eyes, and bowed his head. He remained in that position for so long that Amber went to him, alarmed.

He opened his eyes, but he didn't see her and didn't seem to have heard her either. He moved around the cave, touching the walls, turning in place, closing his eyes or studying the stalagmites. "Tain was here. For many years, he was here. Can't you feel him?"

Amber regarded him worriedly. "The demon could arrive at any minute. He wants you down here for some reason, so I say we meet him up top, in the sun."

Adrian rested his fists gently on a wall. "All this time, Tain was here. He was trapped. I feel his anguish, how he tried to call out and no one could hear him. I could hear him in my dreams, but I didn't know it was real."

"The demon trapped him," Amber tried. "It wasn't your fault."

He nodded slowly, eyes still closed, face to the wall. "Yes, it was. It's what you can never understand. I was angry at him, and I left him alone. I was angry because he wanted to remain with a woman, and I told him he was a fool. I went to fight the things in the valley, and while I was gone, she killed the humans and spirited Tain away. He might have gone willingly at first—at first he'd fallen in love. I blamed him and myself. I didn't understand what falling in love would be like."

"Revelations happen to everyone," Amber said, not really paying attention to the words she chose. "You figure things out—sometimes it takes a long time. But we can talk about this later, preferably while skiing back to the bikes. We'll make camp again, and you can tell me all about it in our nice, warm tent."

He looked up at her suddenly, brow furrowing as though he'd forgotten she was with him. "You must be cold. I will tell Valerian to send for you." He touched the wall, almost lovingly, his voice taking on an archaic lilt. "I will tarry here awhile."

"No, you won't." She planted herself in front of him. "We'll both go and hang out in the motel and watch bad television until Valerian is rested enough to take us back to Los Angeles. Or Seattle. I'd like to go home. I don't want to leave the house empty too long. Predators other than demons are lurking out there."

He seemed puzzled by her vehemence. "I prefer to stay. If I stay long enough, perhaps I will hear the whispers he left, sense the direction he was taken."

"And how long will that take? Years?"

"Perhaps."

"Adrian." She grasped his shoulders and shook him. "You can't stay here for years. You told me the demon lived millennia like *I* lived weeks. Which means they're like weeks to you too, right? Guess what? I don't want to leave you down here for one of those weeks and never see you again. Understand? You're going on about what you feel about me, but how about what I feel about you? Doesn't that count?"

For a moment, he looked fully at her. "I told you not to fall in love with an Immortal."

"Well, too damn late. I love you. Hear me?" She shook him again. "Breaking my heart to stay down here meditating in an ice cave is just"—she groped for a word "—mean."

He kept staring at her, dark eyes fixed. She could never read what was in his eyes, he hid so much.

He spoke quietly. "Finding my brother is the reason I remained so long in your world. I will find Tain and go."

"The only reason? So anyone else you happened to drag into your adventures along the way doesn't matter?"

Adrian brushed a lock of hair from her face and kissed her forehead. "Go home, Amber. Thank you for helping me. Be well."

He raised his hand, and a wave of his power lifted her off her feet. She fought it as hard as she could, but the ripples propelled her upward into the ice tunnel. She scrambled against the walls of ice, hands slipping. She screamed to him to let her go, but his power was far more immense than hers would ever be, damn the man.

The air grew colder as she drifted steadily toward the surface, her tears icing over. She felt the wind above her, which would chill her to the bone if she couldn't get her gloves and mask on in time.

Just before she reached the top, the entire ice tunnel collapsed in a rush. A huge wall of black, freezing water plummeted her down the length of the tunnel back to the cave, splintering Adrian's magic.

The walls of the cave groaned and shuddered, bowing inward. In a split second they broke, and a wall of water spiraled rapidly down to bury the cave, Amber, and Adrian beneath it.

# CHAPTER FOURTEEN

The filthy taint of death magic told Amber the demon had sprung his trap. She saw him in the wall of water, darkness within darkness, blotting out the cool green light of the cave. She couldn't scream because water filled her mouth, the weight of the wave crushing all air out of her. She was going to die. A fire spell and a knack for earth magic wouldn't help her now.

Adrian's power broke the water like a slice of white, cutting the darkness of the demon's magic. His power pressed out a bubble of air around Amber, its white walls shoving the water away. Amber fell to her knees, gasping and sobbing for air, her clothes sodden.

Not two feet from her, Adrian and the demon fought a death match. White and black swirled together, obscuring their bodies, life magic and death magic in a blurred struggle. She felt Adrian's magic like a scythe, a man no longer worried about keeping his enemy alive. He wanted vengeance.

Amber knew that if Adrian lost this fight, she was

dead. The demon would either amuse himself by snuffing out her life instantly or leave her here to suffocate.

On the other hand, if the demon was killed in the fight, they'd never find where he'd hidden Tain. The demon must have had a good reason to go to such great lengths to keep Adrian from his brother.

With dawning comprehension, Amber suddenly understood that this wasn't about Adrian finding his brother. No, this was about the demon trapping Adrian, the most powerful of the Immortals, to keep him occupied while he fulfilled his plans with Tain, whatever they were.

And what if Adrian had been right when he'd told her Tain didn't want to be found? What if the demon wasn't simply trying to thwart Adrian, but trying to protect Tain?

Tain had gone away with whomever had enticed him seven hundred years ago. Adrian believed that Tain had been duped, but what if he'd really gone of his own free will?

What if she wasn't dealing with a powerful demon who wanted to control Immortals, but with an Immortal who wanted to control demons, vampires, and death magic?

"Oh, shit," she whispered, her teeth chattering.

She pawed in her pocket for the radio, but it had gotten soaked, even through its protective plastic covering. There wasn't much chance it would transmit well this far below the surface anyway. She hadn't even bothered with her cell phone.

Hands shaking, she withdrew her pouch of crystals and selected the clearest piece of quartz she could find. With a smaller quartz crystal, she drew a circle around herself in the ice, then closed her eyes and raised the power around her.

Using magic didn't truly require candles, knives, chalices, and censors of burning incense. Those objects helped focus concentration and enhance magical energy, but a true witch could perform magic standing alone in the woods or walking along a beach. She just needed to pull energy from things around her and from inside her, channel that energy, and release it to accomplish her spell.

Having the correct colored candle or the right herb really didn't matter. Magic was about a connection to the deities and the ability to raise energy, not sprinkling the right powder into the right container at the right time.

On the other hand, it never hurt to use whatever was possible to boost strength. Amber sketched the rune for victory in the ice with a piece of carnelian. Then she sat back on her heels, trying to calm her mind, an almost impossible task with the battle raging nearby.

At one point Adrian's sword flew through the air, smashing through the bubble that protected Amber. She gasped, but the bubble sealed again, Adrian's magic holding. The sword skittered and bounced toward her glowing circle. Quickly Amber sketched an opening as the sword morphed into Ferrin and slid faster than thought toward her. He slithered up Amber's leg and burrowed into her jacket, diving into a dry pocket.

Amber gave her pocket a comforting pat, then refocused her energy into the flat crystal.

*Valerian*, she shouted with her mind. *We're in deep shit here, we need you!*

Outside her circle of calm and air, Adrian and the demon fought, through water and through ice, explosions of magic rocking the glacier above them.

*Valerian!*

She continued to mentally scream his name while the

cave grew blacker around her. Adrian fought with magic and muscle, trying to best the demon whose death magic flowed like thick darkness at the bottom of a well. The blackness grew thicker, spreading until she couldn't see Adrian or his white magic, and the walls of the air bubble that kept her safe began to collapse.

Valerian woke from his bored doze when a crackling voice filled the room. "Valerian!"

Startled, he clicked off the television where a national news station reported that a heat wave had hit the Southern states. The voice was Amber's, but it cracked and broke as though she transmitted through faulty equipment from far away. She continued to frantically call his name, and after a few minutes he realized the sound came from the pockmarked mirror that hung above the motel room's dresser.

"Amber?"

"Valerian." Her tinny voice exuded relief. "The demon is going to kill Adrian, and I'm trapped with Ferrin under the ice."

Valerian couldn't see anything in the mirror but his own tall body and wave of blond hair mussed with sleep.

"Where are you?" he shouted back. "What coordinates?"

Her voice shook, fear radiating all the way from the middle of nowhere, as she gave him the GPS coordinates where they were.

"All right. I'll get there." He paused, thinking of the brutal cold. A human could survive with the right gear, but his dragon's blood would freeze, and he'd die. And what Amber needed right now was not human but supernatural help.

"Send someone, send *anyone*," she begged. "Adrian's losing the fight."

"That should piss him off," Valerian muttered. He raised his voice again. "You sit tight, babe. I'll coordinate the rescue mission. Did you say you were *under* the ice?"

"Yes. But any minute it could be under water."

"Crap." His mind worked furiously. He imagined she'd rather be in the Southern heat wave just now, lying on a Florida beach sipping a Mai Tai while Adrian licked her toes. Valerian would like to be on that beach himself, splashing in the waves with a cute werewolf with blond hair.

"Amber . . ." He broke off, having no idea what to tell her.

"Hurry!"

"Hang on," he said, the words sounding lame to him. "I'll find you—I swear it. I owe it to Adrian."

Amber said something else, but her voice crackled and then he heard nothing. Like a cell phone breaking up and dying, her words faded, and then there was nothing.

Valerian swore in many languages including dragon, and dragged the motel-room phone onto his lap. The first number he dialed was Septimus's cell phone. The vampire for some reason was back at Adrian's house—no, he was at Kelly's next door. Valerian's brain filed that interesting fact away as he told Septimus about Amber and Adrian's situation.

Septimus promised things. Valerian heard Kelly's throaty voice on the other end before the vampire clicked off his phone.

Valerian then called Adrian's house and talked to Detective Simon. Simon promised help, too—he'd contact rescue people he knew up in Alaska and get them moving. Before Valerian could hang up, the phone was jerked out of Simon's hands, and Sabina's voice shrilled to him.

"You find her, Valerian, you hear me? Amber's my best friend, and I don't want the pack to have to come after you for getting her killed. We can take down even a dragon if we do it together."

"Hey, I'm doing my best here," he returned. "It's like twenty below on this balmy spring day."

"Just *find* her," she repeated, tears in her voice.

"I will," he said in all seriousness, then hung up.

Having to negotiate with a vampire and being yelled at by a gorgeous werewolf were not making Valerian's day brighter. He looked out the grimy window across the equally grimy parking lot and the slushy snow on the street. Amber might already be dead, and Adrian? Who knew?

He growled, the sound coming from deep within him, startling a mouse that skittered quickly behind the baseboards.

"Oh, what the hell," Valerian muttered.

He grabbed his parka and slammed his way out the door, jogging across the street into the scrub to look for a place to change into his dragon form.

The death magic sucked the power from Amber's spell, and Valerian's voice was cut off. Death magic was winning beneath the ice as Adrian had to divide his concentration between fighting the demon and maintaining the air bubble around Amber.

Amber scrabbled in her pouch of stones. If she could sustain the bubble herself, Adrian could fight without worrying about her. The trouble was, she wasn't certain how to do such a spell, or if her crystals had enough power left in them to help.

Plus, she was terrified, the light was almost gone, and the overwhelming death magic nearly destroyed what energy she had left. She collapsed to the bottom of the bubble, shaking and trying to make out the two forms that fought not far from her.

Pretty soon, Adrian would have to choose between killing the demon and saving Amber. She couldn't be sure which choice he'd make, and she hated that he'd have to make it. But if she'd stayed up top as he'd wanted her to, the demon would likely have found her, snuffed out her life, and tossed her body down the hole to taunt Adrian.

Likely the demon had found their stash of bikes and supplies and wrecked that, too, so even if she did get out . . .

The death magic was depressing her, drawing away her will to live. She needed to keep herself alive, freeing Adrian from having to look after her.

"You don't know any good air spells do you, Ferrin?" she asked shakily.

The snake remained silent in her pocket. He was using her body heat to keep his reptile blood from freezing, and it showed Amber how much she'd come to accept in the last week that she only felt sorry for him.

A thought came to her, though she wasn't certain whether Ferrin had put it there or Adrian. Actually, it sounded like a wisp of Susan's voice: *Invoke the Goddess.*

Amber dumped her stones onto the ice. Of course, the simplest ritual she could do was a spiritual one, to invite the Goddess to her. If nothing else, the chanting of the Goddess's names would calm her down so she might think of a way out of this. And not think about being trapped under a thousand feet of ice and water with two supernatural beings battling it out and her only friend a snake who was doing his best to go dormant.

She drew the circle and closed her eyes to begin a universal chant to the Goddess. "Mother of the moon, queen of the night, blessed be the Goddess, blessed be her might. By Gaia, Isis, Diana, Hecate, Demeter, Ishtar . . ."

Calm eased her aching limbs, her tight throat loosening as she went through the comforting chant. The cold and fear, the icy smell of the water, the hideous noises of the fighting, all receded.

In the darkness, she seemed to see a slim woman in silhouette with thin horns rising from her head. Her dress was a single light sheath bound at one shoulder, her hair black and flowing to her waist. The woman turned her head and looked straight at Amber with eyes large and black and framed with thick lashes, sensual and wise.

Without opening her mouth, the apparition said, "You care for my son."

Amber dashed tears from her eyes and tried to focus on the woman, who grew more blurry the more Amber stared. "Yes. When he's not being a reckless pain in the ass."

"You care for him. He needs that. More than your magic, more than your help, he needs your love."

Amber ground her teeth. "He's not exactly accepting it."

"You must make him accept it. He needs you. In the end, it will be your love that saves him. Hold on to that."

"My love that saves him?" Amber repeated, bewildered, as the goddess began to fade. "Wait a minute, what will save *me*?"

"Friends," Isis said in a faint voice, and then she was gone.

Frantically Amber tried to call up the calm that she'd achieved, tried to reach outside the danger to find the goddess again. Nothing.

As she gathered her stones to try again, the air bubble broke. A wall of water sent her tumbling across the remains of the ice cave, shards of ice slicing through her padded coat to her flesh. She slammed face-first to the frozen ground, tasting blood.

Over the crush of water she seemed to hear an irritated voice uttering every profanity she knew and some she'd never heard before.

"Frigging *cold*, I'm going to have rigor mortis *before* I die."

Amber's body went limp, no air reaching her lungs, her skin feeling strangely warm as she drifted into lassitude. Then something clamped around her like an iron cage and dragged her unmercifully up through freezing water, slamming her down again onto hard, cold ice.

When Amber peeled open her eyes, she found her ski mask and goggles jammed on her face, but twisted so that she could barely breathe. She sat up, jerking her mask and goggles straight with hands clumsy in padded mittens.

She was on the ice again, in open air. Hard wind blasted across the surface, and above her arched a clear sky etched with thousands of stars, the smudge of them blazing to the horizon. Next to her stood an exhausted-looking Valerian in parka and pants and boots. He wrapped a thick blanket around her and extracted a thermos from a box and shoved it at her. "Drink."

It was coffee, the beverage she most hated. But the

steam filled her nose, and she poured the scalding liquid into her mouth, swallowing it like it was ambrosia. The heat burned its way down her gullet, easing her shaking the slightest bit.

Something moved under her coat. She peeked inside to see Ferrin poke a tentative nose from her pocket, and she exhaled in relief that he was all right. Then she quickly scanned the ice, empty of all save herself and Valerian.

"Where is Adrian?" she asked.

Valerian's look was grim. "He disappeared as I pulled you free."

"Disappeared? What do you mean, disappeared?"

"He and the demon vanished together. They're gone. I don't know where."

Amber gazed over the ice again, its unbroken whiteness and the fierce light of the stars making it as bright as dawn. She saw no sign of Adrian or anyone else walking across the vast plain of white. Even the tunnel that had led to the cave was covered and gone.

Grief twisted her, but she had no tears left to cry. She drew her knees to her chest, her hand straying to the pocket where Ferrin hid.

She was not ready to let Adrian go. She was a witch with some skill, and she would dig out the most powerful locator spell she could muster and hunt him down.

"He won't get rid of me that easily," she muttered.

Valerian grinned at her, but his smile was shaky, his face gray-white with cold.

Amber climbed painfully to her feet, the ice so cold it was sticky, not slippery. "We have to find the bikes. Our tent is there too. We can rest there before we ride back."

Valerian shook his head. "I didn't see them. I think the demon already made a clean sweep."

Amber balled her fists. "Fine, then *he* can explain it to the rental agency."

"Don't make me laugh, it hurts."

Amber focused on him. "I thought you couldn't fly so far in the cold."

"I can't. I shouldn't have. I thought if I changed myself back to human and got warm right away, I'd be all right, but I think I've screwed myself over."

"Don't you dare die on me, Valerian," Amber said fiercely. "I'm not living with that for the rest of my life."

He pressed his hands to his stomach. "Yes, ma'am."

His words were nearly drowned by the drone of an engine somewhere above them. Yellow and red lights appeared against the black sky, cutting a swath through the night. A plane.

With the last of her strength, Amber lit her fire spell and let it catch in glittering molecules in the air. At the burst of light, the airplane turned and descended toward them. Not many minutes later, the plane bumped down onto the ice not ten yards from where they waited.

It was a light aircraft, a modified Piper with props on each wing, and both skis and wheels. It looked so normal and *warm* that Amber hugged Valerian in relief.

Her relief was short-lived. The door lowered to form a short stair, and three tall men descended and began to move toward them. Amber caught the metallic tang of death magic, saw the men's fierce silhouettes, and knew she and Valerian hadn't been rescued by friendly ice fishermen or patrollers or environmentalists.

They weren't human at all. They were vampire.

Adrian's battle was a losing one, and he knew it. The demon was far stronger than he ought to be, and Adrian had to use part of his magic to keep Amber from dying. He sensed her shrouded in a small circle of air, a glowing point of life magic like a candle in a small, black room.

Her anger when they'd figured out that the demon had used both Amber and Susan to trap Adrian matched his own. He'd tasted Amber's grief, and knowing the demon had deliberately caused it made his fury grow.

And with it, his magic. He could take apart this frozen ocean and bury the demon in it, but first he had to get Amber free.

Tain had been in the frozen cave—Adrian knew it with every sense. Tain had been there, and he had suffered, and he'd been taken from this place when the demon decided to draw Adrian toward it.

He half heard Amber chanting in her circle, then felt the presence of Isis like a weak projection across a great distance. Even though she'd only arrived as a vision, he sensed her power and comfort, which made him take heart. Isis would help Amber, and Adrian could focus on the demon. Adrian had discarded Ferrin already, knowing the demon might damage the sword-snake irreparably, and Ferrin didn't deserve that.

Adrian felt the cave begin to collapse again, ready to bury Amber. Then the bright hot life magic of the dragon had roared in and snatched Amber out just in time.

The demon snarled, unhappy that he couldn't kill Amber, and opened a black portal with his fist. Adrian felt the demon dive through the portal as water roared past him. At the last minute, Adrian grabbed the demon, muscles straining, and let the demon pull him through.

The vampires advanced on Valerian and Amber, who waited side by side. The fire spell had drained the last of Amber's strength, and Valerian looked ill. She wasn't sure she could work up even a spark now, and Valerian might pass out any minute.

One of the vampires walked forward while the other two flanked him. He was well built, with a raw sensuality that reminded her of the vampire Bryan who'd danced behind her at the club. Vampires seduced and fed; they had no other motivations that she knew of.

These weren't Old Ones, like Septimus. They were everyday vampires, which meant they were only ten times as strong and dangerous as the average human being.

The lead vampire stopped in front of Amber and looked her up and down. In spite of it being night, he and the other two wore sunglasses that obscured their eyes with opaque black lenses. Amber realized after a moment that this meant she could look straight at them without worrying about the mesmerizing magic of their gazes.

"Septimus told us to come and get you." The growl in the vampire's voice indicated he'd rather be having his tonsils pulled out without anesthetic.

"Oh," Amber said stiffly. "That was nice of him."

"About time," Valerian muttered. "Take us back to that crappy motel."

The vampire smiled a nasty smile, making sure his fangs showed white against his lips. "Anything you say, lizard man." He turned abruptly, made a curt motion to the other two vamps, and started back to the plane.

Valerian could barely walk. Amber slid her arm around his waist and let him lean on her as they strove to keep up with the vampires.

The pilot already sat in the cockpit, headphones in place, and the vamp that had spoken to them slid into the co-pilot's chair. The other two vampires waited at the door to assist Amber and Valerian into the plane.

The fact that they wore sunglasses didn't mean they didn't look at Amber. The vamp who helped her climb the stairs gave her the once-over, his gaze sliding suggestively over her body, resting longest on her neck. She tried to ignore him.

As soon as Amber and Valerian were seated and strapped in, the two vamps secured the door and took their seats, and the plane took off.

The plane had no windows, so Amber couldn't look back for any sign of Adrian. They rode in a sealed box that enabled the vampires to travel anywhere at any time—as long as a human flew the plane during daylight. She knew that vamps could easily entice a human pilot to fly for them, either as a blood slave or just because they paid an exorbitant fee.

The vampires had fetched the bikes and their gear, which were now stashed in the back of the plane. Valerian had already closed his eyes and drifted to near-sleep.

Amber sighed and ran her hands through her hair. After a moment, she felt the scrutiny of the vampire who'd helped her in, and turned her head. He watched her from across the aisle, his gaze behind his flat sunglasses making her feel slightly soiled. She frowned at him and turned away.

Now that the immediate worries about freezing to death or dying on the ice had been alleviated, her worry about Adrian returned. It returned full force, threatening to unknot the tension inside her into breathless sobs. Only the vampire's continued scrutiny kept her from falling apart.

The demon held Adrian. Her confidence that she'd be able to find him with her spells ebbed. He could be anywhere, and not necessarily still on this earth.

She had a thought and peeked into her jacket at the

inside pocket. Ferrin was coiled into a tight ball, asleep. She wondered if the snake would be able to sense Adrian or be drawn to him, no matter how far away he was. She'd rarely seen Ferrin more than a few feet from Adrian.

She thought of Adrian's body hard against hers as they'd made love in the tent. And before that, in his bed in his house, tangled in sheets. He'd rested his body half over hers, fingers gently touching her hair. His eyes had been soft, his mouth relaxed—a man content with loving.

The picture filled her mind, and she closed her eyes to keep the tears inside. She'd finally found a man who could make her forget everything that ever hurt her, everyone who'd tried to harm her in the past. A man with whom she could be happy. *And he has to be a five-thousand-year-old warrior with sibling issues.*

Her blissful vision shifted, like a beautiful melody suddenly discordant. In her dream, instead of Adrian stroking her hair, it was the vampire watching her. Slowly he lifted the sunglasses so she'd be forced to look directly into eyes that were startlingly green. She felt herself pulled into his gaze, wanting to lift her neck to him, wanting to feel his fangs biting into her skin as much as she wanted his erection penetrating her opening.

She snapped her eyes open and glared at the vampire across the aisle. His sunglasses were firmly in place, but he smirked, lips parted to reveal his fangs.

"Stop that," she glowered, then leaned against the bulkhead and focused on the wood paneling to shut him out. She heard him laughing softly, but at least he stayed out of her daydreams.

The journey took only a few hours, but the sky had become gray by the time they landed in a tiny airport, which was a landing strip with a wind sock and a shack. The vampires quickly offloaded the bikes and packs, glancing nervously at the horizon.

Now that they'd landed safely, Amber could feel some gratitude. The vampires had made a dangerous journey to rescue them, following orders they hadn't wanted to obey. As Valerian started packing up the bikes, Amber turned to the vampire who had so thoroughly scrutinized her.

"Thank you for helping," she said stiffly. "If you ever need a spell or something . . ." She trailed off, not wanting to promise too much to a vampire.

A cold smile spread across his face. "I could use a blow job." Amber gave him a look of disgust, and he laughed. "Hey, you asked, little blood donor."

"Piss off." She tried to make her tone menacing, but she was so exhausted that the words came out a croak.

He leaned down to put his face close to hers. "If it were up to me, you'd be back on that plane, your legs spread and my fangs in your neck. You'd be begging for it. *And* for my friends to take you while I watched."

The disgusting image he put into her head made her furious. The fact that she was too weak and tired and worried to do anything about it made her angrier still. She unzipped her parka.

He grinned. "Ready for it, are you?"

Amber pulled open the jacket's flap. Ferrin was already rising from her pocket, his neck flaring into a hood.

"I want you to meet a friend of mine," she said clearly. "This is Ferrin, a cobra. His venom is so strong that one bite will make you too sick to feed for months. Wonder what that would feel like?"

To her intense satisfaction, the vampire recoiled. He snarled swear words, grating out the vilest things he could call a woman, before he turned on his heel and stomped away.

Amber let out her breath, her muscles unclenching. He could shout whatever abuse he wanted, as long as he got on that plane and flew far away. Ferrin, after a satisfied look, retreated to her pocket.

The first rays of sun streamed over the horizon as the vampires shut themselves into their windowless airplane. The pilot taxied away and took off, leaving Amber and Valerian alone in the strong morning wind.

# CHAPTER FIFTEEN

Air whooshed from Adrian's lungs, and he found himself flat on his back in snow-covered woods, alone. He looked around in surprise before hoisting himself to his feet.

The last thing he remembered was grabbing the demon and letting it drag him through black denseness. But the demon was gone, its taint of death magic nowhere near this place. The demon had dropped Adrian off here, but where was he, and why?

It was slightly warmer, wherever he was. Adrian divested himself of his ultra-cold-weather gear, most of which was dripping wet from the watery prison. The air smelled fresh, the woods clean and teeming with wildlife. He had no idea where he was, possibly in Canada or the northern United States.

He zipped up his parka, regretting the loss of his compass and global positioning device, which were back on the ice floe, likely hundreds of miles away. Amber had more need of it—she was mortal and would die quickly if Valerian didn't get her to shelter. Adrian would not die in the technical sense, although he could fall through snow pack and get trapped for millennia like the Ice Man. He'd wake up when someone dug him out, snarling and bored out of his mind, scaring the crap out of the anthropologists who found him.

Adrian started walking. The snowdrifts flowed to his knees, powdery snow leaking through the tops of his boots. There was no path, only faint openings here and there amid the dense trees, most filled with scrub and fallen branches. He kicked brush aside in annoyance as he made his slow way through the woods. He could have used magic to blast himself a path, but he thought it wise to lie low, magic-wise, at the moment.

He hoped to Isis that Valerian had gotten Amber to safety and the demon hadn't dumped Adrian in the woods in order to pursue her. Valerian was strong as a dragon and even as a human, but he had his limitations, and he was mortal. The magic protection of Adrian's house in Los Angeles would last awhile even without Adrian there to renew it, but it was a long journey between these snow-covered woods and the city heat of Los Angeles.

Adrian stopped to catch his breath, letting the silence of the woods fill him.

In that silence, he craved Amber. He wanted her with every breath he took. He wanted her laughter and the outraged look she got when he repeated to anyone within hearing that she belonged to him. His blood hurt with longing, his body wanted to hold hers tight against him, to feel the hard nubs of her nipples against his chest and her legs parting to welcome him inside.

Everything about her was beautiful—her softness, her sweet scent, the way her brow puckered as she felt him moving inside her. The little moan she gave just before she came, the languid look in her eyes as they rested together. He should never have made love to her, but when he'd started the flirtation with her in Seattle, he'd thought it would end like his other sexual encounters—enjoyment, good-byes, no regrets.

He started walking, frowning at the trees that blocked his way. She was mortal and he was not, and last he checked, these things didn't work out. He'd have to lose her, and the thought of that cut deep. She had her mortal life to lead and he had his Immortal destiny and all that bullshit he'd been fed as a child.

For now, Adrian needed to focus on the problem of returning to Los Angeles and finding not only Amber, but Ferrin. He'd seen the snake take refuge in Amber's coat as Adrian had instructed him, knowing Ferrin would not survive the cold or the battle with the demon. He'd need Ferrin back soon; he was weaker without his weapon.

He walked for a long time, going over scenarios for retrieving Ferrin that didn't involve taking Amber to bed, and wishing he had better transportation than his own feet. It might not be as cold as on the ice floe out here, but it was still damn cold, and wet too. This boy from the Nile hated cold.

By the time he finally stumbled into a clearing, it was dawn. He stood shakily catching his breath. He needed time to sit quietly and heal; *quietly* was the operative word. No demons, no fights, no nightmares.

The vampire that stepped out from the other side of the clearing in a black leather coat, his eyes protected by sunglasses, probably wasn't here to help him find healing and peace. Faint dawn light edged into the clearing, but the vampire seemed unbothered by it.

Adrian slowly crossed the clearing to him. The vampire could have found him in a number of ways—he was one of the most powerful vamps alive—but the most obvious way made Adrian tighten with anger.

"The sun is rising," he pointed out as the two met in the middle.

"I'm an Old One," Septimus replied evenly. "I can take a little more sunlight than a younger vampire. Why didn't you run when you saw me?"

"I figured there was no point." His eyes narrowed. "Amber had better be safe, or I'll pull your head off."

Septimus made a slight nod. "She is safe. I have no quarrel with her or the dragon. They are resting in that run-down motel, and my vampires will make sure nothing evil comes near them."

"Nothing evil besides your vamps, you mean."

Septimus gave him a smooth smile. As usual, he was well dressed, his leather coat made by an expensive designer, his neatly bound hair tucked inside his collar. "Amber and Valerian won't be touched," he promised. "They are off limits."

"Whereas I am not," Adrian said. "You made a bargain with the demon, didn't you? You had him drop me here, so you could meet me with whatever nefarious plan is floating in your vampire brain to get rid of me."

Septimus inclined his head. "I didn't have a choice. Much as I hated to break a promise to you, he has the power to take me out with the flick of a finger. My club wall was nothing." He removed his sunglasses and let his dark gaze slide to Adrian's neck. "I always wondered what the blood of an Immortal would taste like."

"I don't intend to give you the chance to sample it."

"You will, for Amber's sake. She's safe now, but the

dragon is too tired to protect her. It would be easy to send my vampires in. My orders are to bring you to him—preferably not in a healthy state."

"If the demon wanted me, healthy or unhealthy, he didn't need to drop me here. He had me trapped and was doing fine beating me to a pulp on his own."

"I wasn't talking about the demon," Septimus said.

Adrian stilled. "Then who is the *he* who wants me?"

"I think you know."

They regarded each other in silence. Adrian could stare straight into a vampire's eyes and not be entranced; their glamour had no effect on him. He read in Septimus an arrogance that was not flamboyant, but a quiet knowledge that very few were stronger than he. Adrian also sensed wariness in him, regret that he'd broken the truce he and Adrian had made, and sorrow for Adrian.

"I'm touched you care," Adrian said dryly.

Septimus raised his leather-clad shoulders in a smooth shrug. "I've come to count you as a friend, or at least an enemy I can trust. You'll heal, Adrian. I wish I could tell you it wouldn't hurt, but I promised I'd make it hurt."

Adrian's anger stirred magic deep inside him, magic that could wipe Septimus and every tree and rock from this mountainside.

"Don't do that," Septimus said quickly. "Amber will suffer if you use any magic or fight us, I guarantee it. Besides, I think you truly wish to see your brother again."

Adrian allowed his magic to fade, but his anger remained strong. "Take me to him, then."

Septimus gave a signal. From out of the woods behind him came a score of demons, men in black leather that could make the most hardened motorcycle gang break apart and flee. The demons had no fear of sunlight, so they easily surrounded Adrian and dragged him under deep shadows where Septimus's vampires waited.

The overhead canopy was so thick that barely any sunlight leaked through. Demons and vampires rarely mingled, but this morning they laughed in common cause as they proceeded to beat Adrian senseless, using clubs and knives and fists. A demon thrust a thick sword through Adrian's back, and bright blood poured out his mouth.

Once they had him subdued, the vampires carried Adrian to a Hummer-like vehicle whose windows had been replaced with metal sheets. One of the demons took the wheel while the vampires and demons hoisted Adrian into the back, which was devoid of seats, and piled in after him. They beat him and stabbed him again as the driver put the truck into gear, just in case his rapidly healing body could regain strength. Then they laid him down flat, pinning his arms and legs with thick chains.

Through a haze of pain, Adrian watched Septimus take off his coat and fastidiously lay it aside. The man wore black leather gloves, beautifully supple as they raked through Adrian's hair. Septimus gently tilted Adrian's head to one side, exposing his neck, and traced his jugular with a leather-clad fingertip.

Septimus leaned down and licked Adrian's neck. Then Adrian felt the sharp bite of his fangs, penetrating deep. Septimus began suckling, slowly at first, then with true vampire thirst as though he'd starved himself to better enjoy this pleasure. His lips were hot, his tongue sliding on Adrian's throat like a lover's.

Adrian by this time was too weak to fight him, or even to scream.

\* \* \*

"A dragon wid a cold," Valerian snuffled. He buried his nose in a pile of tissues and made a noise like a spouting whale. "How stupid is dat?"

Amber ignored him. She'd brought Ferrin out of her pocket, and now the snake lay in a loose coil, looking depressed. Filmy white lids covered his eyes, and he didn't move.

"Where is he?" she asked the snake. "Find Adrian, Ferrin. *Please.*"

"He's nod Lassie," Valerian said, wiping his eyes. "He doedn't fetch."

"I know. But I hoped he'd have some clue."

"I hope he cad survive widout Adrian," Valerian added. "He shares Adrian's bagic." He sniffled.

Amber looked at him. Valerian's nose was red, his overly blue eyes luminous and wet. "What happens if you turn into a dragon when you have a cold?" she asked curiously.

He shook his head. "It's nod preddy."

Amber turned away and rummaged through her bag of magic accoutrements again. She had enough charged crystals for a location spell, once she got her energy back enough to perform it, but she wasn't hopeful. Detective Simon, who'd arrived by helicopter a few hours after she and Valerian had reached Alaska, had promised that he had an alert out for Adrian, but he didn't seem sanguine about it.

Simon had gone out to talk to the local police and the park rangers to see what information they had, if any. Before leaving, he'd ordered a pizza and made Amber eat half of it, even though she had to choke it down.

Now Amber sat listlessly in the small motel room, watching Valerian and Ferrin, hating to wait for news.

When someone knocked on the door, she all but tore across the room to answer it. Valerian half got out of bed, his hand on a long knife he kept by his bedside, but Amber threw open the door without waiting. She hadn't felt any evil taint of death magic from outside, and it was broad daylight, too bright for vampires.

The woman who stood on the doorstep was supernatural, but werewolf, not vampire. Amber grabbed her and hauled her into the room before throwing her arms around her. "What are you doing here?"

Sabina returned Amber's hug, then looked at Valerian, who'd collapsed into the bed and pulled the covers over his broad chest.

"What's wrong with you?" she demanded.

"I'b sick. Frob rescuing Amber." Valerian seized a handful of tissues from the dwindling box beside the bed. "Close de door. Dere's a draft."

Amber slammed the door and locked it. She told Valerian, "You didn't have to risk freezing to fly to me yourself. Septimus sent the plane."

"Dno way I'd led you on a plane full of bamps alone. Adrian wud kill mbe."

"Well, now there's a problem with Septimus." Sabina plopped herself on Amber's bed, her mane of blond hair haloing her face. "He's vanished, and Kelly's very upset. She thinks he's betrayed Adrian to the demon."

Amber's heart missed a beat. "Why does she think that?"

"She came over with her cook, both of them very worried. She had sex with him—Septimus, not the cook—and she overheard a phone call when Septimus thought she was asleep. Manny found her this morning wandering around her house wondering what to do, and made her come over to Adrian's and tell me what was going on. Detective Simon had already headed out to come up here and start looking for you."

Amber sat down, feeling numb. "Septimus sent a plane to rescue us, though he didn't come himself. Kelly must have heard him making those arrangements."

Sabina nodded. "She did. When he took *that* phone call, she was awake and sitting next to him. But a few hours later, she heard Septimus in her living room on the phone again, arguing with someone like he was afraid, which surprised her, because who is big and bad enough to scare someone like Septimus? Then she heard him arranging for someone to get him to, she thinks, Montana. She stayed still, pretending to be asleep, terrified what he'd do if he knew she'd heard. He left her house without coming back into the bedroom, and she hasn't seen him since."

"Bastard," Valerian said from behind his tissues. "I nebber liked himb."

Amber balled her fists. "Why didn't Kelly come to you right away? Why did Manny have to drag her over the next morning?"

Sabina gave her a grave look. "I think Septimus made her his blood slave. She let him bite her anyway."

"Whad wad she thinkig?" Valerian asked. "She already escabed one bampire, and only wid Adrian's helb."

"He's pretty sexy, for a vampire," Sabina pointed out.

Valerian snorted. "Oh, blease. He's oberdressed and obercombensanting for a small benis."

"Better than a dragon with a runny nose," Sabina shot back.

Valerian started to retort, then grimaced and bellowed out a sneeze that shook the tiny room.

Amber shut them out and tried to think. If Septimus had betrayed them, they had one more powerful creature out there to contend with. But again, Septimus could be deep in many plots of his own, and whatever he was doing in Montana might have nothing to do with Adrian.

There was another bad possibility: If Septimus had made Kelly his blood slave, she might be feeding them false information. Amber rubbed her throbbing temples. She knew she could walk away from all this, return to Seattle, and try to go on with her life. Go back to planning the Beltane festivities, giving Tarot readings, cleansing houses, teaching beginning magic.

The demon had pulled her into all this by murdering Susan, and here she sat in a run-down hotel with a feverish dragon and a worried werewolf, grieving not only for the loss of her sister but the possible loss of a man with whom she had fallen in love.

Life used to be so simple.

Another complication walked up and tapped on the door. Sabina dashed over to answer it, revealing Detective Simon. He glanced at Sabina in faint surprise, then came inside and closed the door. Amber started to rise, then sank down in sudden lethargy when she saw the grim look on the detective's face.

"What is it?"

Simon scraped the chair away from the desk and sat, balancing himself on the rickety legs. Valerian quieted, wiping his nose in silence, and Sabina perched on the end of his bed.

"I heard a report from some park rangers and state police in the Montana Rockies," Simon began. "A ranger on patrol early this morning found signs of a disturbance in a clearing about a half-mile off a logging road. Someone had driven a four-wheel drive out there, a big one, like a Hum-V."

Simon paused, placing his hands on his knees. He'd looked much like this when he'd first come to tell Amber about Susan's death, sympathetic but no-nonsense, hating that he had to relate things that would hurt her.

"A lot of brush had been disturbed," he went on. "There were definite tracks in the snow—one of a man who'd walked alone across the clearing, and about a dozen tracks of other men who surrounded him. There'd been a fight, a bad one. The whole clearing was bloody with it—large pools of blood." Simon grew quieter. "I'm afraid no one could lose that much blood and survive."

Valerian spoke belligerently. "How do you know it has anyding to do wid Adrian? Besides, he'd Imbordal."

"Because in the woods near the clearing, the rangers found goggles and a mask and other severe-cold-weather gear, more than would be needed to walk around those mountains in late spring. It was gear from an Arctic expedition, and the rental tags were from a store in this town."

Amber sat still, a sour taste beginning in her stomach and working its way up to her throat. Ferrin slithered to Amber and draped himself dejectedly across her knee.

Simon went on. "I'm sorry, Amber. It looks like someone ambushed him, hurt him bad, then dragged him away."

"Adrian cabn't die," Valerian objected.

"I saw the photographs they took of the scene. If he's alive, it's only barely." Simon looked at Amber again, his dark eyes sad. "I'm sorry."

Amber shook her head, some part of her knowing she should reassure Detective Simon that she didn't blame him. But grief clenched her along with gut-twisting worry, and she could not find the words.

"You said this was in the Montana Rockies," Sabina said, looking significantly at Amber.

"What—" Simon began.

"Septimus," Sabina continued, a wolflike glower on her face. "He had something going on in Montana, and I'll give you three guesses what that something was. It would be just like a vampire to get something as flashy as a Hummer for his dirty work."

"Adrian called Septimus an Old One," Simon said. "That sounds bad."

"It means he's ancient and very powerful," Amber said glumly. "Strong enough to take on Adrian if he had help."

"And Sebtimus had a grudge," Valerian put in. "Yeards of being under Adrian's tumb." He sniffled into his wad of tissues. "I bet Sebtimus was habby to get out of dat."

Amber looked at him. "Do you know where Septimus could have taken him?"

Valerian shook his head. "I hab dno idea. Hid club or one of hid hideouts if he'ds on his own, who knowds where if he'ds working for de demon."

"If Kelly's his blood slave, she might be able to find out," Amber mused.

"If Kelly's hid blood slabe, she won'dt tell us jack."

Sabina offered, "She might not be able to resist a really pissed-off werewolf. Or a dragon." She gave Valerian a severe look. "That is, as long as he doesn't have Kleenex stuck to his nose."

Valerian suddenly scrubbed his nose with tissues, glaring at her over them.

"We can start in Los Angeles," Amber said, thoughts swirling in her brain. "I have spells, and I can make Kelly tell us what she knows, which might not be very much. I have the feeling Septimus is smart enough not to spill all his secrets to his lovers."

"He doedn't bite and tell, you bean," Valerian put in.

"Probably not, but I'll get what I can from her." Amber turned to Simon. "Do you have any police contacts in Los Angeles? Maybe if we can present evidence that Septimus kidnapped Adrian, they can raid his club and see if he's there, and maybe raid Septimus's other hideouts. And if the police won't go in, I will."

"With me right behind you," Sabina said.

"Bee too," Valerian snuffled. "Even wid a cold I'll scare the piss out of dem. Dragons sndeeze fire."

Amber's pulse quickened. Valerian could tear down the club chunk by chunk and let the daylight in. She and Sabina could interrogate vampires hiding from the sun—the two of them had enough power to take down one vamp at a time. Plus she had Ferrin, whose eyes were glittering now as he likely imagined chomping any vampire who got between him and Adrian.

Detective Simon got abruptly to his feet. "Amber, can I talk to you? Outside?"

"Id's cold out dere," Valerian mentioned.

"We'll sit in the car. Amber?"

His face was stern, even angry. He wanted to lecture her. She was about to refuse, then got a good look in his eyes. He needed to talk to her, needed to express his fears, and she didn't have the heart to turn away.

Nodding, she gently laid Ferrin on the bed and rose to follow Simon outside.

# CHAPTER SIXTEEN

Detective Simon said nothing until he'd ushered Amber into his rental car, climbed in himself, turned the ignition on, and started the heat running. He firmly gripped the wheel as he studied the dark board walls of the motel in front of them, and she sat quietly, waiting for him to begin.

"Amber," he said at last. "I don't want you going back to Los Angeles. I want you to go home to Seattle."

His cheekbones were stained red, and his wide chest rose and fell with his breathing. He expected her to argue.

"I can't desert Adrian," she said softly.

"I know," he answered. "And you wouldn't be deserting him. I have contacts in Los Angeles, and I'll look into the Septimus angle. I will do it for you." He looked at her directly. "But I want you out of it. I want you home—safe."

She hugged her arms over her chest. "What makes you think home is safe for me?"

"Because from everything you and Valerian have told me, it was Adrian the demon wanted all along, not you.

You were the means to an end. If the demon has Adrian, he'll leave you alone. I've worked on demon cases before, and I know demons are coldly logical. Vampires act on lust and emotion, but demons can be very calculating."

"Everyday demons are logical," Amber said. "This one's different."

"I know, he's an Old One, as Adrian calls him. But if you're right about his modus so far, then he *is* being coldly logical. Ruthlessly so. The demon's got Adrian; he's done with you. That's why I want you out of it. I want him to *stay* done with you."

She shook her head. "I can't sit at home wringing my hands when I could be helping search for him."

"Amber." Simon raised his voice just high enough to cut over her words—a firm tone that he likely used to subdue his detainees. "I know you care for him. I wish you didn't, but I can't change that, so I'll find him for you. But please, for me, go home and lock your doors. Stay safe—please."

Amber let out a slow breath. "I wish I didn't love him," she said. "But I do."

"And the last person you want comfort from is me. I understand."

She gave him a surprised look. "I don't blame you for my problems. You just happened to be the one assigned to Susan's case, and you've been very nice to me. Much nicer than you needed to be. You really cared about how it affected me—I wasn't merely the victim's sister."

"I was just doing my job," he said.

"No, you weren't."

He shot her a sideways glance, then sighed. "No, I wasn't. But how I feel about you is my problem. I'll deal with it."

She swallowed. "I'm sorry—"

He held up his hand. "Please don't launch into the 'we can be friends' speech. I'll find Adrian for you, and then I'll get out of your life. I'm forty-two, I'm experienced in how to move on."

"I'm still sorry."

He shrugged his broad shoulders. "You can't always pick and choose who you fall in love with. I mean, look at your choices—on the one hand, you have a loner cop who's been kicked around a little too much, and on the other a bad-ass warrior with a gleaming sword. I can see how this is difficult for you."

Amber laughed, feeling hollow. "Don't sell yourself short."

"And please don't give me the 'there's someone out there for you' speech or 'I bet you'll have women pounding down your doors.' I'm divorced, I spend way too much time at work, and my social life sucks. But it's my own fault, and I'll get by. Don't feel sorry for me. But do me a favor. Be busy not being sorry for me in your old house in Seattle with all that witch magic around it."

"Susan compromised the wards, and the demon broke through," Amber told him. "I'll have to spend a lot of time cleansing the house again."

"Good, it will give you something to do while I'm investigating in L.A." He gave her a direct look, no longer embarrassed.

Amber gathered her arguments. "I'll make a deal with you. You let me go back to Los Angeles, and I'll wait in Adrian's nice safe house while you and your cop friends raid the club. There's no way I can not know what's going on. At least at Adrian's house I can listen to the police scanner and know right away whether you found him or not."

Simon's eyes were deep blue, like a lake, and his square face was hard and handsome. He *could* have women beating down his door if he'd let himself see that.

"All right," he said finally, his words grudging. "But you'd better promise me you'll stay in that house and not stir a step. I don't want you doing the stupid heroine thing and rushing in to mess up a perfectly good stake-out." He paused while she stared back at him coolly. "But I'll take that cobra with me, if you'll tell him not to bite me. I'm betting he'll be useful."

Adrian opened his eyes as the pain eased off. Sweat stung his eyes, and a lock of blood-soaked hair had matted to his right eyelid. He tried to brush it away, then realized his hands were chained above his naked body, held in place by industrial-strength chains, thick enough to keep even an Immortal tethered.

When he turned his head against the wall, he could see that the wallpaper he rested against was a cheerful pattern; apparently, the inhabitants of this house had decorated even the remote corners in pretty colors. Adrian's blood now covered the charming blues and yellows with streaks of scarlet.

His neck was sore from where Septimus had bitten him, his body weak from loss of blood. The vampire had nearly drained him before sitting back, eyes heavy with satiation, and let his lackeys start beating Adrian again.

Septimus had bailed as soon as he'd delivered Adrian to the house and the vampires had hustled him up the stairs. Adrian had spent the journey hooded by a foul-smelling cloth bag, but he'd known where he was even before they drew it off him. He'd passed out from loss of blood and lack of air, and now the sun was high, two long windows letting in the cheerful sunshine.

He heard heavy footsteps on the stairs, and the demon entered the room and stopped in front of him, eyeing Adrian with his sensual black eyes. Adrian matched him in height, but the demon was cleanly dressed while Adrian was covered in blood and black bruises.

"Submit to me," the demon said. He slowly drew his tongue across his lips, making them wet and red.

"What for?"

The demon smiled. "I hoped you would resist."

He walked to a table and took up a leather whip. "Do you want to change your mind?" he purred.

Adrian told him what to do with himself. The demon took a step back, breaking into a smile, then he began to whip every inch of Adrian's skin, reopening wounds that had begun to heal.

Adrian knew he could free himself at any time with his magic—at least, once he'd rested and healed a little. But he stilled his power, knowing two things: that Septimus held a sword over Amber's head in the form of his vampire lackeys, and that Septimus had hinted that Adrian was on his way to see Tain. Let the damn demon carve him up, and when Adrian saw Tain, he'd free himself and make the demon pay.

When the demon finished with the whip, he dropped it and returned to the table for a fireplace poker. Adrian clenched his jaw throughout the next torture session, getting through the pain by thinking of creative ways to take his vengeance.

At last the demon tossed aside the poker, his gloved hands covered in blood, smiling in afterglow.

Adrian dragged in a breath. "You make a damn boring dom," he grated out.

The demon regarded him thoughtfully. "I see."

He walked back to the table and opened a box, from

which he withdrew a broad-bladed sword. He came back to Adrian and held the point between Adrian's pectorals, nicking the skin.

"Know this, Immortal," he said softly. "If you fight back, what I do to you in this room will be done to your beautiful witch, only much harder. And she'll die. She's not immortal, like you."

Adrian growled. "If you hurt Amber, I'll feel free to let myself go. And then you'll understand the full meaning of the word *retribution.*"

The demon didn't appear to hear, or to care. "I always wondered what would happen if I stabbed an Immortal through the heart. Would he finally die? Would he weaken so much that his goddess would take pity on him and remove the life from his body?"

"You want me to tell you?" Adrian rasped. "Come a little closer. I'll tell you everything you want to know."

The demon's dark-as-sin eyes gleamed, and he bent close to Adrian, putting his lips near his.

Adrian spat blood into his face.

The demon stood up without changing expression. He groped for a handkerchief in his coat to wipe off the blood and spittle before tucking it away again. Then he snarled and slammed the sword straight through Adrian's heart.

Adrian clenched his jaw to keep from screaming. Hoarse, choking sounds came from his throat, but he'd not give the demon the satisfaction of breaking down. He'd stand here and look the demon in the eye and spit on him again.

The demon smiled and pulled the sword out, very slowly. "Does it hurt?"

"Fuck you," Adrian gasped.

"I'll think about it. Maybe I'll do it with this." He

plunged the sword into Adrian's chest again. Adrian's head rocked back against the wall, and the room blurred to black.

When things swam back into focus again, Adrian heard footsteps on the stairs, climbing to the room at the top. A lackey coming to help the demon with his torture session? Adrian's vision was blurred, blood running into his eyes and drying on his face. The demon was across the room again, the sword held loosely.

The footsteps came closer now. No, not a lackey. Adrian knew the step, he'd never forgotten it. Joy flooded through him, overshadowing every bit of pain the demon had doled out.

"Tain," he breathed.

His brother walked into the room. He was as tall, as upright and proud as Adrian remembered him. He'd pulled his thick and unruly red hair into a tail, but wisps straggled from the queue to touch the pentacle tattoo on his cheekbone—Tain had never been able to tame his hair, something women had found irresistible. He wore a casual suit of black cashmere and a plain white shirt with no tie, looking comfortable and relaxed as he ever did, no matter what the fashion of the time.

Adrian started to laugh. Tears leaked from the corners of his eyes to mix with blood and sweat.

"Tain, my brother," he called out, just as he had years ago when they'd trained and fought together. "Cut off this demon's head for me, and we'll go out for pizza. Do you like pizza? I don't even know." Tears slid over his lips. "I know a place in L.A. where they've made pizza an art form. And I met a lady—she's so beautiful, she'll break your heart."

Tain picked up the whip the demon had discarded and studied it as he approached Adrian. The demon stood by, blood-streaked sword held to his side. Adrian knew something was terribly, terribly wrong, but he couldn't stop the wave of happiness and relief that flooded him now that he'd found Tain.

Tain's blue eyes focused on Adrian for a long moment, taking in Adrian's exhausted face and body that the demon had sliced to the bone. His gaze slid up to the heavy-duty manacles and chains that bound Adrian to the wall; then he slowly raised one hand and touched Adrian's jaw.

"You're really here," he said.

"In the flesh," Adrian babbled. "This isn't how I pictured our reunion, but I guess it's better than nothing."

Tain tilted his head to one side, fingers sliding from Adrian's face. "How did you picture it?"

"I don't know. Champagne maybe, or beer. Beautiful women, one for each of us. A celebration no one would ever forget."

Tain shook his head sadly. "No, Adrian. I know you too well. I know what you thought. You pictured yourself rescuing me. I'd be the one in chains and imprisoned, and you'd set me free. I'd fall weeping at your feet, so grateful that you'd saved me. All would rejoice because Adrian had found his brother at last."

Adrian laughed. "Does it matter? I rescue you, you rescue me, I don't care. What matters is, we found each other."

Tain drew back and slapped Adrian across the face with the whip. Adrian's magic stirred inside him, a fiery hot burst ready to be flung at the demon. The demon had to be doing this, playing with Tain's mind, causing the madness that flickered in Tain's eyes.

Tain put his hand around Adrian's throat. "Stop."

Adrian let the magic dissipate. "Let me kill him," he

said in a low voice. "I'll kill him and we'll walk out of here together."

"No."

The demon moved to Tain's side. "I have the advantage of you, Immortal," he said to Adrian.

He morphed seamlessly into the sultry woman Adrian had seen at Septimus's club and in his dream, her long black hair silky, her eyes wide and sensuous. She wore a black satin dress that hugged every curve, her tight nipples against it revealing that she wore nothing beneath.

Tain's grip on Adrian loosened as the woman rose on tiptoe to kiss Tain's lips. Tain drew her up into the kiss, lovingly tracing her mouth with his tongue.

"Tain, she's a demon," Adrian said, fighting revulsion. "An Old One. We kill death-magic beings, remember? Our raison d'etre?"

Tain broke the kiss and looked at Adrian in sorrow. "You will understand, in time."

"I want to understand now."

Tain pressed a fingertip to Adrian's lips. "Not yet, my brother. Not yet."

Adrian bit back a harsh reply as he fought to assess the situation. Tain was mad, and somehow the demon had done this to him. Tain had been imprisoned in that ice cave, the whole damn place had been imprinted with his aura. Why he was free now, and why he hadn't simply fought off the demon or tried to find his brothers for help, Adrian had no idea.

"When, then?" he asked, keeping his voice steady.

"When your pretty lady is here," Tain said. "When she comes to rescue you, then I will tell you everything. I promise."

Chill filled Adrian colder than all the ice floes of the Arctic. "She won't come."

"She will." Tain caressed the demon's beautiful female face. "She will come to you, and when she does, we will slowly torture her to death in front of you. Once she is dead, you will understand." He transferred his intense blue gaze to Adrian. "You will understand my wish to die. Because then you will share it."

*Wish to die? What the hell?*

Adrian shoved aside the horrifying vision of the demon cutting through Amber's flesh and tried to keep his tone reasonable. "We can't die, Tain. We're Immortal warriors. We kick ass through the ages until the Goddess decides we've done enough. Or until the world ends." He remembered the sketches in Susan's notebooks and the words *The end of the world as we know it.* "Ending the world is fine in comic books and movies, but it can't be done. If he—she—told you it can, he's lying."

Tain gave him a patient look. "My wise older brother. Adrian, what would happen if death magic overcame life magic? It's an event we were created to stop." He leaned close and gave Adrian a soft, chilling laugh. "Our raison d'etre, as you say. What happens?"

"Death magic overruns the world. But it won't last. Death magic needs life magic to exist. Life and death must remain in balance. *That's* why we're here. To keep crazy death-magic beings from tipping the balance."

Tain nodded slowly. "And if death magic can't exist, then it too drains away. Then what happens if there is no life magic *and* no death magic?" He leaned toward Adrian, his smile sad. "Everything is gone. And with it, the Immortals. No longer needed." Tain's breath smelled of almonds and spice. "And then we'll be truly free."

"It can't happen that way," Adrian said quickly, although he had no idea whether it could or not. "Why would this demon want to help you drain the world of magic? He'd die too."

"I know he will. He's an Old One, as you say. He is as tired of life as I am."

"Bullshit."

Tain's face darkened. "I'm disappointed in you, brother. I told myself you'd understand."

"I understand this demon has fed you a line, and you've swallowed it whole. Kill the bastard, Tain. Free yourself."

The demon stroked Tain's arm. "Yes, Tain. Do what you want to do. Do what you *truly* wish to do."

Tain gazed down at her for a moment, then smiled viciously, his expression a mirror image of the demon's. Taking a few steps back, he uncoiled the leather whip and beat Adrian with fierce concentration until Adrian's blood rivered from his body to pool on the floor.

Kelly awakened from her nap late in the Los Angeles afternoon knowing he was in her bedroom. She felt his presence in the shadows, though she couldn't yet see him. She lay still, feigning sleep, hoping he couldn't hear her rapidly pounding heart.

She would start work on a new movie next week. She looked forward to the long days at the studio, the early calls, the bustle of cameramen and crew on the lots and the sound stages. She loved the movie life. She'd be surrounded by people, friends she knew and liked, returning to her house only to snatch a few hours sleep, if that. No time for vampires.

She knew Septimus would find her there anyway. He would come to watch her, perhaps to take her out to dinner after the shoot, escort her home, spend the night. The powerful vampire would easily get himself admitted to the lot, and Kelly wouldn't stop it. She had a weakness for vampires, a lethal fascination for them that would have gotten her killed if it hadn't been for Adrian.

She heard a whisper of fabric, a coat coming off; then the bed listed as he lay down behind her. Sensual fingers stroked her hip and the curve of her waist—he knew she was awake.

His hand grazed the swell of her breast and moved to her throat, fingers splaying across her neck and moving her hair. His hot breath touched her skin, and he licked the small wound he'd made on her neck last night.

"You told them what you heard," he said, voice silken soft. "Didn't you, Kelly?"

# CHAPTER SEVENTEEN

Kelly swallowed, but she couldn't lie to him. Septimus would punish her for that betrayal, and her skin prickled in sudden excitement.

She hated wanting it, but she couldn't help herself. Her previous relationship with a vampire had terrified her as much as it elated her, but in the end the terror had won out, and she'd walked. She had the feeling that walking away from Septimus would be much, much harder, if she could make such a choice at all.

He licked her throat and drew his tongue to the shell of her ear, his mouth hot. "It doesn't matter. I plan to tell them all about it anyway. What I did, where they can find him."

Kelly rolled over. The last rays of sun danced on the ceiling above them, but the bed was in deep shadow and Septimus was safe. His eyes, deep and compelling blue, held her. She was no longer afraid to look at him directly, and knew that meant he'd made her his slave.

"You know Valerian will try to kill you," she said, "and so will Amber."

"No, they won't." His voice was low, soothing, wrapping her mind and calming her against her will. "All think Adrian is my enemy, but I have great admiration for him. He has helped me gain more power than I ever would have myself. Death-magic beings can be so untidy. He has an affinity for neatness."

"But you gave him up to the demon."

"I had no choice. The demon is more powerful than any being I've ever encountered. If anyone can survive him, it's Adrian. Adrian has friends. The demon is alone."

"I don't understand. First you betray Adrian, and now you'll help him?"

He touched her face, and she closed her eyes as desire flared.

"The demon is so strong that he has difficulty believing other creatures are anything but weak and crawling. He assumed that fulfilling this obligation would break me, or that the dragon would kill me. And so the demon is no longer paying attention to me."

Kelly's entire body craved his touch, but she sat up and made herself stave off her need. "Then we should call Amber. They're on their way back, and if they find you waiting, I'm betting they'll stake you before you can speak."

Kelly rolled away toward the phone, but he pinned her to the bed before she could reach it. "They will not. I know where Adrian is. They'll listen to me long enough for that information, at least."

His weight held her down, his taut body all kinds of good through his clothes. Her mind fogged, and she reached for the languid relaxation that went with it. She eagerly shifted her thighs open, wanting his swelling hardness pressed against her.

He whispered, his blue eyes feral, "Today I drank the blood of an Immortal. It has made me stronger than I have ever been. I have the power to do anything I want."

"Then why are you here?" She traced the contours of his mouth. "Why aren't you out taking over Los Angeles?"

"Because I wanted to be with you."

Her heart leapt. *If only.* But vampires were skilled seducers; he'd tell her exactly what she wanted to hear.

"I wanted to share my power with you, Kelly. I've been watching you a long time. It's not only been Adrian keeping you safe the last few years."

"You've been watching me?" she asked, startled.

The thought should terrify her. She knew the addictive power of vampires and the danger of falling under their spell. But the thought of Septimus standing in the shadows while she was unaware, his blue gaze hungry on her body, made her want to squirm with excitement. He eased his hand into her blouse, tracing the lace of her bra.

"For some time now, I've been pretending you were mine," he said.

"Why?"

He smiled—a sinful smile that made his eyes glow blue. "Why do you think?" He feathered kisses across her jaw and down to her neck. "Why do you think I waited until you were ready to accept me? Until you healed from what that oaf of a vampire did to you? It felt so good to kill him."

"I don't know."

He laughed softly; then came the tiny prick of teeth in her skin. "I fell in love with you, Kelly O'Byrne. My wild Irish rose."

Her body arched as his mouth closed over her neck, sucking her blood into him. She wrapped her long legs around him, lifting her pelvis to rub herself on his hardened cock while he drank of her.

"But I can't love you back," she murmured sadly. "I don't love vampires; I have an addiction to them."

He lifted his head, gently brushing his finger over the wound to close it. She felt warm and slightly dizzy, hungry for sex.

"You don't. You walked away before without help."

"Because I'm strong-willed and arrogant. You have to be, to survive in Hollywood."

He traced her cheek. "You are strong, as powerful in your own way as I am. You and I will take the world by storm."

"You're an evil, blood-sucking, death-magic fiend," she argued. Then she laughed. "Which puts you several steps above a few producers I've worked with."

"I'm a patient man," Septimus said. His eyes swept briefly closed, dark lashes obscuring the blue. "I am an Old One; I survived by learning patience. I will move as slowly as you like."

She grasped his shoulders. "I don't want you to be slow. I want you to make love to me—fast and hard—right now."

"I feel that. But we'll be slow anyway."

He rolled away from her but only to strip her, maddeningly taking his time. Stockings first, then her blouse, then skirt, then her bra. Before he completed the task, he rose and divested himself of his own clothes, his tall, honed, gorgeous body coming gradually into view. Once he was naked, his shaft standing out erect and long, he skimmed her panties from her hips and joined her again on the bed.

Kelly lifted her body to his as he enclosed her in his arms. "Go ahead, then," she begged. "Make me love you."

Septimus growled a laugh. He pressed her thighs apart and slid himself firmly inside her, filling her empty spaces. She closed her legs around him, and his eyes softened as they began to move together. When he sank his fangs into her neck again, she screamed, coming fast and hard, but still he took his time, showing her for the next several hours just how patient he could be.

Adrian woke from his stupor after the sun was well down and darkness filled the room. The demon wasn't there, and neither was Tain.

Adrian concentrated his magic on healing his body from all the harms he'd suffered in the last twenty-four hours, but he was still weak. His thoughts moved like languid moths, flitting from one idea to the next, images confusing themselves in his pain. The only clarity he could muster was the determination to keep Amber away from here. The demon and Tain were astute enough to know that her death would hurt Adrian more than any of their physical tortures ever could.

Tain had to be under the demon's full control; it was the only explanation for why he'd decided to drain the world of life magic. And yet, once or twice Adrian had caught full reason in Tain's eyes. He spoke calmly of wishing to die, and seemed regretful that the only way to commit suicide was to take the entire world with him.

Perhaps if Adrian could reach that reason, could fan the remaining spark of Tain's sanity to life, he could get Tain to Ravenscroft where he could truly heal. The demon could not go to that otherworldly place of life magic where the goddesses ruled. Get Tain to Ravenscroft, then slaughter the demon before the demon could take retribution on Amber. Seemed like a good plan.

He heard Tain's footsteps on the stairs, alone this time.

Good. He blinked when Tain snapped on the overhead light, the glow of the bulb mundane against Tain's crackling magic.

Tain studied Adrian for a time, a lock of red hair falling over his forehead. He moved to him slowly and traced Adrian's bare, scarred bicep. "You don't have Ferrin. Where is he?"

"Somewhere else."

Tain smiled, the handsome tilt of lips that had always made ladies sigh and follow him with their gazes. "Ferrin is only a weapon. Easily broken."

A weapon bestowed on Adrian by Isis and infused with her magic. "You used to admire him," he said.

"I used to admire you."

Adrian drew a painful breath. "I never deserted you. I've been searching for you since the day you disappeared. I say we scrag this demon and go to Ravenscroft. We can stay there as long as you want, and then go wherever you want, do whatever. I don't know what kind of hold he has over you, but I'll help you break it. Isis will help, and Cerridwen—"

Tain put his face close to his. "Shut up. You don't know anything about healing. I can never heal."

"You look fine to me. He's twisted your mind, Tain— he's a *demon*. An Old One, more powerful than any we've faced. But two Immortals are better than an Old One any day."

Tain leaned his forehead against Adrian's, his eyes closing, his spice-scented breath touching Adrian's mouth. "Please shut up."

"I won't let him have you."

Tain began to laugh. He stood up, his eyes lighting with mirth. "You're too late. He—she—had me centuries ago when she led me away from the battle in Scotland. I didn't notice you stopping her then. I called to you, I waited for you to burst in and rescue me, my big, arrogant brother, but you never did."

"I tried. I searched for you. He hid you from me."

"Well, you didn't look hard enough, did you?" His laughter died. "The most powerful of the Immortals, and you let a demon trick you. I stopped wanting you to come for me a long time ago."

"That's because he screwed with your mind," Adrian grated.

"She *screwed* with many things. And it's made me stronger. I'm so strong now, stronger than you ever were. I asked you to help me drain the world of living magic, but I'm powerful enough to do it on my own." He smiled again. "How do you like that? I've surpassed you."

Adrian said nothing, the pain in his heart having nothing to do with the demon sticking a sword through it. Tain was in there somewhere, his mind as imprisoned by the demon as his body had been in the ice cave.

Adrian leaned his head against the wall, curling his fingers, which had become bloodless and numb. He was a fighter, good at battle and assessing strengths and weaknesses of his opponent, but bad with words and emotions. He had no idea how to persuade without using his mind-touch, and he never could use his mind-touch on his brothers.

He let out a sigh, pretending resignation. "All right. I'll help you if you want."

Tain stared at him a moment, then began to laugh again. "Nice try, Adrian. I don't believe you, but it's a step forward. You will soon understand what I've gone through, why I want to die. And when you watch me drain the life magic out of your witch, you'll grieve with me, and you'll join me. I know you, Adrian. You're not good at dealing with heartbreak."

"What if I told you I don't care about Amber?" he said. "That she's just another woman?"

Tain's smile broadened. "I'd know you were lying. She is precious to you—I've heard how you've protected her again and again, even when you lost ground because of it. You've grown to love her, and losing her would eat you from the inside out. You'd do anything to stop the grief."

Adrian fingered the links in the chain, knowing they were spelled as well as being thick as tree limbs. "Why have you waited so long? If you've been tormented for seven hundred years, why didn't you drain the world before this?"

Tain brightened as though Adrian had asked the right question. "I was not ready. I harbored hope. Once he finally convinced me there was no more hope, we knew it was time for me to die. I saw the young witch riding between while I was in the ice cave. She talked to me, and she was so interesting. She told me about her sister, and I knew Amber would be just the kind of woman you would like. Once you fell in love with her, I would be able to reel you in."

"So you had the demon murder Amber's sister to drive us together?" Adrian passed his tongue over his cracked lips. "Sweet of you."

"I regretted it," Tain said, sounding sad. "Susan intrigued me, and she truly loved her little sister. But I needed to begin, and Amber's life magic was strong. I needed her."

"Then he has stripped every ounce of caring out of you," Adrian said. "You never would have hurt an innocent when I knew you. Hunter, in particular, will never forgive you."

"Yes, Hunter," Tain mused, his look faraway. "The fierce warrior with no mercy. I believe I've surpassed him too."

Two certainties hit Adrian at that moment. The first was that he'd truly lost Tain, and lost him long ago, because the man who faced him now was only the shell of his brother.

The second was that he was facing something far more terrifying and dangerous than an ancient demon: an Immortal warrior turned rogue who nurtured a death wish. The most powerful life-magic being ever created was about to turn on everything he'd been raised to protect.

"Shit," Adrian said softly.

He realized he needed to shift his strategy from trying to rescue Tain to getting himself out of there so he could stop what Tain was trying to do. It was almost a relief to move his brain back to something he understood: escape and fight, worry about Tain and his mental problems later.

Just then the demon glided into the room in female form, wrapped in a sarilike garment. Adrian watched in revulsion as Tain laced his arm behind the demon woman's back and pulled her close. She lifted her garments and straddled his bent knee, making little noises of satisfaction as she rubbed herself against his hard thigh.

Adrian growled. "If you two want to have sex, could you please do it downstairs? Or better yet, unchain me and I'll leave you alone to go for it all you want."

The two in the middle of the room ignored him. Tain pulled the demon up for a long and passionate kiss, his face flushed. "I love you," he said.

The demon smiled at him, her face more beautiful than a goddess's. "It's time," she murmured.

Apprehension filled Tain's eyes. "Can't it wait a few minutes?"

She shook her head. "You know we cannot. The third hour after midnight on the third day. It must ever be so."

"Oh, yeah?" Adrian grated, wondering what the hell they were talking about. "Must be inconvenient when you change time zones."

As before, they didn't seem to hear him. Tain swallowed and nodded. "All right. I will get ready."

The demon stood back with a smile on her face as Tain began to remove his clothes. As the suit and shirt fell away, to be neatly folded and set aside by the demon, Adrian stared at his brother in horror. Adrian's own back and arms were crisscrossed with battle scars, but that was nothing compared to what he saw now on Tain's body.

Wide scars snaked down Tain's back and arms and buttocks in a uniform pattern, running lengthwise down his legs and up under his groin. Not one bit of hair grew on his body now, which was a mass of white, puckered tissue. The wounds looked recent, as though as soon as his rapidly healing body could mend itself, his skin was opened up again.

Every three days.

"Isis help us," Adrian whispered, his own pain forgotten. "Tain, *kill him.*"

The demon lifted a long, curved knife from the table as Tain looked sadly at Adrian and said, "I must do this. It makes me stronger."

He turned, naked now, and placed his hands on the wall. The demon slipped out of her own clothes, then stood naked behind Tain and began to peel the skin from his body in slow, even strokes.

\* \* \*

"He's in my *house*?" Amber asked in shock.

They'd returned to Adrian's Los Angeles home in the small hours of the morning to find Septimus and Kelly waiting for them outside, just beyond Adrian's bubble of protection. Valerian's first move had been to make a grab for Septimus's throat, but the vampire had blasted Valerian back with a wave of death magic. Then he'd calmly explained how he'd given Adrian to the demon, while Kelly stood straight and tall next to him, her arm threaded through his.

"That is where I was instructed to have him delivered," Septimus finished quietly. "The demon claimed that Tain would be there and that Tain wanted to see him."

Amber bit her lip, remembering her conclusions that Adrian finding Tain—or rather, Tain luring Adrian to him—would not be a good thing.

"So now the demon has bod of them?" Valerian asked. His cold had much dissipated as they traveled home via helicopter, then plane, his strong dragon body healing fast.

"It appears so," Septimus answered. He might have been at a board meeting admitting that bar snack sales were down.

Valerian balled his fists. "Good. Thank you for the information. Now prepare to be a dragon snack."

Septimus's eyes flashed dangerously. "You'd choke on me."

"I'm willing to take the risk."

Kelly stepped between them. "Leave him alone. He had to help the demon. He had no choice."

"He made you believe that because you're his blood slave," Valerian returned.

"She isn't," Septimus said evenly. "She is free to leave me whenever she likes. I haven't bound her to me."

Kelly shot him a look of surprise, and Septimus nodded. "It is true. I don't want you tied to me by anything false."

Kelly's stiff expression dissolved, and she reached up and kissed his cheek. Valerian made a retching noise.

"Can we go back to the main problem?" Amber asked. "Why are Adrian and Tain and the demon holed up in my house? What's special about my house?"

"Simple," Detective Simon grunted. "You live there."

"And they want me there? Why should they?"

"I can think of a number of somewhat sadistic reasons," Simon replied.

"I have to agree with him," Septimus said. Kelly nodded next to him.

"What I mean is, I don't have any special powers or talent that they could want. I'm a fairly ordinary witch—good at some things, need practice at others."

Septimus interrupted. "Then obviously they want you as leverage over Adrian. Keep you to threaten, so he'll cooperate. That's what I'd do."

"Of course you would," Valerian growled.

"Be quiet, all of you," Amber said, pressing her hands to her head. "I have to think what to do."

She pushed past them and went across the drive to Adrian's house, entering through the unlocked front door. The others trailed after her, Valerian carrying the duffle bag with their supplies over his shoulder.

Detective Simon reached her first. "You'll do what you promised me you'd do. Stay here and be safe while we investigate ways to get him out."

"That was before I realized he was in my house," Amber returned. "I'm going up there and getting him out. No, wait, I'll throw the *demon* out. He's violated my space, he's ruined a hundred years of witch magic and our sacred spaces, and he's going to pay."

"Amber." Detective Simon's tone was rigidly reasonable. "If Adrian the Immortal warrior can't get away from him, what do you think you will be able do?"

Valerian said, "For one thing, she'll have a dragon with her."

"And a werewolf," Sabina said, arms folded across her chest.

"And a vampire," Septimus put in quietly.

Kelly looked from one to the other. "Oh, hell, I can probably do something. I still have a few underworld connections from my old neighborhood—forget I said that, Detective. But they might have Seattle connections who can help."

Amber paced the large white living room, her thoughts whirling. "The only way to remove a demon infestation in a house is to exorcise him. And to do that I need life magic, lots and lots of it." She again remembered Susan going on about the Coven of Light, how the energy of their circles, connected from around the world, could do wonders. Did they have enough strength to best a demon, even together? She had no idea.

She balled her fists. "All right, here's what I need. Sabina, go through my bags and find every single one of my crystals, spent or charged, and find several small bags for them. Septimus, get us booked on the next flight to Seattle—and pay for it; it's the least you can do for handing Adrian over to the demon. Kelly, set up Adrian's laptop for me. I need to do some heavy-duty e-mailing."

"What do you want me to do?" Valerian asked, dabbing his nose with a tissue as the other three left to start their tasks.

"Get all the way through with that cold, because I'm going to need you at full dragon strength. But just remember when we get there that it's *my* house, and if you tear it up too much, you'd better hope you're good at home repair."

Valerian grinned and took himself off to the bedroom. Through the open door, she saw him flop on Adrian's bed and put his hands behind his head. "Sabina," he called suggestively. "Why don't you look through the bags in here?"

"And me?" Detective Simon asked. "Do you have an assignment for me?"

He stood quietly, disapproval reeking from him, but he knew he couldn't stop her. She also sensed his fury at the demon and his need to help bring him down.

She nodded, giving him a grateful half smile. "When I'm finished e-mailing, I want to talk to you and Ferrin. If this is going to work, I need you both to help me."

# CHAPTER EIGHTEEN

The demon flayed Tain alive, and Tain did nothing to stop her. His blood ran in rivulets down his arms and legs to the floor, and when he wept it was blood, but he did not scream or cry out. Adrian, on the other hand, roared in fury and bent all his strength to pulling the chains out of the wall.

*To hell with it.* He'd get himself out of here and protect Amber from them if he had to lock her in a bank vault and call every goddess in the universe to guard her. White-hot magic shot through him, gathering to focus on the demon and her ruthlessly efficient knife.

Both the demon and Tain turned as one and threw a black spell back at him. Adrian slammed back into the wall, head cracking against the boards so hard they split beneath the wallpaper.

Excruciating pain raked fire through him. He was spent, his usually fast-healing body weak from torture. He was reduced to snarling foul words at them in every language he knew, from ancient Egyptian to Babylonian to modern-day English.

The demon peeled every inch of skin from Tain, carefully setting aside the strips. Adrian didn't want to know what the demon meant to do with them. Tain was clutching the wall to keep himself on his feet, his body covered with blood, mewling sounds coming from his mouth.

Adrian could only watch in furious silence as the demon finished, then carefully wiped off the knife and laid it back on the table, her naked body coated with Tain's blood.

"There now, love," she said softly. "Are you ready to begin the healing?"

Tain nodded, holding his arms out pathetically to her. She morphed into the male demon, still naked, and snatched up the woman's garments to wrap around Tain's exposed body. Then the demon hoisted Tain over his bare shoulders. He turned briefly before he carried Tain out the door, meeting Adrian's gaze, and his eyes gleamed in dark triumph.

Eight hours after their conversation with Septimus, Amber's group gathered in front of the house in Seattle. To the mundane eye, the house looked normal, unchanged, except for the newspapers piled on the doorstep that hadn't been collected. But to Amber's witch's eyes the house was covered in darkness, a wash of death magic enveloping it. Valerian and Septimus and Sabina could see it too and gazed at it in some dismay.

Septimus had geared up his private plane to bring them to Seattle—not, Amber was happy to note, the same plane that had rescued her and Valerian from the ice. They'd landed at Seattle's commuter airport, and, late as it was, Septimus had a limo waiting to drive them to Amber's house.

"What is it?" Kelly asked, unable to see anything unusual. She'd insisted on accompanying them, not out of guilt for falling for Septimus, she told Amber, but because she cared about Adrian and wanted to help.

"Death magic," Amber answered. "He's blanketed the house in it."

Darkness flowed from the rooftops, black and sticky like tar, coating the windows and doors, seeping into the foundations to fight with the wards placed there by Amber's great-great-grandparents. She fumed at the violation at the same time as the magic chilled her inside and out.

Detective Simon, being a normal human, couldn't see it either, but he obviously believed her. He gazed up at the house, hands on hips.

Amber had managed to contact most of the Coven of Light and explain the situation to them. E-mails had flown and the private loop had geared up with ideas, but it came down to one question: "What do you want us to do, Amber?"

Amber was grateful to them for accepting her. They could have told her that she wasn't Susan, that they weren't interested in her problems, or that they blamed her for Susan's death. But the Coven had exuded sympathy and offers of help. They'd loved Susan, and were all for trying to stop the being who'd caused her death.

Amber had explained her idea, and the witches agreed that it could work. She'd then explained it to Valerian, Sabina, and Detective Simon, who'd all tried to talk her out of it.

"No way are you going in there alone, Amber," Valerian said.

Amber studied the curtain of black thick across the door. "I might not be able to get in anyway." She hadn't anticipated being stopped this early and this easily.

"I can get in," Septimus said.

"But you can't help once you're inside," Amber argued. "What I have to do . . ."

Septimus studied her, keeping his gaze from meeting hers directly. "At least I can get in. I might be able to open a way for you once I'm inside."

Before anyone could object, he strode up the steps to the porch. He easily opened the door, which didn't seem to be locked, and walked inside, the curtain of black unmoving.

Three seconds later he flew out backward, his body arcing high, and slammed into the ground at the bottom of the steps.

He was on his feet, unhurt, before Kelly could reach him, his blue eyes flashing grim anger. "Or maybe not," he said.

"So what now?" Detective Simon asked. "If that death magic is strong enough to keep out a vampire, especially an Old vampire, how are we supposed to get in?"

"You don't," Amber said. She slowly climbed the porch steps, picking up the damp newspapers and setting them neatly on a patio table. She absently noted the scratch that she and Susan had made in the porch floor when dragging home a new sofa last year. They'd always been meaning to sand and repaint the floor but never seemed to get around to it.

She stood in front of her closed door, the original ordered all the way from New York back in 1880. The door had weathered time and several refinishings, and was carved and polished and very, very solid.

*My door. My house.* The demon could cover it in death magic, but the wards that had been woven into this house were also woven into Amber. She carried inside her a part of the witches who had made this place.

She'd never truly thought about her connection to it before, but she felt it in her bones now.

She put out her hand and turned the knob, pushing open the door. The death magic parted with a squishing sound to admit her.

"Amber!" she heard Sabina exclaim; then the door slammed behind her, cutting off her friend's voice.

The house lay in absolute silence. Even were she not a witch, even if she hadn't seen the death magic, she would have sensed something wrong. The living room was quiet, the furniture filmed with dust because neither she nor Susan liked to dust and always put it off as long as possible. The usual scent of dried flowers and spices was muffled. The kitchen still bore the dirty coffee and teacups they'd used when she'd sat here and told Adrian her troubles while covertly studying his honed body.

She went out to the hall and began to climb the stairs. A dim glow came from the tower room, filtering all the way down to the base of the staircase. The second-floor landing was littered with debris from the tornadolike wind the demon had shot through the house the night she and Adrian had fled, but no demon strode down the stairs to find her now, no sound came from the upper rooms.

In the shadows of the landing, Amber knelt and removed Ferrin from the pocket inside her jacket. He lay motionless on the hall rug, his glittering eyes meeting hers. She silently removed her small bags of crystals and looped them around his body, gently tightening the drawstrings so they wouldn't fall off. When she finished, Ferrin lowered his head and glided away, silent as mist.

Alone now, Amber resumed her climb. A stair creaked loudly in the silence, but no one came to investigate.

She slowed her breathing, trying to calm and center herself, readying herself for magic.

Her heart started pounding again on the next landing when a man emerged from the tower room and slowly descended toward her. The silhouette was Adrian's, tall, broad-shouldered, firm-hipped, but the light from above glistened on red hair. She knew right away this must be Tain.

She stopped, hand on the railing, and waited. He walked down slowly, in no hurry, not afraid she'd run away. She felt the strong life magic in him, but it was tainted and strange, and her fingers tightened.

He stepped off the last stair and stood in front of her. His eyes were blue, deep and soulful, and she wondered which aspect of the Goddess had made him and who had been his father. His face was square and handsome, and he bore a small pentacle tattoo on his cheekbone. His expression was filled with sadness so deep it had become ingrained in him.

He lifted a bandaged hand and traced her cheek with his exposed fingertips. "You are lovely," he breathed. "I knew you would be."

His touch moved across her lower lip, and it was all she could do not to recoil. "Tain?" she asked softly.

"Adrian did not want you to come. He was afraid for you." He ran his fingers over her lips again. "He was right to be."

She shivered. She remembered the conclusions she'd drawn in Alaska, that Tain would be even more dangerous than the demon, and now, looking into Tain's eyes, she knew she'd been right. Tain had strength like Adrian, but somewhere in the last seven hundred years he'd gone completely insane.

His next words confirmed it. "I wish I could make your

death clean and quick. Painless. But it must be a terrible death. We must make Adrian unable to bear the grief of it." His blood-coated fingers slid to her hair. "If it helps, know that your pain will end mine and the pain of everyone who suffers the world over."

Amber made herself not cringe from his touch. Worse than a madman was an altruistic madman who talked himself into believing that torture and murder were for the good of all.

"Is Adrian all right?" she asked, keeping her voice as steady and normal-sounding as she could.

The sadness in Tain's eyes grew. "He suffers. He begins to understand."

Amber's heart squeezed in fear. "And he's up there, is he?"

"Yes."

Tain did not try to stop her as she pushed past him to climb the stairs. She sensed Tain watching her closely, and only when she reached the top and entered the tower room did she hear him follow.

The tower room had been a project of her mother's. Amber remembered the hours she'd spent up here one summer as a teenager, helping her mother strip the walls and wallpaper them. They'd made a cozy nook where she or Susan could read under the window while her mother sewed on the other side of the room.

After their mother's death, she and Susan had removed the sewing machine and put in another sofa and shelf of books. Just before Susan died, they'd thought about remodeling the room, so they'd taken the furniture out, except for an old kitchen table, which was still there, spattered now with blood.

Adrian stood against the wall across from the table, his arms over his head and bound with thick chains. He was naked, his beautiful body so covered with blood and deep gashes that not a piece of clean flesh showed. He rested his head against the wall, eyes closed, but when he heard her step, he jerked his head up, nowhere near sleep.

"Amber. Get out of here."

"Nice to see you too," Amber said conversationally. "Where is the demon?"

Adrian glared at her, his dark eyes filled with power carefully contained. "Not here. I want you gone before he returns."

Amber went to him. She touched the chains above his head, thinking of a spell she knew that made bonds weak, but she'd never used it before. She'd need time and a place to sit calmly in order to master it, neither of which she had at the moment. "Only if you come with me. You could break these chains."

"There is a reason I don't."

A huge spark suddenly laced through the chains, a powerful spell of electricity that arced through Amber's body and sent her to the ground. At the door, Tain lowered his hand.

"I need you both to stay," he said.

Amber remained seated on the floor and gathered her knees to her chest. "I have friends waiting outside," she told Tain. "They could take you to Adrian's house, where you'd be safe. The demon can't go there."

"I've already tried that approach," Adrian told her.

Amber pressed closer to him, finding comfort in the brawny curve of his calf and the bend of his knee, the scent of his male body. He was still so strong, even chained up and beaten, the muscles of his thighs honed to perfection beneath the firmness of his buttocks.

"Why are Tain's hands bandaged?" she whispered up at Adrian. "What happened?"

"The demon flays him alive every three days," Adrian explained calmly. "Has for seven centuries."

His voice was steady, but Amber heard the horror in it. She gazed at Tain with new, hideous understanding.

Adrian went on. "He wants us to help him drain the world of life magic so he can die."

Amber stared up at Adrian. "You're not joking."

"No," Tain said. "He isn't."

She turned to Tain. "You can't do that. Death magic will take over, no stopping it. Without the balance, nothing will be able to survive."

"I know," Tain said, smiling. "Nothing—including me."

"It would be so much easier if you just let us help you get away from the demon," Amber said.

"I tried that, too," Adrian said.

"No!" Tain strode to Amber, leaned down, and jerked her head back by the hair. "You leave her be."

"Her?" Amber asked, confused.

"Me." Came a sultry voice. The demon flowed in, in the same form as he'd been at the club, a black-haired lady of luscious curves now garbed in a black satin, body-hugging dress. "He knows I want what's best for him."

Tain went to her, and they shared a passionate kiss, the demon's well-shaped hands cupping Tain's buttocks. Amber looked up at Adrian in shock, and he gave her a grim nod. She felt his touch on her mind, then the slight dampening of fear and pain.

She shook her head, eyes wide. "No," she hissed. "I need . . ."

She needed to be alert and clear-headed, but she couldn't tell him that, not with the demon turning around to smile at her. Adrian seemed to understand, and his touch withdrew.

The demon came to kneel at Amber's feet. "We meet again, sweetheart," she said, brushing the backs of her fingers along Amber's cheek. "No truth spell with you this time?"

"It didn't work last time, so why bother?"

"Ah, but it did. I showed you the truth. That I kept my beloved in a cave of ice where no one would ever find him."

"And then tried to kill us with it."

She laughed. "A harmless joke. I knew it would not slow you for long. You're a very clever witch, you know, to find the cave. But then, I knew you would, so I removed Tain from his danger, and brought him here. At his request, you know."

"He asked to come to my house?"

"Not specifically, darling. He asked to come somewhere where he could find his brother and end his own pain. He knew Adrian had been searching for him. He was finally ready to see him."

"And what do you get out of all of this?" Amber asked. "If I understand what he wants to do, you'll die too, right."

"Sweet little witch, I only want what's best for Tain."

Adrian growled, "I've been through all this, Amber. They're both insane; leave it at that."

Amber somehow didn't think the demon was crazy. Tain, on the other hand, gazed at the demon with love in his eyes. He reached down to stroke her hair.

"May we begin?" he asked. "I want to show Adrian what it feels like."

Amber felt Adrian tense beside her, his body going

taut as swirls of power built inside him. Amber slid her arm around Adrian's muscular calf and hung on.

No way would she sit quietly and let the demon peel the flesh from Adrian's body. The spell wasn't ready yet, but she would fight with all her strength if she had to.

"I have an even better idea," the demon woman said. She stood up and stretched her sinuous body, the sultry length of her skin gleaming in the half-light. She walked to a table to pick up a curved-bladed knife and returned to Adrian, who regarded her with arrogant contempt. She touched the tip of the knife to his lips. "We'll let Adrian choose."

Amber didn't know what she meant, but Adrian clearly did. "No," he said harshly.

"Yes," the demon said, drawing her tongue across her lower lip. "You decide, Immortal. Whose flesh shall I lovingly scrape away this time? Your lover's?" She touched the knife to Amber's forehead. "Or your brother's?" The knife moved to Tain's hand on her shoulder.

Tain gave a whimpering moan, but Amber clearly saw his erection tighten in his pants.

Adrian's voice was low and vicious. "Bite me, bitch."

"Decide," the demon said more firmly. "Or I kill Amber here and now."

The knife went to Amber's throat and the blade nicked a small cut in her skin. She felt the tickle of blood on her neck, but she resolutely remained still, not wanting to jolt Adrian into acting before time. *Not long now, not long . . .*

"Do it to *me*," Adrian said. "If you get off on torture that much, flay me instead."

The demon pouted. "There would hardly be any fun in that, would there? Make the choice, Immortal. I'll heal her again once it's done, I promise. And then I'll do it all over again. I want this to last a long, long, *long* time."

The knife bit harder into Amber's neck, and she could not stop a hiss of pain as hot blood leaked to her skin.

Adrian barely contained his rage. He would strangle Valerian for letting Amber get anywhere near here. He also knew from the glances Amber shot him that she had a rescue plan in mind, which stoked his anger even hotter.

She had no idea what she'd walked into, and she'd certainly lose if she tried to fight, even with magic. Adrian could hold his own if it came to a battle and possibly get away, but Amber would be snuffed out before he could save her.

The demon was trying to torture Adrian by asking him to choose which of his loved ones would suffer. But the demon was stupid. If he had posed the question a day ago, it would have pulled Adrian apart to answer. But Adrian had seen what was in Tain's heart and knew that keeping the demon from cutting Tain again would not help him.

Tain had moved into the realm of insanity, and Adrian would have a lot of work to do to save him from the darkness of his own mind. Tain had survived the demon's tortures before, and he'd just have to do it again. Amber, on the other hand, could too easily die, and losing her would be the hardest thing he'd ever had to face. His choice was simple.

He leaned his head back and closed his eyes as though struggling with inner turmoil. Then he answered, "Tain."

Tain moaned. "No. It isn't time yet."

The demon took the knife from Amber's throat, licking the blade clean with a long, red tongue. She went to

Tain, slipping her arm around his waist. "I'm sorry, love. Your brother has decided it's to be you."

"Why?" Tears leaked from Tain's eyes. "Why didn't he help me?"

"Because he loves her more than he loves you," the demon purred. "Undress for me, darling."

Tain shot Adrian an anguished look and began to take off his coat. Adrian felt Amber's fingers tighten on his leg. She couldn't know it, but her touch was keeping Adrian grounded, keeping him sane in this morass of madness.

"When I get the chance to kill you," Adrian said to the demon, "it will feel so good."

The demon smirked. Tain slowly stripped himself bare. He was only half healed, his skin covered with puckered scars, in some places still bloody. He cried silently, tears flowing down his cheeks.

The demon put her hands on his shoulders and ran her touch down the length of his body, bringing her fingers around to stroke his scrotum. She gave him a long, loving kiss.

Removing her lips from his, she said softly, "Face the wall, sweetheart." Then she gently turned him around and helped him place his hands on the wall. Knife in hand, she drew her tongue down Tain's long spine, dipping it between his buttocks. He moaned and pressed his body against the wall, rubbing his erection against it.

The demon stood up and carefully moved the fall of Tain's red hair to bare his neck. She touched the tip of the knife to the first vertebra in Tain's back.

"Amber, don't look," Adrian advised.

The knife dipped into Tain's skin, blood leaking around the cut. Tain made a faint moan as the demon slowly peeled his skin away like she would pare an apple.

Adrian glanced down at Amber, ready to comfort her. But she wasn't looking at Tain and the demon; she stared intently at the black of the open doorway. Adrian felt a familiar presence there, and his pulse quickened in sudden hope.

Across the room, Tain began to sob as the demon started on the next strip of skin, smiling as her dress became soaked with Tain's blood. At the same time, Ferrin slithered noiselessly over the threshold into the room and started across the board floor. Adrian glanced quickly at the demon and Tain, but they were lost in their sickening ritual.

Ferrin flowed on, unhindered, to Amber, where he wound into a coil. He opened his mouth wide, wider, widest, and a clear crystal dropped out to the floor with a tiny click. Amber quietly pressed her hand over the crystal and gave Ferrin a smile.

At the faint sound, the demon swung around. She stared at Amber sitting cross-legged on the floor, her hand at her side; then her black gaze took in Ferrin coiled tightly against Amber's thigh.

The demon sprang across the room with a snarl and plunged her knife down at Ferrin. Before the knife could connect, Ferrin stiffened into a silver broadsword. The blades rang together, sparks stinging Adrian's bare skin.

"Now!" Amber shrieked.

From all corners of the house came bursts of white light, life magic so strong and pure that its power shoved Adrian into the wall. The crystal Amber held glowed incandescent as though it channeled the power of the sun itself. Amber opened her mouth and sang a clear note, and a harmony of female voices joined in the music.

Adrian sensed the magic of the witches joined together, forming a circle of life magic so strong that the hair on his body stood up. The circle encompassed the house—Adrian imagined Ferrin slithering through the dark, dropping crystals in each room so the witches could drape a net of life magic over the entire house. In his mind he saw a blur of women, each kneeling before a crystal or flame or water chalice, chanting and singing, all connected, sending their magic across the miles to focus on the stones Amber must have charged to receive them.

Adrian laughed. Mirth rolled from deep within him, and pride, and relief. He let his own pent-up magic blast from him, adding to the witches' magic as he laughed. His chains burst into metal shards, and he reached down and scooped up Ferrin, growling in joy as he brought the sword around.

No death magic could exist among all this life magic. The demon screamed and snarled, becoming male again, the dress tearing into shreds and falling away. He pointed at the ceiling, opening a hole darker than night, and dove upward into it.

"Tain," Adrian said. He felt a surge of joy. He could grab Tain and get him to Ravenscroft, where Isis could come and no demon could touch him.

Tain gazed at the fading black hole in anguish. "No!" he screamed. "Don't leave me."

"Tain, let him go, I'll take you home."

Tain looked at Adrian in pure rage. "I want to die. I want to *die.*" He blasted out with his own magic, and despite his bloody and ravaged body, his power was hard and raw and stronger than Adrian had ever known it to be. It slammed Adrian back into the wall beside the hook that had anchored him in place.

The black hole widened and the demon's hand snaked through. Tain shouted in delight and grabbed it, to be whisked upward and out of sight, the hole slamming closed before Adrian could reach it.

Amber closed her mouth, and abruptly the music ceased. She slumped over, the crystal rolling from her hand, the light fading. One by one, Adrian sensed the crystals in the house dim, but the shell of living magic remained, reinforcing the witch wards that glowed stronger than ever.

The door downstairs slammed open, and he heard snarls and claws scrabbling on wood as a werewolf bounded inside, followed by quick human footsteps. Something flashed at the window, and a huge face appeared, a dragon snout bending down to reveal two huge, unblinking blue eyes.

"Everything all right in there?" Valerian asked.

Adrian growled a laugh as he sank to the floor and drew Amber onto his lap. She raised tired eyes to him and smiled as he bent to kiss her lips.

"I guess it worked," she said.

# CHAPTER NINETEEN

Adrian rested his head against the cool tiles of the shower. The steam rolled over him and the heat soothed the aches in his body. Water slid down his back, rolling in rivulets over his thighs to pool at his feet.

He smoothed back his hair, the water sluicing down his spine and sliding between his buttocks. The blood had long since washed down into the drain, healing water wiping away signs of his ordeal.

The demon had Tain, and Tain was ready to destroy the world. Adrian alone had not been able to stop him. Amber's ruse with the circle of life magic had been clever, but even with her at his side, his power had not been enough. Tain was mad, and he had to be stopped.

Sometimes it was hell to be an Immortal.

The bathroom door opened, the draft rolling steam through the room. He knew who it was, having learned her step and her scent and the way she moved.

He glanced through the wavy-glass shower door to see her pause in the middle of the room, her silhouette motionless. Then the colorful pieces of her clothing began to fall to the floor until she was a pale peach smudge of nude body. She moved to the shower and opened the door, stepping in next to him without embarrassment.

His heart beat faster. The shower plastered her short ringlets to her head and beaded on her breasts, her nipples already dark and tight. He leaned down and licked water from her lips, his thumbs pressing the corners of her mouth to open her to him.

She laced her arms around his neck, her breasts pressing his chest as he took her mouth in savage strokes. He'd almost lost her this day—almost. The *almost* made him know he never wanted to lose her again.

The kiss went on and on, both of them hungry. When they parted, Adrian held her face between his hands, studying the woman who had become the most important thing in his existence.

"Why did you tell the demon to torture Tain and not me?" she asked, her voice hollow against the running water.

He remembered his sickening horror when the demon had pushed the knife against Amber's throat, making a line of blood. "There was no question."

Her tawny eyes held worry. "You spent so many years trying to find Tain. You could have taken him to safety while the demon busied himself with me."

He gave her an incredulous look. How she could think that? "I would have done anything to stop him from harming you."

"Including sacrificing your own brother?"

She didn't understand. He stroked her face, touching skin smooth with water. "To him it was just one more step in the demon's hold over him. He could stand it."

She looked at him in sudden compassion that warmed his heart. "It must have been difficult for you."

"It was not difficult at all. The demon knew that the only way to break me was to hurt you. He wanted to see how far I'd go to keep you from harm."

"And you played right into his hands."

Adrian cupped her face in his hands, fingers brushing water from her cheekbones. "I don't care about his games. I care that you are safe from him."

"But I'm only a mortal witch. I'll die someday."

"I think you're missing the point."

She closed her mouth, but her sudden answering spark showed that she understood. "He hurt you so much." She rested her fingertips on his chest, tracing the line of his collarbone. "I wish I'd been able to reach you faster."

"I wished you hadn't reached me at all."

She looked puzzled. "You *wanted* me to leave you chained in my tower room while the demon used you as a pincushion?"

"I wanted you well out of this. Valerian knows he should have kept you away, which was why he looked so sheepish downstairs."

Valerian, human-shaped once more, hadn't wanted to look Adrian in the eye. Valerian was lucky that Amber and the Coven of Light had prevailed, or Adrian would have wrung his dragon neck, and the shifter knew it.

"Valerian did what I told him to do," she said.

"A sixty-foot dragon backing down from a five-foot-five witch? He's losing it."

She gave him a look of defiance. "He wanted to save you. He felt responsible for not being able to save you from the ice cave. He thought my plan a good one."

Her glare told him she expected him to agree that the plan had been brilliant. And it had been, except for the fact that it had put her square in danger. She took his silence in a negative light and scowled.

"It got rid of the demon, didn't it?" she asked.

"Before I was able to get Tain away from him."

"Get Tain away from him?" She pressed her hand over the closed wound in his chest that still ached and throbbed. "You were chained up and being tortured. The demon stabbed you through the heart."

"I can't die, Amber. He would have tired of the game after a while."

"Not until you were in so much pain you couldn't think straight. You said he was trying to break you. How much pain could you stand before that happened?"

Adrian couldn't answer. He didn't know.

"He would have had two Immortals under his power," Amber said. "He still has only one."

"Yes, and I can't stop them. I could probably take out the demon alone with enough effort. But not both him and Tain." He leaned forward, hands taking his weight on the wall on each side of her head. "I've never before faced anything I couldn't stop."

She studied him for a time, and then her lips curved in a faint smile. "Welcome to how the rest of us feel most of the time."

He let out his breath. "I learned today that it's easy to be brave when you have nothing to fear."

"You are brave, Adrian. If you weren't, you wouldn't have bothered following the demon to rescue me in the warehouse in the first place."

He fell silent, letting her believe what she wanted. She didn't understand the immense power of an Immortal—she'd only seen what Adrian had let her see of his own power. Immortals were so strong that if one of them decided to turn against the world, the world was in trouble.

"I didn't come here to argue with you," she said, her voice softening. "I came here to wash your back."

His blood heated, his arousal tightening. This was more like it. "My back?"

The sly look she slanted him made his cock rise all the way. "Well, we can start with your back."

He growled and pressed her shoulders into the wall, his body crushing hers, but she only laughed.

Amber assumed he'd shut off the water and carry her out of the guest bathroom to the bed waiting conveniently in the room outside. Instead he wrapped his hand around the bar of soap and drew it slowly up her body. She stilled as he lathered his hands and rubbed them, slick and wet, across her collarbone, then down her breasts, palms cupping her with a wet sound before sliding to the curve of her waist.

He soaped her hips, moving to her back, then down between her buttocks. He lathered his hands with soap again and slid them between her legs, parting her petals without coyness and rubbing fingers over her.

Amber braced herself on the shower wall and let her feet move apart so he could wash the insides of her thighs, down the backs of her knees, then her calves and ankles. He even lifted each foot to wash it thoroughly. Then, kneeling next to her, he rinsed her off, rubbing the clean water all over her.

He pressed her against the wall, his hand on her abdomen, and teased his tongue over the already swollen bud at her mound. Amber slid her fingers through his wet hair, letting the shower pound on her breasts and shoulders, her head tilted out of the line of falling water, her heart beating hard with rising excitement.

Adrian teased and rubbed with the tip of his tongue until she was tingling and jerking. Then he closed his mouth over her and sucked. His tongue was fiery hot, grating on her with just the right friction. Streaks of heat shot down her legs, her toes splashing little fountains on the bottom of the shower.

He alternated between licking and suckling, teasing and heating. His hands were strong on her thighs, pressing them apart, his fingers hot bands on her skin. She arched to his mouth, the shower wall cold and slick on her back.

"I'm supposed to be healing *you*," she moaned.

"You are. You always heal me."

He renewed his teasing between her legs while she rose on her toes, a scream escaping her mouth to ring in the steam-filled bathroom. "Adrian . . . dear Goddess."

He pleasured her without mercy, his tongue doing its magic. He spread her thighs, licking her all the way to her opening, pressing inside to drink her.

By this time, she was screaming with climax, begging him to do all kinds of erotic things to her that she'd never dreamed of wanting before.

He rose the length of her, pressing her against the tiles, hands finding her waist. Water streamed from his black hair, dripping in rivulets down his face. His eyes swam with white sparks, the dark of them fathoms deep.

*There was no question*, he'd said in that heart-stopping voice when she asked him why he'd saved her instead of Tain. Something in him had settled, uncertainty gone. He had made up his mind what he'd do, with a honed ruthlessness she found terrifying.

"Do you still want to argue about belonging to me?" he asked in a deep voice.

"Not really."

"Good," he rumbled. He lifted her, hands on her buttocks, parting her thighs to let her wrap her legs around his hips. "You're mine, Amber. Never forget that."

"I thought you wanted to make me forget," she said, slanting him a coy look.

"Never. I want you always to remember you belong to me."

She smiled into his kiss, which was brutal and filled with excitement. He move his mouth restlessly to her neck and throat, to her breasts, back to her mouth.

He stopped kissing her only long enough to position his tip in her cleft, and then she found the hardness of him widening her and pressing into her, deep.

She scrabbled for hold on his slick shoulders, sinking fingers into his skin. He'd scarred over where the demon had cut him, angry red marks a reminder of the pain he'd suffered. She pulled him tighter into her, squeezing him hard, wanting to comfort him.

He closed his eyes, water beading on his dark lashes. He pressed her back into the shower wall, muscles working as he moved inside her. His hand beside her head closed to a fist, his other hand hard under her buttocks.

He made love to her in a frenzy, his teeth scraping her lips. He punched the tiles next to her, his strength cracking one.

Her back ached from being pressed against the wall, his teeth hurt her, but she didn't care. She squeezed him as he pumped into her, feeling him stretch and fill her fuller than she'd ever been, even with him. His cock reached high inside her, hard and tight.

She couldn't believe the wildness he made her feel, this raw, beautiful man. He gentled his strength for her, his muscles cording as he held back, not wanting to hurt her.

His tender consideration melted her, her body becoming as hot and fluid as the shower water around her. She had no idea what she babbled to him, but he'd reduced her to incoherence and soft, flowing joy.

He muttered something fierce and ejaculated at the same time, his seed hot within her. He caught her screams with his mouth, his eyes closed, face tight.

She lifted her head as he opened his eyes. What she saw in him told her he wasn't sated by a long shot. Her excitement stirred again, her opening swollen and ready for more.

When he shut off the water and slid her legs off him, she started to protest, but he lifted her wet body and carried her out to the guest-room bed.

Their lovemaking after that was unlike anything she'd ever done. He took her from behind on the bed, her hands and knees sinking into the wool blankets, his body hard behind hers. They slammed together, rocking the headboard into the wall, the bed scraping across the floor.

She screamed his name, but he was completely silent, focusing on riding her as hard and fast as he could. He came in silence too, his body shuddering and sweating with sudden release.

Tears wet her cheeks as she fell beside him on the bed, but not of sadness. She'd never felt such climax in her life, and all she wanted to do was lie here and kiss him over and over again. He stroked her face, brushing away the tears, kissing her mouth and forehead.

"Thank you," he said, voice harsh.

She smiled, weak and spent. "It's not a hardship having sex with you."

"For finding me. For coming to help me."

"I thought you were mad at me for that."

He brushed back a lock of her wet hair. "Only because Tain was right: I'd want to die if you were hurt. But thank you for not making me face it alone."

She studied his dark eyes, opaque yet full of emotion. "I'm always here for you, love. I don't want anything to hurt you either."

He kissed her fingers in silence. He was a big, bad warrior, probably not good with females who declared their undying devotion to him. She had the feeling that saying *thank you* had been hard for him.

He concluded the discussion by rolling her over and making love to her again, this time more gently but with no less intensity.


Valerian rocked back on the chair on the porch and took a long swallow of the beer Kelly had brought home from the grocery store. After the crisis ended, the starlet had decided they all needed food and drink, so she and Sabina had headed to the store at the end of the block.

Valerian's cold had gone for good, and he enjoyed the balmy air of late April, the cool humidity that felt good on his face. Poor Adrian. Valerian felt sorry for the man, not so much for getting beaten up and battered, from which his incredible metabolism would help him recover, but for finding out that his long-lost brother was a madman.

Valerian had known Adrian a long time, ever since they'd fought side by side against a nasty nest of vampires in what was now the Czech Republic a few centuries ago. They'd become friends over the incident, and after they'd known each other fifty years or so, Adrian had told him about Tain's disappearance. Valerian had volunteered to help in his quest to find Tain, but neither of them had found a trace until now.

Poor guy. Valerian had no siblings that he knew of, dragons moving fast and far from their own kind not long after hatching. He barely remembered his own mother, and he had no clue who his father was, but that suited him just fine.

Adrian was different. He'd had camaraderie with Tain and somewhat with his other brothers, as much as Adrian snarled about them. One big happy Immortal, demigod family.

"Crazy," Valerian said.

"Who's crazy?" The porch door swung shut as Sabina walked outside and plopped herself on the porch swing, lifting one jeans-clad leg and tucking her foot under her.

"Adrian and his brothers."

Valerian sipped his beer while surreptitiously giving Sabina the once-over. She was slim and taut, her muscles honed for fighting, her gorgeous legs long and strong.

"You've known them long?"

He shook his head. "Only Adrian. I've never met his brothers."

"Amber and I have been best friends for years." She sighed and ran her hand through her tangled mane of blond hair. "Did you come out here to be alone, or to get away from the noise upstairs?"

Valerian grinned. "Are they making noise again?"

"I was sitting in the living room, but there was so much bumping and banging, the ceiling plaster started coming down. Septimus and Kelly are cooing in the kitchen, so I thought I'd give them privacy."

"I don't blame them," Valerian said. "Amber and Adrian, I mean. They've had a hell of a week."

Sabina agreed. "So have I, come to think of it. It's not every day I have to rescue my friends from some freezing motel in Alaska and help fight a demon, not to mention an Immortal with a death fixation."

"Same goes for me."

Valerian studied his beer bottle a moment, watching condensation bead on the label. He rose and moved casually to the swing and sat down next to Sabina. She looked up at him, but didn't scoot away.

"Want a beer?" he asked. "I'll grab one for you."

"Not with all the magic floating around here."

He lifted his brows. "What's that got to do with it?"

"If I drink too much close to a huge flood of magic, it makes it more difficult to control the change. And I've never been close to magic as strong as this."

He looked into her golden eyes and carefully moved a strand of hair from her cheek. "It's a werewolf thing?" he asked, and she nodded. "Dragons don't have that problem."

"You get colds."

"I was born in the tropics. My blood's made for warm weather. I can stand it—almost—as a human, but not in dragon shape." He took a sip of beer, his booted foot pushing the porch floor to move the swing slightly. "Wolves have fur coats."

"I'm not much for warm weather."

Valerian looked down at her. "Couldn't work, could it—a werewolf and a dragon?"

She made a slight shrug. "It could while we were in human form. In a temperate climate."

"That's a good point." He leaned down and slanted his mouth across hers, tasting warm lips and an incredibly sweet mouth. She rose into the kiss, lacing her hands behind his neck.

They kissed for a long time, lips and tongues tangling. If he'd had her with him while flying around the icebergs, Valerian thought, maybe he wouldn't have been so cold.

They kissed a little longer, exploring each other. Valerian brought his hand up to cup her breast through her thin shirt.

After a time they eased off. Sabina rested her head on his shoulder and they sat enjoying the quiet of the evening after battle.

"I need to check in at home soon," she said at last. "My dad's already been on my cell phone, asking me what kind of death magic was going on here and why. They'll all want to see me in person before they believe I'm all right."

"Your wolf pack?"

"Something like that."

"You know, I was just thinking how dragons spend their lives alone—no parents, no brothers and sisters, no pack."

Sabina gave a short laugh, her breath warming his neck. "I've had nothing *but* family my entire life. Can't go anywhere without them wanting to know every last detail about what I do." She looked up at him, head moving on his shoulder. "I can't put it off any longer. We're only five houses down. Want to come?"

Valerian took another sip of beer, then set the bottle carefully on the porch floor. "Sure, what the hell."

He rose, and Sabina walked down the steps of the porch, holding out her hand. Valerian slipped his larger hand in hers and let her lead him away.

# CHAPTER TWENTY

The phone rang in the darkness and Amber rolled over to pick it up. Adrian stirred beside her, his healing sleep deep. His head was pillowed on his arm, his hair black against the stark white of the guest-bedroom sheets.

"Hello?" she mumbled.

"Oh, sorry, Amber, I didn't mean to wake you."

Detective Simon sounded embarrassed. The digital clock beside the bed read nine-thirty p.m.

"No, I was just resting. What's up? And where are you?"

"Home," he said. "I'm sorry I left without saying goodbye, but I thought it was best."

"That's all right." Amber tried to remember when he'd left. Maybe when Kelly and Sabina had ducked out to the grocery store, but she had been climbing the stairs to be with Adrian and hadn't noticed.

"Amber." Simon hesitated a long time, as though he couldn't bring himself to say what he'd called for.

"Thank you," she said into his silence. "For helping me—us. For everything you did."

"It's not over yet," he reminded her. "Your vampire friend told me he'd gotten reports of a slew of demon attacks in Los Angeles, with about a hundred people killed. Looks like your demon's going on the rampage."

Amber's mouth went dry. She knew that banishing the demon and Tain from the house wouldn't stop them, but she thought they'd need a little time to recover. She looked over at Adrian where he slept, head on his bent arm. She hated to wake him, he looked so relaxed. *You've done so much, but you can't stand down. Not yet.*

"Amber?"

"I'm here."

"I also wanted to say I was sorry for not being able to get Susan's killer. I have a warrant out for the demon's arrest, and the paranormal department is on it, but—"

"Don't worry, I understand if you don't bring him in right away. An ancient demon from before the dawn of civilization will probably be a little hard for ordinary police to catch, even the paranormal unit."

"I wanted you to know that I haven't walked away from the case. That I'm here—in a professional role, I mean. It's my job to solve crimes, and I know your demon and Adrian's brother won't stop. I'll help with whatever you need. You just call me, all right?"

"That's nice of you."

He sighed. "No, it isn't *nice*. It's natural, because I'm still assigned to the case. I'm trying to tell you I'll help because it's my job, not because I'm stalking you or anything." He trailed off, then drew a breath and started again. "What I mean is, I don't want you hesitating to call me just because I spilled my feelings for you up in Alaska. I'm a big boy, I'll get over it. I don't want you in danger because you were uncomfortable about calling. Am I making sense?"

"Perfect sense. I promise I'll call for help if I need it." She paused. "I'm sorry it can't be different."

He snorted. "Stop that. You aren't sorry you're with Adrian, so don't pretend you are."

She sensed Adrian lifting his head, awake and watching her with fathomless dark eyes. "All right," she said.

"And don't be sorry for me. Like I said, I'm a big boy."

"You're breaking my heart, Detective. I already feel bad enough."

He snorted again, and she realized he was laughing. "Don't. You be happy with your macho Immortal warrior. He ever hurts you, though—"

"I'll tell him." She smiled into the phone. "Thanks for calling me. Good night, Detective."

"Good night. Tell Adrian good night too."

"I will," she said, and they both hung up.

Adrian stretched his hand across the bed to lightly stroke her thigh. "He's in love with you."

"He did imply in Alaska that he wanted to be more than friends. But that he'd back off because he knew how I felt about you."

"Hmm." Adrian gave her an unreadable look and continued to caress her. She wondered what was going on in his head. Jealousy? Amusement? She remembered how he'd told Detective Simon in Los Angeles that he was glad there's be someone to watch over her when he was gone.

"There have been more attacks?" he asked. "I heard him."

She lay back down, not bothering to pull the sheets over her. "Worse than before, it sounds like." She studied him a moment. "When you go after your brother and the demon, don't argue against me coming with you."

He was silent a moment, doing nothing but touching

her gently, his fingers brown against her pale skin. "I'm not going after them, not alone. It wouldn't do a damn bit of good if I did."

She stilled in surprise. He looked delectable, as he always did lying with the sheets twisted around his limbs, black hair fanned out on the pillow. But his eyes held a grim light, his jaw tightening as he admitted what she sensed he hadn't wanted to say out loud. *I can't do this alone.*

"I'll help you," she said hurriedly. "Whatever it takes, you know that. And Detective Simon just said that we could count on him any time, and Valerian—"

Adrian sat up and pressed his fingertips to her lips. "I need more than that. I need more than your unique magic and a dragon and a werewolf. I need more than Septimus and the Seattle Police. I need even more than your Coven of Light. I need an army, a powerful one that can rope in my brother and kill the demon and stop Tain from doing what he intends."

"And you need me to help you recruit?"

Adrian's sternness dissolved into low laughter. "You wouldn't know where to begin. What I need is an army of Immortals. Alone, I'm not strong enough to stop Tain. But all of us together . . ." He grimaced and scrubbed his hand across his unshaven face. "I really hate to admit this, but I need to find my brothers." He fell back against the pillows and groaned. "Isis, help us all."

"Is finding your brothers so bad?" Kelly asked several hours later as they gathered around the table in the clean and well-stocked kitchen.

Amber had made coffee for everyone and tea for herself and Septimus, who also didn't like coffee. Valerian and Sabina sat side by side, very close together. They avoided looking at each other, but they didn't throw sarcastic barbs at each other either. Amber found that interesting.

"You have no idea," Adrian said, shaking his head. "My brothers and I were made for a common purpose, more or less, a long time ago. You'd think we could work together, but it's more like herding cats in the dark."

"Each one of you always thinks he's right?" Sabina asked brightly. "Sounds like my family."

"I haven't seen them in centuries," Adrian added, running a blunt finger around the rim of his cup. "After the goddesses made it clear that they weren't too worried about losing Tain, I basically said *up yours* and went my own way. I assume Kalen and Hunter did too, because I never saw them again. Darius I think went back to Ravenscroft like the responsible Immortal he thinks he is. Don't know if he's still there."

"We could do locator spells on them," Amber ventured. "I *think*. And the Coven of Light could help. They're all over the world."

"It might not be that simple," Adrian answered. "Locator magic doesn't necessarily work on Immortals. If my brothers don't want to be found, they won't be found."

"So, no putting up 'Wanted' posters, then," Valerian observed. " 'Anyone with information leading to the whereabouts of Immortal warriors, contact Adrian. Description: Bad attitudes, big swords, cranky as hell.' "

Adrian gave him an acknowledging nod. "But Amber is right, the Coven of Light could help. There's a spell of summoning, the Calling, that was used in the old days to call the Immortals to fight evil—demons, vampires, and otherwise. It hasn't been used in centuries, and knowledge of it might be lost."

Amber gazed at him in interest. "You mentioned it when we were driving to Los Angeles. Don't you know it?"

"No, because I was always on the receiving end. The spell is known as the Calling, and witches used it throughout the ages whenever death magic grew too powerful. I have no way of knowing whether the spell even exists anymore, or whether my brothers will respond to it if it does."

"The Coven could research it." Amber's fingers warmed as her fascination increased. Searching for the perfect spell was a game she enjoyed, the more cryptic and archaic the spell, the better. "I've already asked them to research the demon's name. If they can find that too, we can bind him."

She could tell by Adrian's expression he didn't think it would be that easy, but he said nothing.

"The Calling spell," Septimus mused. "I've heard of it."

"I hope you've decided whose side you're on," Valerian growled at him. "Tain erasing life magic from the world should make you happy."

"Not really." Septimus sipped tea and licked a drop from his lips. "If Tain unmakes the world to kill himself, he unmakes me with it, and I enjoy my long life. You do know why vampires become vampires, don't you? The Turning is only successful when one truly fears death. Most humans accept death in the end and welcome the peace. Vampires will do anything to avoid that peace. I imagine the Old vampires will be more amenable to helping you stop Tain. The young are short-sighted."

"Vampires today," Valerian breathed in a mocking tone.

"I'll contact the Coven of Light," Amber said. "They've all noticed the sudden increase of death magic. Some say they've been sensing it for almost a year, but it's escalated. They're fairly powerful witches. One of them may know of the spell already."

"We need to find it fast," Adrian said. "Tain is getting stronger all the time. The demon attacks in Los Angeles will seem tiny by comparison in a matter of days. We have to grab him, and we have to stop him. None of us is safe until we do. We're the only ones who know what they're really up to, so they will go for us first."

"I feel so much better," Valerian muttered.

"A spell like the Calling will need much power," Septimus added. "Do we have that kind of power? No offense to you, Amber, but in my experience the deep magic necessary to call ancient ones like Immortals takes power and planning and timing."

"Casting the spell on a day of power would be best," Adrian said. "A time when we can focus as much magic as possible into an intense ritual. The moon is waning, and I don't want to wait all the way to another full—"

"Beltane," Amber interrupted.

"Beltane?" Kelly asked. "What is that?"

"A Sabbat," Amber answered. "The night of April thirtieth on into the first of May. A power day and a major celebration. Beltane is about rebirth, the end of winter, the Goddess and God joining, rejuvenation and fertility."

"The power of sex." Valerian grinned. "I can go for that."

"Figures," Sabina muttered.

"Beltane is the epitome of life magic," Amber continued. "A perfect time to raise the spell, if we can find it by then."

"Needless to say, I won't be attending this life-magic fiesta," Septimus commented. "Better I get back to Los Angeles and stand by to enforce order, if I can. I don't want the demon turning *my* vampires against me—or killing them if they refuse to do as he bids."

"The demon will hurt you," Valerian pointed out.

"Really? If I get into trouble, I'll be sure to call on you, dragon. You can burn him out."

Valerian laced his hands behind his head. "I'd be happy to."

Amber ignored him. "Witches who dabble in death magic might know of this spell too," she mused. "If you happen to hear of anything—"

"You'll be the first to know," Septimus said.

"Susan was to have been High Priestess this year at the Beltane festival, wasn't she?" Sabina asked softly.

"Yes." Amber thought of the clutter in the workroom upstairs and their plans for the garlands, the circle, the maypole, the ritual. She and Susan had been working on writing the ritual for a while, wanting to have everything just right.

"I guess we know who will be High Priestess instead," Sabina said, looking pointedly at Amber, then at Adrian. "And High Priest."

The High Priest and Priestess guided the ritual and represented the God and Goddess; some said they even manifested the Deities inside themselves. The Beltane ritual was quite powerful, and any magic done afterward would be strong. If Adrian needed intense magic for the Calling, they would certainly find it after the Beltane ritual.

Valerian wasn't entirely wrong about the sex part. A powerful priest and priestess raising energy through the act of sex could work highly charged magic. Never mind crystals and candles—sex magic could render amazing things.

His dark eyes warm, Adrian slid his hand over Amber's and sent her a smile that hinted of sin.

"I'd be happy to," he said.

Amber began her search for the Calling spell that day. She contacted the witches in the Coven of Light and told them what Adrian had decided, asking once again for their assistance.

"We need Immortals to stop an Immortal," she wrote on the loop. "This has moved beyond avenging Susan's death into something much bigger. We need to find the spell, and we need to find it quickly. We have ten days until Beltane. Will you help?"

The response was an enthusiastic *yes*. The witches online promised to pass the word to others in the Coven who couldn't access the loop on a regular basis. Then they signed off to start the search.

The Coven looked in libraries, bookshops, manuscript collections, and records of their coven and others'. They interviewed elder witches, utilizing the technology of the Internet, and poked around dusty, forgotten shelves in shop corners. A few traveled to the place where the Immortals had last been called—the fateful day Tain had disappeared—to see if knowledge of the spell lingered there, but they found nothing.

Amber contacted covens in Seattle and searched every book on witchcraft, published and unpublished, she could get her hands on. One never knew how knowledge could get passed around, to whom and where. Seven hundred years was a long time.

They searched around the clock, Amber barely looking up from her computer. Adrian didn't like her leaving the protection of the house, so she spent most of the time on the phone and the Internet, or going through books Valerian got for her.

Beyond her frantic researching, she sensed the danger outside, the growing darkness in the city, Adrian's grim expression every time he came home. Tain and the demon had begun their quest to drain life magic from the world, and vampires and demons were no longer shy about attacking and killing people they'd lived side by side with for years. Adrian and Valerian had seen no sign of Tain, but the demon knew where they were, and it was only a matter of time before he decided to mount another attack.

So they researched and watched the clock, and Valerian and Adrian went out armed and came home blood-streaked and tired. Detective Simon called often to check on them. He sounded strained and stretched as well. The paranormal unit was working double shifts trying to keep the city safe, and failing miserably. The vampires were too well organized, the demons happy to break free of restriction. Septimus, who might have been able to help keep them in line, had his hands full in Los Angeles.

When a witch in Amber's local coven was murdered—stalked to her house and slaughtered just outside her door—Amber invited the rest of the coven to stay at her house. They arrived, white-faced and frightened or stern and angry.

"The Goddess will take her retribution," one of them said.

"Or Adrian will," Amber promised.

The dozen local witches overran the big house. It drove Valerian crazy, but they helped with research on the spell and keeping in touch with the others in the Coven of Light.

But as much as they searched, Beltane drew near without their coming close to finding the spell. The problem was, one member of the Coven pointed out, the Calling spell had probably been passed along in oral tradition back when most witches were illiterate, plus it had been dangerous to write out spells in case the witchfinders came across them. Adrian had told her that the last Calling had occurred seven hundred years ago, and it was possible that any information about it had later been destroyed by the Inquisition in the fifteenth and sixteenth centuries.

Then again, another member pointed out, the Inquisition had kept copious records on everything. Coven members in Europe were sent to comb archives to see whether the Inquisition had "questioned" a witch who'd known of the Calling spell.

Adrian, when he wasn't out defending the city against demons and vampires, helped in the research and also attempted to locate his brothers on his own in case the spell proved too elusive. But he made no move to leave Seattle. He more or less moved in with Amber without ever stating that he was doing so, sending for things from his house in Los Angeles and settling in without making a production of it.

He also melded his magic with that of the witches staying in the house, to cast even more protection over Amber's abode than he had over his own. The demon would definitely return, he explained, and they needed this place to be a fortress.

Valerian stayed in Amber's house as well, when he wasn't visiting Sabina and her werewolf family or helping Adrian. He complained about the house being overrun with women and never having any time in the bathroom, but he stayed and sat on the porch most nights, guarding the house. When Amber thanked him for it, he stared at her and made a smart-ass remark about staying outside only to get away from female chatter. Amber smiled at him and left it at that.

As April drew to a close, the Coven of light still had no leads. Adrian also hadn't succeeded in finding any sign of his brothers, who were proving more elusive than the spell.

"You should have pagers," Amber told him one morning as she drowsed in bed with him in the growing daylight.

They always shared a bed when Adrian wasn't out fighting, but though he made love to her with thoroughness and sometimes in a frenzy, Amber sensed she was losing him.

She had the feeling that once the other Immortals appeared, he would leave her. Not in a cruel and thoughtless way, but to keep her safe while he fought the battle with Tain that needed to be fought.

Perhaps a clean break would be best, she'd tell herself. *I get on with my life, he goes back to being an Immortal warrior ready to save the world. He'll move on through the centuries, and I'll live out my life as a normal person.* She'd stop and decide that was the most sensible course of action.

Then pain twisted her heart. *But I'll miss him.*

"That's what the Calling spell is," he answered, his voice rumbling in the darkness. "An Immortal pager."

"I meant something more up-to-date."

He laughed softly, tracing light patterns on her bare back. "I can't even keep track of my own cell phone. If you gave Hunter an electronic pager, he'd probably eat it."

"Why?" she asked, startled.

"Because he's crazy. Not like Tain, but . . . he does his

own thing. He likes to act insane to scare the bejesus out of his enemies. It works."

Amber thought about that. She'd grown used to Adrian, a powerful being who kept his power in check so he wouldn't blast holes in the walls and flatten everyone in his path. She'd seen the insanity in Tain's eyes, which had been terrifying.

What would the other Immortals be like, Kalen, Darius, and Hunter? Would they gentle themselves for the less powerful around them, or see no reason to keep their power in check?

Adrian's eyes held impenetrable darkness that could grow warm with desire or ice-cold, shutting out everything and everyone. She skimmed her hands over his strong body, feeling his contained power thrumming beneath his skin. He should frighten her, but she craved him, the demigod who gentled himself for her.

He stopped her questions at that moment by kissing her and making love to her again.

As usual, that evening after sunset he took himself and Ferrin downtown and didn't return until nearly dawn.

"Vampires again," he told Amber and Valerian in the warm kitchen of the still-sleeping house. "An Old One was guiding them, one who doesn't share Septimus's views on keeping the balance. They've been killing—an awful lot of people."

"And what did you do?" Valerian prompted.

"Killed the Old One." Adrian smiled ferociously. "I enjoyed it. Kicking vampire ass never loses its charms."

He rose, the kitchen light glittering on Ferrin's coils on his arm. "Tain and his demon are going through the world like evangelistic crusaders. I'm going back out to do some crusading of my own. Come with me?" he asked Valerian.

"Sure." The dragon-man got to his feet. Adrian strode out the door without a good-bye, his attention fixed on finding dangers of the night. Valerian started to follow, then stopped, snapping his fingers like he'd forgotten something. "You go ahead," he called. "I'll catch up."

It was an obvious ploy to talk to Amber out of Adrian's hearing, but Adrian merely nodded in the shadows and moved away, his boot heels clicking on the porch floor.

Valerian leaned his hands on the table, thick knuckles whitening. "Adrian really loves Tain," he said to Amber in a low voice. "That's all I've heard for years, how Tain was his favorite and the wonderful things Tain did. Adrian never came out and said he adored him, but you can tell, you know?"

"I know." Amber nodded. "That's how I felt about Susan."

"Then you'll understand what I'm about to say." Valerian's usual good-natured expression had gone. "When Adrian finds Tain, he'll try to help him. The rest of us need to make certain Tain and the demon are stopped. If that means putting an eternal binding spell on Tain or chopping him up and shoving the pieces into separate boxes, we have to. Because Adrian won't."

Amber chewed on her lip. "I've thought of that. You know Adrian will hate us if we do."

"Exactly. So are you going to be able to handle this?"

"Because I'm in love with him?" She paused a moment, then sighed. "I have to handle it, don't I? I got a good look into Tain's eyes. He's crazy and he's ultrapowerful—not a good combination."

"Well, maybe Adrian will be able to sweet-talk Tain and make him all better," Valerian said without conviction. "But if he can't, the rest of us have to do something.

Will you promise me that if you can't put down Tain—if you can't hurt Adrian like that—you'll at least stay out of the way so I can?"

Amber thought about the warring love and hate in Tain's eyes when he'd gazed at the demon, how he'd barely acknowledged Adrian except as a means to an end. Tain had closed himself off from his brother a long time ago, and if he felt any regret, he didn't show it. He had turned into a monster willing to sacrifice anything and anyone to ease his own pain, and she had the feeling that Adrian patting him on the shoulder wasn't going to stop him.

She also knew that Adrian would never forgive her. He might understand that it was necessary, but whatever affection he felt for her would turn to dust.

When she nodded to Valerian, she felt the distance between herself and Adrian grow greater. "I promise," she said. "And I'll help. I swear this."

With extra witches working in the house and helping with research, Amber at last found out something tangible about the demon.

"We already knew he could change gender and appearance," she told Adrian one afternoon. "He told us he was a son of the Egyptian snake god Apep, but he knew that wouldn't help, because Apep apparently had hundreds of sons. Or at least, many demons claim to be his offspring." She shoved a fat book one of the local coven witches had found at him and touched the page. "This one has appeared in many guises to many cultures. The Egyptians, Etruscans, Romans, Celtic peoples, Norse— all have a name for him. In ancient Egypt, he called himself Bakira. Ring a bell?"

"I didn't know him as Bakira." Adrian sat back in his

chair, his gaze going remote, reminding Amber once again that he was an ancient, mysterious being. "He took that name later. I knew him as Kehksut, and I battled him and bested him. He got away before I could kill him—saved by Seth, as a matter of fact—but his powers were greatly diminished. He changed his guise and his name through the years, but his strength had been reduced, and we ignored him. His power has grown tenfold." He stopped, a frown pulling at his mouth. "We should not have ignored him. It was a mistake."

"You don't seem very surprised," Amber remarked. "Did you already know this?"

"I suspected it, when I was in the tower room. He knew exactly how to get to me, knew that turning Tain from me would hurt me more than swords. He knew me." Adrian's tone was resigned as he glanced at the page. "Your finding confirms it."

Amber leaned toward him over the book. "I thought you'd be more excited. If we know his real name—what did you say it was? Kehksut?—then we can bind him. We Call Tain, bind the demon—done!"

Adrian shook his head. "Kehksut is not his true name, just one name of many he is known by. You'd probably not even be able to pronounce his true name."

"So we'll learn demon language. Work with me here."

He started to smile. "A being's true name isn't a word. It's music in his heart." He touched his breastbone with his fingertips. "My name isn't really Adrian, any more than yours is Amber. It's what we call ourselves, and what we let others call us. Our true name is an inexplicable part of us, which is why knowledge of it can give others great power over us. You know that in many cultures of this world, humans are given one name in a religious ceremony—at baptism, say—but are always called by another name by friends and family. It is why so many of you have nicknames."

Amber sat back, disappointed. "Fascinating," she said. "But not very helpful."

Adrian's smile turned genuine as he came back from whatever sphere of existence he'd been visiting in his head. "It might be. You will find his true name, Amber, just as you will find the Calling spell. I have great faith in your abilities."

His eyes and his smile warmed her from the inside out, as did his confidence in her. He'd always believed in her, which was a wonderful, heady feeling. She only wished she shared his faith.

On Beltane Eve, the thirtieth of April, Amber at last found the Calling spell.

She had located it in a small museum in Rome, where its archaic writing had been framed and used in an exhibition called "Witches of Our Past."

Amber had seen the spell listed on the museum's tiny online catalog and had asked Christine Lachlan, a powerful Coven of Light witch living in Rome, to see it in person. Christine had called Amber excitedly and told her she thought it was indeed the Calling spell.

The spell had been written in Latin, apparently by an elderly magus who had wanted to preserve this bit of folk magic. According to the curator, the page had been lost for centuries and turned up recently in a crumbling collection donated by a widow who had cleaned out her attic.

The curator and a history professor from a nearby university worked to translate it into modern Italian, then into English for Amber, and Christine faxed copies to her.

Amber excitedly scanned the fax, her fingers tingling in relief and anticipation. She dragged her Book of Shadows to her desk and began to write up a ritual that would incorporate the spell and its powerful magic into their celebration.

Outside, Amber's neighbors had decided to put aside their fears for one night and hold their spring celebration as usual. They'd more or less turned Beltane into an annual barbecue and drinking fest. If the local witches wanted to gather in a circle and chant and dance, that was a small price to pay. Even those uncomfortable with paganism felt the power of this night, the magic of the God and his festival, and defied the darkness to enjoy themselves. They helped Sabina and Valerian and the witches set up the Maypole festooned with ribbons in the strip of green that ran behind Amber's house, and decorated porches with paper lanterns and garlands.

Amber glanced at the activity with a pang in her heart as she worked.

Her family had always hosted the annual Beltane celebration, and Amber felt a sudden longing in her heart for a family that would take the tradition into the next generation.

The longing was more than just to have someone to carry on a tradition—Amber was alone now, the laughter and dynamic of families absent from her life. She longed for family, and she knew who was the impossible man she wanted family with.

Amber finally finished the ritual, typed it up, and sent it to the Coven of Light loop, explaining what she needed them to do. Because there wasn't time to gather the Coven in person, they would participate in the circle by means of scrying, either in stones or crystals or water or fire, as their talents dictated, just as they had when

Amber tapped their power to banish the demon from her home. On Amber's end, their powers would be gathered in crystal stones held by local witches, friends of Amber and Susan, who would also lend their powers.

The spell itself was fairly simple, but it needed a very careful focusing of great amounts of magic. The Coven of Light had warned her that even with all of them joining in, the spell might not work.

But Amber had an Immortal at her disposal, and she'd already asked Adrian to act as a conduit for the Coven's power and enhance their magic with his own.

And he would—if he showed up in time. Adrian had gone out very early that morning, before she'd gotten confirmation that the spell was indeed the right one, and now, as the sun was setting, he still hadn't returned.

In the growing dark, Amber hastened through her house, already in her blue satin robes embroidered with crescent moons and the horns of the goddess Hathor. She ground her teeth with worry when she found Adrian's cell phone on the table beside her bed, the battery run down. No way for her to contact Mr. Immortal and see if he was all right.

She wondered if she could face the other Immortals if the Calling actually worked, without Adrian at her side. Would they listen to her and ask what she wanted them to do? Or sneer at her, blast her with their powers, and disappear into the night? Adrian's descriptions of them hadn't been particularly reassuring.

Darkness increased, and she lit the paper lanterns, glowing like colorful flowers against the night. But still no Adrian.

Amber opened the refrigerator and removed crowns of flowers and fresh leaves that Sabina and other witches had made that morning. Valerian had grumbled that they'd left no room for the beer he'd wanted to stock for the night.

She carried the crowns outside and gave them to the local witches, who were already gathering in the place they would cast the circle. The ceremony would begin soon, and if Adrian remained absent, she'd need a stand-in for the High Priest.

"Valerian," she said in passing.

The dragon-man turned and held up his broad hands. "Don't ask me where Adrian is—I have no idea."

"If the demon and Tain have caught him—"

"I thought of that," Valerian said. He lit the last paper lantern on the porch and tossed down the spent lighter. "I'll go look for him."

Amber wanted more than anything to go with him, but she knew she needed to stay behind. Being High Priestess, at least for the night, meant she had to be everywhere, watch everything, and answer a million questions. Technically, she didn't have the seniority or experience to be High Priestess, but the local witches had agreed that Susan would have wanted Amber to take her place tonight.

Fire pits began lighting up the strip of green, and backyard grills were wheeled out, picnic tables laid with food and drink. Beltane for her neighbors had become a grand celebration of spring, an acknowledgment that the wet, cold winter had turned and good weather was just around the corner.

All knew about Susan's death, and the neighbors hugged Amber when they saw her and expressed their condolences. They were distressed by Susan's loss, a young woman most of them had known since her childhood. Tears filled Amber's eyes as she moved from group to group, talking about Susan and remembering her.

When it was fully dark, the waxing moon rising in its backward *C* crescent, the witches beckoned Amber to prepare the circle. The neighbors moved back to their tables to eat and drink and watch as the witches performed their strange rituals. *Odd girls*, the neighbors seemed to think, *but harmless*, and their robes were pretty. The other witches had already donned their flower garlands, but the High Priest would crown Amber during the ritual.

If he ever appeared.

Amber drew a circle with her wand lightly in the earth; then she and the others placed flowers around the circumference. It was a big circle this year, with all the local witches participating, eager to witness and participate in the Calling spell. The witches said prayers as they worked, asking for blessings and remembering Susan and the witch who'd been killed.

They placed fat green candles at the four quarters, east, west, north, and south. They set the altar on the north side of the circle, with a statuette of the Goddess and one of the God, a censer of frankincense, a bowl of water and one of salt, stones for prosperity and fertility, and more green candles. Streamers of multicolored ribbon hung from nearby trees, completing the beauty of the circle.

Behind them rose the Maypole, a seven-foot post decorated with long ribbons and flowers. The neighborhood kids liked to do the Maypole dance, weaving ribbons in and out and around it, innocent of its symbolism. Or maybe not innocent. Kids knew so much these days.

"Stop looking at the Maypole and thinking of Adrian," one of the witches murmured to Amber, her garland swaying as she laughed. "You'll get to play God and Goddess soon enough."

The comment only made Amber's nervousness increase. When Valerian and Sabina appeared on her back porch, she abandoned the circle preparation and raced to them. "Did you find him?"

Valerian shook his head. "I flew all over this damned town. Never saw him."

"Not a scent of him," Sabina put in.

"It's unnerving how you do that," Valerian said to her.

"I'm a *wolf,* dragon breath."

Valerian put his hand on the small of Sabina's back. "Want me to keep looking?" he asked Amber.

"No, we'd better start the ritual without him," Amber said, resigned. "The important thing is to Call the other Immortals, although whether they'll listen to me without Adrian here is anyone's guess."

"Well," Sabina began philosophically, "if the Calling summons the Immortals, maybe it will Call Adrian too."

"I guess we'll find out. Valerian—want to stand in for High Priest?"

The tall man eyed her in trepidation. "What do I have to do?"

"Stand by the altar and read a chant. It's all written down—then present me with a sword and give me the garland. That's it."

"I thought Beltane witchy stuff was all about sex," he asked suspiciously.

"It doesn't have to be," Amber said. "You're a powerful life-magic being—your magic will help infuse the circle with power. There's no better candidate to ask."

"Oh, what the hell." Valerian shrugged. "As long as I don't become a sex object."

"Don't sound so disappointed," Sabina said.

He grinned. " 'Course, I could be one *later*."

Amber hurried away, too agitated to be amused by her friends' banter. She went back to the circle where the witches were taking their places and told them about the change of plans.

Just before closing the circle, Amber placed the crystals that would bring the Coven of Light inside on the ground near the four quarters. Valerian approached, looking out of place and uncomfortable. Magic was already rising in the circle, and she vividly sensed Valerian's dragon life force, a strongly contained essence that wrapped him like white-hot fibers.

Amber positioned him near the altar and thrust a piece of paper into his hands. He studied it, chewing his lip. "I'm not good at reading out loud."

"Just do your best," Amber said, turning away.

The other witches were in place, hands folded, falling to silence, waiting for her to start the circle. The outsiders too quieted to watch, and Sabina sat down cross-legged in the grass, grinning at Valerian. Kelly had returned to Seattle that day in order to see the Calling ritual—"Honey, I wouldn't miss this for the world. My director can lump it"—and now sat demurely in a lawn chair near Sabina.

Septimus was nowhere in sight, but he wouldn't be. Beltane was a celebration of life, a reinforcement of life magic to last another year. A death-magic being like a vampire wouldn't be welcome even if he could draw near.

In the sudden hush, Amber took up her wand and

walked the circle again, this time infusing power into it all the way down into the ground. A blue nimbus flowed from her wand and glowed around the circle, rising above her in a dome, closing the circle. She knew the non-magic people outside wouldn't see the bright hue of the magic, but the witches and Sabina and Valerian would.

She had started her walk on the north side, behind the altar. She ended the large circle in the same place and looked up to see Adrian standing calmly in Valerian's place on the God side of the altar.

Amber jumped, and glanced quickly over at Sabina. Valerian sat next to her, grinning at Amber, his arm around Sabina's waist. He gave Amber a little wave.

Adrian regarded her calmly, as though he'd been there all day. He'd dressed in medieval garb, surcoat and boots and a dark cloak fastened at his shoulder with a gold clasp in the form of a Celtic harp. Not to forget his Egyptian heritage, he had adorned his forearms with gold bands in the form of serpents. Ferrin, now a sword, rested between his gloved hands, the sword's point touching the earth between Adrian's feet. Adrian's black hair was bound at the base of his neck, his dark eyes as enigmatic as ever.

There was no time for Amber to glare at him and demand to know where he'd been. She let out a little breath of relief and took her place beside him, resolving to question him later.

A hush fell over the circle, over which she distinctly heard the hum of magic. The High Priest was to be the first to speak, and Adrian began his chant in a loud, clear voice. He didn't have the paper Amber had thrust at Valerian, and the words he spoke were similar but not the ones she'd written, as though he'd done this ritual before, but in a different time and place altogether.

"We hail the Goddess and welcome her return to earth," he said, his baritone voice rumbling. "With her comes life and new hope and love and prosperity. Hail to the Goddess, the bringer of life."

The others in the circle touched their hearts and kissed fingers to Amber, now the representation of the Goddess on earth. As they did, Amber felt a shadowy presence behind her, similar to the one she'd felt under the ice cave before Isis had appeared. She couldn't turn around to look, but when Adrian left his place to face Amber, he made a faint acknowledgment to something over her shoulder.

He went down on one knee, lifting the sword high in both hands. "My pledge and power are yours, Lady, as well as my love, to you, the bringer of life." He lay the sword at Amber's feet, then gently placed his palm on her abdomen and leaned forward to press a kiss there.

His lips burned through the silk of her robes, reminding her how little she wore beneath them. She felt an ancient and powerful magic in his touch, as though he were indeed invoking the fertility of the earth and every person on it.

He moved his hands to her hips and gazed up at her, eyes filled with strange power. She looked down at him a long time, her fingers curling at her sides to keep from touching him. She sensed his body merging with that of something even more ancient than he was, the prehistoric god who had evolved into a deity for primitive farmers, a deity who loved and revered his wife, the Goddess of the Earth.

Amber had never felt the manifestation of the deities

so strongly in a ritual as she did now. Adrian looked up at her with the God's eyes, while behind her, Isis touched her shoulder with transparent fingers, her magic flowing into Amber. "Love my son," she whispered. "As I loved my husband."

Amber could not answer. Her love for Adrian filled her as much as did grief for Susan, and she sensed Isis grieving with her.

*She was a good woman*, the Goddess told her. *She was true to you and loved you from her heart.*

Tears filled Amber's eyes, and she saw the same tears in Adrian's. She leaned down and kissed his forehead.

Adrian climbed to his feet, but he remained in front of Amber, resting his hands on the curve of her waist.

In a voice that rang with the power of the God through the centuries he said, "Goddess, thou art *mine*," then crushed Amber in his arms and kissed her hard on the lips.

An energetic madness filled Amber through their joined mouths. As she held him, returning the kiss, the circle, the soft night and its fires, the bright paper lanterns, Valerian and Sabina and Kelly, the interested neighbors and children playing in the dark—simply vanished.

# CHAPTER TWENTY-ONE

Amber found herself beside Adrian on her back in a green field with trees swaying above her, decorated with the same streamers that she'd helped to hang a few hours ago. The trees looked the same, but the houses and the people had gone. In their place, woods and green grass surrounded her, sharp moonlight glittering through the branches. Ferrin, as a sword, lay in the grass beside them like a sentinel.

Before Amber could ask where they were, Adrian's mouth was on hers, his body pinning her to the grass while he pushed aside her robes. A fierce longing rocked her body, and she found herself tearing at his clothes as much as he tore at hers.

He pushed her robes off and had her panties down and crumpled in the grass before she could do more than fumble with the old-fashioned laces that kept his leggings closed.

"I want these off," she said frantically.

Adrian threw off his cloak and surcoat in silence. He wrenched open and pushed down his leggings, kicking off the boots as he did so. Amber ripped the laces of his linen shirt in her haste to untie them, pulling up the shirt to bare his scarred torso.

She skimmed her hands over his flesh, fingers splaying on his chest where curls of black hair twined her fingertips. Down his ridged abdomen her hands went, feeling every rock-solid muscle, to the erection that reached for her.

She explored his cock as though she'd never felt it before, sliding fingers over every slick crease and ridge. He lay back, naked, on one elbow, spreading his legs so she could see him all the way to the base, his eyes dark with desire. Wiry black curls twisted against his inner thighs, stark against his skin.

"My sweet Lady," he whispered.

Someone else spoke along with Adrian in a deep masculine voice that held almost, but not quite, the same timbre as his.

"It has been so long, my Lord," she answered. Another woman spoke with her—*the Goddess,* Amber thought in wonder as she watched her God with hungry eyes.

"Drink me," Adrian said, reaching for her.

Amber moved to lie down beside him, pillowing her head on his welcoming thigh, and took his cock in her mouth. She felt the excitement of the Goddess as they tasted him together, feeling the velvety edge of his shaft. He laced his hand through her hair, pushing himself into her mouth, his breath coming faster.

"I love you," he said, the two male voices overlaid.

"I love you, my Lord," the Goddess responded.

Amber licked and explored, using her lips and tongue to taste her way along Adrian's shaft to its base. She gently probed the stiffness of his balls.

He groaned softly as she licked him, raising himself

on his knee so she could better reach him. She loved this man, every inch of him, loved his firm skin and the hard muscles that flowed beneath it. She loved the masculine scent of him, the taste of him in her mouth, the feel of his cock under her fingers.

She moved back up his shaft to nibble his tip, then closed her mouth all the way over him. She felt the frenzy of the Goddess build up inside her, felt her need for her God, and she worked him strong and hard.

Adrian twisted his hand through her hair, but she barely felt the pain. His own frenzy excited her as did the sound of his hoarse breathing and broken voice. "Amber. Love."

He pumped his hips upward, shoving himself farther into her mouth, and she didn't mind a bit. The Goddess knew how to pleasure him to the utmost, and fire built between Amber's legs, hot liquid inside her.

Suddenly he moaned and ejaculated hard into her mouth. He tasted of salt, and of honey and mead, the good things of the earth as well as the spicy bite of male. Amber drank him while the Goddess laughed in glee, needing him as much as Amber did.

When Adrian could give her no more, Amber fell back onto the grass, smiling, her head landing on his cloak. He rolled onto her, pinning her wrists with strong hands, and kissed her lips and face and throat, licking and biting her as she had him. The Goddess within her lay back in rapture, spreading herself bare before her God.

Adrian cupped each breast while he suckled her, his lashes thick and black against his cheeks. He licked the crease between her breasts, then slid his tongue to her navel to tickle her. Amber laughed for the joy of it.

He nibbled the skin beneath her navel, his hot breath stirring excitement. Then his tongue swirled in patterns across her abdomen and down to her mound. He knelt back, hands on her thighs to widen them for him, then dipped his mouth to her.

Adrian had pleasured her like this before, but tonight the God within him went wild, wanting to please his Lady. His tongue worked magic all over her, making her writhe, heat cascading through her body. She threaded her fingers in his hair and pulled him closer, lifting her hips as he'd lifted his to her.

"Adrian." She laughed out loud and the Goddess chimed in. "My Lord, you please me wondrous well."

Amber started to laugh harder. She'd never thought the word *wondrous* in her life.

Adrian raised his head. "Think it's funny, do you?" The fire in his eyes and the dark-as-sin way he looked at her wiped the smile from her face.

His fingers on her thighs were bands of fire, pushing her open and drawing him up to her. He licked and sucked, then delved his tongue into her until she was gasping and groaning. Then back to the hard little nub that made her arch to him. A wave of tingling darkness suddenly rolled over and over her until she screamed.

He went on and on, pleasuring her through her orgasm, her body writhing, fists clenching, her cries echoing up through the trees and the colorful streamers floating on the wind. At last he lifted his wonderful mouth away and sat back on his heels, a satisfied smile on his face.

The breeze cooled her, but not by much. She touched the curls at the joining of her legs, finding them wet and slick. "Please."

Adrian's eyes swam with sparks, the power in him building with his excitement. "Turn over," he commanded.

Amber rolled onto her belly, wriggling all the way onto his cloak. He covered her body with his, his warm chest pressing against her back, his teeth finding purchase in the shell of her ear. "I love you so much," he whispered in that strange, double-timbre voice.

Before she could respond, he grasped her hips in firm hands. Over her shoulder she caught a glimpse of his huge hardness glistening in the moonlight, before he dragged her back to him and filled her with it.

Her voice rang out, already broken with screaming. He drove into her in wild, mindless sex, no gentle lovemaking this time. The Goddess inside her laughed, and the God in Adrian buried his fingers in Amber's flanks and rode her hard.

He sexed her for a long time, his sweat dripping to mingle with hers, their bodies locked together, her breasts swaying over the earth. Amber came long before he did, and then twice more, her body squeezing to a single point of pleasure that suddenly was set free. Adrian pumped into her as she climaxed, then threw his head back and shouted to the watching sky as his seed burst into her.

They fell together to the cloak, out of breath and sweating, too exhausted to say a word. Adrian touched Amber's flushed body with gentle fingers and kissed her swollen lips.

After a long time, the Goddess that filled Amber spoke. "My Lord, I missed you."

"And I you, my Lady."

"You are as virile as I remember."

He smiled. "And you as ripe and sweet as a peach in summer. We chose well, my Lady. Their love is strong."

"As strong as ours?"

"Maybe," he said. "Kiss me again."

Amber lifted her head and met his mouth in a long, warm, after-lovemaking kiss. The intimacy was complete, the coyness gone, the only thing left pure enjoyment of body to body.

Amber felt the Goddess and God fade away, and then it was Adrian alone kissing her. They lay on his cloak in the deserted clearing, and she tasted him and only him.

He touched her bruised lips. "Did I hurt you, love?"

"No. That was . . . powerful."

"That is one word for it."

He smiled and kissed her again, just a touch of lips on lips, his dark eyes languid. He pillowed his head on her breasts, making no move to leave.

"Where are we, do you think?" she murmured.

His voice rumbled pleasantly against her body. "The same place we were when we left. They brought us to the heart of the place, what is truly here, if that makes sense."

Amber looked around in sudden trepidation. "No one can see us, can they?"

"I don't think so. They must have made it so we are obscured or so no one notices we've gone."

"You don't *think* so?"

He kissed the side of her breast. "Don't worry. The God and Goddess know what they're doing."

She still glanced around nervously, expecting to be propelled back to the circle naked and in Adrian's arms at any moment.

To distract herself, she asked, "What happened to you today? Did you find out something?"

"Today? No." He sounded surprised.

"So why were you late? I was worried about you."

He raised his head, eyes darkening. "You don't know how much I love it that you worry for me."

"Why wouldn't I? There's a demon wanting to snare you, not to mention your insane brother, plus power-hungry vampires and other nasties."

He smiled slowly, as though she'd complimented him, and kissed her with the heat of their lovemaking still on his lips.

"I was not fighting vampires," he said in a low voice. "It took me all day to find a Renaissance clothing maker with a surcoat in my size."

She gasped. "You're kidding."

"I am." He laughed at her outrage, then went somber. "A demon horde moved into one of the residential neighborhoods and started a reign of terror. I met with some of Septimus's people and Detective Simon's team, and we took them out." He paused, stroking her thigh as though reassuring her it was all taken care of. "Then I really did have to pick up my cloak and surcoat. The artist I'd commissioned wasn't finished, and I had to wait. I'm not used to having someone worry about me."

She pressed a kiss to his forehead, afraid to say the wrong thing.

"We'll have to go back soon," he said. "And start the Calling."

"I know."

She shivered. She might be lying with him for the last time, because if the spell worked and his brothers arrived, they'd go after Tain. Once he found Tain and killed the demon, his quest would be over. He and his brothers would likely return to the place called Ravenscroft, and Adrian would forget about the mortal witch he'd made love to. She touched his hair, swallowing a lump in her throat.

He rolled over and covered her body with his. "I want to make love to you again. Just you and me this time. No God and Goddess listening in."

She smiled and nodded. He kissed her—Adrian's kiss, which combined loving with fierce possession. He spread her and entered her again, not with the frantic frenzy of a God who'd not coupled in half a year, but with the loving thoroughness of Adrian who wanted to pleasure her.

After they dressed, Adrian drew Amber to where the north quarter of the circle had been and pulled her into his arms for a kiss. She sensed the world shift, and as they eased out of the kiss, the noise of the Beltane revelry came to her, along with the houses, the people, the dogs barking in games with the kids.

The circle was still glowing magic blue, the witches with garlands in their hair still watching them, Valerian and Sabina on the grass with Valerian's arm around her shoulders, Kelly in her lawn chair, delicately sipping a drink through a straw.

As Adrian ended the kiss, everyone in the circle applauded. "All hail the God and Goddess," one of them said, and the cheering started, followed by the throwing of flower petals. Adrian lifted the crown of flowers and streamers from the altar and placed it on Amber's head.

As the cheering went on, Amber whispered to Adrian, "What just happened? Didn't they notice we'd been gone?"

"We were tools of the God and Goddess," he explained. "They likely fixed everything the way they wanted it."

"It doesn't bother you to be a tool?"

His smile became strained. "I've been one all of my existence. Created to serve the goddesses, to help fight their fights."

Her fingers tightened on his. She could still feel the

warmth of him inside her, and she wondered, when the God and Goddess had exchanged their flurry of fertility, if Adrian had impregnated her. The thought made her heart flutter.

She remembered when they'd first slept together, how Adrian told her he could get her with child or not, as she liked. She assumed he'd held back in their subsequent encounters, but this time they'd been in the hold of deities who likely did what they wanted for their own purposes. If they thought Amber would be better off bearing Adrian's child, it would happen.

Adrian raised their clasped hands to his lips and kissed Amber's fingers. "Ready to try the Calling spell, love?"

Amber gave him a long kiss, possibly the last one. "Thank you for all you've done."

His brows rose over dark eyes. "Got you trapped in an ice cave and nearly killed by a demon?"

"You know what I mean. Thank you for coming into my life." She kissed him lightly on the lips, then turned away, drawing a deep breath.

"All right," she said. "I'm ready."

Adrian's feelings were mixed as Amber moved away from him to reinforce the circle. The reveling witches settled down and moved to the quarters to begin the more serious spell.

He felt stoked. The coupling with Amber had raised his power to a height he'd not felt before. The magic tingled through his limbs and along his scalp; even the roots of his hair thrummed with power. He was ready, itching to begin.

Amber's kiss before she turned away had held a note of finality. She was telling him good-bye, because she thought he'd leave her after the spell. What she didn't understand was that he was bound to her now. It had nothing to do with the God and the Goddess using him, nothing to do with what Isis wanted. It had everything to do with what was in his heart. She'd sealed her fate a long time ago in the warehouse, when she'd lifted a tawny gaze to him filled with challenge.

They couldn't have their forever, because she was mortal, and it would hurt like hell when he lost her, but he would take what he could. Drink of the cup of life, as the Beltane celebrations told him to. He would not avoid joy just to avoid grief.

Beyond the circle, the night had moved on. The younger children were being herded inside, protesting all the way, but the smallest ones were already asleep in the arms of parents. The adults, on the other hand, brought out more wine and beer and settled in to enjoy themselves, city people celebrating an ancient farmer's ritual. Adrian had fought all day to protect people like these so they could enjoy their night in peace.

The Calling spell was fairly simple, Amber explained. All they needed to do was join hands and chant the ritual—enhanced if they wished by crystals and candles. But not just anyone could stand and say the words and Call an Immortal. It took power—power that only experienced and strong witches possessed, witches like Amber and her sister Susan and those in the Coven of Light. No mere mortal could frivolously chant the spell and find her living room full of Immortals.

Each witch in the circle picked up a crystal to use as a conduit for the Coven of Light and held it in cupped hands. Valerian and Sabina were let into the circle to enhance the spell with their ambient life magic. Amber stood at the head of the circle with Adrian. All power would fuse through her and him as she said the actual words.

The witches were nervous but excited, and Adrian tasted crackling energy in the air. Amber slipped her hand in his and smiled at him, her face framed by the silk streamers of her crown.

"Are you ready?" she asked.

"More than ready," he said, trying to keep his voice calm. He held her hand firmly, letting her fingers imprint on his. "The question is, are you ready for my brothers? You should know—I'm the nice one."

"I'll risk it."

"Never say I didn't warn you." He firmed the muscles in his jaw to keep his mouth from shaking. Confronting his brothers wouldn't be easy, but he looked forward to it. He hadn't had a good argument with Darius in a long time, and truth to tell, he missed that.

A hush fell, and all gazes turned expectantly to Amber. She closed her eyes, her right hand enclosing a stone that she lifted to head height. Adrian felt a spark of power dance into her hand, and he deliberately sent his own magic into her. As long as he held her and grounded her, she'd be all right.

"I summon thee," she began. "I summon thee, warriors of light, across seas and deserts, across woods and hills. Hear me, for the need is great."

A faint breeze sprang up in the branches above, rustling leaves and streamers and ribbons. The crystals in the witches' hands began to glow, the Coven of Light adding their power.

"I summon thee by Isis, by Kali, by Sekhmet, and by Uni. By earth and fire and water and air, I Call."

The breeze died, and all was silent. A darkness seemed to settle outside the circle, dimming the people and the fires there.

Adrian squeezed her hand. "Keep going."

Amber closed her eyes and continued the chant. "By the power of the Mother Goddess and of the Horned God, I invoke thee to help us in our time of need. Thou who art created to aid against the powers of Death, gifted with the strongest powers of Life, I summon thee to me!"

She shouted the last word, a burst of magic arcing from her lips to rumble into the sky. A sudden gust of wind whipped through the clearing, billowing people's robes and Adrian's cloak, ringing wind chimes on houses all along the green.

Then the wind died and all was silence.

"Damn them," Adrian whispered.

The sounds of the party drifted back to them, the people carrying on without noticing what the odd witches did in their flower-strewn circle. Even Kelly chatted with one of Amber's neighbors, not paying the least attention to Amber and Adrian.

Amber looked around in disappointment. "It didn't work."

"Try it again," he answered, holding his voice steady. "Sometimes my brothers need to be kicked in their lazy butts."

"Maybe I'm not a strong enough witch," Amber said in a reasonable tone. "Maybe one of the others of the Coven of Light should say the words."

Adrian shook his head. "No one else in the Coven of Light was infused by the Goddess this night. And you have me and every bit of my magic you need. Try it again."

Amber gazed at him a moment, her golden eyes beautiful. He leaned down and kissed her. "Go on."

Amber drew a breath and nodded. She began the words again. "By Isis, by Uni, by Kali, by Sekhmet . . . I invoke thee to our need."

The stones glowed again, darkness settling once more outside the circle. Adrian felt Amber's power suddenly surge, everything given to her by the Goddess released. He added his own power, pouring his life magic into her through their joined hands, bracing against the backlash so it wouldn't hurt her.

Amber opened her eyes. They glowed like the sun, magic radiating from them to light the circle and slice through the blue nimbus to the sky. She raised her hands to the heavens, and her voice rolled from her with a deep note that shook the earth. "I summon thee to ME!"

White light shot from stone to stone in the startled witches' hands to meet with a crash in the middle of the circle. The whiteness solidified into one luminous spear that joined the golden light from Amber. The spear pierced upward, ripping open the night sky.

The tear burst into brilliance, the noise of it deafening. Adrian held tight to Amber's hand, feeling his power sucked out through her and into the rip in the fabric of reality. Fires in the pits leapt high to meet the sky.

Forms appeared in the tear, and Adrian's heart sped. Darius, his face twisted in pain, Hunter snarling, but each face disappeared as soon as it formed.

*Come on. Come on.*

The tear shrank. Amber clenched her fist, her face twisting in concentration as she willed the Immortals to come to her and do her bidding. Adrian wasn't sure that anyone so powerful had ever Called them, but the spell had not been used in seven hundred years.

Amber's strength increased. The hole in the darkness enlarged again, and then, incredibly, Adrian saw Tain's face, his youngest brother compelled to respond to the spell he'd been created for. If Tain would come, and then his brothers, they could take Tain and all would be at an end.

Tain's face was broken and bloody, blood leaking from his eyes even as he put up his hand to try to stop the spell. Hunter coalesced again near him, his face taking on a "what the hell?" look before disappearing.

Then the demon appeared. Kehksut, millennia old. His unnaturally beautiful face blotted Tain's, and he broke into a gloating smile.

Amber's hand jerked out of Adrian's as her body rocketed upward toward the hole. Adrian grabbed for her, but couldn't catch her before the demon Kehksut closed a tendril of dark magic around her, yanking her to him. Her scream was cut off as the dark magic crushed her throat; then Kehksut flung her body away.

Amber crashed through the white and blue light of the circle, her body whirling before she slammed to the ground twenty feet away. The white stones burst one after another with the sharp staccato of popping glass. The witches screamed.

The demon made a sharp gesture, still laughing. The tear in space, the tenuous faces of the Immortals, and the Calling spell exploded. Shards of the spell burst outward, glittering against the black air. Adrian grabbed his sword and launched himself upward, using a surge of magic to propel himself to the hole. Around him, the shards of the spell splintered into smaller fragments, then dissolved into mist.

# CHAPTER TWENTY-TWO

Adrian latched on to the demon's lower body, gritting his teeth as he struggled to pull the bastard down. Kehksut lashed out, a knife between his fingers, catching Adrian across the jaw. Adrian never felt the sting. His berserker instincts took over, and he fought as he had in the ice cave, relentlessly hacking at the demon with his sword, blasting out with his own magic.

Kehksut fought to get away, and Adrian tasted triumph. If he could kill the damn demon, he could Call Tain and his brothers back and begin helping Tain without interference.

He smacked Kehksut's face with the hilt of his sword, liking the feel of bone crunching under the blow. Out of the corner of his eye, he saw Valerian morph into dragon form, and smiled in glee when Valerian's huge face snaked around to look Kehksut in the eye.

"Mmm, a demon snack."

Adrian continued to grapple with the demon, holding hard when Kehksut tried to twist free. The demon managed to turn himself and launch a stream of darkness at

Valerian, who roared in rage as he was shoved backward, his wings beating for balance. He couldn't simply flame Kehksut with Adrian in the way, so he settled for wrapping the demon in one clawed fist.

Kehksut laughed. Darkness exploded from his body and shot up Valerian's foreleg to penetrate his chest. Valerian recoiled and dropped him, his wings ceasing to beat in midair. Adrian wrapped his arm around the demon as Valerian dropped to the ground, morphing back into a man along the way. He fell with a sickening crunch, and Sabina in wolf form skimmed across the ground to him.

There was no way to tell whether Valerian was all right. Adrian raised his sword. He was so filled with rage and light from the spell that the death magic the demon threw at him glanced right off him. Kehksut looked worried, and Adrian grinned as he lifted Ferrin for the killing stroke.

"Adrian!" Kelly screamed below him. "Amber is dead!"

Adrian looked down for one split second to see Kelly on the edge of the circle, its flowers scattered across the grass. Her model-perfect face was twisted with weeping, tears glittering in the red strobe light of the ambulance behind her. Men in dark clothes and reflective tape rushed a stretcher toward Amber's form that lay still upon the ground.

Kehksut took advantage of the distraction. He kicked Adrian in the face, wrested himself free, and dove upward into the closing hole. Adrian's gaze riveted to the men kneeling over Amber's twisted body and her trailing robes that stirred slightly in the breeze.

Above him the hole in space closed with a crushing sound. White light flared once. Then it was gone, and Adrian fell to earth. Only at the last moment did he remember to use his magic to slow himself to land without harm.

Then he was striding across the grass, but he wasn't aware of his feet moving. Faster and faster he moved, passing Sabina, who wept over Valerian, whose naked body lay broken and motionless. Detective Simon was striding from a police car as fast as Adrian. They met over Amber just as one of the EMTs regretfully pronounced Amber dead at the scene.

Simon looked at Adrian over the stretcher, his square face like thunder. Adrian barely saw him. His sword fell with a muffled thud as he dropped to his knees beside Amber.

She lay so still on the stretcher, her face gray and bloodless in the glaring lights of the emergency medical team. She was dead. Her heart didn't beat, her blood didn't flow, and her life essence was rapidly draining away. The backlash of the power had been too much, and she'd had nothing left to save her when she fell.

His hands unbuckled her from the stretcher, not even feeling the men who tried to stop him. He brushed them away and lifted Amber against his chest, feeling more hollow and empty than he ever had. He'd lost mortal humans he'd cared about before, but he'd felt only sadness at their passing, not this all-consuming, gut-clenching grief.

He sensed a darkness beside him, but it was Septimus kneeling down, careful to keep his pristine slacks from the mud. Adrian realized dimly that the demon had washed so much death magic over the faded festivities that Septimus and other dark creatures could now emerge to cause trouble.

"Adrian," Septimus was saying in his low, silky voice. "I can bring her back." His fangs touched red lips, his eyes glowing with anticipation of a Turning.

Adrian hesitated only a moment. If he gave Amber to Septimus, she'd live again, in a way, and she'd be nearly as strong and immortal as Adrian. He could be with her. But she'd be undead, a creature of death magic, and she would grow sick of him, her love eventually turning to loathing. She would become like the female vampires in Septimus's club, a sensual being who lived to taste blood and have sex with her victims while she drank them.

"No."

"Better than losing her."

"No." Adrian's voice grew sharp. He rose and lifted her, brushing off the angry touch of Detective Simon, who was shouting something at him. "Hand me my sword."

Septimus picked it up gingerly between his fingers, as though he could barely stand to touch something so infused with life magic. Adrian gripped the hilt as he held Amber and used the blade to slice open the night. A slit appeared, faint light flowing through it. As Septimus and Detective Simon stared, Adrian walked with Amber through the slit.

The night disappeared behind him as though it had never existed. Cool ocean air greeted him, a sun rising beyond a wooden Japanese-like terrace and a white sand beach. Home. Ravenscroft.

Adrian lay Amber's body on a low bunk on the woven matting floor. She lay motionless, her breath gone. He gently removed the garland and ribbon crown she still wore, and straightened her robes with a shaking hand.

"Isis," he called softly. He lay his head on Amber's unmoving breast and waited.

After a time, he wasn't sure how long, he lifted his head to see the sun full in the sky and Isis standing on the edge of the matting. Her translucent Egyptian wrap hugged her body, and her head was crowned with horns that seemed to grow straight above her ears.

Isis glided to him and rested her hands on his head. "You grieve, my son. 'Tis natural."

"It isn't *natural*," he said in a broken voice. "Give her back to me. You can."

Isis shook her head. "She is mortal. They end."

Adrian's face was wet with tears he didn't remember spilling. He wiped them from his jaw and found his hand smeared with blood.

"In thousands of years this is the first time I've ever found happiness," he said harshly. "You could at least let me taste it for five minutes."

"And what would you do with it?" Isis asked in her contralto voice. "This five minutes of happiness?"

"Love her. Be good to her. Do anything in the world for her."

"And if it is best for her to die?"

He snarled. "Cease the cryptic goddess speeches. You know I love her, you know what she means to me. When you lost Osiris you didn't cease until you found him and brought him back to life. I need her in my life. *Do this for me.*"

Isis watched him a long time in silence. Adrian placed his hand on Amber's still chest, missing the beating of her heart, of her life. He leaned to kiss her forehead, his lips trembling.

"What will you give up?" Isis asked him.

Her eyes resembled his, dark and fathomless, thoughts behind them that couldn't be read.

"Immortality," he snapped. "Power. Magic. Whatever you want."

"It would be difficult for you, adjusting to mundane life without your magic. You might grow to hate it."

"So I'd learn to use a can opener and take out the trash. I'd be with her. That's the difference."

Isis smiled faintly. "I need you to remain Immortal, Adrian. I need you for what's to come. Your brothers will help, but you must be in place in the end, to help Tain."

"And for that you'll let Amber die?"

"That is not what I said. I asked what you would give up. You told me immortality and your great power. Let me choose something more difficult. Give up Tain. You step back and let your brothers take on the quest to find him. Heal Amber, teach her, love her. Let Tain go."

He swallowed, heart squeezing. "They might hurt him."

"They might."

"Why do I have to sacrifice one for the other?" he demanded. "Kehksut wanted the same thing from me."

"Not a sacrifice. That is not what I ask. I ask you to trust them to find him. It must be so, Adrian, so that all the pieces fall into place."

"Please don't tell me this is all an elaborate game of the goddesses to test their children or something."

She laughed. "You are much too literal, Adrian. You always have been. Think on my offer. Stay with Amber, heal and love her. Let the others take up the quest for Tain."

Adrian took Amber's limp hand in his and pressed a kiss to it. Isis said a *choice*, but it wasn't a choice.

Tain and his demon had singled out Amber and her sister because they knew Amber was just the woman to pierce Adrian's heart. They knew Amber would distract Adrian from his search for Tain once Tain was ready to begin draining the world of life magic.

"My brothers aren't even aware of the problem," he said. "The Calling failed."

"But the Coven of Light is aware. Send them to find the Immortals, and they will finish it. Tain needs you."

*Amber needs me more.*

He knew he could put his love for Amber behind him, enter the fray, live for his vengeance. At one time he would have done that in a heartbeat. But now with Amber lying before him, near to touch but so far out of reach, he knew that a life of vengeance was an empty one.

"Bring her back to me," he said. "I have been doing what you want for thousands of years. Do this one thing for me."

"You will leave Tain to your brothers?"

"Yes." He heaved a sigh. "May the goddesses help him."

"We will." Isis drew closer. She stooped her tall figure, and pressed a kiss to Adrian's forehead. "It is done."

Amber's eyelids fluttered, and she made a soft gasp but no other motion. She lay still, breathing quietly, while Adrian held her hand between his, watching her. It was a few minutes before a spark of awareness entered her beautiful eyes; then she looked at him in surprise.

"I was with the Goddess," she said, her voice weak but full of wonder. "And I missed you so much."

Adrian gathered her in his arms. Isis had vanished, and the shadows were lengthening on Ravenscroft's beach, but this was a place outside reality, and time moved differently here. He pressed a kiss to her hair, reveling in the silkiness and the warmth that meant her life.

"I missed you too, baby," he whispered.

In the dark of early morning of the first of May, Amber looked around her kitchen table at her friends. Kelly had transported Manny from her house to Seattle, and the Italian banged pans while he made fluffy pancakes, omelets, and breakfast bread.

Amber had come to herself in Adrian's arms as he knelt in the mud beside the ambulance. She'd reached up and touched his face, bloody and rough with beard, but his smile and his eyes so warm.

She remembered a dream of the Goddess, her welcoming embrace, and her own regret that she'd left Adrian behind. The regret had turned into acute longing, and then she'd seen him in the dream as he leaned to press a kiss to her hair. Then she was back in the clearing and saw the ambulance and Detective Simon mad as hell and Kelly crying.

She was touched they were all so worried about her. *But I'm fine, really,* she'd protested. Adrian had cradled her and kissed her, and despite the failure of the spell, she felt happy and even blessed.

The paramedics insisted on taking her to the hospital. Valerian rode in the same ambulance, grumbling all the way. Sabina admonished him to keep still and let the EMTs do their job. He'd ended up with nothing more serious than a broken arm. The emergency-room doctors had pronounced Amber fine, seeming surprised at her radiant good health, and sent her home.

Now she poured herself more tea to wash down Manny's heavenly bread, and surveyed her friends. Even Septimus had stayed, sitting comfortably in the kitchen, unworried that the sun would rise in an hour or so.

"So," Valerian said. "The Calling failed, the demon—what did Amber call him? Kehksut?—and Tain are still running around loose, and we have no clue where the other Immortals are."

"We have to find them anyway," Amber said. "We need

to bring them together, by conventional methods if nothing else."

She expected Adrian to join in with ideas on where to start, but he remained strangely quiet. He reached for her hand and closed his fingers around it, but offered nothing to the discussion.

"I suppose this will involve flying around," Valerian grumbled, lifting his splinted arm to the side. "My wing is broken."

"That's all right, sweetie," Sabina said. "They might let you on a plane."

Valerian grimaced. "I hate airplanes. The last two were full of vampires."

"You seemed happy enough to get into them at the time," Septimus pointed out.

"Flying Vamp Air was marginally better than dying on an ice floe," he growled. "Marginally. The second time, I was anxious to get up here and save Adrian's butt."

Septimus gave him a smooth shrug, and Amber waved for attention.

"We have no way of knowing what the spell did," she said. "We don't know whether it brought the Immortals together, or tossed them around the world, or didn't do anything at all. It will be a long time before I'm ready to attempt something like the Calling spell again, and who says Kehksut won't shatter it the same way next time? We have to search for the brothers without using big magic."

"Sounds tedious," Valerian grumbled.

"But we have a good team." Amber looked around the table. "A dragon, a werewolf, a powerful vampire, a movie star, a police detective if he wants in, not to mention another Immortal." She squeezed Adrian's hand, wondering at his quietness. No, he more than quiet. *Resigned.* That worried her.

She went on. "And the best resource of all, the Coven of Light. They live around the world, and the Immortals could be anywhere. I already posted a message explaining that the spell failed. They're standing by, asking what I want to do next."

"And what do you want to do next?" Septimus asked quietly. He flicked his gaze to Adrian, as though he too wondered why Adrian wasn't taking over the conversation.

"Sleep for a week." She laughed a little. "I'll tell the Coven of Light to search for the Immortals using any means necessary. I'm asking everyone here to help them, even if it means flying to Nepal to search the top of Everest. We can use this house as a base, now that Adrian has strengthened the warding. Bring the Immortals here, and then we can figure out how to find Tain and stop him."

Septimus put in smoothly, "From what I understand about the Immortals, Adrian might be the only one able to drag them back here by the hair. They don't necessarily listen to anyone else."

Valerian nodded in agreement. "What does Adrian the Magnificent say?"

Adrian's eyes darkened as they did in his most inscrutable moods. He sat back in his chair, releasing Amber's hand to cradle his coffee mug. "I won't be joining in the search."

They stared at him in stunned silence. Valerian's expression turned amazed, Sabina's mouth opened, and Septimus raised dark brows. Only Kelly watched him speculatively.

"What do you mean, not joining in?" Valerian demanded. "Why should we be doing all the ass-busting work? Tain is *your* brother."

"I will be here to help Amber coordinate efforts," he said. "I'll find a way to kill Kehksut and free Tain. But finding him and the other Immortals is up to you."

Valerian's expression grew more incredulous. "So not only do we not know where to start looking, but now you're bowing out?"

"Not bowing out," Adrian corrected him. "Lying low. Let my brothers take care of problems for a change."

"I see—you want four crazy Immortals running around loose instead of just one."

"I can't tame them," Adrian said. "But if they realize the danger is great enough, they'll help. The problem isn't convincing them to find Tain, it's convincing them not to hurt him when they do. That's what I need you for." His gaze included everyone at the table.

Valerian shook his head, eyes glumly on his coffee. "Oh, this just gets better."

Adrian's lips quirked into a smile that did not reach his eyes. "Kehksut you can chop into little pieces, I don't care."

Amber sat in silence. Adrian had not mentioned his decision to sit back in Seattle and have the Coven of Light and his friends scour the world without him. She'd expected he'd be out of here as soon as he had a shower and a meal. If anything, he needed to renew the quest with vigor, to prevent Tain from doing more damage than he already had.

Adrian's gaze slid to her, his eyes unreadable. She wanted to blurt out questions, and she sensed the others did too, but she held her tongue.

There didn't seem to be anything more to say. Amber pushed her tea aside and announced she'd contact the

Coven. The others dispersed and left her alone to fire up her computer and post to the loop.

She spent the next hour answering questions and explaining what the witches needed to do: look for the Immortals—Darius, Hunter, and Kalen. She had no idea what they looked like, though Adrian had filled her in on a few of their characteristics, and that they each had a pentacle tattoo somewhere on their bodies.

Amber added some of her own deductions based on what she'd seen of Adrian and Tain: well built, handsome in a raw way, possessing brute strength and incredible magic. The Coven agreed to search and post results daily, the online witches promising to keep those without Internet access as up-to-date as they could.

Finally Amber sighed, flexed her aching fingers, and stood up. The house was quiet. She'd heard Septimus and Kelly depart together with Manny, and Valerian telling Adrian loudly that he was walking with Sabina to her house. He seemed taken with the werewolf family.

Amber went in search of Adrian and found him, incongruously, shoving dirty breakfast plates into the dishwasher.

"You have to rinse them first," she said, leaning against the doorframe.

Adrian lifted a syrup-coated plate between his sinewy hands. "I thought the dishwasher was supposed to clean it."

She came slowly into the room. "It does, but not as well if you don't rinse them first."

Adrian shrugged, tugged out the plates he'd put in, and dumped them in the sink. He turned on the water, the noise effectively halting any conversation she'd want to start.

Amber reached around him and snapped off the tap. "When were you going to tell me?"

His face went innocent a moment, as though he'd say, *Tell you what?* Instead, he leaned his fists on the edge of the sink, fixing his gaze on the pile of wet plates and pans.

"I hoped you wouldn't notice me hanging around."

She laughed shakily. "Right, Adrian. You're hard not to notice. For one thing, you have a cobra on your arm."

He looked down at her, his dark eyes quiet. "I made my choice. Remember when Kehksut asked me to choose whether to spare you or Tain from his torture? I chose you. For always."

She frowned at him. "What has the demon got to do with you searching for your brothers?"

"I don't know," he said. "The goddesses have something in mind, I don't know what, but Isis doesn't want me interfering. She told me to put aside my obsession with Tain and let my brothers take up the task. She offered to let me stay here with you, to be with you, and I took it."

Amber's lips parted in shock. "Why should you? Adrian—I'm flattered you like my company, but staying here will make you crazy. I'll come with you—give me a few days to rest and I'll be raring to go."

He cut off her words by pressing her back against the counter and kissing her. He cupped her shoulders with strong hands, his tongue slicing into her mouth. She tasted need in him, felt the sharpness of his teeth against her lips.

"You're worth the price," he whispered.

His eyes were dark, pupils black and wide. She glimpsed the swirling stars from when they'd first made love, and her body craved those sensations again.

He slid his hands down her back, fingers inching beneath her waistband, his erection rubbing brazenly against her. The seams of her jeans began to rip, Adrian's strength tearing the fabric so he could massage the mounds of her buttocks. She leaned into him, lips accepting his hard kisses.

A thought cut through the stirring madness, and she opened her eyes.

"What price?" she asked against his mouth.

Adrian parted his hands, ripping fabric until her jeans pooled at her feet in a pile of warm denim. He hoisted her in her bikini briefs onto the counter, fingers hot on her thighs.

She tried to push him away, but he was a mountain of muscle. "Adrian, what price?"

He parted her legs with firm hands and stepped between her thighs, hooking her knees over his arms. She glared at him, though her body begged her to shut up now and ask questions later.

His eyes swam with white sparks. "A promise I made to Isis that I really don't want to talk about now."

"I do want to talk about it."

He stretched the strings of her bikini briefs until they broke, and she felt cool air on the curls between her legs.

"I do," she said, her voice carrying less conviction.

"Later." He bent to kiss her mouth again, hungry.

"Now." She put stilling hands on his wrists. "What did you promise Isis? That you'd stop pursuing Tain? Why?"

"Hell." Adrian raised his head. He didn't step away, but she felt him withdrawing, the sparks dying in his eyes. "I didn't want to tell you."

She waited, her heart pounding.

"It was the price of your life," he said in a low voice.

"Isis gave me back your life, and in return, I let go of my obsession with Tain."

Amber stilled. "My *life?*"

She remembered flashes of last night, the demon grabbing her with death magic and the backlash of the spell, sickening pain that filled her body, then peace, then opening her eyes to find Adrian smiling at her, his face blood-streaked, his surcoat in shreds.

"I was in danger of dying? The doctors said I was fine . . ."

"You did die." Adrian's eyes were flat. "Kehksut killed you, breaking the spell. I took you to Ravenscroft, and Isis gave you back your life."

Amber stared. "Why should she? I'm just a mortal witch, I'm nobody important."

"Because I asked her to. I asked her to do it for me. I wasn't ready to give you up."

"Oh." Her stunned mind tried to take it all in. What he told her was unbelievable. Dead, Ravenscroft, Isis, her life returned. "I'm not like a zombie or a vampire, am I?"

"It is true life. Infused with the life magic of a goddess."

She smiled shakily. "Well, no wonder I felt like shit when I woke up."

"I wasn't ready to let you out of my life," Adrian said. He smoothed her hair from her forehead. "But if you want me to leave, I will. Just say the word, and I'm gone."

Amber watched him for a long moment, studying his hard face, the lines that feathered about his eyes, the dark hair sweeping back from his broad forehead. He was so strong, and so eaten up inside, laughing when he went for a kill and weeping when he'd first found the drawings of Tain.

She touched the cold silver of Ferrin who hugged his bicep. "I need you to stay," she said.

"I've dragged you through hell—you died because of me."

"Not entirely because of you. If I got hurt last night, it was because I thought I could handle the spell. Because I thought I could help you find your brothers and Tain and save the world. I should have let a stronger witch perform the spell. I'm just as egotistical as Susan was. And as stupid."

"Not stupid. Brave." He traced her cheekbone, his silver ring cool on her skin. "Susan had no idea what she was getting into. You did know, and you went after the demon anyway. You saved me from his torture. You helped me every step of the way."

"Don't get maudlin," she said softly. She brushed a kiss over his warm mouth. "We were just getting to the good part."

His eyes sparked again, his smile turning wicked. "Good part?"

"I'm hoping you had set me up here and ripped my pants off for more than just stopping my questions."

His eyes darkened. "Maybe."

"Well, then." She slid her arms around his neck. "Let's get on with it. We'll have to think of *something* to do while the others are out hunting your brothers down."

He licked her bottom lip. "Why do you think I said you were worth the price? So I could do *this* as much as I wanted."

He moved his hands to her thighs again, sliding them up to bury his thumbs in the thick honey that flowed to meet him. He lifted one hand to his lips. "So I could taste you as much as I wanted."

Amber cupped his face between her hands and kissed him hard. "Make love to me."

"Why do you think I tore your clothes off?" Adrian answered in a voice dripping with heat. He unbuckled and unzipped and kicked his pants to the floor, revealing that, as usual, he hadn't bothered with underwear.

Amber rocked her head back and laughed to the painted ceiling as Adrian parted her legs and drove his thick hardness into her. He gathered her into his arms and began to make love to her in wild, hard strokes.

"I love you," he said, his eyes heavy. "I love you, my witch."

"I love you too," she whispered, then moaned as her climax began to take her—too soon, much too soon. "Welcome home."

Created at the dawn of time to protect humanity, the ancient warriors have been nearly forgotten, though magic lives on in vampires, werewolves, the Celtic Sidhe, and other beings. But now one of their own has turned rogue, and the world is again in desperate need of the

# IMMORTALS